WOEBEGONE

kasey kubica

Woebegone contains content that may not be suitable for some readers. A list of these elements can be found at the end of the book. Please note that some of the warnings may be spoilers.

ONE

Red.
Blue.
Red.
Blue.
Black.

From the flat of her back, Annemarie sluggishly rolled toward the radiating lights in the distance. Her tawny-brown eyes fluttered shut from the immense pressure amassing in her head. A groan escaped her bloody lips; she realized she retained some semblance of a voice. "H—" Her mouth opened to call out, but only a huff of hot air slipped from her. "H-help!" The sound came as a croak—raspy, high-pitched, dry. She barely recognized it as her own. "S-someone, please." Practically a whisper this time, and now, the attempts hurt as if her trachea were in a vise.

No voices, no faces, no movements. Only flashes of light, the colors no longer discernible from behind closed eyelids.

She continued to squeak for help for ten minutes. She thought if she exercised her vocal cords, gave them a good warming up, her voice would return. No improvements came as her cries and whimpers carried on, however.

An explosion of white washed over her. It startled her even with her eyes closed. The once-alternating blinks of colors in the distance became a singularity of brightness. Annemarie attempted to open her eyes, though the combination of her temples throbbing and the light focused on her made it impossible.

A muffled voice came from nearby. She strained to hear; it felt like her ears were packed with sopping-wet gauze.

"Over here!" The voice was louder, though not any clearer. Suddenly, hands caressed her face; gentle touches moved near her neck, to her collarbone, across her shoulders. More noise, more lights.

"Annemarie! Annie! Can you hear me?" Sturdy hands clenched either side of her already aching head, followed by another set on her shoulders, her hips, and her legs. "One, two, three." Her body easily rotated to return her to lying flat on a plastic backboard. A wave of nausea reared its head, causing her stomach to churn, the feeling of vomiting imminent. "Annemarie?" The voice and caress came again. A stiff device wrapped around her neck, forcing her to stare straight up.

Before she could confirm the source of the voice or the touches, straps stretched across her upper chest, hips, above the knees, and ankles, keeping her tightly secured as her body levitated off the crunchy grass.

Fingers pried open her eyelids, cracking through the collection of blood trickled down from her hairline, and her pupils constricted from the assault of the penlight. She flinched and tried to shake away the meddlesome person. Bound by the brace and foam blocks, she instead scrunched up her features in displeasure—the most she could manage.

With her pupils returning to normal, she noticed the sky was the darkest shade of blue with a shocking lack of twinkling stars. Every other clear night yielded a view of millions, as there were so few lights on Port Harrow to obscure them. But tonight, with the flood of red, blue, and white on the roadway, everything washed out, everything was gone.

Red, blue, white, how patriotic, she thought. Searching for any familiar marks in the sky to determine where she might be, Annemarie finally closed her eyes in defeat when she knew it was no use. The night sky looked no different between the southside and the north; it did not matter where it happened, but rather, what had.

"Annie, honey, stay with me." The same voice from before.

"Wh-what happened?" It hurt to talk, to form words. Her throat ached and burned with every breath. There was a lump firmly lodged in place, creating this pain. She could feel a bruise blooming across her neck.

"You were in an accident."

The lump doubled in size and discomfort.

The lightheadedness and cognitive fog lifted. "What? Where am I?" She tried bolting upright, momentarily forgetting the restraints holding her in place and thusly knocking the wind from her lungs. When she caught her breath, she groaned out, "W-where's Jesse?"

The man simply replied, "We need to get you to Brownstone."

"Where is Jesse?" Annemarie repeated. She attempted to sound forceful, demanding. Her voice betrayed her, when instead, it cracked mid-sentence, revealing her tremble.

Through the blear of double vision, she recognized there were others surrounding her, but she could neither put a number on the head count nor discern who they were beyond emergency responders. No one in the haze said a word to her. The only noise came from seemingly far off in the distance. Muffled voices chattered among themselves. "What . . ." She tried to coax an answer from anyone who could hear her, but the words never formed in her tight, sore throat.

The backboard slid over top of an elevated stretcher where they secured her with two final straps. They quickly moved toward an ambulance, its doors open, ready to receive her. The wheels and legs of the stretcher collapsed beneath the frame and slipped over the vinyl floor of the ambulance's back compartment; two loud *thunk*s bounced around in her chest cavity.

Annemarie strained to lift her head at a ninety-degree angle to her body. She failed to make it more than an inch up, instead causing extreme vertigo where the floor was falling out from underneath her. Her stomach lurched. Her heartbeat increased. Involuntary tears streamed down her cheeks.

Why am I crying? she asked herself.

A blurry, dark-haired man in dark pants and a light-colored top climbed into the ambulance near her feet. He reached for her bound hands. The warmth he exuded instantly comforted her. It was familiar.

"I'm here, Annie. I've got you."

"Oh, Jesse! Thank god!" A weight lifted from her chest. The lump in her throat dissolved. All her muscles relaxed. The heat of his hands spread throughout her body. She could breathe again.

As he shuffled sideways between the wall of the ambulance and the stretcher, his face moved closer to hers. Softly, the words came:

"No, Annie. It's Alistair."

"What? No, Jesse, w-why . . ." Annemarie blinked twice in quick succession, a vain attempt at escorting the tears from her eyes. His voice did not sound quite right anymore. Despite knowing her husband inside and out, she was no longer certain what, or *who*, she was hearing. It could still be Jesse playing a trick, though—he liked to mess with her as often as he could. *What a cruel joke.*

"Annie, you with me?" A warm hand touched her cheek, causing her to instinctively lean into the gesture with a fluttery gaze and a tentative smile on her lips. When she opened her eyes, the feeling of the floor dropping out from under her returned, but she was not dizzy. Her vision finally cleared and she saw who stood beside her.

There was no mistaking tall, trim Chief Deputy Sheriff Alistair Lucas for anyone else.

He settled onto the bench alongside her and the ambulance doors shut, locking them in. Two heavy, rapid thumps signaled the driver could head off.

"Okay," he said with a heavy breath. "I know you've got a fuzzy head. Bear with me." His elbows propped up on his knees and he pushed the tips of his thumbs into the inner corners of his eyes. He sighed. "You and Jesse were driving on Wildwood. On-on your way home from the festival. Far as we can tell, J-Jesse was driving and got to th-the blind spot at Sycamore. Y-you know the one." A nervous laugh escaped him despite trying his best to remain composed. The duties and responsibilities of the role as sheriff had long since left Alistair; the professionalism always on display was nowhere to be seen. "There was a truck coming from Sycamore. The driver blew through the stop sign and T-boned you g-guys. Jesse, he . . . We d-don't know how you got out. There was no point of ejection. No open door. We actually didn't even know you were w-with—" He hesitated to continue, wondering if she even wanted the details right now. "The car's in such a totaled state . . . It was a miracle you even got—"

Alistair abruptly stopped talking at the sight of Annemarie's convulsing, every inch of her trying to break free of the restraints. He flinched when her earsplitting wail overtook the small space. Tears flooded her face, most of them pouring into the soft tufts of her copper sideburns and disappearing behind the nubby tragus of each ear. Her chest heaved, her breathing at a rapid-fire pace. Hyperventilating.

Needing her to calm, Alistair reached a trembling hand to her cheek in an attempt to comfort her again. He wanted to speak confident words of reassurance, but knew nothing he could say would allay her. Annemarie recoiled in anger, horrified and upset, but once again, the neck brace thwarted much movement.

Dig Kimball drove with reckless abandon. The curves on Wildwood Highway were already precarious when going the speed limit. Annemarie may have been secure where she lay, but Alistair slid across the bench with every wrench of the steering wheel. He banged the palm of his hand on the wall separating them and yelled, "Take it down a notch. We don't need any more fatalities tonight." The moment the words nonchalantly tumbled out of his mouth, he realized his mistake.

Her pained wails cut deeper through the interior of the truck, cut through Alistair, Dig, and Steven Huang, the paramedic-in-training in the passenger seat. A blast of crackling static poured into the cab from the speakers, startling an already edgy crowd. The gruff male voice that followed paused Annemarie's lament.

"Port Harrow Fire, this is James Errol with Brownstone Medevac. I'm coming in for a landing at Hawthorn Park. We'll be ready to transport the patient in three minutes."

Dig reached for the receiver hanging from the dashboard to respond. "Brownstone Medevac, this is Dig with Port Harrow Fire. We're en route to your location. Looking at an ETA of five minutes."

"What's the condition of the transport?"

"Stable. Concussed but alert. Possible spine injury, couple broken or fractured ribs, and generally banged up real good."

Annemarie listened intently at their back-and-forth. She knew James. She grew up with his son, Nic. The Errol family lived on Port Harrow for several years when the kids were in school, but at the end of James and Christina's divorce, she took everything, forced him to move off the island in search of affordable accommodations, and split custody of their son. Because the high school was over in Brownstone, on the mainland, Nic could still attend classes regardless of which parent he stayed with. Once in a while, when Annemarie visited the mainland, she would run into Nic and play catch-up. Over the years, she introduced him to Jesse, who in turn formed a solid friendship.

Jesse . . .

Her crying regained momentum, though not as heartbreaking or earth-shattering as it had been. She was far from coming to terms with what happened—frankly, she still did not know anything. However, she knew a commotion would not garner her answers. She choked on her silent sobs, the pain in her throat ever present. Again, Alistair attempted to soothe her, to calm her nerves. In the mess of her crying and James's call, she managed to ease out of hyperventilation. It was the distraction she needed, albeit a temporary one.

The ambulance teetered to one side as Dig jammed around a sharp corner, then all the passengers violently lurched to a halt. He poked his head of shaggy brown hair into the back compartment to squeak out an apology, but a preoccupied Alistair shuffled around Annemarie, readying her for the helicopter transport. Steven and Dig took over for the sheriff, hauling the stretcher out of the ambulance and wheeling her to a waiting James.

Alistair approached him with a quickened pace, hand outstretched. "Jimmy, thanks for coming so fast."

"Anything for you folks, Sheriff." James paused to take a second glance at Annemarie, to be sure he saw properly. "Oh, Annie, sweetie! What happened?"

She gave him no response. Tears continued to stream down her face. Her ears felt like they were full of water, like climbing out of the ocean after a swim. She wanted to shake it out, shake out the sensation, but *the damn neck brace . . .*

"Nasty accident up on Wildwood." Alistair shook his head. Annemarie saw this motion and envied him.

"Well, I'll get our little lady to Brownstone a-sap. I'll give Jesse a ring when she's officially been admitted. I'm sure he'll be on the ferry soon anyway."

Alistair's blue eyes narrowed and his expression darkened. He grimaced; his brow furrowed with an emotion James could not place. "Actually, Jimmy, that won't be necessary. Jesse McCready is dead."

TWO

Feet beating on the dirt, breath huffing loudly, Annemarie followed the slight twists and turns of the forest trail, attempting to keep up with her red merle Australian shepherd, Moose, who was faster than lightning. Both familiar with the paths, she allowed the dog without restraint as she focused on her breathing, her heart rate, the fluidity of her muscles and bones guiding her forward. Running became cathartic for her after the accident, admittedly after much prodding and encouragement from outside parties. It was almost the one-year anniversary, and now more than ever, she needed these halcyon moments to occupy her brain.

Most mornings, she struggled to get out of bed, but barring a physical ailment, she laced up the well-worn sneakers, slathered on sunscreen over her sun-kissed skin, and packed a pocketful of treats for the big galoot who never let her out of his sight. But even if somehow, some way, Moose did not demand their habitual run, the few times Annemarie managed to "call out sick"—literally unable to leave the couch or the bathroom or her bed—it set her into such a rotten headspace, made her feel off, she regretted not going outside. The catharsis assuaged her physically and mentally, so she pushed.

It had seemed to work the last five months. It did not always distract her, but here she was, pumping her toned arms and legs in tandem, gliding through the woods at peak condition and strength, her biggest worry being having to clean Moose's furry undercarriage of sticky burrs and pods he gathered as they raced for miles.

The tall trees surrounding her morning routine reached forever into the sky, their tops creating a shaded canopy to keep most of the sunshine, and the warmth, at bay. It also provided a cover for her depression. Doctor Striker was a stranger to her prior to the catastrophic accident, but based on who Annemarie claimed to be before Jesse's death and the husk of a human being showing up to the initial office visits, she understood what a toll the disorder had already taken in such a short period of time. The doctor's first "prescription" for Annemarie was a demand to take up a hobby. It did not matter what: exercise, fiber arts, photography, something in the community, anything to help take her mind off the pain. It was not a cure-all, but it would help to lighten some of the burden the depression caused. Medication was on the table, but at the very least, Annemarie wanted to try a hobby before jumping into a potentially never-ending cycle of side effects while she found the just-right pill and dosage.

So here she was, running.

The trail neared the edge of the woods, leading to the bright morning sunshine pounding on the ecru sand of the shore of North Beach. Annemarie sharply whistled for Moose to reroute and follow her. He was quick to shift gears, to leap over the random fallen branches, to meet her at the entrance of the wide-open space.

Not another soul was in sight as she emerged onto the beach, awash in the morning sunshine aggressively spilling over the tops of the old, wind-worn hemlocks and narrow lodgepole pines. She stopped running the moment she met the clearing, using this opportunity to catch her breath. Before the accident, she spent an inordinate number of her days on this stretch of sugary sand, using her free time to explore both land and sea. After the accident, it took months before she even considered venturing out to the place she had formed innumerable memories with *him*.

Sometimes, it still hurt to think or say his name.

As her mind slinked away from the task of running, Moose barked once, bringing her to the present. She wanted to believe he could read her mind or her body language and was calling out to her, reaching out to help back her away from the ledge. But she knew he was a silly dog who liked attention and barking was his way of demanding an answer to the question, "Why aren't you playing with me?" She snapped out of her dark trance and surveyed the beach, trying to locate the rascal. A scan from east to west fell short as a silvery glint off in the distance caught her attention. The element-worn sea cave, eroded through the rock over time, sat at the water's edge some two hundred yards away, and an intermittent glistening near its entrance mesmerized her.

"Flying fish must be active again," she muttered.

Another bark drew her attention to the opposite side. Moose had moved further along the expanse, landing beside an enormous pile of bladder kelp. He play-bowed once at the green-brown mass, let out an excited *raff*, and looked between Annemarie and what was in front of him. His gaze shifted back to the mound, his eyes remaining fixed directly ahead. He lay down at once, paws stretched out in front of him.

She closed the gap of about thirty yards, wondering what captivated him so expertly. As she approached, he stood, inched toward the kelp, and whimpered. *Maybe it's a dead fish,* she thought. There was a good chance the smell of a rotting carcass was alluring, but the poor dog did not know what to do with it. Moose was smart, but some things—*dog things*—sometimes alluded him.

The pile of kelp was the size of a supermini car. Though not uncommon to see dotted along the beach in mounds from locals reeling in the long, thick strands of the abundant plant life to stop it impeding swimming and fishing, ones of this magnitude were rare, but not unheard of. She had seen bigger a couple times before; a storm passed through and churned the waters so violently, much of the anchored kelp broke loose and washed ashore. It was piled upon itself by the beachgoers, oftentimes children trying to see how tall they could build them.

Annemarie met Moose on his side of the pile, eager to see what had him in a tizzy. When she saw it, she gasped and tripped over her own feet as she tried backing up too quickly.

A bloody hand peeked out from under the edge of the sea sludge.

A scream rose from her diaphragm, into her chest, and tried to escape from her throat, but it never materialized. The bile surging up in her was fighting for its own spot too. Shock froze everything in place. Moose continued to eye the hand, his ears pinned back in a show of confusion and dismay. She, too, did not react. She did not know how to.

The fingers moved ever so slightly. Like whoever they belonged to knew someone was watching, could feel their presence, and this was their final attempt to signal for help. Overcome with adrenaline, Annemarie dropped to her knees and dug. She tossed away handfuls of sand and clumps of kelp one after another. She pounded the ground with her fist, commanding Moose to help. He followed her lead, though much less organized and pointed. Her hand brushed against the slow and erratic-moving fingers. The skin was icy, drained of any warmth a normal, healthy body possessed. Against her better judgment, she cupped the hand in her own, giving it a gentle squeeze to reassure whoever was buried under the mess that help was here. It barely squeezed back.

With every glob of organic streamers she pulled from the bottom of the pile, a little more toppled from above to replace it. The attempt was futile, but she had to give it her all. She needed to try. Wrapped in the sounds of her heavy breathing, the slush and slurry of sand and kelp slapping each other, the waves crashing nearby, she did not hear the noise Moose had. His mismatched red and silver ears perked up, prompting him to abruptly stop digging. He stood stock-still for one long moment before loosing a bark and running at the tree line. Too slow, Annemarie reached out to grab his collar—missing completely as he was long gone—and she fell over into the sand, elbow first.

She turned her attention back to the pile, knowing Moose was smart enough to stay out of trouble, knowing she could not give up on this rescue mission. She never carried her cell phone when she went running; who would want to carry around such a large, cumbersome, yet equally delicate and expensive glass-faced toy when the main goal of running was to jostle and bolt and fly? For a short minute, she wondered if she should continue the seemingly fruitless endeavor or sprint out to the highway, about a mile and a half as the crow flew, to flag down an oncoming car.

With one more genuine attempt to dig at the body, she focused on trying to find their head. *Can a person breathe when tangled up in kelp?*

"I'm trying to help, I promise!" she yelled at the pile, hoping the person could still hear. She flattened herself onto her stomach, using this new angle to shove both arms into the debris, fishing around for more than the first four inches of their one exposed limb. It did not take much meddling to bump into a soft, pruned, rounded object—presumably a head. A bald one. It was not too far from the edge of the mound. She knew no strength she could ever possess would allow her to pull them free, but having a location made it easier to focus on an end goal.

She dug and dug, using every fiber inside her to grab at the long strings of plants. She glanced over her shoulder to find Moose. All she saw was a flash of silver in the distance, him no doubt hot on the trail of his quarry. She whistled once, loud and long, in the hopes it, too, would echo in the trees to recall him. She did not have time to wait for a response.

Finally making a dent, she revealed the bald dome, obviously belonging to a man. Several handfuls later, she freed the entirety of his head. His face was bloated, waterlogged, bruised in shades of purple and blue, the shape of him not natural, indicative of broken bone.

"Peter!" she cried.

Peter Arthur—Port Harrow's long-time resident mechanic.

"Oh my god, Peter!" He did not flinch at the shrill sound escaping her. His hand still grasped at the air, like the presaging death knell before he drew a final breath. For now, though, he was alive. She snaked her fingers up against his neck, feeling for the carotid artery. His pulse was thready, but at least it was there.

A bark emanated from the woods. Annemarie quickly looked up to see Moose trotting out from the forest's edge, panting and looking pleased with himself after what had to be the squirrel-chasing of a lifetime. Attention rerouted to Peter, the excavation continued, trying to be careful to pull more kelp away from higher up on the pile to stop it from crashing down on his face. She imagined the sheer weight of it all was creating immense strain on his lungs. As she revealed a little more of him, now down below his chin to his neck and the top of his chest, she saw his blue button-down whorled with pink pineapples was soaked with blood. His blood? She could only assume so if his hand were any indicator.

The further she dug at the body, the more she wanted to stop. She choked on the taste filling her mouth: briny, hot, decomposing ocean matter mixed with the unmistakable stench of metallic pungency. She shot a hand to her face to stifle the gag reflex, to try to keep down the vomit threatening to make an appearance, when she noticed blood dripping from her fingers. She groaned— one of disgust and exhaustion. She dragged the wetness across the sand, picking up more morsels and tidbits than leaving anything behind.

Peter let out a moan. Annemarie's ears perked up as she strained to listen to anything he might say. If he was even capable of that. "Peter," she said firmly. "Peter, it's Annemarie McCready." She identified herself as if it mattered. "I'm here with you now, Peter. I'm here to help you." She said words she hoped Jesse heard in his last moments of life. She never knew if anyone had been with him when he died or if he was already gone when found. No one offered up that information, she did not go seeking a police report, there were no details during the court proceedings, and she never thought to ask. Never wanted to know, if she were being honest. She *needed* to save Peter, to help him go home to his family.

He let out a deflated sigh, like the weight of the kelp on his chest was eking out the last of his life in little pained squeals. She reached for one more clump of green glop, now stained red, and she gasped at what she inadvertently revealed: His torso was ripped to shreds. Her hands were covered in more of his blood. She pushed herself backward, falling off her bent knees into the sand. She wiped her sticky fingers on her day glo orange shorts—an appalling contrast of colors.

Maybe the kelp was keeping him from bleeding out.
What if I just passed down his death sentence?
Should I try to stopper it with more seaweed?

Will that introduce harmful bacteria to his bloodstream and cause an infection?

Why didn't I bring my cell phone?

How long does he have?

Half a dozen thoughts and questions clouded her mind, keeping her stuck in this fallen-over position. Moose barked again. He had plopped down six or seven feet from her, out in the open, watching closely. This snapped her out of the torrential swirling down the drain.

Annemarie pushed up onto her feet, giving herself a brief moment to shake out the pins and needles in her legs, waiting for her own blood to recirculate. She continued to wipe as much thick fluid off her hands as she could, which led to more on her shorts, up her white T-shirt, and even accidentally onto her face as she fought the wind blowing loose strands of her messy hair into her eyes. She clicked her tongue against the back of her teeth, signaling Moose to be ready.

"I'm gonna get help!" she announced. She snapped fingers at Moose, called *heel*, and began a rapid run toward the densely packed trees to Wildwood Highway. If she was lucky, she would be on the road in under ten minutes.

She made good time as she weaved around the trees, jumped over logs, skirted unruly shrubs, and dodged clouds of hovering bugs. Still half a mile from where she needed to be, she could at least see the pavement up ahead. She balanced being mindful of her footsteps with keeping her eyes on the prize of reaching the road. Glancing down for a brief moment, she hopscotched over a tiny but muddy creek bed littered with broken, slippery rocks. But before she could look up again, her entire body collapsed as something large and heavy crashed into her—or she into it. She did not see it. Not really. All she witnessed was a flash of grey across her field of vision, followed by her knees buckling and all the weight of the world knocking her flat onto her back. Moose was right beside her and did not even flinch; it happened so quick.

The wind beaten out of her, she propped up onto her elbows, looked at her bloodstained torso—presumably still all Peter's—and checked around herself to see what took her down. Nothing was in sight. She heard the sounds of the day: birds chirping high above in the canopy, some kind of wildlife scampering from underbrush to tree trunk, the gentle hum of the few cars passing by on the little two-lane highway.

The cars.

She used what breath and strength she had left to propel herself back onto her feet to sprint the last leg to civilization. The shoulder alongside the road was only a foot wide, overgrown with dandelion, thistle, wild strawberry, and white daisy. Annemarie normally marveled at the colorful weeds and flowers that persevered year after year despite the island's city council doing what they could to eradicate pesky weeds, but today, she could not care less. She trampled across the brilliant bursts of yellow, purple, white, and green, concerned more about flagging down a vehicle.

Of course, none were in sight.

Home was about four miles away. She resigned herself to making the trek along the shoulder, en route to retrieve her cell phone. In that amount of time, surely someone would come across her. Port Harrow was a small enough island community where anyone would recognize Annemarie, and given her disheveled, ghastly features, most anyone would stop to help. She double-checked that Moose was by her side, relegated to the edge of the woods instead of out in the road like her. Her feet pounded on the pavement, picking up the pace. As they rounded a sharp curve, she spotted a vehicle accelerating toward her off in the distance.

When it got closer, she realized it was her mother's little CUV. Whether it was Cecily or her father Ken, she did not care. Short of the car belonging to the sheriff's department, this was the best possible outcome.

Annemarie wildly waved her arms above her head. She knew what she looked like at that moment and could only imagine what the person driving thought. As the vehicle approached, she saw it was Cecily behind the wheel. Her mother slammed on the brakes. She threw the car in park, unbuckled herself, and clambered out onto the highway, leaving the driver's door open.

"Annemarie, oh my god, what—are you okay?" Cecily rushed over, a flash of grey with her salon-perfect, cinder-block tresses falling to her shoulders, pewter faux leather jacket over similarly colored blouse and chinos, and strappy silver flats.

"I'm okay, mom. But I need your cell phone, now."

"Whose blood is that? Is it yours? Where's Moose? Oh my god, is Moose okay?"

"Mom! Phone!" Annemarie snapped her fingers, trying to pull Cecily's attention. Cecily did not move, however. Annemarie hurried over to the passenger side, knowing the purse was waiting there on the seat. The door swung open. Annemarie reached for the leather bag, unzipped the front pouch, and pulled out the hot pink device with a gaudy gold grip on the back. She stabbed in the numbers of Cecily's lock code.

For a fleeting moment, Annemarie was not sure if she should dial 911 or default to calling Sheriff Lucas directly. She relied on the former, in the event Alistair was busy and could not answer his phone or get to the beach quick enough; he was often off-island at the sheriff's hub in Brownstone.

"Azure County 911, what's your emergency?" a man with a deep voice asked.

"My name is Annemarie McCready. I'm on Port Harrow at North Beach and I need help here. There's a dying man buried under a gigantic pile of kelp. He's b-bleeding out. I c-couldn't help him." Her voice came out coolly at first, as if she had rehearsed the lines of this play for weeks, but the composure quickly dissolved while she uttered the words to describe this reality.

Eavesdropping on the call, Cecily's brown eyes widened and darted between the beach off in the distance and her blood-soaked daughter. Her hand rose to her mouth to shush a gasp.

"Okay, Miss McCready. Is the man conscious?"

"Yessir," she said quickly. "At least, he was when I left him."

"You left him, miss?" Annemarie could not tell if he was asking incredulously or for clarity's sake.

"Yes. I didn't have a phone and I was alone, so I ran to get help."

"Okay. Do you know the identity of the man?"

"His name is Peter Arthur."

Cecily's eyes flared an expression of confusion. Peter had been her and Ken's go-to mechanic practically all their adult lives. She often invited him and his wife, Yongsoo, over for Sunday brunch, always brought back a slew of pastries from his favorite bakery whenever she visited Cedarbrook, and gave the couple an open-ended invitation to join them for Thanksgiving and Christmas—Peter was more than their mechanic, he was their friend.

"And what is the nature of Mr. Arthur's injuries?"

"I don't know. He was bleeding from the torso, and that looked really torn up. Like he'd been attacked." Annemarie shook her head in disbelief.

"Attacked?" Keyboard keys clacked in the silence between question and answer.

"By an animal? I don't know." She paused. "He wouldn't open his eyes and he didn't speak. Only groaned a bit. His pulse was weak. I managed to dig him out up to his chest area, but I think the rest of him is being crushed. I don't know, I don't know. Please get someone out here. Sheriff Lucas, if he's available." She was beyond losing her cool. She knew she needed to provide adequate information for the man to do his job—something Alistair had kindly lectured her all about—but she was regretting not calling him directly. He would drop anything for her, no questions asked.

"Okay, Miss McCready. I'm dispatching emergency services now. Can you tell me exactly where you are?"

"North Beach. Uh, I think I'm between mile markers twenty and twenty-one. I'm on the side of the road with a grey car. I'm covered in blood, so they definitely can't miss that."

Cecily heard this and shook her head dramatically while snapping her fingers to catch Annemarie's attention. "Seventeen and eighteen!" she corrected.

"Oh, sorry. Between seventeen and eighteen." She was further away from home than she had originally thought.

More keyboard typing. "Okay, Miss McCready. A crew is on their way. Please stay safe on the side of the road there. They will be to you shortly."

"Thank you," she said meekly. The call disconnected. There was no reason to stay on the line. Annemarie placed the phone back in the purse and shut the door. She noticed a smudge of red on the handle. She looked down at her clothes, trying to find a clean spot to wipe away the mess she had left behind on the car.

"Why is Peter Arthur dying on the beach?" Cecily yelled. "What happened?"

"I don't know. I-I was out running with Moose—*shit.* Where's Moose?" Annemarie wildly spun in place, arms flailing out to either side as she searched for her dog. He was last seen tromping through the roadside weeds with her as they made their way home, but he, unfortunately, became the least of her concerns upon Cecily's arrival. "Moose!" she called, cupping her bloody, sandy hands around her mouth. A few pieces of grit stuck to her lips, causing her to spit and blow puffs of air to rid herself of the tainted articles. "Moose!" She faced the tree line, thinking another squirrel caught his attention when no one was watching.

"Annemarie! There!" Cecily cried, but as the shrillness in her voice trailed off, laughter filled on the upswing. She pointed straight ahead of her.

Annemarie looked at Cecily then followed the invisible line she had drawn to her car. And inside, perched in the driver's seat, was Moose in all of his rust and silvery, fluffy glory. He had helped himself to a safe place to sit, having climbed into the front seat beside a completely oblivious Annemarie on the phone. He was panting, tongue lolling from his mouth, never looking prouder.

"Ridiculous beast," Annemarie muttered.

"What happened to Peter?" Cecily returned to the more-pressing matter.

"I don't know, mom. We were out running, Moose got all excited about a big kelp pile, and I found Peter buried under that. I tried digging him out, and just . . ." She released a deep, heavy sigh, quaking from the depths of her lungs. It was a mix of frustration and exhaustion. "I felt utterly helpless, trying to get at him." Her head hung low, her chin coming to rest between her collarbones. "I hope someone gets here quickly. I don't know how long he has left."

Annemarie thought she should be panicking more, as if her reaction of cool, calm, and collected was not adequate given the situation. She should be howling and bawling every single emotion out of her right now. But she was pretty certain after six months of doing just that—coupled with an endless binge of alcohol, few chewable calories, and not leaving the couch for much more than using the bathroom and opening the front door to collect her delivered groceries—she could only muster superficial feelings; her well had not been replenished.

She wanted to sprint back to the beach, to sit with Peter, hold his hand, promise him help was on the way. But she knew she had to wait for someone to arrive on the scene.

Cecily walked over to the open door of the vehicle, leaned in across Moose's body, grabbed a small pouch out of the center console, and made her way back to Annemarie. She clicked open the soft-sided plastic container, revealing wet wipes. "Here." She handed over a polyester towelette. "Clean up some of the mess. You look horrible."

Annemarie raised both arms over her head to look down at her bloodied ensemble. She made a face, lips scrunching up into a puckered grimace. The bridge of her nose shortened, causing wrinkles around the creases of her eyes. She plucked a wet wipe from Cecily and first cleaned her hands. The cloth turned red and brown as she ran it over her skin. There was nothing she could do about her clothes, so she did not bother. She bent to clean spots of sand and blood from off her shins.

Upon straightening her spine, a stab of pain exploded from her lower back. "Ah!"

"What, what?" Cecily startled and she dropped the package of wipes.

Annemarie had forgotten about her fall. The sudden pain reminded her of the weird circumstances in which she met the ground. As she rubbed the sore spot with her free hand, she opened her mouth to respond, but was interrupted by the sound of a distant siren.

The women waited a bit impatiently for the quickly approaching screaming vehicle to reach them. For a brief moment, Annemarie contemplated covering herself up in some fashion, so as to not alarm whoever was about to join them. She realized she did not care enough to try.

The grey and blue sheriff's department SUV roared around the curve half a mile up the road and finally came into view. The blaring siren quieted. The vehicle slowed as it passed Cecily's car, pulled a tight U-turn, and came to park behind her on the shoulder. The light bar flashed, alerting oncoming traffic to the scene, warning them to keep a buffer.

Out of the vehicle stumbled Chief Deputy Sheriff Alistair Lucas, neatly stuffed into the department's tan button-down and pressed dark brown slacks. As always, his brown scissor-cropped hair was in perfect order and his face was clean-shaven. His fair skin was tinged red while his ocean-blue eyes flashed a deep dread, of fear and distress.

"Oh my god, Annie, what—is that your blood? Are you okay? What happened? Where's—" He asked a flurry of questions, seemingly the theme for the morning, practically forgetting why he was even there. As he gave Annemarie a once-over, grabbing her arm, twisting her around, checking for any wounds, the passenger door of the police vehicle opened. Both Cecily and Annemarie jumped at the sound of Deputy Riggs making an entrance; neither woman realized he had been along for the ride.

Still being manhandled by Alistair, Annemarie pushed her hand against his chest to stop him. "Alistair, come on. I'm fine. We need to get to the beach." She was ready to sprint the whole way, but his grip remained on her arm.

"Where exactly is he?" Alistair asked. "Riggs'll wait for the paramedics to catch up." Riggs had tucked his blond head into the back of the SUV, rustling around for a bit and returning with a black duffel bag. He walked it over to Alistair who heaved it out of his deputy's arms and over his own shoulder.

Annemarie raised her free arm to point north. She hesitated a moment then turned to face northwest. "That way. On the beach. About a mile and a half. There's no trail, so be careful." As she readied herself once more, knowing Alistair could easily keep up despite his moderately constricting uniform, she turned to Cecily. "Mom, can you take Moose home?"

"I, uh, uh . . . Yeah. We'll be at your house," she begrudgingly replied. She did not want to leave Annemarie alone, but she also did not want to bear witness to any more of this incident than she already had. A bloodied daughter alongside the road was not something Cecily dreamed would ever happen—and now in one year, Annemarie had twice been found in such a manner. So she wanted to retreat to the comfort of somewhere safe and familiar. She knew Annemarie was in good hands with Alistair. He always had her back.

THREE

Best friends since forever, they raced off together into the woods, Annemarie leading the way and Alistair a few steps behind with his duffel bag of supplies.

Adrenaline coursed through her veins—the thought of possibly finding Peter still alive, being able to save him, drove her forward, faster than she had ever run before. She was mindful of her steps, as she had been on her way out of the woods, but worried Alistair might be falling behind. In his work pants, with that heavy duffel, not having a clue about the terrain, there was no way he could keep up. She turned her head slightly, the tip of her ponytail slapping at the side of her head, and saw he was right beside her, keeping pace with ease. He did not notice her watching him, as he was too focused on not tripping on a forest made entirely of roots.

Emerging onto the beach, Annemarie recentered herself and tried to locate the gigantic kelp pile. It was not immediately in front of her like she thought it would be. It was to their right a few hundred feet. She pointed at it, barked, "There!" and led Alistair to Peter.

They approached the mound of slimy, green-brown bladder kelp. In the time she had been gone, the tide had come in enough so the occasional wave would crash up and lap at the hill of decomposing sludge.

"That thing is *massive*," Alistair murmured. Like Annemarie, he was used to seeing piles of washed-up kelp and seaweed along the beach, but never ones this size. "He's *under* that?"

She nodded shallowly. "Yeah, he's right—" She stopped short, both in speech and movement, when she focused on the spot where Peter had been. His body was no longer present. "Wait. He was here. Right here!" She pointed at the edge of the kelp and stomped a foot in protest. "Where the hell did he go?"

Alistair dropped the duffel on the sand to give himself a bit of breathing relief. He was in excellent shape, but even that run was a little much, especially right after a heavy breakfast. "Annie, I think—" he started, but she interrupted him.

"No, not a word. He was here. If he wasn't, where did all this blood come from?" She flailed at herself, showing off the handprints and smears over her shirt and shorts.

Alistair held up a finger to stop her, but refrained from speaking. He reached for her arm, the one he had been holding onto while at the road, and tried to show it to her. The entire backside of her upper arm was scratched and already trying to scab over as the blood dried. "Did you fall at some point?"

"If you're implying I hit my head . . ."

"No. But this is a pretty nasty mess back here. It was bleeding before. Maybe . . ." He trailed off. "Maybe that's where all the blood is from?" He framed it as a question instead of the pointed statement he meant.

"I-I did fall. But not until after I left Peter to run to the road. I didn't have my phone so I needed to get help and

I tried to dig him out as much as I could. I tried, Alistair, *I really tried* I'm not crazy he was here I swear to god he was here!" Her sentences ran together, not allowing her to take a breath. Each thought progressively grew in volume, leaving her practically shouting at him.

Alistair lifted both hands in front of him, hoping to slow her panic. "Annie, Annie, it's okay. Cal—"

"Don't tell me to calm down. I'm calm."

"I beg to differ," he muttered, but he had said the quiet part out loud. His eyes grew wide when he realized what he had done.

"I'm not crazy."

"I didn't say you were."

"But you're looking at me like I am." She paused. "He was here. I was trying to help him."

"I believe that you believe you were."

"Alistair!"

"Okay, then if he was here, if you had been helping him, where did he go? Where is he?"

"I-I don't know." Her eyes darted down to the kelp. The spot where her knees dug into the sand, where she wiped so much of his blood off her hands, where she had separated the tendrils to try to free him, were all gone, all washed away with the incoming tide. "Stop looking at me like I've lost my mind."

"I'm not. I'm looking at you. I'm seeing you. I'm seeing a woman who was out for a run, who fell and hurt herself, who's still dealing with the death of her husband—someone she couldn't help before he died— and I'm seeing a traumatized woman approaching the one-year anniversary of that death." Alistair tried not to bring up Jesse's death if he did not have to. It was rare he did, but using his best judgment, trying to be as unbiased as he could, he saw exactly that: trauma resurfacing.

Annemarie raised her eyes to meet his. Mouth agape, bottom lip almost quivering, tears welling up and threatening to spill over, she stopped herself from slapping him. Every ounce of her wanted to reach forward and hit him. She could not believe he was bringing *that* into this.

"Crazy. You think I've lost my mind. That I'm seeing things. I can't even—" Before she broke into tears, she staunched her sentence. "How could you . . ." She looked away for a moment, willing the redness in her face to dissipate, and she saw the glide of flying fish sparkling in front of the sea cave off in the distance again. Her mind drifted away with a thought of Jesse bringing home fresh-caught fish once a week and teaching her how to gut, clean, and properly fry up each species he reeled in.

"Over there!"

Annemarie's attention snapped back to the present. She whipped around in place to find Riggs and two paramedics stomping their way through the last few feet of forest, making their entrance onto the beach. Alistair left his bag at Annemarie's side and headed over to update the men on the situation.

Feeling helpless, hopeless, and utterly confused, Annemarie stood beside the pile, dumbfounded, not knowing what to do. She eyed the mound suspiciously. Before she comprehended what she was doing, she was down on her knees, ripping out handful after handful of kelp, throwing it back into the ocean as the waves came closer. She dug in as deep as she could. She heard a startled cry come from the men behind her.

"Annie, stop!" Alistair called as he approached with a quickened pace. His arms circled her entirety, wrapping her in a warm embrace, pulling her away from the pile that threatened to collapse in on itself, onto her. "Let's have Marc and DJ give you a once-over before I take you home, okay?"

Tears freely fell from her eyes now, triggering a deep burning in her chest and throat and a struggle to breathe properly. She tried to push herself away from Alistair, from the comfort he was providing. He did not believe her and she could not stand to look at him, let alone be held by him. She did not want to be coddled and she definitely did not need rescuing by someone who thought she was losing—or had lost—her mind.

"Let. me. go," she said through clenched teeth.

"Come on. Let's get this over with." He ignored her demand. He pulled her up onto her feet and found that she was not willing to move of her own accord. He dragged her. She struggled to free herself. Annemarie was strong, but unfortunately for her, Alistair was stronger. Had he thought it would not result in incessant shrieking, he considered picking her up and throwing her over his shoulder. The last time he did that, years ago, he ended up with an errant foot slamming into his balls, and he was not ready to deal with that kind of pain again. She was so upset, he was not sure that scenario could be avoided even if he tried.

Instead, he transported her all the way up to the tree line, where paramedics Marc Allan and DJ Harcourt waited with Riggs.

"All right, gents. Give her a quick checkup and we can be on our way." He let go and gently nudged her in their direction. While the men readied their tools to check her vitals and make sure she was physically okay, Alistair excused himself to head back to the kelp mound. He intended to retrieve the duffel, but took an extra minute to walk the perimeter. He owed that much to his friend, and to a 911 caller in need. He would do the same for anyone else. It was part of the job.

Careful of the rising tide, he inspected what he could. Any evidence of a crime had been washed away. If Annemarie had not imagined Peter Arthur's body under the kelp, he was no longer around and there was nothing to prove. As much as he hated to doubt her, he needed to use his best judgment. Taking on the role of a law enforcement officer meant remaining unbiased, regardless of his opinions and feelings on the matter. He did not have the time or resources to follow a baseless lead. He crouched to examine the dent Annemarie created with her digging, hoping it had gone undisturbed by the waves. Nothing out of the ordinary, nothing to see.

A small, albeit powerful wave crashed a dozen feet off shore and sent a thick spray of foamy water racing across the flat sand, aiming directly for Alistair. He paid no mind until it overtook his black leather boots. Standing, he let out an annoyed groan. He carefully stepped out of the remnants of the froth left on the beach as the water receded, picked up his bag farther up the shore, and headed back to Marc, DJ, Riggs, and Annemarie.

Much to his surprise, she was not with them.

"Where is she?" he asked a ruddy-complexioned DJ. His fair skin in the bright, warm morning sun was giving him away.

He shrugged. "We were done with her, so she left."

"She okay?"

DJ scratched a spot on his forehead. "She's scraped up. A little rattled. We offered her a bandage for that arm, but she refused. Not much more we could do for her especially considering she was so unwilling to cooperate."

Alistair shook his head. "Sorry you guys had to come all the way out here for nothing." He paused. "Don't get me wrong, I'm glad there wasn't a body to retrieve." Marc and DJ nodded. "Let's head back."

The paramedics led the way into the woods, keeping a brisk pace to shorten the amount of time they were walking. Riggs rounded on Alistair, sidling up alongside his boss. "What do we put on the report?" he asked.

Alistair chewed on his bottom lip for a moment before responding. "I'm not sure. She says she found a body. There're no signs of a body. Should be open and shut, right?" Riggs nodded. "I don't want to discredit her based on the fact that Jesse's one-year anniversary is coming up soon, but I also know I shouldn't simply take her side because of our history. Something about her conviction though . . . *man*." It was obvious to Riggs that Alistair was no longer talking to him, rather speaking out loud, working through what just happened. "She's so sure he was there. And that arm wound couldn't have produced *that* much blood to get it smeared all over her clothes like that, could it?"

"You could test the blood on her clothes," Riggs reminded him, but otherwise said nothing else. He cared for Annemarie as much as Alistair did, but he was more concerned in that moment about picking and choosing his steps as they navigated nature's debris field of branches, mud puddles, and on-alert critters. The remainder of the mile-long walk was quiet—Alistair having made temporary peace with the clashing thoughts in his head and Riggs trying not to fall into anything thorny. How any of them made it to the beach in a flash without succumbing to some kind of injury was unknown. Annemarie was right when she warned them that the route was treacherous. Riggs was not the least bit surprised to hear she had fallen herself.

Back at the highway, the paramedics had already departed, en route to the station at the south of the island. Alistair's SUV sat alone on the shoulder, lights still awhirl. Cecily was long gone, too, which caused him to wonder where Annemarie was.

He threw the duffel into the back of the vehicle and climbed into the driver's seat. Riggs spent a minute stomping dirt out of the treads of his boots. Alistair started the engine, waited for a passing sports car to zip by, and pulled another U-turn to head east along Wildwood. Riggs did not question the direction.

The speed limit along the highway was a rambling thirty-five. Alistair kept to that, knowing he would catch up to Annemarie, who no doubt was walking or running home, seeing as how she had no other means to get there. They had all congregated at a curve in the road, making for low visibility in either direction. As soon as the SUV came out into a straightaway, he spotted a white and orange figure up ahead. He contemplated sounding his siren once, to catch her attention as he approached from behind, but thought better of it. He knew she would not be pleased to see him.

She walked along the shoulder, stepping over bundles of weeds and flowers infiltrating the gravel, not minding anything else. Alistair pulled up alongside her, rolled down the window, and cleared his throat.

"Annie, I'm sorry," he offered genuinely.

"Not talking to you, *Sheriff*."

He continued to slowly roll forward to match her speed. "I don't think you're crazy."

She remained silent.

He repeated, "I don't think you're crazy. I just think you saw something that maybe wasn't there."

Still no let up. Her walking turned aggressive, setting down each step a little harder. She was hoping to send a message; he was hoping to *hear* her say that message. At least that would mean she was talking to him.

"Come on, Annemarie. You have to understand where I'm coming from. You have to at least see it from my perspective." The sound of the rubber tires plodding against the asphalt echoed in the wheel wells, filling the silence between them loudly. "Come on, *please*."

"Begging me isn't going to change anything, Sheriff." She abruptly stopped in place, causing Alistair to panic and slam on the brakes needlessly. Despite barely topping three miles per hour, the vehicle still seized violently, and a distracted Riggs—who had been texting on his cell phone—lurched forward. He started to yell out a protest of, "Ow! What the hell, Al?" but it was lost in the moment.

Alistair put the vehicle in park, turned on the light bar, and climbed out to stand on the road to talk to her. "Look. Let me do my job. Please let me take you home and get a statement from you, okay? Let me take your clothes for DNA testing to prove one way or another. There's no reason you need to walk the rest of the way to your place when I can get you there sooner and we can figure out what's going on. Please? I wanna help." He set one foot ahead of himself, as if taking a step, but the glare she shot him told him to stay back. In all their years together, he had never seen her this angry. Not directed at him, at least. "Please." It was no longer a question, but a plea.

With her arms folded across her chest, she stared hard, sizing up him and his apology. If she were being honest with herself, she was not mad *at him*, per se. She did not like the fact that he was not willing to believe her story, but she had a hard time believing it herself, and she was the one who witnessed it all. Deep down, she knew he was right to question her. He was doing his job. As the sheriff overseeing all of Port Harrow, his plate was full and she recognized the fact that without hard evidence of any kind, he was going to dismiss this. But to be *dismissive* of her was what hurt the most.

She did not say anything further. She dropped her arms to her sides in a show of yielding and crossed the road to hoist herself into the back seat. Alistair climbed in after her. He shifted gears to allow the vehicle to roll forward gradually, then accelerated them down the road to her house.

Ignoring the awkwardness between the two, Riggs glanced up from his phone, aimed a smile at Annemarie over his shoulder, and said, "Hi, again, Annie," in an upbeat tone.

"Hey, Riggs. How are you?" She, too, skipped over the thick air between herself and Alistair.

"Good, good. Been glued to my phone all morning waiting for news on my mom's surgery. I hate it," he admitted. He bowed his head to stare at the lit-up screen in his hands, then stabbed a side button to shut it down. He turned to look at her again.

"I hope whatever news you get about her is good," she said with a pleasant smirk. "Tell her I said hi when you talk to her next."

He nodded shallowly and gave her a tight-lipped smile. "Will do."

Alistair slowed the vehicle as he approached Annemarie's driveway. It dipped down slightly from the road, creating a bit of a blind spot when trying to leave the property. Cecily's car sat beside Annemarie's green sedan and Alistair parked behind them both. All three stepped out of the SUV onto the weed-littered gravel, slammed the doors simultaneously—causing quite the ruckus—and Cecily appeared on the front porch with an excited Moose by her side.

"Any news?" Cecily asked.

Annemarie walked up the three steps to the small covered landing in front of the door and muttered, "Al doesn't believe me. That's something." She pushed past her mother, entered the home, and disappeared out of sight. Cecily grimaced. She looked down at her grey flats, trying not to make eye contact with either of the men.

"Hey! I want your clothes for testing!" Alistair called after her, hoping she heard and would not throw the soiled outfit directly into the washer or trash can. His attention returned to Cecily. "Cec, I *want* to believe her. I do. I just—" he started, but stopped when he saw the look of sadness on her face.

She closed her eyes and heaved out a deep breath. "It's about Jesse, isn't it?"

"I—" He paused in order to find the right words. "I honestly don't know. She was already mad at me for not believing her from the get-go, and the moment I brought him up, she kind of went off the deep end." He scratched at a spot behind his right ear and scrunched up that side of his face in thought. "Problem is, whatever the case may be, there's no evidence at the scene. We'll test the blood on her clothes to make sure it's not hers. But beyond that, we've got nothing to go on besides her word. That's not enough. I wish it were, but, y'know, protocols dictate otherwise. I can't—" He did not bother finishing the sentence. Cecily was a logical woman, just like Annemarie, just like he was—but nothing he could say would make either of them understand that his doubt was not personal. Annemarie expected him to take her side and he could not; not yet.

They awkwardly stood in silence. Riggs continued to stare at his phone, occasionally typing a fast text, once again taking a back seat in the conversation. After a few minutes of shifting from one foot to the other, crossing and uncrossing arms, and exasperated sighs, Cecily spoke.

"Seeing her like that, on the side of the road . . . It brought back a lot of horrific memories." She choked on a sob that lingered in her throat.

"It did for me too," Alistair admitted.

"Is this what her life's gonna be from now on? A series of nonstop traumatic events?"

"I don't think so. We all hit stretches of bad luck." He shrugged then glanced at his watch. "We should conduct the interview and get on with our days."

Cecily sidestepped to allow both men to march up the porch and into the house where the low thrum of the running shower filled the living room. She left the door open to allow Moose to come and go as he pleased. "I was gonna make Annemarie a snack. Can I get either of you anything? Something to eat or drink?" Riggs took a seat on the charcoal lounger. Alistair sat beside him on the adjoining couch, leaving enough space for Annemarie and Cecily to sit when they all reconvened.

Riggs shook his head and responded, "No thanks, Mrs. Mitchell," without even looking up from his phone.

"I could use a glass of water," Alistair said. The run to the beach, the walk back to the road, the time in between left him parched.

"Sure thing." She walked through the doorway connecting the living room and modest-sized kitchen. The sound of the faucet turning on and dishware rattling echoed behind them. The refrigerator door opened and closed several times, followed by more clinking and tinny ringing. Alistair never heard the shower turn off, so he was surprised to see a dripping wet, towel-clad Annemarie barge out of her adjacent bedroom. For a moment, her eyes met his and she appeared shocked, as if she forgot he was there. She glided across the room toward the kitchen, not saying a word to either of the men.

"Mom, would you mind making me—" She ran into Cecily who was on her way out to the living room, holding a glass of water for Alistair and a plate with a sandwich meant for her daughter. "Oh, you read my mind." She grabbed the glass with both hands and chugged down half of the liquid in two big gulps. Taking the plate from Cecily, she moseyed over to the opposite end of the couch from Alistair, sat, and unceremoniously shoved the sandwich down her throat, barely chewing by the looks of it. *Ducks eat with more grace,* Alistair thought with an internal laugh.

Cecily immediately turned to head back into the kitchen to retrieve another glass of water. While Alistair waited, for both his drink and Annemarie to finish her meal, he nonchalantly nudged Riggs with his elbow to catch his attention and gestured with a cock of his head to invite him into the conversation.

Alistair pulled a moleskin notepad out of the pocket of his shirt along with a pen, opening it up to a fresh page. "Whenever you're ready, we'd like to get a statement, as well as collect your clothes."

"Clodes er en dere," she said through a mouth full of sliced ham, cheese, and thick bread. She threw a balled-up fist with her thumb extended over her shoulder, to indicate the clothes were in her bedroom and bathroom, and she was giving permission for one of them to retrieve it.

"I'll go get an evidence bag," Riggs said quietly. Alistair nodded him off. He waited patiently, trying not to stare at her while she ate. Cecily returned with another glass of water meant for Alistair. She handed it to him as she sat between them. Annemarie's towel had slipped down an inch from where she had tucked the edge into itself, revealing the top of her left breast. She did not seem to care. Cecily, on the other hand, did. At least in mixed company such as this. She reached out to try to fix the problem, but Annemarie swatted her away.

"Iss fine, mom. I'm almose done here."

"I was just trying to save some embarrassment from happening is all," Cecily replied.

"Not like iss anything Alistair hassn seen before."

Cecily's eyes widened as she looked back and forth between the two. She pointed at Annemarie, then to him. "You two have . . . But in high school, you said you . . ." Her hand shot to cover her shocked mouth.

The tops of Alistair's cheeks blushed rosy pink. He hesitated a moment before saying, "No, Cec. She just means . . . breasts in general."

Annemarie shrugged. "Yeah, sure. That's what I meant." Alistair and Annemarie knew that was not what she meant, but for Cecily's sake, that was what they were going with. Annemarie finished off the last corner of her sandwich. "I'll go get dressed." Excusing herself from the couch and empty dishware, she sauntered into the bedroom, out of sight, leaving Cecily and Alistair to sit in awkward silence once again. He doodled on his notepad while he waited. She cleaned under her fingernails.

Riggs returned with a large plastic evidence bag and a pair of black nitrile gloves already on his hands. As soon as he reached the living room, he rounded the corner into the bedroom to gather the dirty clothes.

Before Alistair or Cecily could say anything, Annemarie shouted, *"Riggs!"* and watched as the blushing, tail-between-his-legs deputy scurried out of the bedroom.

"I'm sorry, I'm sorry!" he called back at her.

With a bemused chuckle, Cecily said to Alistair, "Now it seems Riggs's seen some too."

FOUR

Over the course of the following thirty minutes, Alistair questioned Annemarie about the incident, getting everything jotted down in his notebook. She meticulously divulged details, doing her best to not stray from the story with personal opinions. She knew the routine from having to give statements about the accident last year to hearing anonymous stories from Alistair's and Riggs's time on the force. The more she talked about it out loud, the wilder it sounded, and the closer she was to understanding why he hesitated to take her seriously. She knew what she saw, but she had no way of explaining any of it.

Near the end of the interview, Alistair closed his notebook and set it on the coffee table in front of him. He cleared his throat. "I-I don't want to have to bring this up, but I have a few questions relating to . . . Jesse's death."

Annemarie gulped audibly. When last he brought up her dead husband, mere hours before, she lost her cool completely. She had made peace with her anger toward him from it; would she be able to get over it this time too? "Okay," she said softly.

"How are you holding up in relation to the one-year anniversary?" he asked, cutting to the chase.

"Not fucking good," she muttered.

"I imagine as much. But in all seriousness, have you been seeing anything out of the ord—"

"*In all seriousness?* Who's fucking joking, Al?"

"I didn't mean it like that," he said quickly.

Cecily guided her hand over to Annemarie's lap to offer a spot of comfort, and to attempt to calm her. In all the years Annemarie and Alistair had been friends, she had never spoken to him in this way, and seeing this sort of outburst worried Cecily.

"I've not been hallucinating. I don't see his face smiling back at me when I look at flowers. I don't hear his voice whisper my name on the breeze. I'm a vision of picture-perfect health. Ask my therapist." She practically spit out the last sentence.

"I understand this is a touchy subject, Annie."

"You're goddamn right it is! You're trying to tell me that my encounter with a dying Peter Arthur didn't actually happen, that I hallucinated it. That I'm longing for my husband who died a horrific death, and I couldn't be there to help him, so obviously I feel guilty or something. *Oh*, and that I've hit my head, which must also be the cause for these hallucinations. Does that sound about right, Sheriff?"

Alistair closed his eyes to take in all her vitriol and to breathe in deep. Maybe he deserved it, maybe he did not, but he was going to let her get it out for as long as she needed. When she finally stopped, he retorted, "I'm sorry to have even brought it up." He pushed up from the couch, retrieved the notepad from the table, pocketed it, and motioned for Riggs to join him. "You're obviously *just fine*."

Her face turned bright red at this admonition. Cecily saw the anger rising in her features and squeezed

Annemarie's clenching fist once. "I think we've all had a long morning. It'd be best if you got on your way, Sheriff. Annemarie needs some time to decompress."

"Mom, I—"

"You *need* some time to *decompress*," she repeated, using what weight she had behind her slim frame to hold Annemarie down on the couch, to keep her from bolting to her feet. Cecily feared if she let this continue, Annemarie might hit Alistair, and she did not want to think about the consequences, whether it be the assault of an officer or her best friend of thirty-odd years.

"Have a nice rest of your day," Riggs said to them as he followed Alistair out of the house, holding onto the sealed evidence bag.

"You too, Riggs," Annemarie called, though the door was already closed. The SUV's doors opened and slammed shut, the engine started, and it disappeared out of her driveway, spitting a bit of gravel back at the house as it went. "I had a handle on it, mom," Annemarie protested.

"No, you didn't. He was only trying to get to the bottom of this, to help you understand why this whole thing is problematic, and to see if he—if *we*—should be worried about you. He was doing the right thing, and you were being a bitch."

Taken aback for a moment, Annemarie gaped at her mother, but did not say a word. She could only blink at her as she processed what had been said.

"I'm sorry to be so blunt with you, but it's true. You've *never* spoken to him like that before. Why now? What's so different now that you're suddenly so vicious about everything he's saying or asking? Is it Jesse? Is that the issue?"

"I'm not having this conversation with you right now."

"No, I think it's time we do. This last year has been beyond devastating for you and I cannot even begin to pretend I know how you feel. For *six months* you hid away, only showing your face the few times you chose to show up in court, and there was nothing me, your father, or your sister could do to help you. You were killing yourself. A nonstop supply of alcohol and eating an apple every six hours was killing you."

"I mean, apples have fiber and beer has calories . . ." Annemarie interjected, trying to lighten the mood. She worked the rubber band off her wrist and loosely tied back her hair.

"Annemarie Bailey McCready!" Annemarie's eyes went wide and she promptly slammed her lips shut, holding back the silly rebuttal she had. "You were killing yourself because of this unfathomable thing. And when you needed help the most, you wouldn't let any of us in. Except Alistair. Alistair, who found you on the side of the road after the accident, who was a guard at your side the whole time you were in the hospital, who . . . who *loves you* so thoroughly and is willing to risk his job—"

"Mom."

"—just to take your side on something you may be one hundred percent wrong about, who—"

"Mom."

"—has been a part of your life since you were in diapers. And you think he needs to be treated like the villain. Annemarie, you—"

"*Mom!*" she finally snapped.

"What?"

"I'm tired."

"I know you're tired. It's been a horrible year and I want what's best—"

"No, mom, I'm tired of all this." She gestured out in front of her and in the air. "You should leave too." Annemarie moved to the lounger portion of the couch and stretched out onto the soft material. She pulled a blanket from off the back to drape across herself. She turned over and closed her eyes.

Cecily did not appreciate being treated like she was the bad guy either, but she took it in stride. The anniversary did not excuse the behavior, but it helped to understand it. She picked up the dirty plate and empty glasses to take into the kitchen. She cleaned the small mess of breadcrumbs, the paper sleeve from the sliced cheese, and the dishes. As she gathered her few belongings in the living room, Moose watched her every move with a steady eye from the threshold of the bedroom. She walked past him as he let out a short whimper.

"Need to potty, Moose?" she asked in a hushed tone, trying not to bother Annemarie further. His long, fluffy tail wagged. "Come on." She opened the front door to usher him outside. He bounded down the steps into the driveway and high-tailed it to the side yard where he found his favorite mole hill to urinate on. He snuffled around in the grass, wanting to follow the trail of something delightful, only to lead to another lifting of his leg up against a shrub by the house. Cecily gave a soft whistle for him to come back to her. He trotted along to her side. She pointed at the front door and commanded, "Go inside," but he sat his rump down in the gravel at her feet. "Moose, inside, now." His head lolled back, allowing his tongue to flop out of his mouth and to show off his pearly fangs. "You're being silly, young man. Inside. Now." She slipped a foot under his butt to urge him to stand and move along. No budging. "I don't know who's more stubborn: you or your mother."

She walked over to her car in order to put down her purse. As she opened the door, she heard another whimper. She peered over her shoulder to find Moose scooting closer to her. "Oh, I see how it is. You wanna come home with me?" She stepped away from the vehicle, allowing him to launch himself into the front seat, much like he had when they were out on the highway. "Well, hang on a second." She walked back into the house, still careful of the loud footfalls echoing on the front porch. On the small table under the wall-mounted television sat a stack of brightly colored sticky notes and a pen. The top slip read "unsalted butter, peaches, that good rum, toothbrush": a shopping list. Cecily removed it from the pile and set it aside so she could write on the next blank page.

"Took Moose for a sleepover. -Mom" She removed this piece of paper too.

Unsure where to position it so Annemarie would easily find it when she woke—because Cecily sure as hell was not going to wake her up to inform her of the impromptu plan—she stuck it on the face of her cell phone on the coffee table. She silently excused herself from the room once more, making her way to the car to take Moose home for a night in with her and Ken, who loved Moose like the son he never had.

FIVE

The bright, glittery CON-GRAD-ULATIONS banner hanging in the foyer went unnoticed by every single person who entered the house—each of them more interested in finding their friends, the kegs, and the snacks. The day had been one nightmare after another for the seniors of Brownstone High School who already had one foot out the door, with the graduation ceremony unexpectedly relocating from the leaky-roofed gym to the muddy football field, all thanks to a thunderstorm that had rolled through the night before. Chairs needed setting up and arranged, a podium of sorts constructed for the class council and speech givers, and rerouting everyone to pick up their cap and gown packets in the cafeteria, mere hours before the ceremony. Even those not directly involved with the planning pitched in, but it was a lot of hard, stressful work, culminating in a windy event that saw more than one mortarboard tumble off a head, never to be seen again.

But with the pomp and circumstance behind them, the real party could begin at Christina Errol's home—a sprawling residence tucked into the forested southeastern tip of Port Harrow. Graduating son, Nic, had been given permission to throw an epic soiree for his classmates to commemorate a job well-done.

Loud pop music blared over speakers in the living room, muffled only by the sounds of dozens of seventeen- and eighteen-year-olds gushing to and gossiping with one another. For most of them, graduation and the ensuing party was one of the last times they would see their friend groups in one place—summer jobs, travel, and preparing for college in the fall begged to occupy their time from here on out.

Nic's mother was awarded the family home in the nasty divorce and she gave her only child run of the place, so long as he and his friends did not break the valuable art. Despite Nic's propensity to give exactly zero shits about anything, he always made sure he stashed all of the expensive possessions in her bedroom and locked the door, making it impossible for his friends to cause irreparable chaos.

And that was all the students cared about—anarchy, but in a privileged sense. None of the residents of the island community, their children included, knew hardship intimately. Most families came from money and those who had to work hard to be a part of the elite upper crust were considered to have "made it" if they bought a home on Port Harrow.

As so many of the privileged offspring hunkered down for a long night of debauchery, two of them casually sipped beer from plastic cups as they pressed themselves into a corner near the staircase that led to the second floor of the home. Annemarie's copper hair with her signature streak of bubblegum pink she meticulously touched up every Sunday night fell past her shoulders, parted down the center with an elaborate zigzag pattern adorning her scalp. She constantly tugged at the upper hem of her tube top to keep it in place over her small chest *and* have her midriff revealed to some extent. Meant for someone with a more ample bust and a slightly longer torso, she was practically drowning in too much material. But the motion became second nature as she was easily captivated by the dark-haired, blue-eyed hunk leaning dangerously close to her.

Alistair kept one hand wrapped around his cup while the fingers of the other were idly scratching against the belt of Annemarie's low-rise jeans in a slow, methodical manner. She said something, but under the din of the noise bouncing around the house, he did not hear her. He leaned in closer, resting a cheek against hers, trying his best to ask, "What did you say?" without screaming in her ear.

The gentlest of mischievous smirks darted into the corner of her mouth before she replied, "I said I bet you're so glad to be done with school."

It took a delayed moment to understand, followed by a single nod. "Only for a couple months, though. Honestly, I can't wait for—"

He was not allowed to finish the thought as several bodies stumbled into them, shoving Alistair into Annemarie, pinning them both in their little corner. She let out an audible *oof* as she took the brunt of the force, but she was okay. Alistair used all of his weight to muscle the trio away from them, and once successful, returned his attention to her.

"You good?" he asked.

She nodded. "Perfect." Her fingers fluttered over her ear to push back a chunk of hair. "What were you saying?" she practically shouted at him.

He assumed the position again, opened his mouth, and only got out "I can't wait—" before being interrupted again.

This time, Nic snuck up behind the two and kneed Alistair in the back of the leg, causing Alistair to buckle and lose balance. "Hey, dipshits!" he announced. He threw both of his arms into the air, brandishing a beer in each hand and showing off the bottle-blonde clinger he had wrapped around his waist. She embraced him tightly, holding on for dear life. When she lifted her head to glance up at Alistair, Annemarie gasped.

"Marissa!" Her hand shot to cover her mouth, more to hide the smile and laugh threatening to escape her than in shock. Her sister, one year her senior and graduating alongside Alistair and Nic, was sloppy drunk. She needed an anchor in order to stay mostly upright and her flavor of the week happened to be the host of the party.

"Hey, little shishter. What're you doing here?" Marissa slurred her words as she struggled to keep her head lifted.

Trying to be heard over the noise, Annemarie leaned toward her collapsing sister and yelled, "Alistair brought me!"

With a knowing nod, Marissa managed to make eye contact with him. She loosened her death grip around Nic's waist in order to point a wobbly finger at Alistair. "You take care of my shishter, mishter." She snorted. "Shishter, mishter. Mishter shishter." Another *snerk* escaped her before she returned to clutching onto Nic's midsection for stability.

The corner of Alistair's mouth perked up into a grin. "Don't need to worry about us. You, on the other hand . . ."

"Oh, she'll be taken care of, believe you me." Nic shot him a wide smile and gave a quick wink.

Alistair's mouth dropped open and he moved close to Nic's ear. "Dude. You're not . . . really . . ." He raised both eyebrows as concern filled his face. "She's—"

But before he could get any further, Nic rested his hand—still gripping a bottle—against Alistair's chest. "I'm putting her up in mom's room so she can take a break from partying and have somewhere safe to be."

Alistair huffed out a relieved breath. He always liked Nic, and the mere thought he might take advantage of someone completely blitzed made his stomach churn and his skin crawl; hearing it was not Nic's intention allowed the tension to ease.

Still leaning close together, Nic tried to whisper, "You, though. You need to find yourself an empty bedroom, stat." He pointed past Alistair's shoulder at Annemarie who was gnawing on her bottom lip, fluttering her lashes at him once they locked eyes. It was no secret she was a bombshell—both Mitchell girls were. She had been Alistair's best friend all of their lives, but only in the last year or so had he developed more than platonic feelings for her and fought with himself for almost six months to ask her out. She did not hesitate with her answer, though he sometimes wondered if she only said yes because she was the last of their large friend group to bag a significant other—she promised Alistair that was not the case and she had true love for him.

They spent their free time making out wherever they could, often getting detention for so blatantly ignoring school policy about gratuitous public displays of affection. Annemarie even went so far as to sneak out of the house when she had been grounded for said infractions and hoofed it twenty minutes to Alistair's dad's house so they could make out some more. None of their private sessions ever progressed past third base, and he never wanted to push the fact that he was ready to be her first if she was ready to be his.

But tonight—the alcohol loosening up his reticence, his inhibitions, seeing her standing there with that bit of midriff exposed because of those hip-hugging jeans riding low, and that perpetual pout as she continued to while away the time by burying her upper teeth into her bottom lip . . . Nic's suggestion did not seem like a bad one.

Alistair turned back to look at Nic, but he was already halfway up the stairs, both hands free of the beers as he carefully guided Marissa to the safety of his mom's bedroom. Staring for a bit too long, his concentration broke at the caress of a hand on his bicep.

"Earth to Alistair!" Annemarie called over the music. A lopsided grin graced his lips as he swiveled on his heel to face her. "There you are."

He stepped toward her, fished an arm around her waist, and pulled her close. "I was always here."

She pursed her lips before planting a kiss on his still-smiling mouth. He started to say something but she interrupted with a quick, sultry, "I wonder if there're any empty bedrooms."

"Let's go find out." Alistair slid his hand into hers, tugging, urging her to follow him. It turned into a competitive race up the stairs and a flurry of rattling door handles and walking in on other couples, which resulted in becoming moving targets for classmates to throw random objects at when they interrupted something.

Two doors remained at the end of the hall. As they approached, the one on the left swung open just wide enough for a body to squeeze through and Nic emerged. He stopped in his tracks when he saw Annemarie and Alistair. He gestured vaguely over his shoulder. "Mar-Mar is gonna crash here tonight." His eyes darted between the two. "This room's off-limits, but that one's open." He shot an over-exaggerated wink at them before hustling down the hall, out of sight.

In the small bedroom, Annemarie had worked Alistair out of his red button-down shirt and their fingers fumbled with the buckles on each other's belts as they kissed in a feverish frenzy.

"I wanna . . . do this . . . with you . . . all summer," she said in between gasps for air. It took a moment for the entirety of the sentence to hit Alistair, and when it did, he immediately, and inadvertently, stopped making any advances. "Did I say something wrong?" she asked. She stared up at him through her eyelashes, her mouth slightly ajar as her wet bottom lip threatened to quiver.

He shook his head. "No, I just—" She took his answer at face value and closed the gap between them, trying to get him to crane his neck down to continue where they had left off. He stopped again. "Annie, I . . . We need to talk."

"Can't it wait?" Her eagerness knew no bounds.

After a delay, he shook his head again. "No, I-I don't think so." He placed his hands on her shoulders and set her down at the edge of the bed. He sat beside her, leaving a sizeable space. "You know I'm going to school after this." She nodded. "And I'm leaving sooner than later." Another nod. "Then you know that this—" He motioned between them with a hand. "—won't last much longer. That is, unless you're willing to try long distance, but I don't know how well that'll work out."

She gave a noncommittal shrug. "I mean, I don't graduate for another year, and you'll only be up in Gunnison. That's not *that* far."

"No, but think about the ferry commute, the mainland traffic, making our schedules line up. College is intense. I'm not going there to party. But I can't . . ." He let his voice trail off before he said something he would regret.

They were both thinking it, though. "School's your priority," she said with a knowing, albeit sad nod. "It always has been and it always will be." She sighed. "Am I ever gonna see you? Like, honestly?"

"Honestly?" he echoed. Her nod was shallow. "I'd like to. In an ideal world, I'll have weekends free. But really, I don't know." He lifted both hands in the air to accompany his shrug.

"But you're not leaving next week, right?"

"No, but I need to figure out an apartment, I'll be working a ton . . . Our time is limited, a-and I don't want to have an amazing night with you and then go run off. I don't want you thinking I used you. I don't want to lose what we have either."

Annemarie cocked her head. "Alistair, you're my best friend. I would never think that, and nothing could ever ruin this. Even if we break up tomorrow. We've got too much history to let it go to the wayside."

"Do you promise?"

"I promise."

She stuck her pinky into his face, goading him to reciprocate the gesture. They linked little fingers, twisted till taut, and kissed their respective thumbs.

He pulled away from their promise tradition and sheepishly rubbed at the back of his head. "I wanna be sure, is all. I don't want—"

She grabbed his chin between her thumb and forefinger, averting his shy gaze from his lap to her eyes. "Hey, you let me take care of myself, okay? You let me worry about me." She fell into his arms up against his bare chest. He brought her close, wrapped her in a tight embrace, and pressed his lips against her forehead.

"Annie, I'll never not worry about you."

SIX

The sound of an upbeat rock song filled the living room. It played through the chorus once, then on to a second time before Annemarie roused from her angry, irritated sleep. Without bothering to roll over, she extended her arm backward toward the coffee table to blindly grope for the obnoxious, vibrating noisemaker. Managing to swipe it with her hand, she nearly dropped it when the unfamiliar edges of the sticky note caught her off guard. Begrudgingly, she rolled onto her back to allow the use of both hands to remove the note. Her eyes flitted across the screen to see "Sheriff Lucas" was calling—Alistair on his work phone—and though she answered, her attention was on her mother's handwriting.

"Hey." Her greeting was groggy and solemn.

"Were you sleeping?"

She opened her mouth to answer, but a yawn caught up first. A variation of "yeah" came out with her exhale. "Sorry."

"No, I'm sorry for waking you." The apology was immediate.

Her hand reached up to scratch her scalp and noticed her ponytail was askew. "It's fine." The rubber band fell into her palm as she worked her fingers through the slightly damp hair. "What time is it?"

"Uh . . ." There was a break in his voice for a moment. "One thirty."

Annemarie grunted a pain of recognition. "Shit. I'm gonna be late. Gonna have to make this quick. What's up?" She needed to get to the library to relieve Katherine, but she knew even if she left right now, she would be behind schedule. While she waited for Alistair to mumble his way through an array of *I really shouldn't be telling you this* and *I thought you'd want to know*, she pulled the phone from her ear in order to navigate to the messaging app. The last text sent to Katherine was from two days prior when Annemarie confirmed she could cover the last half of the shift. As she finished apologizing profusely and promising she was leaving soon, Alistair finally got to the point.

"I got a phone call a bit ago." He paused. "From Yongsoo."

Annemarie shot upright and almost sent the phone flying across the room. *"What?"*

"Yongsoo called into the station to report that Peter's missing. She said he didn't come home this morning and he hasn't been answering her calls. Even her texts are going unread."

Her breath caught in her throat, only allowing a strangled, strained gasp to escape her lips to fill the silence between them, the silence created by his purposely stopping to maybe elicit more than a few words at a time from her. "Are you saying you believe me?" she finally managed. Part of her felt relief that she was not losing her mind—Cecily and Alistair had kind of impelled her to believe that her grief had caused a pretty convincing hallucination—and part of her pushed her heart so deep into her bowels, she was afraid to hear anything further.

"I'm saying Peter Arthur is unaccounted for at this moment." Matter-of-fact. Unwilling to cave, even a little, to give her the benefit of the doubt. *Good ol' Al,* she thought.

Annemarie buried a hand in her hair to grip at her roots, tugging some. "W-what happens next?" Her voice quivered with the question. She readjusted her position on the couch, tucking her toes underneath her folded legs. Any thought of ending the conversation in order to get on the road to the library fluttered away like the sticky note that was now on the floor.

"Standard protocol is to send an officer to the person's last-known location, but given that Yongsoo saw him at home two mornings ago as he was on his way to the marina for a couple days of fishing on their boat, and she says no one in the harbor recalls seeing him motor out, we don't have a good 'last-known location.'" He cleared his throat, more of an awkward segue than an unclogging of the passageway. "I hate to admit it, but this is a weird situation. Because we never deal with missing persons here, and so few of us have that experience, *and* add to it we have some strange eyewitness testimony—that's you, by the way—it's kind of a tricky thing. We're expediting things as best we can. I've got deputies going around the island on the lookout for him and his boat, plus another headed to Brownstone right now to search their marinas and shorelines. This is one of those times where I wish you—" He stopped short.

Annemarie thought she knew how he intended to finish the sentence, but assumed he was trying to not piss her off any more than he already had. She let it roll off her shoulders. She was cranky about that morning, but more than anything else, she was physically sore and mentally exhausted, and it was time to carry on with her day. She did not love what she had seen on the beach, hallucination or not; she needed to believe the sheriff's department would handle it. Alistair and his crew were more than capable.

"Well, let me know if—"

"Tell me something." His words were followed by the sound of a writing utensil scratching along a papery surface.

"Like what? A joke? The recipe to my rum peach pie?" She amused herself and smirked.

But Alistair's response came across deadpan and professional. "Did you see what he was wearing?"

"Excuse me?"

"Peter. When you were digging him out, did you see what he was wearing?"

"I don't see how that has—"

"Yes or no, Annie." The sudden, to-the-point demeanor was so unlike how their conversations normally went, which made her feel like *she* was on trial for murder. It reminded her too much of the line of questioning presented in the courtroom when Travis Kelly and Nowell Reid were facing manslaughter charges for the death of her husband.

The memory lit a fire in her to comply with Alistair as much as possible—thereby ending the phone call, her now number-one priority. "Um, yeah. It was a blue shirt. W-with pink pineapples all over it." Every detail about that morning would remain etched into her brain forever. She knew she would never not see the horrific scene, especially the button-down being slashed and bloodied once she revealed that part of him with her digging. "I-is that a note for the file?"

"When Yongsoo called in, she said she last saw him wearing a floppy fishing hat, cargo shorts, and his favorite 'blue button-down shirt with peach-colored pineapples on it.'"

SEVEN

The sun blazed high above the street, beating heat on the necks of passersby making their way to and from work for the lunch hour. Annemarie sauntered along the worn, cracked sidewalk, sporting jean Bermuda shorts and a tight-fitting tank top. Having blasted the air conditioning the entire journey into Brownstone from the island, the warmth of the day was welcome on her bare shoulders.

With nothing more than her small bifold wallet tucked into a back pocket, keys half hanging from a front, and her cell phone in hand, she made her way to the entrance of The Sloe, a gastropub known for their expansive menu of food and drink to suit any appetite, and one of the only bars in the area open before three p.m. It was often the go-to for Annemarie and her best gal pal, Nina Novak, to meet when they arranged a lunch date; it was halfway between the ferry dock and Nina's office, making it easy walking distance for both of them.

The large, faux-bronze door leading into the establishment was propped open a few inches with a rubber stop, allowing fresh air to filter into the space whose air conditioning was on the fritz. Annemarie pulled on the handle to let herself in. The heat in the room was mildly oppressive, more muggy than hot, and stifling. She was grateful to be in lightweight clothing.

Annemarie did not see Nina at first. She assumed her friend had not yet arrived. Nina mentioned via text that her morning deposition might run through the lunch hour, but she would try to get there as soon as possible. Annemarie waved at Cale, the server, who often tended bar during the day shift. He gave her a warm smile, followed by an uplifted chin-nod, pointing to the far-left corner. Annemarie's eyes tracked the invisible line Cale created, spotting a briefcase leaning up against a booth seat. She nodded back as a reply of thanks.

Nina pored over a yellow legal pad of paper, furiously scribbling notes with her left hand while her right rested on the smooth, cool glass of her beer. She paused from her writing to take a drink, allowing her to look up and spot Annemarie approaching. She followed through with her swig, gulping down the refreshing IPA, but quickly greeted her longtime friend with a wiggle of her perfectly manicured fingers.

Annemarie slid into the booth across from Nina. She set her phone face down onto the mosaic tile tabletop and smiled. "Really going for the Farrah today, huh?" Nina's long, black, feathered locks lifted and pulled away from her dark skin, framing her full cheeks, drawing attention to the smear of ruby on her lips.

She chuckled, nodding emphatically, causing the hair to flutter. "Someone's gotta bring it in this city of beige." She set the pen in her hand on top of the legal pad and pushed it off to the side. With Annemarie here, work could wait. She was clocked out for the rest of the day anyway, free to get up to whatever hijinks she wanted. Sitting in a bar at noon on a Tuesday, about to catch up with her friend, sounded like the perfect reward for a job well-done. "You're looking good," she mused.

Annemarie laughed. She thought she looked like the train wreck she was. "That's sweet of you to say." She paused, then changed the subject. "Have you ordered food yet?"

Nina nodded again. "Yep. Got the *ushe*. Cale was making fun of me, like always." She rolled her eyes. "*I get it.* I order the same damn sandwich every time I come here. 'No sense of adventure,' he says." But the slightest of smiles accompanied her words. She always acted annoyed when he poked fun at her choice of a grilled chicken and mushroom melt, even though she not-so-secretly loved the silly, flirty banter they exchanged.

"I'm gonna go put in my order. I'm starving," Annemarie announced.

"Well, hurry back, I've got to tell you all about this girly I've been seeing."

Annemarie's eyebrows raised in surprise. "Will do," she said with a slight grin. She set a hand on Nina's shoulder and gave it a firm squeeze. "I've missed you." She walked up to the U-shaped bar in the middle of the art-deco room. "Afternoon," she said as she leaned against the counter with her elbows propping her up. This move stretched the skin at the back of her upper arms, causing the scab on the big wound to tug and pinch. She grimaced, but held the position.

Like a scene out of a movie, he stood there, monolithic, drying a glass with a white bar rag. He casually dressed in jeans and a black T-shirt with the bar's logo printed in baby blue over his left pec. "What can I getcha, Annie?" he asked.

"Chicken Caesar salad, please," she said with a sweet smile.

"Anything to drink?"

"Just ice water right now."

He poked a finger at the computer screen beside him, ringing up her order. "Want me to leave it open in case you decide to add something?" He sidestepped to grab a pint glass, filled it with ice, and topped it off with water from the soda gun hidden below the counter. He set the drink in front of her.

She shrugged. "Sure. Thanks, Cale." She rapped her knuckles twice on the perpetually sticky-feeling bar top and returned to the booth. She slid into her seat and greeted Nina once again with a warm smile. "Okay, dish."

Nina's cheeks grew visibly rosy. "*Oh, Annie.* She's wonderful. She's smart and funny and she's as much of a pessimist as I am. She's gorgeous. Oh my god is she ever gorgeous. Thick and luscious and . . ." She fanned her hand at herself, overwhelmed at the mere thought of the woman.

"What's her name? Where'd you meet?" Annemarie folded her hands and placed them on the table as she leaned forward, eagerly awaiting more details.

"Her name is Zuri and she's a bailiff. We met in court." She wiggled her shoulders like an over-sugared child being told to sit perfectly still and was incapable of doing so.

"Is . . . that legal? Like, are you allowed to date court employees?" Annemarie pulled up both of her legs onto the booth seat to cross under her, making herself more comfortable.

"Nothing says we can't. She holds no conflict of interest in any case of mine, being a bailiff and all. We're professional as hell when we're in the building, but the second we get home . . ." She blushed deeper.

"How long have you been seeing each other?"

"Six months, give or take."

"Wow. Has it really been that long since I last saw you?" Annemarie's jaw hung low at the thought—for as close as Nina and she had been all of their adult lives, the last year found Annemarie inadvertently shunning everyone to focus on her trauma. No one begrudged her for it, but it did mean she missed out on a lot; and the distance between Port Harrow and Brownstone seemingly grew with each day she refused to talk to anyone outside her four walls.

"Not quite. But things weren't serious then and I wasn't sure if it was a *fun only on the weekends* kind of deal, if you know what I mean." She gave an overexaggerated wink.

"Is it serious now?"

"I mean, I would *die* for that woman, if that's what you're asking." Nina snickered. She took another gulp of the beer and wiped her mouth delicately with the back of her hand, careful to not smudge her lipstick.

"Aww." There was a happy lilt in Annemarie's voice. "I'm so happy for you, babe. That's wonderful. Really." She was excited for her friend who had struggled to find a healthy, happy relationship with men for years, especially after coming out as bisexual and deciding to navigate the world of dating women after years of wading through the bachelors of Azure County. But Annemarie's enthusiasm wavered as she spoke, tattling on her.

The sparkle in Nina's dark eyes faded and her features scrunched up as she observed Annemarie. "Are you okay? You seem like something's bothering you. It's not because I—" Her hand shot to her mouth when it dawned on her; did her gushing about finding love when Annemarie had lost hers strike a nerve?

Annemarie shook her head quickly, the ponytail slapping at the backs of her ears. "Oh, god, Nina, no. No, no, no. I'm genuinely happy you've got something good going on in your love life for once. Truly." She paired it with a toothy grin to convince Nina she was sincere.

"Then what's been going on with you? I feel like we haven't spoken *at all* recently."

Annemarie nonchalantly but emphatically shrugged. "This and that. Some . . . odd things have been happening back home. I don't even know where to begin or how to describe any of it." She paused for a moment, hesitating to say anything further while Cale set their meals on the table. She continued. "Have you ever felt like . . . *oh fuck.*" Annemarie quickly turned in her seat to face the wall, awkwardly trying to hide herself in plain sight. She was no longer making eye contact with Nina.

"What's wrong?" Nina glanced around their immediate area, looking for something out of the ordinary. When her search yielded nothing, her eyes shot across the room to the doorway where two men stood idly. She focused on the taller of the two. Light hair, light eyes, a slightly crooked nose veering to the left. He looked like an average nobody to her; the smaller one was cute, but unknown to her as well. "What's wrong?" she repeated.

Annemarie could not help but look. She did not want to. She knew she should not. But . . . maybe she was mistaken. She turned in place, slowly easing her gaze toward the men, and narrowed in on the taller of the two. "It's . . . Nowell Reid."

"Why is that—*oh fuck* is right. That's . . ."

"Yeah." It came out of Annemarie's mouth so softly and smoothly, like it did not hurt her to say so. His was a name she disliked saying, hearing, *thinking*. Nowell Reid was half of the reason Jesse was dead. It was Nowell's vehicle swerving into oncoming traffic that caused Jesse to no longer exist beyond a box of bones in some soil back east. Even though the courts acquitted him and the driver, Travis Kelly, of any charges and Annemarie came to terms that it was an accident beyond their control, she could not help but hold a grudge; and no one could blame her. She still spent nights crying over the fact that anyone was capable of causing something so catastrophic in another person's life, even as an accident.

At one point in the last year, in a fit of torment, she pulled a dictionary from off a shelf at the library and looked up the word ACCIDENT. An unforeseen and unplanned event or circumstance; lack of intention; an unfortunate event resulting especially from carelessness. *Carelessness*. That was what the men exhibited on that night nearly one year ago when they T-boned Jesse and her. Annemarie's wounds, though dire, healed; save for a few scars, no one would have been the wiser that she had walked away from such a horrific accident. The mental scars, however . . .

The last thing she needed during her little visit from her own microcosmical world was to run into the reason for her depression, the reason for her will to not carry on, the reason she now checked the *widow* box on all appropriate forms.

Travis passed away five months ago after an unfortunate boating accident. It was deemed a "tragic incident" and used to stress the importance of safety in all bodies of water at all times of the year—at least, that was how *The Brownstone Beat* posited it. Annemarie found herself torn between emotions: relief that she would never have to see his face ever again and utter sadness that his family lost a loved one due to more carelessness.

With Nowell, she knew he was around—knew he lived in Brownstone—but in a city of fifty-two thousand, what was the likelihood of running into him? She never saw him prior to the accident, as far as she knew, and she had successfully gone this long without seeing him. Until now.

She could not help but stare. She did not care if it was rude or unbecoming of her character to be two seconds from pointing him out, to call nasty accusations; but Nina pulled her back to earth with a few words. "Mistakes and accidents happen. Wishing him dead won't bring Jesse back, hun. An eye for an eye rarely garners the closure we so desperately seek."

Annemarie turned to face her friend. Nina half expected to be chewed out for trying to make light of the past. She was pleasantly surprised—or rather, shocked—

when a thin smile came over Annemarie's pale face as they locked eyes. "Spoken like a true attorney," Annemarie said with a reluctant chuckle. "You're right. As always. I just . . . It's a knee-jerk reaction to want to hide, and to hate him. And I don't know how to deal with that. It's not like I ever see him. But here? Now? What're the odds?"

Nina gave an understanding nod. She knew Annemarie was hurting and found it difficult to move on. She did not blame her for not being able to. If her long-term partner was ripped away from her, especially so unexpectedly, she would not know how to be strong. A distraction was in order. "So, forget his ass. Tell me . . . What's been going on back home? This weird stuff, I mean."

Annemarie traced circles around the rim of her water glass. She had not taken a drink from it yet. She regretted not ordering a martini. She wanted to. She longed for a hard drink; Cale made them *so* strong for them. With Nowell in her vicinity, every fiber of her being wanted her to grab hold of a thin-necked glass and drink it down to its last drop in a single gulp. *A deep drunk is what I need,* she thought. But something inside her refrained from flagging down Cale and she returned to the conversation Nina was attempting to have with her.

"I'm not exactly sure how to explain it. Or even where to start. I guess . . ."

Before Annemarie could get out another word, Nina lifted a finger to interrupt. "I'm sorry. Hold that thought. The floodgates need some pressure relieved." She slid out of the booth in one smooth movement. "Be back in a jiff!"

Her head of fluttery hair bounced as she pranced across the expanse of the bar, quickly disappearing through the plaster arch leading to the bathrooms.

A heavy sigh escaped Annemarie. *I don't want to be here right now,* she thought. Her fingers still played with the glass. She watched the back of Nowell's head as he talked with Cale. When the server walked away to punch the details into his computer, Nowell turned to look at the interior of the establishment, eyes taking in every surface, and finally caught sight of Annemarie in his scan. At first, he did not recognize her—or at least chose not to react when he saw her. He had glanced away but immediately darted his eyes back to her booth. She quickly shot her gaze down at the salad and wished she could disappear from existence in that moment.

The sound of footsteps followed by the scraping of a chair on the hardwood floor echoed in her ears. She looked up and saw he was sitting beside her, having pulled up a seat from a nearby table.

He forced a weak smile across his face and both eyebrows were perched high on his forehead, soft and arched, a sort of demonstrative peace offering.

"What the shit, dude?" The words forced themselves out of her mouth and she had no way to catch them. His expression dropped away immediately. A burp rose from her stomach. She wanted to let it out, but quickly realized it was not a bubble of gas; it was bile. Her body was trying to make her vomit.

Nowell raised both hands in front of his face, hoping to stifle any anger that might fly his way. "Look, I know I'm the last person you want to see, but I'm not here to harass you. I promise. I don't want anything but five minutes of your time. I need to talk to you."

"You have sixty seconds." Her eyes widened when she realized those words came out of her mouth. Was she really going to listen to him?

His eyes popped at hearing it too; he assumed she would bite off his head—and he would deserve it. Nowell sucked in a deep breath and held it for a moment. He released it and quickly stuttered, "T-that night-t . . ."

Her eyes rolled. *"Seriously?"* She could not bother to close her ajar mouth. "You wanna talk to me about the night you were involved with the death of my husband? And you don't consider that harassment?"

He sighed, understanding her skepticism with his intention. "I know, I know. This probably isn't the best time. You're obviously here with someone. But I've been waiting a year for the right time and I don't think it'll ever come, so I gotta do this now. If you'll let me." He paused. "And I still have forty-five seconds."

Annemarie pressed her lips together to suppress a laugh. She studied him. She had spent hours in the courtroom staring at him, memorizing every flaw of his face, every remarkable spot the naked eye could see. Now, his face seemed unfamiliar, harder, a little more weathered, a tinge of pink from the bright sunshine outside—or maybe it was a wash of embarrassment or unease silently outing him that he knew he was in the wrong for approaching her. His face was slender compared to the last time they were in each other's presence, eleven months prior. The creases in his forehead were prominent, but not in such a way to create permanent wrinkles yet. The light brown tuft of hair he wore during the trial was buzzed down to stubble. She had not been sure it was him when he walked in, but that slight crook in his nose was unmistakable. He looked more like a poor effigy of the youthful man who stood trial—rough around the edges, unrefined, disparate.

"Are you okay?" His question interrupted her thoughts. The tone in his voice made Annemarie think he was sincere in not wanting to upset her or wanting to cause any harm. However, regardless if he meant to hurt her or not, whatever he needed to say was not going to be easy to stomach. The bile tucking itself back into her gut was a great indication of this.

"I—"

"Hey! What do you think you're doing?" Nina came flying into the scene, a predator swooping in to catch its unsuspecting prey. The bar quieted enough to hear the *brrt* of butts awkwardly pivoting on the vinyl seats and creaking of wooden chairs as all attention was drawn to Annemarie, Nina, and Nowell in the far corner. Nowell's companion stared curiously with everyone else. Even Cale had his eyes fixed on them, his hands slowing to a complete stop while he worked on inputting an order at his screen.

Nowell's face drained of all color. He was not scared of Nina, but temporarily frightened by the unexpected attack. She reached out her arm to wrap her long, skinny fingers around the collar of his shirt, ready to yank him out of his seat. As she made contact with the cotton top, she gripped it tightly and pulled. Nothing happened. The material stretched a little before returning to Nowell's neck. She overestimated her strength, or underestimated his staying power.

He slid from the seat, happy to give it up if it meant Nina would retract her claws. There was nothing he liked less than an angry, shrieking woman directing her ire at him. "I'm sorry," he apologized quickly, almost tripping over the two words as they came out. "But Annemarie . . ."

"You think it's okay to bother the woman you widowed?" Nina lashed out.

Annemarie stood from her seat and tried to silence her friend. "Nina, stop. This isn't—"

"No, Annemarie. *This* isn't appropriate. He needs to walk his scrawny, loser ass out of here right now. He—"

"Nina." The word seethed from between her clenched teeth. Annemarie quickly took stock of the other patrons, seeing all of their eyes locked on the unfolding scene. "Nothing to see here, folks," she called, hoping it was enough to get them to stop staring. Cale looked seconds away from hopping over the bar counter to come to their rescue; she held up her hand to signal that it was okay, he could stand down.

The small crowd grumbled indeterminate words at Annemarie's proclamation and returned to their conversations, though several of them kept glancing her way, watching out of the corners of their eyes to see what else might happen.

"Can I please use the remainder of my minute?" He was begging now.

"Your minute?" Nina barked. "You think Annemarie's going to—"

"Nina, thank you for your services, bill me later, but I've got this." She turned to meet Nowell's pleading eyes. "No. Your time's up."

She watched how all of him deflated, how his mouth sagged the instant she denied him, how those peace-offering eyebrows dropped so low his forehead went taut. All the tension in his body released, and as he turned to walk away, defeated, Annemarie noticed his broad shoulders had visibly sunk.

"You like burgers?" she called after him.

He faced her and those eyebrows were up again. "Uh, yeah. Yes. Who doesn't?"

"I don't," Nina muttered under her breath.

"Enough!" Annemarie snapped at her.

"Sorry, hun. Old habits . . ." Nina chewed on the inside of her lip, twisting her mouth to the right in an attempt to keep silent about anything that was to come.

"I'm in town for the night. Meet me at Grey Barn at six tonight and you can have your five minutes." Annemarie was not sure why she was giving Nowell the time he wanted. Under normal circumstances, she would be more than willing to let anyone talk to, or at, her. Under these circumstances, she should not have cared to hear a lick of what he, specifically, had to say. But even she had shocked herself when she gave him sixty—well, fifteen—seconds. And here she was doing it again.

Nowell stuttered silently for a moment before nodding emphatically, saying, "I'd have to move some things around but—"

"It's a one-time offer."

"I'll be there, then. T-thank you." He beelined for the front door, motioning for his buddy to follow him out of the place. Within a minute, the friend returned to the bar, slapped a ten-dollar bill on the countertop for the two beers Cale had poured for them, and raced back out.

"How strange," Nina murmured.

Annemarie groaned. "Don't even start."

"No, I mean it, what the hell was that all about? The whole thing. He waits for me to disappear to make his move? What did he even want? Why does he think he can bother you like this? Why are you *actually meeting him*?" Nina wanted to reach out and grab Annemarie's shoulders to give her a hard shake.

"I don't know, Nina. Let me meet with him tonight and I'll fill you in. I'm as confused as you. I ..." She trailed off. Her mind was a mess of a thousand cogs, all struggling to work together to formulate a single, coherent thought, and all she was on the receiving end of was a bunch of jumbled images, words, and feelings. "There was something in his expression that said he wasn't messing around."

"It's called *guilt*."

Annemarie waved her off. "No. It was ... I don't know. Color me intrigued." She cleared her throat. "And had someone not dive-bombed the conversation, I might have gotten it out of him right now."

Nina pointed at the door. "Oh, you want me to go chase his ass down and drag him back here?"

Annemarie smiled. "Something tells me you running after him, hollering and screaming his name, is gonna put the fear of god in him. Assuming you didn't already."

"I mean, I try. But I might be losing my game." She huffed on her nails and buffed them on her blouse.

"I appreciate you sticking up for me. It's sweet." Annemarie grabbed Nina's hand and intertwined their fingers. "Something in me is telling me to go." What she neglected to acknowledge was that her stomach was roiling again; the anxiety, the dread, the grief had a vise grip on her insides and the nausea was coming in tsunami-like waves. Chills ran up her spine.

"I'm just looking out for you. Alistair's got you covered when you're on Port Harrow and I've got your back when you're here. Oh, and speaking of—how is Alistair? I haven't talked to him in months. Since Christmas, maybe. You know, he called me on—"

Annemarie could not help but think about Nina's visceral reaction, about how she felt guilty—almost ashamed—that she agreed to meet with Nowell when she knew what her parents or Alistair or Marissa would think and say if she told them of her grand plans for the evening. She could hear it now: *How could you meet that murderer? You're betraying Jesse's love by talking to him. What were you thinking? What were you doing*?

What *was* she doing?

EIGHT

The outdoor seating section of Grey Barn was abuzz with customers in conversation with their dinner companions as they looked over the menus, procured the merriment of the restaurant's famous cocktails, shared their appetizers, entrees, and desserts, and took their time enjoying the cool evening air with a typical orange and blue sunset peeking out from behind the buildings further down the street. In the far back corner of the patio, nearest to the sidewalk, Annemarie waited for any sign of Nowell. Her feet bounced with anxiety, with agitation, shaking the table and causing her glass of water and pint of her favorite imperial stout to vibrate. The menu laid flat in front of her, never opened. She knew what she would order—the same bacon avocado chicken breast sandwich she ate every time she dined at Grey Barn—and did not think fiddling with the pages of the worn cardstock menu would distract her enough.

Since she had not expected to spend more of the afternoon in Brownstone, she was still in her tank top and jean shorts; she found herself lacking a jacket and severely regretting it. The particularly hot days did not often lead to chilly evenings during the summer, with the sunbaked asphalt, concrete sidewalks, and buildings holding in the heat well into the late-night hours. The slight wind caused her to shiver now and again, but hearty gulps of the beer helped warmth course through her body. She glanced around the space again, craned her neck in either direction to see pedestrians coming and going, and finally spotted a familiar face.

But not the one she was expecting.

Adonis incarnate, with thick, blond hair perfectly coiffed into a pompadour, bright jeweled eyes, and a mouth full of dazzling white teeth permanently on display topped off an otherwise lean and bronzed swimmer's body packed into tight jeans and a form-fitting black tee. He had a hand shoved into the back pocket of another strikingly handsome man whose darker features and more pensive expression were a humorous match to his companion. The couple was deep in discussion, of what, Annemarie could only guess, and had their gazes so intently fixed to each other, they breezed up the sidewalk and almost past the outdoor seating area of Grey Barn before giving anyone around them a second glance. When the blond turned away for a full-body guffaw at whatever his partner had said, he locked eyes on Annemarie and immediately stopped in place.

"Oh, *honey*," he cried out before the other man had the opportunity to register what was happening. The blond stepped over the rope separating the pedestrians from the restaurant patrons and wrapped Annemarie in the tightest of hugs before she could even stand from her seat, pulling her taut to his torso. When she was finally up on both feet, he made sure to lift her off the ground in the way he always had. Adam Ebert was no slouch when it came to letting his chosen family know they were loved. "Baby doll, what're you doing here? Are you alone? Is everything okay?" The questions came rapid-fire.

Annemarie returned to her chair, a dim smile on her lips, feeling a tug of sorrow and elation at their sudden presence. Adam's husband, Rory, finally joined them at the table. "Hey, Annemarie," he said softly, giving her a half wave. Despite their long history as friends, Rory was always the shy, quiet one who let a raucous Adam run the show.

"Hey, Rory," she replied meekly. She turned her gaze up to Adam's glowing face. "I'm meeting a . . . friend."

She hesitated long enough in her response to cause one of Adam's eyebrows to perk up in intrigue. "A friend, huh?" Before she could say anything more, Adam reached for the empty chair on the opposite side of Annemarie and seated himself, then rustled up another one from the nearby table, giving Rory a spot to join them.

"It's just business."

"Business? In Brownstone? Did you finally leave the library world behind?" Adam prodded.

"No, nothing like that." It was then it dawned on her how awkward and stilted the conversation was—she wondered if either of the men felt it too.

Adam, Rory, Jesse, and Annemarie had been close friends. They used to do most things together, and it helped that Adam and Jesse were coworkers—the latter being the former's boss. There was always a playful air within their relationship, one of Adam having an obvious, outward crush on Jesse, but keeping it light and fun because they all knew Jesse would never leave Annemarie. Immediately following the accident, Adam and Rory reached out to see if they could do anything for her, but her spiral into grief and depression saw her not returning their phone calls. They even attempted to visit her, but she refused to come to the door, leaving them feeling it had all been for naught.

At the time of the trial, finding Travis and Nowell not guilty, the Eberts were nowhere to be seen. Annemarie chalked it up to them having their own lives, and while they were so deeply entrenched within the McCready household, there was no obligation for them to hover over her, especially when she had made no effort to reach out to them.

So seeing them both for the first time in almost a year not only caught her off guard, but made the hairs on the back of her neck stand at the thought that Adam was the last person Jesse spoke to before his death. It brought back all sorts of grieving feelings. But here they both were, sitting in front of her, trying to act like it was the good ol' days, and all she could manage back was small talk.

With a deep breath, she added, "It's been a while since I last saw either of you." She was as guilty for that as they were.

Rory nodded knowingly. "Sorry about that. We've . . ." He trailed off in thought. "We weren't sure if you wanted to hear from us. Seeing as how—"

"No, I'm sorry, I wasn't saying that like I'm annoyed by any kind of disappearance." She paused. "Shit. That word sounds awful too." She shook her head. "I'm happy to see you. And I'm sorry that I didn't ever call. It's been . . . a really fucking shitty year."

Adam reached his hand across the table to grab hers, which was holding onto the half-full glass of beer. After a reassuring squeeze, he let go. "You don't have to apologize for anything." He chewed on his lower lip for a moment. "After Jesse, well, after all that, our crew got a new supervisor and he was beyond unbearable, so I asked to transfer to a mainland-based team and that prompted us moving over here too. They have me working up and down the coast all the time. I sometimes go an entire week without seeing Ror because I'm holed up in some bedbug-infested motel. And Rory—"

"You never told me they had bedbugs." Rory's eyes grew big at this admission.

"Not the right time, babe," Adam muttered with a shoved elbow into his husband's side.

Annemarie could not help but snort. "Like I said, it's fine. I was in no shape for company for the first six months anyway and I feel like I'm only now getting back on my feet. I have Alistair to thank for that."

"Oh, yeah, how's Sheriff Lucas doing these days?" Adam leaned forward against the table's edge as if ready to hear all manner of juicy gossip.

"The same as before. Stubborn, cocky, annoying." She rolled her eyes but laughed. "But he's also been great. He's been my rock, even when I didn't want him around or interfering."

Adam flopped a hand at her. "Well, of course he stepped up."

"Huh?" She cocked her head ever so slightly.

"I said of course he stepped up. He'd do anything for you, doll." He paused. "I mean, a lot of people would. But him especially."

She shrugged. "He's my best friend, so sure, I guess so."

"That's not what I mean."

A terse sigh escaped her. "I know what you mean, Adam, and things aren't like that. That's way in our past. We had our fun when we were younger, got that out of our systems, and we've both moved on. He's made himself available because that's what friends do. That's—" She stopped herself when she heard her own words. If she said anything further, it would once again sound like she was taking cheap shots at them. She glanced up from the table to search the sidewalk. She saw another familiar face coming toward her, his eyes locking onto hers from a distance away. But when he went to raise a hand to wave, it quickly shot down when he saw Annemarie had company.

Nowell walked past the outdoor section without looking at her again and ducked into the entrance of the building at the opposite end of the seating area, disappearing inside. He did not reappear.

"Anyway, I'm glad I ran into you both tonight. I understand life's taken us in all sorts of fun directions the last year, but I would really like it if we could stay in touch. I know it's a two-way street, so I'll do my best too, if you still, y'know . . . want to be friends. I know Jesse was kind of the glue sticking us together."

Adam's eyes lit up at this. He reached for her hand again. "Oh, honey, *of course* we want to stay in touch.

We'll find time to get together soon. Promise." He pulled her arm clear across the table and kissed her knuckles. "You always have a place in our lives."

"Definitely," Rory added. "We're having a party in a few weeks for my birthday. I'll shoot you an invite."

"I'd like that." A genuine smile plastered itself across her face. Knowing Nowell was still waiting for her somewhere inside, she glanced at the screen of her phone and said, "My company should be here any minute," but did not continue with additional details.

Adam slapped his hands on his thighs. "Yeah, we have reservations too. We should get going to that." All three stood at the same time and exchanged hugs and kisses on cheeks. Feeling Adam's warmth against her still-chilled skin made her shudder for a moment, but the familiar scent of his cologne, a fond memory of only a year ago, soothed her. "Take care of yourself, honey. We'll talk soon."

Annemarie waved at them as they made their way back the way they came from the sidewalk. They disappeared down the block and were out of sight by the time Nowell reappeared in the doorway that exited onto the patio, his eyes scanning the crowd. Annemarie lifted her hand in the air to catch his attention. He acknowledged her with a quick upward tilt of his chin and worked his way through the full tables, taking care not to bump into others.

"Hey, sorry I'm late," he said as he reached to pull out his padded chair. "I also didn't want to intrude on whatever . . ."

"No worries. I haven't been waiting long." A lie. Even though Nowell was over ten minutes late, and Adam and Rory had eaten up a chunk of time, she had been sitting in that spot, fidgeting and anxiously waiting, for an hour prior to that. But he did not need to know that; it had been her choice to get there so early.

She took stock of him, noticing that he was not wearing the same clothes as before. He had dressed down considerably for his hangout at the bar; now, he was in nicer, clean jeans, and a colorful rugby shirt. He wore a black baseball cap, but it immediately came off the moment he sat. He balanced it on his bent knee under the table. He looked up and noticed her sizing him up, but only smiled in response.

"I've never been here before. Walked by dozens of times, but never actually stopped," he mused. "I'm assuming it's good, if you suggested it by name."

Annemarie shrugged sheepishly. "I've been known to come here once or twice." She paused, then with an easy smirk, added, "A week."

He laughed. "That bad, huh?" He winked, which made her chuckle along. "So, what's good here?"

"Pretty much everything. I don't think I've ever had a bad meal. But . . ." Her voice trailed off. She instantly remembered early in the prior year when Jesse and she had dinner at Grey Barn for their thirteenth wedding anniversary and he got violently ill. The vision of Jesse hunched over the toilet with his face practically buried in the water of the bowl made her simultaneously laugh and shed a tear. She did not finish her original sentence to Nowell. Instead, she said, "Everything is good."

Two members of the front of house staff walked around the outdoor area turning on the propane patio heaters. Annemarie shivered again. She regretted not asking Nina to borrow a jacket or a pair of pants when they parted ways, but also knew she would never hear the end of it, her choosing to meet Nowell, her indiscriminately falling into his asking her to hear him out about . . . whatever he had to share.

A waitress with curly black hair worked her way over to them, smiling as she sashayed around this table and that, eyes locked on Annemarie's face. She was a regular-enough customer that the waitress did not even need to ask what she could get her; she knew. Maddie scribbled down Annemarie's order onto her pad of paper, then looked to Nowell and asked, "What'll it be, sweetheart?"

His cheeks flushed slightly. "I guess I'll get the pear gorgonzola flatbread."

"Anything to drink?" she asked, batting her eyelashes at him in an obvious attempt to flirt.

He reached for the drink menu sitting in the middle of the table, but tossed it back without even opening it. He pointed to Annemarie's pint glass. "One of whatever she's having. And please put her drink and meal on my bill."

Maddie nodded and scooted off before Annemarie could respond. Her jaw went slack for a second, a hand reached out to stop the waitress, but she was gone in the blink of an eye.

"You don't have to do that."

"I know I don't. But I want to. It's the least I can do for agreeing to meet with me."

"Well, full disclosure." She paused. She reached for her beer, put the glass to her lips to take a full gulp, swallowed, and set it down. "This is number three for me. You *really* don't have to pay my way."

Nowell tutted. "Seriously, it's not a problem. Have another, if you want."

She smiled meekly as her thanks. "So . . ." she said slowly, trailing off. She knew what she wanted to say; she did not know how to say it. Her hand instinctively reached to the beer, holding onto the glass to steady herself, to provide support and comfort. Her nails clinked against the side, hoping to allay the uneasiness swirling together with the beer. She had turned to alcohol way too many times in the last year as a means of mitigating unpleasantness. Early days, it was the only calories she consumed. These days, that was no longer the case, but drinking to drown her sorrows was the common thread. She wanted desperately for it to not be a crutch, but she wanted desperately to be able to cope.

He reached a hand behind his head and tenderly rubbed at the nape of his neck. "Yeah. So." He chewed on the corner of his mouth, part of his lip disappearing behind his teeth. Annemarie could see he was as nervous as she was. "H-how are things?"

The muscles along her jaw went tight. This was exactly what she was hoping would not happen. *Small talk.* She hated small talk. It also did not seem appropriate coming from this man in particular. She brought the beer to her mouth and took a long, drawn-out sip. She intended to take a single gulp, but kept going once the liquid hit her tongue. The last four inches of her beer disappeared in a few seconds. She set the empty glass with its dregs of foam and brown liquid onto the table, wiped her mouth with the back of her hand, and stared hard at Nowell.

"I don't mean to be a jerk, but you said you needed to talk to me about something, and that's why we're here. Can we please get to that?" They were not friends. They did not know each other prior to the accident. Whatever Nowell had to share with her seemed urgent, like it had been eating at him for the last year the same way Jesse's death—his sudden extraction from her life—had pulverized her. Deep down, she hoped deciding to hear him out, to allow him to speak his piece, would help her move on. That it would ease her another inch away from the ledge.

A little taken aback, Nowell blinked a few times at her. "Yeah, okay. Sure. Sorry. That's exactly why we're here." He nodded as he spoke, not sure what else to do to show he agreed with her sentiment.

Maddie reappeared with the imperial stout. She set it in front of him, and with a smirk, said, "Haven't seen you 'round these parts before. And definitely never with our dear Annemarie." She glanced over at her customer, who had diverted her own gaze to her lap. Feeling the tension between the two rising, she asked, "Get you another, sweetheart?" motioning to the empty beer glass.

"No thanks, Maddie. I'll stick to water." Annemarie flicked a quick, reassuring smile at her.

"No problem. Your dinners should be out soon."

Nowell said "thank you" to her so softly as she walked away that it was lost in the surrounding sounds.

"So. Whatcha got for me?" Annemarie pressed her lips together to form a thin, flat line. Her eyebrows raised in genuine curiosity, creating wrinkles on her forehead.

Nowell audibly inhaled deeply through his nose. He held it for ten seconds before letting it go with a big huff. "All I ask is that you let me tell you everything without interruption. This has been hard for me to come to terms with—"

"Yeah, I wouldn't know anything about that." Her tone seethed her annoyance. She instantly closed her eyes. "I'm sorry. I shouldn't have said that. I'm not the only one this affected. I know that."

"It's okay. I know our actions have made your life unfathomably difficult this last year." He cleared his throat. "For that, I'm sorry." He paused. "I do still ask that you let me get through all of this. It's a lot. And-and I'm not sure how to even explain this to you." His eyes were wide, the blue of the irises so bright but so dark all the same, and his gaze was vacant as he looked at her. "I have a sinking feeling I'm gonna say this, you're gonna get mad at me, and you're gonna storm out." He raised both hands in front of him to stop her from reacting. "I wouldn't blame you either. Like I said, it's a lot. It's almost kind of too much."

Annemarie sighed heavily, an angry half groan accompanying it. She rolled her eyes. "Just do it, Nowell. Put up or shut up."

He stared down at the table, let out a quick breath, and nodded, ready to start. "Travis and I had been at Oak Bay for the better part of the afternoon. We always came over to Port Harrow to fish on the Fourth. We met a couple chicks and they ended up emptying out our cooler by about nine or so. Trav has never—" He stopped himself. "Trav *had* never been a huge drinker to begin with, so after a couple he was done anyway."

"He blew like a .003. He wasn't drunk. I know that," Annemarie interrupted. She closed her eyes again and shook her head. "Sorry, sorry." She was trying to obey his simple request. The excess of beer gave her a catty confidence she could not shake. The truth serum her semi-drunkenness was concocting could not stop her tongue.

"That's not the point," Nowell added. "So, we were done drinking by, like, nine. The chicks were pissed we ran out of beer and walked off. No idea where they ended up. And honestly, I don't even know how they got there. We never saw a car. T-that's beside the point." He shook his head. "Sorry."

Maddie returned with her hands full with their entrees. She gently set them down. "Watch your mouths. Food's hot. Anything else I can get either of you?" Annemarie and Nowell shook their heads. She left without another word.

"We weren't catching anything and a thick fog rolled in. The kind where you can't see five feet in front of you. We packed up everything and Trav offered to drive." He gulped, and Annemarie noticed a change in his demeanor—a hint of agitation settled in his voice. "When T-Trav was pulling out of the lot, he almost hit a guy who was walking across the road. He honked at the dude but he totally wasn't fazed by us. Then, like, he disappeared."

Annemarie quirked an eyebrow. "Travis did?"

"No, the dude. I guess the fog swallowed him up or something. When Travis thought it was safe to move, we got onto the road, uh, onto Locust. He was taking it slow, y'know, 'cause of the fog, and I saw this weird flash of light in the side-view mirror. Kinda thought it was a car pulling up behind us." She opened her mouth with the intention of urging him to move the story along, but he lifted a hand to silently plead her to let him finish. "Travis said he saw a flash of light too, but ahead of us. We were comparing notes, then out of nowhere, something hit my truck. Like, crashed into the hood and went up and over." He took a sip of the beer and choked on a cough. "Shit, that's strong. You've had *three* of these?"

She smiled without showing her teeth, accompanied by a shrug. "I'd rather drink a couple and feel something instead of a dozen and then have to pee every ten minutes." A knowing smirk flashed across his face. "So, what'd Travis hit?"

"The fucking dude."

NINE

There was an audible intake of her breath at this. "But instead of, y'know, landing in the truck bed or on the ground, he held onto the roof and immediately punched a fist through the windshield. Trav panicked and hit the brakes but the dude didn't budge. So, he floored it, not knowing what else to do. But everything got really quiet and we thought maybe he was gone. I was looking out my window and suddenly, *boom*." He slapped his hands together, causing Annemarie to jump. "I'm face-to-face with the guy, only the glass separating us. He slammed a fist through the window and grabbed me by the hair." Even though Nowell's hair was buzzed, he used his fingers to push back some of the stubble at the hairline and leaned forward, showing off a three-inch scar.

A chill ran down her spine. He was no great storyteller, but the details were enough to make her shiver. Nowell had been watching her the whole time, gauging her reactions to the things he was saying, but he neglected to notice how little she was wearing until the evening breeze kicked up. Without hesitation, he reached a hand over his head, behind him, and removed his long-sleeve. He balled it up, then handed it to her.

"Uh, what?" she asked, briefly staring at it like he was offering her a dead animal.

"You're freezing." She had not realized she had wrapped her arms around herself for warmth. She dropped them to her sides and still refused his shirt. "I know how you feel about me, but please stop being stubborn and making yourself uncomfortable just to prove some kind of dumb point." He pushed it at her again until she reluctantly accepted it. She gave it a once-over before wriggling into the warm confines. She fixed the floppy collar and rolled up the sleeves, catching a hint of the savory rosemary scent attached to the material.

"Thank you."

Nowell took this break from his story as an opportunity to work on his flatbread. Now cooled enough to bite into, he ripped off a big chunk, folded it in half, and stuffed it into his mouth. He waited until he finished chewing to continue. Annemarie followed his cue and took a hearty bite from her sandwich. It splashing down in the vat of beer of a stomach made her momentarily grimace.

"The guy got a hold of me and slammed me into the glass. A shard cut that scar in my scalp—" He pointed to it again, as if she needed reminding. "—and he broke my nose." He used the same finger to push on the side of his nose to straighten it, demonstrating what it used to look like. Annemarie's eyes went wide upon seeing it and marveled at how much of a difference such a little change made. "While it had a hold of me, Trav had one hand on the steering wheel and one on me, trying to get me free. The whole cab lit up with this super-bright light, and the next thing I remember, I was waking up inside the truck, post-accident. Trav was alert, but pinned 'cause of the caved-in dashboard. The cops showed up not too long after, and, well, you know what happened next." He purposely did not repeat the gruesome details of the crime scene—how the vehicles were steaming piles of gnarled metal, that Jesse had to have died upon impact or shortly thereafter with the way his head was stuck in the shattered windshield, or the way he had puked out his guts when the gravity of the situation hit him.

A few tears rested on Annemarie's cheeks. She buried her face in her hands to silently sob. There was no holding back the tidal wave of emotions. Nearby guests noticed what was unfolding—a bawling woman accompanied by a man who was reaching across the table in an attempt to stop her from making a scene. In reality, Nowell wanted to comfort her, to wrap his arms around her and apologize for their mistake, for the pain he and Travis caused, to tell her he understood. But . . . they were not friends. He was part of the reason why her husband was dead.

Maddie came by the table to check on them, but stood in place with her mouth agape at what she saw. She pushed past Nowell and crouched beside Annemarie. She glared over her shoulder at him, squinting as she judged every fiber of his being. "Annie, sweetie, do I need to make him leave?"

It took Annemarie a few moments to compose herself. When she could finally speak, she said through sniffles, "No, it's okay. It's not his fault. I'm having a rough day."

"Are you sure? I can send him packing like *that*." Maddie snapped her fingers to bolster her statement.

Annemarie flopped a free but wet hand at the waitress. "It's fine. Promise."

Maddie pulled a clean paper napkin from her apron and handed it over. "Okay, if you're sure . . ."

"I am. I promise. It's just really close to, y'know, Jesse's anniversary. I've been beside myself." She gestured to Nowell across the table. "My friend here was reminding me of what I lost." She realized how that sounded the moment it left her mouth. "In a good way!" She laughed a little, enough to ensure Maddie and the surrounding customers would leave her alone, to understand that Nowell's presence was not the problem.

With hesitation, Maddie eventually stood from her crouched position, gingerly touched Annemarie's shoulder, and excused herself from the area. But not without glaring at Nowell one final time. He clenched his teeth as she walked by. He both wanted to avoid any further confrontation and to speak his mind about how tired he was of being seen as the bad guy. He knew the latter would garner him no support from anyone, so he remained quiet.

"I'm sorry," he said softly. "I didn't mean to make you cry."

Annemarie motioned for him to stop. "I know." She wiped away the last of her tears with the napkin, deeply sniffed once, and cleared her throat.

She stared at him for far longer than was comfortable; a deep groove impressed itself upon her forehead. She said nothing at first, afraid whatever might come out would be a series of squeaks and squeals instead of actual words. She did not know what *to* say anyway. She instead chose to push the remainder of the onion rings around on the plate, no longer making eye contact with him.

He took this as a sign to continue. "As you know, we got tossed into jail for the night in Brownstone. The sheriff wasn't the nicest guy." Annemarie glanced up at this admission, her eyes wide and concerned. Nowell took a long pull from his beer.

"Was Alistair rough with you or . . .?"

"Alistair?" he asked. "Oh, you mean Sheriff Lucas. He was just rude." A nonchalant shrug rolled off his shoulders. "He wasn't, like, abusive or anything, but the questions were hostile from the get-go, like we were absolutely guilty. And I get it—out of context, sure, we totally were. But we didn't know the guy, didn't know his ties to you, or your . . ." He did not finish the sentence.

"He had no love for Jesse, I can tell you that much," she replied somberly. Her lips puckered into a tight frown in the corner of her mouth.

"Well, he was acting like, uh . . ."

"It's okay. You can say his name."

Spit stuck in his tight throat for a hesitating moment. "He was acting like Jesse was his best friend." She shook her head, both in admitting that was not the case and in an act of disbelief. "It doesn't matter at this point anyway. What's done is done, I've got no beef with the guy. We fucked up, we got off, Trav killed himself, and you're down one husband," Nowell stated quickly and matter-of-factly. "Not a day goes by where I don't think about what's happened." He finally took another bite of his meal. The night air quickly turned what was once a piping hot, soft, fancy pizza into a congealed, floppy block of carbs.

"Wait, wait," she interrupted. Nowell looked up from the plate. "You got off because you both said you were swerving to avoid hitting a deer."

Nowell nodded. "When we told our lawyer what happened, he said we were crazy to insist that some dude flung himself at us like a damn sugar glider, but the story was so bizarre and our individual recaps were identical. I don't think he believed us, but I think he was so worried about losing a case, so he told us to lie under oath. Using the deer excuse would provide us with a better chance at getting off without prison time. We didn't like the idea of lying, but we also understood how insane what we were saying sounded. Our lawyer told us the state believes in acquittal of vehicular manslaughter charges if there's enough evidence that Trav swerved 'cause he had to. We figured we didn't have anything to lose at that point." He pushed the half-eaten flatbread away from him toward the edge of the table. He had had enough. "You know how the court proceedings went. Travis and I didn't talk for a little while. We were trying to figure our own shit out. Sure, we weren't convicted, but we were still involved, and that was getting around. He got—" He made finger quotes. "—'laid off' at his job and several other places he applied to afterward were conveniently having sudden hiring freezes when they came across his application."

Annemarie continued to process everything he had been saying, almost on a delay. She raised a hand to signal for him to slow down. "You said Travis killed himself. His death was ruled an accident. That he accidentally drowned in a riptide."

"I mean . . . I wasn't there. But I knew what was going on with my best friend and I know he knew better than to go swimming in an area known for its strong currents that have killed before. Plus, swimming? Out here in

February? No one does that." He paused. "If that's where he was found, he did it himself." Nowell chewed on his lips, keeping them busy, to stop them from quivering as he conjured up memories of his best friend. "The guy was haunted after the accident."

"Like ... he was seeing Jesse's ghost haunted?" Annemarie knew it was a stupid question to ask, but the amount of beer and her incredulity with the whole night made her need further clarification, ridiculous or not.

Nowell shook his head. "Not quite. Um. When we started talking again, about a month after we were acquitted, he told me everything that was going on. He started drinking. Heavily. He wasn't getting any job leads. He was super depressed, reclusive, all that. Um. He said he was seeing things. Things he couldn't explain in the periphery of his vision." He motioned to either side of his head. "He swore he kept seeing flashes of light. That sometimes, when he would be out by himself, in the woods, or fishing, h-he'd feel eyes on him. He'd see outlines or silhouettes in the distance that he couldn't explain. He told me regularly of the shit he was seeing. He said it was driving him nuts, that seeing and hearing all these inexplicable things was making him crazy. He offhandedly mentioned to me that if it got any worse, he'd take death over living. He also laughed right after that and changed the subject to my son's softball team. I didn't take him seriously. I should have taken him seriously."

Now, it was his turn to let loose the waterworks. It was no more than a few dribbles of tears and he was able to quickly wipe them away with the collar of his shirt. Annemarie noticed how tense his entire body had become. He did not utter anything else. He stared down at the tablecloth and fingered the hem of the material. For fear of returning to the tears, he did not know what else to say.

"I'm sorry Travis died," she said softly. Nowell only nodded his appreciation; he could not look her in the eyes. "You have a son?" she asked, piping up a little louder, hoping to ease the tension, to relax him.

He finally looked up at her. "Yeah. Dylan."

"How old is he?"

"Almost five."

"I had no idea." She paused. "I mean, I don't know much about you, and I guess a courtroom is no place for a kid . . ."

"His mom had him the night of the accident and he stayed with her for a while through the proceedings. I didn't get to see him much. That was pretty rough. I've had primary custody for almost all his life, so besides day care and time with her, we don't spend a lot of time apart." A small smile crept into the corner of his mouth. "He's a pretty rad kid."

Annemarie was happy to see she succeeded in diverting his attention from the troubling thoughts surrounding Travis's death. Unfortunately, she wanted to know more about his theory that the drowning was not an accident, but she knew returning to the topic would be difficult—at least right now.

"You're looking like you've got something to say," he said quietly, almost as if he were addressing himself, not her.

Annemarie tapped her fingertips on the tablecloth, trying to hold her tongue. "I just . . ."

"What?"

"I'm flabbergasted by the whole thing. I'm having a hard time believing your story. I mean, what was the guy? Some supernatural being?" She shook her head. "But on the flip side, if it wasn't true, why would you bother going out of your way to tell me? I mean this in the nicest way possible: I already kinda don't like you, and you probably couldn't care less what I think of you, so it's a bit too elaborate to be a story you made up to try to convince me you're not guilty." She ruffled her hair with both hands and opened her mouth to speak again.

But he interrupted her. "Maybe I want you to not hate me."

Her mouth remained ajar as she stared at him, a tad aghast. "Are you saying that you're willing to lie to me so I won't hate you?"

He squeezed his eyes shut for a moment. "No, no. It's the truth. But this is me being selfish. I've not had an outlet for this information since before Travis's death. I needed to get it off my chest but I don't feel comfortable telling a therapist the sordid details of an accident where I was a party to killing a man, and how I lied under oath to avoid prison. In talking to you, I'm coming clean and hoping you'll absolve us of our mistake. The court letting us go is one thing. You, on the other hand, are far more important to me when it comes to setting me free." She studied his facial expression as he said it, looking for any signs of bullshit. They did not know each other—why would he care?

She mulled over his words. What was she supposed to say to that? Maddie suddenly reappeared to clear the table of the picked-over food. "Any to-go boxes?" she asked.

"Not for me," Annemarie replied.

Nowell shook his head as well. "Thank you," he said. Maddie ignored him. He rolled his eyes, but she did not notice. As she neatly piled the dirty dishes to whisk away, she pulled the padded folder with their bill inside from out of her apron. She set it in the middle of the table.

At the same moment Nowell began to say something, Annemarie blurted out, "I forgive you."

Startled, he asked, "You do?" He blinked a couple times to better focus on her face. He wanted to clearly read her eyes as she responded.

"Yes. I believe you. Since your acquittal, I've been angry, but not necessarily at you or Travis. The evidence proved neither of you were drunk, and even though I didn't—don't—know you, I know it wasn't a malicious act. I'm pretty sure my therapist is the only person not upset with me for not wishing an eye for an eye. I don't have the energy in me to hold a grudge. Not anymore." She gave him a weak smile. He could see she meant every word.

"Thank you," he said with a shallow bob of his head. "I appreciate your forgiveness. I—"

Before he could continue a new sentence, he was interrupted by Annemarie's cell phone ringing. "Oh, sorry." She reached for her wallet tucked between her outer thigh and the arm of the chair. She fished out the loud, vibrating phone. The screen read "Alistair." She swiped across in order to answer. "Hello?"

"Hey, Annie," he greeted her quickly.

"Hi."

"How are you?"

"I'm all right. Bit tipsy. What's up?" She felt rude having this conversation in the presence of company.

"I wanted to make sure you were okay. After what happened the other day, I . . . I just wanted to make sure you were okay. I just got off work and was curious if I could swing by." A trait Annemarie found simultaneously endearing and pesky, Alistair constantly did wellness checks. Considering her track record of not being *well* the last year, she appreciated the concern and effort—knowing he had a duty as sheriff and was compelled to as her friend—but he also did so unnecessarily at times. Including if her mother could not get a hold of her in a timely manner, she would sicc Alistair on Annemarie under the guise of it being a wellness check, when maybe she had been busy with library patrons or out on a run.

"Oh, yeah, I'm fine. I came over to Brownstone to see Nina and decided to stay the night. I texted mom an hour ago to see if she could keep Moose." She had done that, knowing she was too drunk to catch the ferry home. She could have sobered up on the long ride across the channel, but she wanted to remain impaired. Even without running into Nowell and hearing the story of Jesse's demise from a different perspective, she was already feeling agitated, unsettled, with the anniversary of his death so near. She knew alcohol was not the appropriate answer to forget her problems from the last twelve months, but it sure felt good to feel nothing. And besides, no one else could offer her a better solution for coping.

"Oh, okay, great." He paused. "Are you staying with Nina?"

"Uh, no. With Marissa."

"Okay, well, when you get back to town, give me a ring. I'm waiting for a return call from Yongsoo, which I expect by morning. There's news about Peter."

Annemarie tensed her whole body. "There's news?" Her voice shriveled up from the confident tone it had taken a sentence earlier.

"Yeah. We'll talk tomorrow, though. I'll have much more information then. Have a good night with Marissa and Charlie. Tell them I say hi."

"I will. Thanks for the call." She pulled the phone from her ear, pressed the end call button, and set it face down on the table. "Sorry about that. Island business." She rolled her eyes half-heartedly.

Nowell had diverted his attention to emails on his phone as he waited for her to finish her call, trying not to eavesdrop on the conversation. He glanced up from the glowing screen to meet her gaze when she acknowledged him. "No worries. It gave me a chance to check my inbox. Despite all this internal tormenting bullshit, business has been booming for me. It's enough to keep me distracted most days."

She slightly tilted her head. "What is it you do?" There was never any expectation to know a thing about Nowell, or Travis, but she realized in that moment that she well and truly knew nothing about him.

"Construction. Remodels mostly, but I've been dipping my toes into new builds. The county's growing at such an intense rate and there's more vacant land than there are homes needing a rework, so I go where the money is. Thankfully, I've got a good crew under me that makes it possible." The moment he ended his sentence, it dawned on him that he had spent the entire evening talking about himself. Which, to be fair, she was asking all the questions, but that made him feel like even more of a self-absorbed, selfish jerk. Caught in thought, he stopped short of asking anything of her as he remembered that this was not a date. This was not bonding time, outside of him sharing his experience with her in the hopes of finding redemption and forgiveness. He kept his mouth shut on offering up any additional information.

"Neat." It was a forced response met with her eyebrows being forced up her forehead. It was not that she did not care. The phone call from Alistair played heavily on her mind. "I have something to tell you," she finally blurted out after a prolonged moment of silence.

"What's that?" An eyebrow cocked upward.

"That phone call. It was from Alistair. Uh, Sheriff Lucas. He apparently has news about something I'm kinda involved in." She paused for a moment to think. "It's something you might be interested in."

Now, both eyebrows were involved as a means of showing his intrigue. "Oh yeah?"

"I found a body on the beach two days ago. I was out running with my dog and I—"

"Wait, *what*?" His voice was an octave away from a shriek. "Like a body-body? A person's dead body?"

She nodded, acting as if it were no big deal. "Yeah, well, I mean, he was alive when I found him, and when I got back there with the cops and paramedics, he wasn't there anymore, so I don't know *what* I found, honestly. Anyway . . ." She waved her hand in the air as if the details did not matter and gave a huff of a deep breath that cycled through her lungs. She did not know what the point was of telling Nowell any of this, but it felt good to say anything at all to someone who may not brush off her experience as ludicrous. "Alistair, he . . . he means well. He's my best friend, and has been for most of my life. But sometimes the line between sheriff and friend blurs, or he outright says things in his professional capacity that rubs me the wrong way personally. In this case, he inferred— no, well, he flat out *said* with it being so close to Jesse's, um, anniversary, that maybe I was seeing things. That maybe Peter wasn't actually there."

"Peter?" Nowell was trying to follow along.

"The man I found. He's a friend of my parents." She cleared her throat in an attempt to keep the story going. "His wife reported him missing, there're no last-known whereabouts, and like I said, I may not have even seen him." She placed the flat of her hand against her temple and pushed it through her hair, allowing a blank, hollow stare to take over her face. "I'm starting to think Alistair may be right."

"But h-his wife! She said he's missing. Coinciding with you seeing him."

"*Thinking* I saw him," she corrected.

He shook his head, ignoring her self-doubt. "That's gotta mean something, yeah?" Nowell was becoming as insistent as she had been with Alistair at the scene of the maybe-crime. It filled her with a smidge of warmth that someone else felt similarly about the events, regardless of what had happened.

"He said he'll have more information in the morning, so I suppose I get to wait and see what's going on." She sipped at the dregs of her water. "That's not the part that I thought would interest you, though."

"Oh?"

"It's a long, sordid story, but when Alistair and I were at the scene of the . . . well, where I thought I saw Peter clinging to life, we were having a big argument. I thought I saw flying fish. Y'know, how they glint in sunlight when they leave the water? I didn't think anything of it, not really, but you telling me what you saw . . . I can't help but wonder . . ."

"You think you saw my guy?"

"I don't know what I saw." She said it too forcefully, almost like defending herself against a heinous accusation. She did not mean to sound exasperated, but her intent was to be firm that she had no idea what she was dealing with. Enough speculation could lead her down any number of roads. Both Alistair and Cecily did a good enough job convincing her it was all in her head.

After a few solemn moments, Nowell replied, "That's . . ." Before he could even think of a way to finish the sentence, he shook his head, then sighed. "Now I think I know why you're so willing to believe my story." She nodded. "Shit. I'm sorry."

"Why are you sorry?" She cocked her head.

"I'm sorry that this isn't one big, crazy dream. I wish it were." He leaned to one side and reached around behind him to remove his wallet from his back pocket. He pulled out a hundred-dollar bill and tucked it into the fold of the padded booklet. He set it at the edge of the table for Maddie to collect whenever she came by next. "It may not have been my fault your husband died, but I still feel responsible. I always have. And I'm sorry for that." He lowered his head in shame.

"Please stop apologizing."

"Sorry," he said in response to her request. She narrowed her eyes at him. He opened his mouth to apologize for apologizing, but stopped himself. He diverted his attention to the screen of his cell phone to check the time. Just after nine. "When's the next ferry?"

Annemarie shook her head. "In twenty minutes, but I'm not headed home tonight. I need a night away from the island. From my life, if I'm being honest." She took the pause in their conversation to plant both hands on the table to help steady herself as she stood.

"Then where are you staying?" He followed suit.

She shrugged. "I told Alistair my sister's. But I know if I go over there, she's gonna want to know why I'm here this late, why I've been drinking, and so on, and I'm not a good face-to-face liar. She's not gonna be happy with me when she hears I've been out with you. I can already hear her diatribe about how lecturing me is her way of loving me and looking out for me and *blah blah blah*." She screwed up her lips into a thoughtful frown.

"Oh." It was the best he could muster. They walked from the gated seating area, back into the restaurant, and out the front door to end up on the sidewalk, mere feet from where they had been sitting. Without thinking, Nowell blurted out, "You can crash at my place if you need to."

Annemarie slow-blinked at him a couple times, processing his offer. They stood still beside the road, him having awkwardly shoved his hands in his pants pockets and her staring at him a bit blankly. In her head, she worked through her choices: Nina yelling at her, Marissa yelling at her, renting a hotel room, or crashing on Nowell's couch.

"You live around here?" she finally asked.

He made a fist with the tip of his thumb sticking out and motioned over his shoulder. "A couple blocks up that way, on Western. I walked here."

"Let me go pee and yeah, I'll take you up on your offer."

"Yeah?" he asked in order to confirm she was genuinely accepting his invitation.

She nodded. "Wait here."

Annemarie ducked back into the restaurant. Her head swam as she weaved around employees and customers in the ambient dark of the dining area and had to squint the moment she pushed into the brightly lit bathroom. Stumbling into the first stall, she unbuttoned her shorts and let them fall to the tile floor. She hiked up the bottom of Nowell's shirt to keep from sitting on it.

"Okay, Annemarie. It's an innocent offer. He's asking you to crash on his couch. It doesn't mean anything more than that. Don't get worked up over nothing. You've got this." She pep talked her way through her time in the bathroom.

Before she could say anything else, a voice interrupted her. "Stand your ground, girl!" a woman in the adjacent stall cheered.

Cheeks red, mortified, unaware she had company, she reached for a strip of toilet paper to fold up and finish in a hurry, hopeful to not meet the other woman at the sinks.

TEN

The walk to Nowell's condo had not taken them long; just like it had not been more than a few minutes before he offered her something to drink, including but not limited to water, soda, and alcohol. He was nervous having her there—for no other reason than the wife of the man he and Travis had killed was sitting in his living room, and she was not there against her will or in a hostile manner. In all truthfulness, *he* needed the drink more, but she was not in any way at ease either.

They spent the better part of the first hour dawdling with their conversation—not really talking so much as giving knowing glances in between mindless mutterings. Under normal circumstances, one might view it as two people sweet on each other, either of them afraid to make the first move, unsure if the other person even liked them. Given who Nowell was to her, even with his extraordinary tale softening her resentful, jagged edges, the situation was clearly one they were both uncomfortable being a part of.

Nowell was regretting inviting her over; Annemarie started to doubt that the decision to agree was the right one—until their second drinks eased the tension enough that she fell into blithe spirits. Out of nowhere, she regaled him with how she and Jesse met, how she had fallen head over heels for him with only one glance, how she knew they would spend the rest of their lives together after an unfortunate sailing accident left him wounded in the hospital and she dropped everything to be there for him; it was a relationship simultaneously enthralling and hurtful to talk about. Nowell hung onto every word as best as he could, trying to not fall asleep sitting up because it was late and he was full of warming alcohol while perched on his cozy couch.

When she had had her fill of rambling and intermittent crying, she passed the baton to him, once again placing him in the spotlight. He brought up his ex-wife, his son's mother, and trailed off into nearly incoherent babbling about the drama surrounding their breakup. Annemarie found her mind wandering through the entirety of it; the couch they were settled into was exceptionally comfortable, and with each passing minute, she sank into it a little deeper. Before long, she slipped into a deep sleep, incapable of feeling an ounce of guilt for passing out during his story.

He took no offense. Admittedly, he was ready for bed immediately after showing her the couch, the kitchen, and the bathroom. He kept up the charade to benefit her, thinking she wanted to remain awake. He pulled a lightweight comforter from within the ottoman coffee table and took care to drape it over her sleeping form. He tiptoed out of the room, en route to his own, flipping off the overhead light before disappearing into the darkness.

The vehicle glided to a stop along the gravel driveway, the brakes creaking to match the groan that fell from Annemarie's mouth at the little jolt that came with the car settling into park. After a long twenty-four hours away, she was finally back home, and much worse for the wear. Brownstone always felt like a second home—between it being where the high school was and the friends who lived there now—so it never exhausted her or made her feel appreciative of the quieter existence of Port Harrow. But after last night ... Though she was not one to sneak around, deceive, or hide the truth from her loved ones, her meeting with Nowell needed to stay hush-hush and required the utmost anonymity and secrecy. She did not want—or need—the questions of what she was up to there as the topic of conversation, the way Adam had tried to wriggle it out of her.

When she woke up in Nowell's apartment, she was confused by the unfamiliar home—having startled out of a nightmare about losing Jesse, which was a recurring theme—and instantly wanted to flee. As she gained her bearings, slowly picking through her foggy brain's memories of the previous night, she calmed down. She took her time gathering her wits as she still was moderately drunk. Her phone showed it was after six, and the morning light trying to filter through the slats of the curtains on the nearby window confirmed that. The first ferry of the morning back to Port Harrow had sailed, so there was an hour before she needed to be down to the dock.

Nowell must have been dead to the world as she rattled around the apartment; making frequent trips between the bathroom and kitchen as she chugged enough water to drown a horse and unsure if she needed the toilet for urinating or vomiting. But by the time she was ready to make the fifteen-minute walk to the waterfront, silence still permeated the space. She snuck out without a goodbye or thank you and hoped she would be able to make it the whole way home without an emergency stop of any kind.

Now, here in the driveway, her full bladder trying to push its way out via her abdomen and her stomach roiling and burbling with the unease of the previous night's nonsense, she could breathe a sigh of relief. She rested her head on the steering wheel for a moment before taking a deep breath and pushing herself out of the car. She was grateful her parents had taken Moose—one less responsibility to worry about in her current state. She needed the morning to recuperate without his sassy, needy ass in her way.

A foul stench infiltrated her nostrils the moment she shoved her way into the house. She scrunched up her features as her stomach unceremoniously lurched. *The trash can,* she thought. She dropped her wallet on the couch and stumbled her way into the kitchen. She gagged as a wave of a week's worth of rotting vegetable matter and just as many hastily emptied wet dog food cans rushed up into her face upon cinching the plastic bag closed. She thought she might need to reopen it to catch her vomit but was able to keep everything inside of her.

She cautiously took the four stairs leading into the yard. As she lifted the lid of the garbage bin, her stomach reeled and she fought the urge to puke again. The lid fell from her grip and landed with a heavy thud.

"What the fuck . . ." she asked with an incredulous, disgusted tone. "What died?" She held her breath and lifted the garbage bag to dump into the can but stopped. Sitting on top of the other white bag was a scrap of clothing she did not recognize. She reached over the lip of the bin and picked up the blue shirt. It was damp with blood. It reeked. She tried to scream out in horror, but it was choked by vomit rushing up her throat.

She dropped the piece back in the can and the garbage bag on the ground. She raced up the steps, any semblance of drunken unbalance gone, and aimed straight for her wallet where her phone was tucked away. She dialed Alistair's number.

"You've reached Chief Deputy Sheriff Alistair Lucas on Port Harrow. I'm sorry I missed your call. If this is an emergency, hang up and dial 911. Otherwise, please leave your name, number, and a brief message, and I will return your call as soon as I can. Thanks." Then the line beeped.

"Alistair, it's Annemarie. I found something in my trash can and-and I don't—I need you to come here." She hung up. She pulled up the number for the sheriff's office and hit dial.

"Azure County Sheriff's Department, Port Harrow—"

"Riggs it's Annemarie is Alistair there?" It flew out of her in one breath.

"Hey, hey, slow down. No, Al's not here. What's up? Can I help you with something?"

She paced the living room, moving from the front door to the entrance of the kitchen and back. "I f-found something out back. In my garbage bin. I think it's Peter Arthur's."

"What?" he barked.

"I need someone to come up to the house right now."

"I'm on my way. I'll be right the—" The line went dead before even finishing his sentence.

Annemarie refused to go back outside until she was accompanied by someone. She could not face it alone again. She did not think her stomach could handle it either.

A rapid knock came twenty-five minutes later. She flew from her seat on the couch to answer the door. Riggs stood on the stoop, his blond hair slicked save for one chunk flopping forward as he lowered his head to pick at a string near a buttonhole on his uniform shirt.

"Hey, Annie," he said in a quiet tone. He did not wait to be invited in. He stepped past her and headed for the kitchen. He knew every inch of her property like his own, including that the bin was out the back door and the fastest way there was straight through the house. When they reached their destination, Riggs pulled a pair of nitrile gloves from within his pants pocket as well as a clear evidence bag.

She held her breath and flipped up the lid of the black can so it flopped against the side of the house and stayed open. She peered in to double-check the clothing was still there, still in the state she had found it. Part of her thought she might have imagined it.

Riggs choked back an involuntary retching noise. He grabbed at the stained material, giving it a once-over. She watched him inspect it closely. Blue shirt, pink pineapples, shredded halfway down the chest, still a little wet with blood in places.

"What on earth . . ." He trailed off. He carefully folded the dregs of the shirt with the one hand in order to stuff it inside the bag. He removed the dirty glove, dropping it in with the shirt, and sealed the zipper teeth. Annemarie took the opportunity to throw away her full garbage bag before closing the lid. Riggs set the evidence on top of the can and removed a notepad and ballpoint pen from his shirt pocket. "Okay. Tell me what happened."

"I was taking out the trash, opened the bin, and saw the top of the shirt. I didn't recognize it at first, so I picked it up to see what it was. Then I realized it matched what I saw Peter wearing when I found him up on the beach, and Alistair told me he was last seen wearing it. I dropped it and went right inside to call him, then you."

Riggs scribbled notes for a minute after she stopped talking. "Is that everything?" She nodded curtly. "Okay. Well, I'm sorry Al couldn't be here. You didn't hear this from me, but he's with Yongsoo right now."

Annemarie's eyebrows rose. "Oh?"

"We—he—found Peter's body." He lowered his voice as if trying to hide it from a larger crowd. "It was in the sea cave up on North Beach. His entire torso was shredded like-like . . . I don't know. Like pulled pork. It was . . . fucking *awful*."

Images of finding Peter under the kelp and the description was too much—Annemarie rushed to the natural fence line of bushes and violently threw up several times. The sound of all that morning's water evacuating her guts caught the attention of Alistair who was hurrying from his cruiser to the front door. He diverted around the side of the house to beeline to the noise.

He came up alongside her. "Hey, you okay?" His voice was warm, soft, comforting as he rested a hand on her upper back and rubbed gently. She jumped at his touch, unaware of his presence. She barely nodded. She kept her mouth open as wide as she could, letting drool stream off her tongue. He turned his attention to Riggs. "What's going on?"

"She found Peter's shirt," Riggs replied as he motioned to the evidence bag.

"What? Where?" Alistair scuttled over.

"In the garbage. Sitting on top of her trash. She touched it at first, but—"

Alistair grabbed Riggs's notepad to look over his slanted scribbles. "I've got this from here. Head on back down to the station and I'll finish it up."

Riggs nodded, another chunk of his hair falling onto his forehead, giving him a boyish quality. He reached into his pocket and retrieved a tissue. He handed it to Annemarie as he walked past her still bent over at the waist. "Feel better, Annie."

A bubble of gas uprooted itself from the depths of her stomach and made its way out of her in an abrupt burp before she could weakly reply, "Thanks, Riggs."

He disappeared around the front of the house before Alistair approached her again. "What's going on? You okay?"

"I will be. Riggs just . . . He told me a little too much about the manner you found Peter."

Alistair groaned with the tail end coming out as a growl. "He shouldn't have said anything."

"No. He really shouldn't've." She straightened her spine as she stood and spread her hands out in front of her, as if putting herself on display. "But he did. And here I am."

"Let's get you cleaned up before I ask any more questions. That sound good?" He motioned a hand forward to escort her into the house. She trudged up the stairs, Riggs's tissue pressed to her now-closed mouth. Alistair grabbed the evidence bag and followed closely behind.

"I'll be right back." She held up her hand to stop him from following her into the bedroom and connecting bathroom. She shut the door behind her. She meant to brush her teeth with a mouthwash chaser, but Riggs's description coupled with the stench from the trash can came rushing back in vivid flashes, forcing her to double over. She barely made it to the toilet. After several more minutes of dry heaving, of thick saliva slavering out of her mouth, her stomach was empty and incredibly uneasy. How much of this was because of last night's overindulgence and how much was from that moment?

Alistair sat in the living room, one leg crossed over the other as he flipped through Riggs's notepad. The incident seemed straightforward, but he had questions. He needed answers in order to finish off the report.

Annemarie exited the bedroom, a perfumed wave of wintergreen and citrus chasing after her. She could not escape the smell in her mind's eye, even if it was long gone. "Sorry," she muttered.

He dropped his feet to the floor and leaned forward to rest his elbows on his knees. "You good to talk?"

She released a huff of breath and nodded. "I don't think I have anything left in me to hurl up so we should be good."

He patted the seat beside him. "Come on." She settled onto the couch, bringing her knees up to her chest as she positioned herself to face him. He readied his pen. "Tell me what happened."

"I got home a bit ago and went to take out the trash. I noticed there was an awful smell when I opened the bin. I looked inside and saw part of the shirt. I didn't know what it was, so I grabbed it and saw that it was covered in blood. I freaked out and dropped it and came inside to call you."

He finished scratching out his notes, knowing what Riggs had jotted down was exactly the same, but wanting to verify it himself. "I'm sorry I missed your call," he said quietly.

She shook her head. "It doesn't matter. I needed someone here and you're my go-to. You're also usually on the move so potentially closer than someone at the office." She flashed him a feeble smile before her mouth returned to its permanent frown.

"Is there anything else?"

"No. That's all that happened. I mean, besides Riggs coming up and taking my statement too."

"Okay." He flipped shut the notepad. He shoved it and the pen into his pants pocket. He reclined on the couch, allowing him to post his left ankle onto his right kneecap again. "Are you okay otherwise?"

She shrugged one shoulder in a glib manner. "I'm hungover as fuck and my stomach feels wretched, but I'll be fine. That . . . was not how I wanted to start my day, y'know?"

"Hungover? You get up to something fun last night?" He smirked, trying to prod at her a little.

She realized her mistake in saying anything. She did not want to admit where she had been. Alistair would not have understood. No one would. It did not matter anyway. "I told you when you called last night that I was already kinda tipsy. I ended up having too many drinks, is all."

The cheered smile spread over his face melted into a concerned frown and lowered eyebrows. "Dooooo I need to worry about that?"

She flopped her wrist at him limply. "I'm fine. I promise."

"You sure?"

"Yeah. Just fine." She knew Alistair would always worry she would spiral again, especially at any mention of drinking on her own. She wanted him to be at ease on the subject. "Please don't worry about me."

He brought his hand over to her tense shoulder and gave it a squeeze and a gentle rub. "I always will." He lowered his head and averted his gaze to his lap. "I'm sorry."

She reached out to caress his cheek and gave it a solid pat. "Don't be sorry that you care. I'm sorry you have to. I never thought I'd need looking after. It's been tough knowing I may never be okay."

Alistair ran his own hand along his cheek, still feeling the warmth from where hers had been. He scratched at his jaw. "Well, I don't think it's as fatalistic as that. It's only been a year. I'm proud of you for making it this far, given the circumstances."

She opened her mouth to say something snarky, something about how he must have had little faith in her, but she knew he meant well with the comment—and if she were being honest, she had no confidence she would make it to the next morning when she was in the thick of her grief. She did not *want* to make it. It had been hard enough losing Jesse, but compounded by the fact that she was not physically well either made overall recovery seem nearly impossible.

She sat with her thoughts, as did Alistair and his own. They were done with the police work, but he was not ready to leave, not yet. A gurgling cough interrupted their silence. Annemarie's hand shot to her mouth to cover any further noises, or potential vomit, from resurfacing.

"You sure you're okay?" Alistair cocked his head as he watched her deliberately trying to hide her queasiness—the paleness of her skin, the light sweat beading around her hairline, the negligible tremble in her hand as she struggled to keep composed. She only nodded. "Marissa must be a wreck too, huh? She never could hold her liquor, especially after she had Charlie." Annemarie could only grimace, willing the corners of her mouth to slide up into a forced smile; she hoped it looked sincere but was certain she looked like a caricature of herself. Alistair parted his lips, ready to ask another question, but the trill of his phone interrupted the move. He fished out his work phone from the pocket opposite the pen and notepad and thumbed the screen to navigate to the text message.

She was too in her own head to notice his eyes widen as he read what was on the screen, then narrow as he glanced up to stare at her. She chewed on her bottom lip as she mulled over whether she needed a slice of bread or the whole damn loaf to settle her stomach. *Never again,* she thought. *One drink will be my limit from here on out.* She knew it was a lie.

"So, it's the second."

Her ears pricked up. "Hmm?"

"Today's the second," Alistair repeated.

"All day," she mused, a slight smirk on her lips.

"I just mean . . ." He trailed off as he reconsidered the words he intended to say. "The fourth is, y'know, the day after tomorrow."

She shrugged, indifferent to the information he was sharing that she already knew. "You ever consider a career as a calendar? You'd be pretty good."

He snorted. "Nah, the pay's shit."

"Is being a cop in a sleepy hamlet much better?"

"You're changing the subject," he said flatly.

"Yep."

It was like trying to pull teeth with her. "Wiiiiill you be joining us at the festival?"

"Maybe. Probably not. I don't know." She stood from the couch in a flash, practically startling him. She squeezed herself between his legs and the coffee table— the fastest way to breeze past to the kitchen. She disappeared inside where all Alistair could hear was the rustling of plastic.

"It might be good for you," he called.

"Or it might be the second worst day of my life—the first being one year ago when I lost my husband in a horrible car accident on our way home from *the festival*." He could not see her face, but he knew she was leaning hard into the derisive statement. She returned shortly with two pieces of wheat bread slathered in chunky peanut butter, the corner of one piece already missing and her mouth silently champing like a cow.

"I'm trying to be helpful. I think it would be helpful. Facing it, head on—" He stopped himself before he could say anything more. His poor choice of words was glaringly obvious the second they slipped out of his mouth, but the deer-in-the-headlights look Annemarie was giving him—her eyes wide, absolute stillness including the methodical cud-chewing of her jaw— confirmed that. Feeling he needed an excuse to leave, he checked his watch and huffed out a breath. "Oh, look at the time. I've gotta go file an incident report." He shot up as suddenly as she had and was all the way to the door in seconds. He looked over his shoulder just long enough to catch her gaze. "Feel better, Annie. Let me know if you need anything." Her eyes darted down to the bread in her hands and she did not say another word.

ELEVEN

Annemarie eased the car against the curb in between two vehicles a quarter of a mile from Hawthorn Park where the island's annual Fourth of July Festival was happening. She ran her hands through her shaggy mane, giving it a good ruffle as she scratched her nails across the scalp. A heavy, exhausted sigh came out. Despite the library being closed for the holiday, she took advantage of the vacant building to clean the first-floor space from top to bottom as best as one person could in approximately six hours. She wanted to tackle the basement too, but neither time nor energy allowed. She was happy to take on the task— especially with Moose being at her parents' and Jesse offshore with his marine ecology crew all day—but it did not make her day any less tiresome.

She slapped down the visor to reveal the small, dusty mirror. With her paisley-print clutch of makeup in tow, she fished out a glass bottle of liquid foundation and the beige nub of a blender to cover a budding bruise along her jawline. During her spree, she pulled down a bucket of cleaning supplies on her face and her reward was the new discoloration. Satisfied with her color-matching quick fix, she plucked a tube of her favorite brick-red lipstick to apply to her pale lips. She leaned in close to the mirror, pressing the waxy stick firmly, when suddenly, the entire car violently swayed from side to side, increasing in intensity with every second. Completely caught off guard, she was concerned regarding her safety while stuck in a vehicle during an earthquake. When the tremor dissipated, no one else around her seemed fazed.

Faint laughter came from somewhere nearby. Annemarie's eyes darted to the rearview mirror. A splash of brown flitted from behind her. As she turned to the driver's side window, a tanned, bare torso filled the entirety of her view, causing her to throw herself out of her seat while screaming, except . . . she was still buckled in. The shoulder harness snapped into place, restraining her, forcing her to take a second look. In the moments it took to calm her racing heart, she recognized the vibrant mauve stinger tattoo emblazoned on one pectoral muscle, as well as the pronounced dimple of flesh to the right of his navel where he had been impaled on the sailboat all those years before.

She pounded a fist on the window and shouted, "Jesse Alexander McCready! I want a divorce!"

The awful chortle of delight came again, only this time, it was dangerously close. Jesse backed away from the car, his drying wet suit peeled to his waist, the arms flopping as he bent to rest his hands on his knees. He convulsed with laughter, his wide, lapis eyes fixed on her. She shoved open the car door at him, causing him to leak back several steps.

"That wasn't funny." She tried to keep the tone of her voice level.

He pointed at her face and then to the car. "*That* was hilarious. What wasn't funny was you kicking me into traffic." He motioned over his shoulder at the road.

"You mean *that*?" She pointed to the motionless bumper-to-bumper vehicles.

"They could've run over my feet!" he interjected, emphatically showing off his black water shoes. He stuck out his bottom lip in a pout. "I need my feet. I *like* my feet."

Annemarie rolled her eyes but she chuckled all the same. "You were never in any danger, babe. Promise." She reached to pat his cheek, but he playfully jerked away.

He pushed back his shoulders and stuck out his chest. "I'm mad at you."

"*You're* mad at *me*?" She crossed her arms. "You scared the ever-living shit out of me not three minutes ago. If anyone should be mad, it's me."

He made a fist to gently punch her shoulder, rocking her in place. "Aw, I was just goofin', babe."

"You're such an ass," she muttered as she leaned back into the car to retrieve her purse and the lightweight jacket draped over the passenger headrest.

"What was that?" he asked with a melodic hum in his voice.

"I've asked you repeatedly not to scare me. I don't understand why you think it's so funny to see me screaming my head off and getting so riled up." She slammed the door shut. "It's not funny, and I'm tired of it. I really am." She narrowed her eyes at him, fixing her gaze on his expression to see what he had to say for himself.

After a long pause, he looked down at his feet and finally said, "You're right. I'm gonna be forty soon and it's probably time I grow up. I mean, yeah—" He shrugged. "—it's funny on the outside, but . . . is it funny when it's at your expense?" He fixed his eyes on her, peering up through his eyelashes, a hangdog expression on his face. Then a massive grin broke out. "Yep, still pretty funny. But I'll stop. No more scaring you."

"Promise?" she asked.

"Promise." He placed the tiniest of kisses on the tip of her nose, one of her favorite gestures of his. Changing his tone, he asked, "Is the back open?"

"I haven't locked up. I figured you'd want a change of clothes first." She motioned to the back hatch of the car with a slight lift of her chin. "Tank top, board shorts, boxers, and shoes. In the bag."

He kissed her cheek. "You're the best, babe." He moseyed over to the rear end, popped the fifth door, and immediately peeled off the remnants of the wet suit. Beneath the neoprene, his board shorts remained dripping wet from the layer of water the suit held onto during his dives. He unzipped the backpack in front of him to reveal the dry clothes and a big, clean towel. He tied the terry cloth around his waist in order to strip out of the shorts and boxers, now naked under the towel in front of the long line of traffic.

A couple of catcalls and whistles came from the cars.

Annemarie slid into her jacket and tucked her purse under her arm. She moved to the hatch to lean against the car in order to watch Jesse change.

"Pervert," he muttered with a cheeky grin.

"So, all these strangers are allowed to watch you undress, but your own wife can't?"

Still in only a towel, he closed the gap between them to plant a kiss on her lips. He lingered for a moment longer, but was interrupted by someone calling, "Ew, gross! Get a room, you two!"

Jesse and Annemarie broke their intimate moment to look up and see Adam approaching their car with Rory in tow.

Jesse snorted. "Ah, the pot's calling the kettle black again I see."

"What? I can't help it if he drives me wild." Adam leaned over to plant a sloppy kiss on Rory's cheek, causing Rory to playfully scrunch up his face and wipe off his husband's spit with the back of his hand. Adam wrapped an arm around Rory's neck and pulled him close to nestle into his side. "And speaking of driving me wild—" He pointed a finger at Jesse. "—when you gonna leave her and come over to the dark side?" Annemarie laughed into her hand, watching as Jesse's entire face suffused bright red while he scratched at the back of his head and tried to hide his shy smile.

The couples usually spent their days off together, whether it was a bonfire at one of the beaches, a meal over in Brownstone, or a game night in either of their homes, but recent weeks had found them headed in all different directions, never able to connect. But despite being physically absent, outside of Jesse and Adam working together, they kept up on their group text chat. The other three loved to pick on Jesse about Adam's innocent crush on him, Annemarie and Rory usually the instigators.

Despite Jesse not minding that a male employee lusted for him, it still made him blush when the topic was brought up. He thought highly of his accomplishments in life, but less so about himself as a person; a childhood filled with being mentally beaten into the ground by his father and bullies at school had taken its toll even far into his adult years. He marveled at the idea that Annemarie could love him for who he was—he did not think he was anything special, though she always made sure he knew he was wrong, in the most loving way possible. Taking compliments was not his strong suit and knowing Adam, and Rory to an extent, had a playful, wandering eye turned him into a bumbling, stuttering dork. He never minded it, but he also never knew what to say in response.

Shifting gears, Adam directed his finger at Annemarie and started, "Hey, Annie, did you know—"

Jesse nonchalantly shoved his elbow into Adam's ribs, forcing him to abruptly stop his sentence. Adam raised an eyebrow at Jesse, who gave a barely perceptible shake of his head as he chewed on the inside of his upper lip.

"—it's been a while since we last saw you," Adam continued.

"I was indeed aware of the fact it's been a while. But you embarrassing Mr. Unembarrassable here completely makes up for the lack of recent hang outs." She pointed at Jesse and his ever-reddening cheeks.

"Well, we'll let you continue your very public striptease for everyone. If we don't hook up with you in the park, we're having a bonfire at our place afterward. You guys should swing by," Rory offered.

Adjusting the towel, Jesse said, "Yeah, absolutely. We'd love to."

"You'd love to hook up in the park?" Adam asked with mock enthusiasm, once again catching Jesse off guard and getting to witness a full-body flush this time.

"Consider it a date," Annemarie piped in before her husband could stammer himself into a heart attack, clapping her hands together once for added emphasis. Adam and Rory faced her and both smiled. She let out a mischievous cackle.

The Eberts left the McCreadys on the side of the road. Jesse shimmied into the clean pair of boxers, followed by the dark blue board shorts, finally allowing him to remove the towel. He ran it over his head, wicking away what moisture he could. He spread it out in the back of the car in order to have a place to dry his wet suit and shorts. Annemarie fished out the white A-shirt before he closed the door of the hatch.

She handed him the top. He leaned in for another soft kiss. "Thanks again." As she turned to watch for traffic, he snaked a hand into hers but pulled her back. She twirled into his arms where they shared one last passionate kiss. But before she could pull away, he brushed his lips against her ear and whispered, "Your face is red."

She pulled away from him and scrunched up her features. "Huh? I'm not mad anymore."

"No, I mean it's really red." He started to point a finger at her, but she slapped it away.

"Har, har, Jesse. I'm beyond that. You apologized." She shook her head and rolled her eyes so hard she could practically see the backside of her skull.

With a disgruntled sigh, he said, "I'm not talking about that. Look." He reached a hand out to her cheek, rubbed his thumb over the skin, and pulled away to show her a red smear.

Annemarie gasped, spun on the ball of her foot, and stared at her reflection in the driver's side window. A three-inch-long stripe of brick-red lipstick stretched across her cheek. In all the hubbub of him shaking the car to scare her, she lost track of where the tube of lipstick traveled and accidentally colored on her own face. "What—I—How—when were you going to tell me about this?"

"I'm telling you now, aren't I?" He grinned, all of his teeth on display.

"You said no more pranks!" she protested.

"I promised to not *scare* you again." He stuck out the tip of his tongue in a taunt.

"You're the absolute worst." She smiled—this time, providing the tender, corner-of-the-mouth smirk she reserved for only him. Once more, she turned to stare at herself in the glass, wanting to remove the smear of color.

Over her shoulder, she glanced Jesse's reflection coming up behind her. He wrapped his arms around her, pressed his bare chest against her back, and whispered, "No, leave it." He could not hold in his laugh for long despite delivering the line completely deadpan. He buried his face in the valley where her neck met her shoulder, causing her to momentarily squeal.

"I am *not* hanging out with all our friends and family looking like a second-rate clown." She worked at the decreasing smudge a bit longer before deciding her cheek was now red more from friction than the lipstick.

With a chuckle, he said, "At least you're *my* second-rate clown."

They waited for a break in the traffic to cross the two-lane Wildwood Highway toward the entrance of Hawthorn Park. Jesse took a moment to pull on his tank top and seamlessly moved from adjusting the bottom hem across his waist to slipping his hand into Annemarie's. She did not look at him or even flinch when he did this; he nailed that move every time.

Hawthorn Park consisted of twenty-two acres of well-manicured, rolling green grass butted against a combination of rocky, sandy, and cliff-face shoreline. It overlooked the ocean and gave way to a distant view of nearby Derry on the mainland and was the largest park on Port Harrow, playing host to the town's annual Fourth of July extravaganza. A fireworks barge parked in Hawthorn Bay offered viewers tens of thousands of dollars' worth of entertainment packed into twenty boisterous minutes, and every year, they upped the budget to bring in more and more attendees. While the local city council never charged for parking or entrance fees, the ferry service saw record numbers and benefited from the increase in money, and local vendors, artisans, and food trucks got to participate and reap the uptick in sales. For a town of barely eight hundred permanent residents, the population almost quadrupled for one day a year with eager visitors in search of the best fireworks display for three counties.

Par for the course, the park was already packed with every type of person imaginable: singles; families of two, three, four, and more; the elderly who were either turning down their hearing aids or pocketing napkins to ball up and stuff into their ear canals should the display get too loud; packs of teenagers conspicuously eyeing the beer garden; several generations spread out over copious piles of blankets, every single one of them enjoying what the event had to offer.

During most of Annemarie's youth on the island, she stayed close to her parents and sister during the festivities. They usually camped out in the middle of the park—Cecily insisting they arrive early to pick the best spot—and visited with friends and neighbors, eating hamburgers, hot dogs, chili cheese fries, and guzzling ice-cold soda and water on what was inevitably an extremely hot day. As a teenager, she wanted to wander with her friends, Alistair included, hoping to snatch up the remnants of someone's forgotten or abandoned beer, but not before getting high together in the adjacent woods where no one would catch them. Now, as an adult, and with Jesse in tow, their new tradition was to walk around the grounds visiting with the townsfolk and catching up with those whom they did not see regularly, before settling down with her family to eat dinner and watch the fireworks.

Their first stop was the bright red-and-black plaid blanket weighted down by Cecily, Ken, and Annemarie's niece, Charlie. The five-year-old focused on her coloring book and box of crayons, occasionally pushing her crown of ginger curls out of her eyes with her chubby fingers, barely paying attention to her surroundings.

Cecily spotted the couple first and climbed up off the ground to greet them. "Annie, Jess, hi!" She embraced her daughter in a tight hug. When they broke apart, she continued over to her son-in-law to give him his own hug and a kiss on the cheek. As she finished, Ken got to his feet to share in the greetings.

Annemarie hugged him. "Hey, pop."

Charlie's eyes darted up to the adults and she released a squeal of excitement. "Jesse, Jesse, Jesse!" she cried out. She bounced in place until she lost balance and fell forward, but quickly recovered to scramble across the blanket and stand beside her uncle.

"Hey, kiddo," Jesse said as he mussed the tangle of hair on her head. She immediately scaled him like an overeager climber taking on the highest peak in the mountain range. Charlie used her feet to propel herself up his legs, his torso, and finally wrapped her arms around his neck where she hung onto him tightly. He raised his left arm perpendicular to his body to allow her free access to swing on him like a monkey in the trees. He smirked at her willingness and trust to tackle him, though he turned his focus on the conversing adults. Occasionally, he grunted or winced in discomfort as she accidentally kneed his kidney or full-body-slammed into his legs.

"Saw your research vessel off the north shore this morning. Doing anything interesting out there?" Ken asked Jesse, referring to his job as a marine ecologist for Azure County.

"Nothing super out of the ordinary. Someone spotted a couple of dead seals floating up there, so we went to investigate. Looks like they were attacked by something, but whatever it was didn't bother to finish the job. That in and of itself is a bit weird, but stranger things happen around here. The ocean and marine life are getting a bit unpredictable with the climate change we've been experiencing. Desperate times, y'know?" Jesse shrugged at the same time Charlie climbed up his core to sit on his shoulders. He gently grabbed hold of her petite ankles to keep her secure. Knowing she was safe, she tipped backward to hang upside down with her back pressed against his and her long curls trailing down even further.

"Charlotte Leigh! What do you think you're doing?" a voice yelled from behind Annemarie and Jesse.

In between incessant giggles, Charlie said, "Hi, mommy."

Jesse turned in place to look at his sister-in-law, Marissa, walking toward them with a quickened pace. Though Marissa and Annemarie were only a year apart in age, they could not have looked any different. Marissa's honey-highlighted blonde hair was kept in a messy, pixie fringe, and her ruddy-brown eyes were always surrounded with a thick coating of mascara. She had several inches on Annemarie and proudly owned the little extra weight in her midsection with a steady stream of crop tops and low-rise jeans.

"Get down before you hurt yourself," Marissa instructed. Charlie did not budge and her face slowly changed from joyful to puzzled. "Don't know how, do you?" The amused hum in her voice added to the ridiculous scenario.

Charlie shook her head. "Nuh uh." She giggled again. She attempted to perform a sit-up, but barely made it halfway before flopping back into place against Jesse. They both grunted.

Marissa swooped in to wrap her arms around her daughter, hoping to disengage her legs from Jesse's neck. She set Charlie on the ground and *tsk*ed at her. "You know you have to be careful, honey. What would you do if you broke your Uncle Jesse?"

Behind them, Alistair emerged from a crowd of attendees, dressed in dark blue jeans and a light-colored collared shirt. Hands shoved in the front pockets of his pants, he sheepishly smiled at the Mitchell and McCready clans when they all locked eyes.

"Allster!" Charlie shrieked, her eyes growing wide as she, too, recognized his familiar face. She struggled away from Marissa's embrace. The moment she broke free, she leaped at him. She had complete faith he would catch her.

"Hiya, Charlie." Alistair greeted her with a grunt as she tightly wrapped her arms around his neck. She gave him the biggest hug her little frame could muster and he petted her hair. Having such close ties to Annemarie and Marissa's family, he was like another uncle to Charlie, and she cherished him almost more than she did Jesse.

Alistair carefully released his grip on her small body, allowing her to dangle off him like Jesse had. She giggled as she used her strength to continue climbing all over him.

Ken reached out his hand for Alistair's. "Al, how's it going, son?"

He accepted the gesture with a firm handshake. "Doing just fine, Ken. Been busy training a few new recruits for Derry's office."

Ken scratched at his salt-and-pepper beard, the hollow sound of fingernails on coarse hair echoing loudly before he responded. "Yeah, I thought I saw a couple unfamiliar faces down by the station the other day. They Derry boys, you say?" He paused. "Shame the county won't give you more."

"Ah, well, it's no big deal. We've got a good team here. I couldn't ask for a better group of folks watching our collective backs." Alistair smiled, but his expression melted away as Charlie launched herself up and over his shoulder to hang off him from behind. He tilted back slightly, trying to accommodate the weight now pulling at his Adam's apple.

Marissa intervened between Alistair and her father. "Daddy, I'm sure the last thing Alistair wants to talk about when he's off duty is more work." She sidestepped around the men, cocked her head at Charlie, and smiled. "Whatcha doing, monkey?" Still latched onto Alistair's neck, she used her feet to gain purchase as she scaled his back, folding herself into a compact triangle. When she completed the task, she laughed maniacally. Marissa turned to Jesse, winked, and said, "Sorry, Jess. You're dead to her now."

The group laughed.

With a casual shrug, Jesse replied, "I've got time to win her back." He grinned, but it slid from his face as he locked eyes with Alistair. "Sheriff."

Alistair gave a curt nod. "Jesse."

It was no secret the two men were not friends. No matter how hard Annemarie tried to force them together—certain that similarly aged men with similar habits and similar personalities would gel, if only they would let down their stupid, stubborn, tough-guy exteriors—they could not seem to make it work.

Alistair tried his best to rein in his overall feelings and be accessible when he and Jesse were around each other—which happened often considering how close he was with the family as a whole—but since cultivating a friendship was not priority number one, the most he could ever muster was small talk. Jesse did not seem to mind the lack of effort and never attempted anything more either. In fact, he carefully treaded water around the man, his wife's best friend, the island's beloved sheriff. He never intended to make enemies of anyone, but the intimate history Alistair and Annemarie shared—and the gigantic figure she painted of him for Jesse with her innumerable stories—caused him to believe that Alistair was a threat. Alistair's actions, initial unkind welcome, standoffish attitude, and career intimidation did not necessarily prove that notion wrong.

Much to either of their displeasure, Annemarie constantly begged for civility and maturity. They both agreed to try to try.

In an attempt to be humorous, Alistair asked, "Did you solve your seal murder mystery?" The call for the dead seals came into the sheriff's department first and Deputy Riggs relayed the information to Jesse's team to investigate. Unless people were suspected of causing harm to the wildlife, the sheriff's department had no need to get involved. No one tagged back after the call was transferred, meaning the marine ecology crew had it covered. Alistair never heard the outcome.

"I don't deal with *murder* in my line of work, Sheriff. It's referred to as the circle of life." Jesse practically spit as he emphasized the word. They often badgered each other about their respective careers, usually leading to arguments of who had the better job, who was more important.

Quick to retort, Alistair said, "And thankfully, neither does Port Harrow with me in charge."

The air between everyone went quiet and thickened, leaving them with little to say in regard to the ongoing pissing contest, with no clear direction as to how to move forward. Annemarie and Marissa exchanged annoyed glances, simultaneously shook their heads in exasperation, and muttered, "Boys."

Jesse broke away from his shared death stare, realizing how immature and stubborn he was being. He leaned over to plant a kiss on Annemarie's slightly rubbed-raw cheek and muttered, "Sorry, babe."

"Now that we've determined your winkies are equally big, let's move on and try to enjoy the rest of the party, okay?" Cecily finally piped in, hoping she might embarrass the men enough to stop the constant ridiculousness.

"Mom!" Marissa exclaimed with an incredulous laugh.

"Yeah, we still have a bunch of folks to go see," Jesse replied, mainly addressing Annemarie, but announcing to everyone his intention to leave. Annemarie nodded. He abashedly raised his hand in an attempt to say goodbye to the group.

As Annemarie followed him away from her family, she blew a kiss to everyone and gently set a hand on Alistair's shoulder, giving it a squeeze. He reached up and touched his hand to hers. She caught up with her husband, slipped her hand into his, and cuddled up to his bare, sun-bronzed arm, acknowledging him trying to move past his issues. "I'm sorry, hun. I don't know why I let him rub me the wrong way. Especially when I know he's not actively goading me." Jesse took the opportunity to properly apologize. "He bothers me so much sometimes. I want to be polite, and I see he's trying too, but I always get the feeling he's scheming to sweep you off your feet when I'm least expecting it. When I'm at my worst, probably, which he manages to bring out of me every damn time."

"I don't understand what the big deal is. Or why neither of you can manage to get along." She stroked her thumb along his. He lowered his head, ashamed of the admission.

"It wasn't a big deal when we lived across the country from him. But now that we're here and he's around *all the time*, it's hard to ignore the way he looks at you."

"The way he looks at me?" A slight head shake. "He's my best friend. Always has been and will be until the day one of us dies."

He stopped walking to look at her directly. "Yeah, but you dated. He's—" With a flourish of his hand, he made a suggestive wave over her body. "—he's seen you naked. You two have *been together*." The red tinge to his cheeks caused him to avert his eyes to the ground again.

She slipped her hand from his and crossed her arms over her chest. "Jesse McCready, are you jealous of my high school boyfriend?"

He shoved his hands in his pockets and kicked at a spot in the grass. He muttered, "Yeah, maybe I am." His eyes raised to look at her expression to gauge whether she was about to lecture or laugh at him.

Annemarie stepped forward. "Jess, I'm sorry my past with Alistair makes you feel this way. But that's exactly what it is." His eyebrows lowered. "The past. There're things he and I have done that you and I will never experience." He opened his mouth to interject, but she had a hand ready to press to his lips to silence him. "And you and me?" She ran the same fingers down to his chest, tapped it once, then motioned to herself. "We've done and *will continue* to do things that he and I won't. This isn't a matter of one being better than the other. It's not a competition." She cupped his cheek. "I chose you and I always will."

"I know."

"Alistair means well. Well . . . well enough. But if he were truly an asshole, he wouldn't be as well-loved as he is. The town doesn't feel any kind of obligation because he's sheriff. And you know, people here love you too." She grabbed hold of his chin with her thumb and index finger, focusing his gaze on hers. "Especially, and most importantly, me." She pushed her lips to his, sealing her words with a delicate, meaningful kiss.

When she pulled away, he lowered his eyes and said, "Yeah, but you're only sayin' that 'cause you *have to*."

She smiled. "I'll try to do better. We'll never be best friends—"

"I don't expect that."

"But I honestly haven't tried to get to know him. So, I promise I'll try."

She shrugged and raised both hands. "And if it doesn't work, then at least you tried. Now, can we stop all this sad, mushy feelings crap and go have a good time?"

Jesse reached for her hand and said, "God, yes, please."

For the next few hours, Annemarie and Jesse made the rounds of Hawthorn Park, saying hello to neighbors and old friends and occasionally helping out patrons in need; whether it be a visiting father struggling to carry several meals and drinks to his waiting family, cleaning up the overflowing trash cans, or pointing lost people in the right direction. It was not until the sun started setting that they got any time to themselves.

They returned to the family blanket with sloppy burgers, crinkle fries, battered and crisp cheese curds, fried pickles, and big cups of ice water to watch the fireworks; both of them famished and parched after an evening of constant walking and talking. They ate to their heart's content, both of them stealing each other's food and generally being ridiculous together. Once hosed off from the mess of grease, they nestled in for the show. Cuddled up against his side and his arm wrapped around her body to bring her in even closer, she nuzzled her nose into the hollow of his neck, allowing him to gently rest his chin on the top of her head. They stayed that way for the full twenty minutes of the display. He periodically kissed the top of her wavy hair and breathed in the scent of her citrus shampoo, with a hint of lingering fried food and sunshine. He softly chuckled into her hair and she smiled every time he did.

When the festivities concluded, the crowds vacated as quickly as they could, trying to be the first back on the road home or to the ferry terminal to catch the next boat. Typical of any event at Hawthorn Park, the highway would be packed for the next hour as it drained the two thousand patrons. Knowing not to bother with the hurry-up-and-wait traffic, Annemarie and Jesse stayed to help clean up the park and break down the vendor booths. Yet another tradition they started four years prior when Annemarie returned to Port Harrow with a husband in tow.

By midnight, the park was back in tip-top shape, cars on the road were near nonexistent, and Annemarie was falling asleep on her feet. Her early morning play session with Moose, the cleaning spree at the library, and now hours of sunshine, schmoozing, and fun left her drowsy where she stood. Being at the far end of the park, she begrudgingly began the march up the gentle slopes. Jesse watched her struggle for a couple minutes before swooping in to lift her into his arms.

"W-what are you doing?" she groggily asked.

"Sweeping you off your feet," he whispered into her ear. She half laughed with the tiniest of smiles, wrapped her arms around his neck, and closed her eyes. He made his way across the giant field toward their car, the only one left parked at the curb.

With the keys in his hand and Annemarie nestled cozily in his tired arms, he used the fob to unlock the doors. Careful not to jostle her awake, he tried to open the passenger door with his fingertips, but failed several times; the handle loudly snapped back with every attempt. On the fifth go, he succeeded. The door swung open, allowing him to set Annemarie on the seat. He pulled the seat belt out and around her body, fastening it to keep her safe on the drive home.

Jesse climbed into the driver's side, shutting the door quietly. He pulled out his cell phone from his pocket and saw Adam texted a few minutes earlier.

> **[Adam]**
> You're probably still at the park,
> but we're going till two or three
> if you and Annie want to swing
> by.

Jesse considered the invitation for a moment, wanting to see everyone in a much smaller capacity. He glanced from the illuminated screen to Annemarie's peaceful face. He responded to Adam.

> **[Jesse]**
> Need to get A home. Long day.
> Brunch tomorrow?

> **[Adam]**
> You sure? She can crash in the
> spare room while we drink and

you can just stay here when we
close up for the night.

Jesse typed out, "Yeah, OK, be there in ten," but he hesitated. He knew Annemarie would not mind, but as his finger hovered over the send button, he quickly backtracked and deleted the message.

> **[Jesse]**
> Would love to but need to get
> home to Moose.

[Adam]
No worries. Grey Barn @ 12?

> **[Jesse]**
> Sounds good. See you in the
> morning.

Jesse tucked the phone back into his pocket. He started the car. As he shifted into gear, Annemarie stirred and "I love you" softly escaped her lips. They pulled onto Wildwood Highway to head home.

TWELVE

Despite Annemarie telling everyone she had no interest in going to the event, there she sat in almost the same parking spot as one year ago. One year ago, she gathered with all her family and friends. One year ago, she last saw Jesse alive. There had not been enough time between his death and now for her to heal. While she functioned like a well-oiled machine most days, the fireworks and communal picnic felt like too much too soon; every person she was about to encounter would give their condolences, share stories and kind words, and treat her like she was seconds from shattering. While it was true she still needed to be handled with care, she despised that sort of treatment, be they friend or family. Besides, she had zero interest in revisiting a place where many of her fondest memories were created with the person she cared for most.

Her coworkers at the library insisted it could be cathartic, that it could do her some good to face off with the traumatic experience, to make new memories. Cecily tried to convince her of the good time she would have hanging out with Marissa, Charlie, Alistair, Riggs, and everyone else she normally enjoyed the company of. They would all eat delicious food, watch the fireworks, help clean up . . . The same as every other year. But when Annemarie loudly countered it would not, in fact, be the same in Jesse's absence, Cecily had little to say in response.

Now, here she was, a mixture of anxiety and guilt burning deep into the center of her bones.

Parked with the engine still running—giving her the opportunity to flee at the last minute if she decided she could not follow through with the plan—she sighed deeply, if not a tad exaggeratedly, releasing a long huff of breath she had been holding in. Her knuckles were stark white and aching, not wanting to let go of the steering wheel.

"You can do this," she murmured to herself. "It's only a few hours. Mom and Marissa will be there. They'll keep me distracted. New memories mean moving forward not moving on, or that I'm erasing Je—" She could not get his name out before the tears welled up, pushing diligently against the brims of her eyelids, trying to break the levy wall to cascade down her cheeks. Letting go of the steering wheel meant turning off the engine, opening the door, climbing out, attending the party, and acting normal. She did not want to do any of it, face any of it—ever again if she could help it. She closed her eyes and exhaled deeply.

A single knuckle rapped twice against the driver's side window, startling her to the point of crying out. Her hands instinctively covered her mouth, embarrassed at the noise that escaped her lips. The tears that threatened to give her away finally poured out, soaking the tips of her fingers.

The door swung open against her silent wishes, revealing her upset, crying form to the public. Alistair crouched beside her.

"Oh, Annie, Annie, Annie. Hey, I'm sorry. I didn't mean to scare you." He reached forward to her protruding elbow as she continued to involuntarily sob into her trembling hands. "It's okay." His tone was soft, comforting.

"I can't go out there, Alistair. I can't face everyone." Her hands moved from over her mouth up to her eyes to hide the tears. She did not know why. Alistair had seen her at her worst; this sobbing, bawling mess was nothing to him.

He brought his arms back to his body and readjusted the crouching position to something a little more comfortable. "You don't have to. No one's forcing you to be here." He looked over his shoulder at the traffic on the busy road, making sure he was not causing any kind of hazard by being there. "You can drive off right now. Car's already running, traffic isn't too bad. You could be home in forty." He balled up his fist with the thumb sticking out. He motioned behind him toward the south side of the island. "Or better yet, let's both go. We can sneak off to my place. I'm not on duty tonight." He gestured to his button-down and grey joggers. "I've got a fridge full of beer, several boxes of cereal, a couple frozen pizzas, other random shit to eat. We'll leave and not deal with any of this bullshit anymore."

She lowered her hands, tears still streaming from her beet-red eyes, but no longer hiccupping her way through hyperventilation. "Yeah?" she asked with a sniffle, her voice possessing a hint of hope.

"Yeah! You and me. Let's get outta here." He stood, finally giving his knees a bit of relief from the stalled position. He stopped moving when he saw the look on her face. The tiny crook of a smile that appeared in the corner of her mouth with that hint of hope melted away.

"I can't."

"What do you mean you can't? Do you want to be here?"

Sheepishly, Annemarie replied, "No." She wiped away tears from her cheeks with the back of her left hand. She sucked in a deep breath through her nose.

"Do you want to go home?"

"No." This was not the answer he expected.

"Then what do you want?"

"I . . . I don't know. I wanna go hang out with you guys, but I know I'll spend the entire time thinking about Jesse. I wanna go home, but I know I'll pick up a six-pack on the way there and that's not what I need right now. I just—" She cut herself off before finishing the thought. A fresh barrage of burning-hot tears returned.

Alistair leaned forward and planted a kiss on her forehead. He put his hands on either side of her face, awkwardly balancing over the threshold of the vehicle. "Annie, everyone will understand if you go home."

"I don't want anyone thinking I wasn't willing to at least try."

"You have! You're here, aren't you?" He paused. "Look, you've got two choices, hun: you muster up the energy to hang out or you leave. It's not that simple, but it kinda is." He patted her jean-clad knee closest to him. "I'm gonna head in. Whenever you figure out your plan, let me know." He hoisted himself up to stand and walked away.

He realized nothing he could say or do would give her the courage to act one way or another. He gave her an excellent escape plan, and while she seemed intrigued at first, it was obvious her heart was not in it. But neither was it in the celebration. He said what he wanted to say and hoped she would make the best decision for herself. Whatever it may be.

He stuffed his hands into his pockets, waiting for traffic to ease up to cross the two-lane highway. A small pickup truck stopped long enough for him to walk to the other shoulder of the road. He waved at the driver, long-time island resident Merle Doss, who gave back a little salute of acknowledgment before stepping on the gas to continue his journey north.

As he meandered along the sidewalk toward Hawthorn Park, he heard, "Alistair, wait up!" He peeked over his shoulder and saw Annemarie tearing across the roadway to catch him. He did not stop, but slowed his pace. She closed the gap between them—all her therapeutic running paying off—and playfully punched his upper arm.

"Thanks," she said with a faint, closed-mouth smile.

"For what?" He shrugged before she could answer, acting as if he did nothing. In reality, he *had not* done anything.

"You know what." They walked in silence side by side, occasionally stealing glances at each other that made either of them smile in turn.

Because Hawthorn Park was a large public gathering place, there was no single entrance. A parking lot accommodating up to fifty vehicles was packed with tourists and locals alike, loading out their trucks, SUVs, and sedans of the family and supplies they brought along. Throngs of ferry passengers on foot from the terminal rounded out the boisterous crowd. This was the premiere event for Port Harrow. Nowhere else in Azure County could even come close and everywhere within seventy-five miles stopped trying.

Alistair and Annemarie followed the sidewalk until they reached the parking lot, falling in line behind a crowd of attendees making their way toward the paved paths of the park. Like every other year, the layout of the event included a long wall of booths filled with artisans hocking their jewelry, artwork, specialty items, and anyone else wanting to turn a profit with their handmade items. The Port Harrow Community Council charged a premium price for space, which helped pad the island's bank account to present the annual events.

Behind the clutter of kitsch and artistry, a smaller but still impressive lineup of food trucks had ferried over from the rest of Azure County. Everything from greasy burgers with ostentatious toppings to fully loaded dessert waffles ran this year's gamut.

Alistair thought everything sounded and smelled incredible. Annemarie did not. The acrobatics her stomach performed in that moment made every single item sound repulsive—even the healthier options not laden with batter, breading, butter, and grease. Food was not what she needed. Not right now; maybe not at all on this particular night.

To the right of the shopping booths and food trucks, the grassy, green field stretched on forever, full of colorful blankets topped with families awaiting dusk, still a couple hours away. There were no bad seats in the house, so long as eyes were fixed on the waterfront and skyline some half a mile ahead.

Annemarie scanned the crowd hoping to find any other familiar faces—Alistair was always a welcome companion, but she needed to surround herself with more people. If she were to survive the night, she had to be distracted. Thankfully, her family was never in short supply of entertainment. She just needed to find them.

An elbow abruptly jabbed her in the ribs, breaking her concentration. "I'm grabbing a dog. Want me to get you anything?" Alistair asked, motioning to the food trucks with his head.

She thought for a moment. "A brat. You know how I like it. I'll pay you back." A weak smile crept into the corner of her mouth as she feigned interest in existing anywhere outside the four walls of her house, of anywhere other than here.

"I'm on it." He cut through the crowd and disappeared before she could change her mind. She slipped her hands into the back pockets of her jeans as she rocked back and forth on her heels.

"Annie!" a deep, gravelly voice called from behind her.

Caught off guard, she whirled around to see who it was. Dig Kimball's neatly styled mustache and beard juxtaposed by the shaggy mop of hair on his head made him stick out like a sore thumb. Annemarie rarely saw him around the island, but he was the comforting, familiar sight she was after.

"Hi, Dig. How are you?" Annemarie stretched her arms to embrace him in a hug. He smelled of pipe tobacco and motor oil—his signature scent. It had followed him around all the years she knew him. If he was not at work, he was busy working on one of his classic cars; his jeans were often spattered with a myriad of automotive fluids, and today was no different.

"I'm good. Doing good, thanks. Been keeping busy with work, and when I'm not strapped into the rig, Eileen's pulling me away from the garage to run circles around the property with all of them damn honey-dos." He gave a hearty chuckle. "Work keeping you busy?"

She shrugged, but was mirthful with her delivery. "Off and on. I stepped back severely during my recovery, but I'm trying to pick up more shifts—"

"Oh, hi, honey! I'm so glad you came!" Cecily swooped in from behind to give a startled Annemarie a warm hug.

She turned her head to look at Cecily and spotted a train of Mitchells trailing not too far behind her. Marissa dragged a wheeled cart loaded with blankets, pillows, an overstuffed backpack, and a big, blue teddy bear with an amber eye gone missing. Charlie marched behind the wagon, stopping every ten feet to spin around and growl like a predatory cat at Ken, her hands raised up in the air like razor-sharp claws; he pretended to be scared with each of her outbursts, crying out with expert dramatic flair. Charlie was beside herself, thinking she was scaring him every time. Marissa could only roll her eyes as she walked up to Annemarie to plant a quick kiss on her sister's cheek.

"She's been doing this the whole way here." Marissa glanced away and saw Dig standing awkwardly off to the side. "Hey, Dig!"

"Looks like the gang's all here," he announced, counting each of the Mitchell heads. "Well, all except Al."

As if summoned out of thin air, Alistair sidled up to the group, hands full with food. He handed a cardboard box stuffed with a charred bratwurst and a massive pile of golden waffle fries to Annemarie who was more concerned with rallying round with her family than eating. Alistair, on the other hand, dived face-first into his food, famished after not eating all day while tending to work matters on the mainland.

The crowd of seven milled about in a loose circle, idle chatter filling the air as the family caught up with Dig. Alistair had his loaded hot dog shoved into his mouth when his eyes lit up, spotting a familiar face in the distance. He let out a muffled, "Mmf" and motioned with his head, primarily catching the attention of Dig and Ken. Their eyes shot across the field to see what Alistair was directing them to.

The telltale height, buzzed haircut, and slightly crooked nose was enough to catch anyone's attention, alerting them to the arrival of Nowell who plodded down the sidewalk with five-year-old Dylan beside him. Nowell had his hands buried in the pockets of his pants and his head lowered, watching each of the steps Dylan took.

"Motherfucker."

Annemarie turned to face Dig who had muttered the word, obviously pointed at Nowell.

"Leave it be," she said quickly.

"The audacity that man has, coming back here like this," Dig continued.

"Leave it be, Dig," she repeated. She tried to sound stern with him, hoping the voice she used with Moose to drop the squirrels he caught would work on humans too.

He ran his hands through his hair, smoothing back the strays as he tied the loose locks into a low ponytail. He spit on the ground then wiped his upper lip with the edge of his forefinger, looking ready for a fight. Before Annemarie could reach a hand out to his arm to hold on tight, he was gone. Barging straight for his quarry, he made it to him in record time, ending up mere feet in front of him, forcing Nowell to abruptly stop.

"Oh, excuse me," Nowell said as he tried to sidestep around Dig and ushered Dylan with him.

"No. Excuse *me*." Dig extended his arm in front of him and put a pointed finger into Nowell's chest. "You're not welcome here."

Nowell swatted away his hand. "Don't touch me, pal," he cautioned.

"Dig, stop!" Annemarie called from their group. She had to raise her voice to be heard. When he did not respond to her, not even a glance, she lifted a foot to walk in his direction, to physically restrain him if she had to, but Cecily grabbed her wrist tightly and kept her from getting far. *"Mom,"* she snapped; Cecily did not let go.

"I'm not your pal. No one here is." Dig was seconds away from growling.

"Bro, I'm just here to watch the fireworks with my kid," Nowell replied as he set his hand on top of Dylan's brown, shaggy bowl cut.

"I'm not your bro either."

"Okay, my mistake. Doesn't change the fact that I came here with my kid. I don't want any trouble." Nowell puffed up his chest a little, straightening his spine, trying to make himself look like less of the slouch that he was. He gently guided Dylan off the sidewalk toward the food trucks as an attempt to get around Dig.

"I *said* you're not welcome here." Dig reached for the collar of Nowell's green and yellow rugby shirt and yanked hard, causing Nowell to stumble backward for a moment. A fist came swinging through the air, aiming right for Nowell's nose, but he ducked at the last minute and it instead sailed past. Dig recentered himself and tried again. This time, Nowell was not fast enough. He had been too busy shooing away Dylan to see Dig's uppercut aiming for his jaw. When he landed the punch, Annemarie cried out, startling Cecily and allowing her to rip free from her mother's grip.

She rushed across the field separating her from Dig and Nowell. "Knock it off!" she yelled as Dig swung a fist again. She inserted herself between them, hopeful that Dig would not try to punch Nowell if there was a risk of hitting her. But it did not deter him.

Other attendees of the festival stopped in place to watch what was unfolding. Dylan shuffled far enough away to be out of harm's way and kept his face hidden so as to not have to see what was happening. As Annemarie stretched out her arms to plant a hand on each of the men's chests in an attempt to keep them in their respective corners, Dig completely ignored her and jutted out to one side in order to get to Nowell. Nowell received one more punch in the ribs—a lucky hit—before he tackled Dig to the ground. Dig's head narrowly missed slamming into the sidewalk, but they both still landed with a loud *thud*.

"Alistair, do something!" Annemarie shouted. He had not moved from his spot among the Mitchell crowd. If he were being honest, as a civilian, he did not truly care what happened to Nowell Reid; but as the sheriff, he knew he had to step in. He handed the remainder of his food to Cecily to hold while he intervened, albeit casually. He slowly approached the scuffling men, wiping leftover grease on the back of his pants, hoping Dig might get another lip buster in if he took his time. But when he saw Dig's nose was bleeding profusely and Nowell was leaning over his body, he knew he had to do the right thing.

"All right, boys. Enough's enough," he said in a loud, clear voice. "Go about your business, folks!" he called to the crowd, frozen in place, rubbernecking at the explosive pre-fireworks show happening in front of them.

Dig put up his leg to kick at Nowell, touching him just enough to get him to fall backward, but without the proper force to cause any damage. Nowell landed on his ass with another *thud* and a pained *oof* escaped his lips. As the

160

commotion settled, Dig tried to climb up onto his knees and took the moment of quiet to lunge at Nowell one last time. Alistair properly intervened, swiping at the back of Dig's T-shirt to keep him from doing any further damage.

"Cool it, Dig," Alistair instructed.

"He's not supposed to be here," he protested.

"No one asked you to be Annemarie's bouncer," Alistair replied. He glanced around, his eyes darting to the faces of the few people still milling about. He noticed Annemarie had moved over toward the food trucks where Dylan was hiding behind his hands. Her fingers gently tugged at his little arms, coaxing him to come out from his shell.

"It's a public event, asshole. It's open to everyone," Nowell spat out.

"Not to murderers." Dig's return was quick and to the point.

Nowell's eyes immediately shot down to the grass below him, refusing to make eye contact with anyone else. He had been hoping to go unnoticed the entire night; there were enough people present who had no idea who he was and it was entirely possible to hide within the crowd and have a fun night with Dylan. But hearing Dig using *murderers* in a clear, loud voice would absolutely raise concerns. And most importantly, it was a word Dylan had not yet learned to associate with his father. He wanted to shelter him from that information as long as humanly possible.

"Now, now, Dig. He has every right to be here, like you, or me, or all these other people. Leave it be, or *you'll* be asked to leave." Alistair paused for a second. "As it stands, Mr. Reid is allowed to have you arrested for assault." He hated how the words sounded coming from his mouth—the last thing he wanted to do was arrest Dig.

Nowell shook his head. "I'm not pressing charges." He rubbed the palm of his hand along his jaw. "I just want to be left alone." He finally got the gumption to look up to search for Dylan. Annemarie was crouched into a small ball beside the boy, brushing his hair away from his face and wiping a couple tears from his cheeks. "Dyl!" he called. Dylan looked up, almost startled, and zipped away from Annemarie to dive into Nowell's arms. The force of his landing caused Nowell to go flat on his back; it elicited a small, reserved chuckle from them both.

Alistair reached out a hand to help Dig off the ground. He begrudgingly took it, but as he got to his feet, he muttered at Nowell, "I should press charges against *you*." Alistair grabbed a stack of napkins from the nearby waffle cart and handed them to a still-bleeding Dig who bunched them up in his hands and daubed away the blood.

Trying to extract Dylan from around his neck, Nowell struggled to get upright. Alistair extended a hand to help him as well, which Nowell happily accepted. "Thanks, man. I appreciate it."

"Don't thank me. Thank the woman you widowed." As Alistair walked away from the scene, he mumbled under his breath, "I'd've let him wail on you a lot longer if it were up to me." Part of him did not care if anyone else heard this; the other part of him regretted it the moment it slipped out. No one seemed to flinch at its delivery, however.

The Mitchells were already moving on in search of where they would set up their blankets and pillows to watch the night's show. Alistair trailed not far behind, giving the occasional glance over his shoulder to Annemarie's whereabouts. "You coming, Annie?" he called when he saw she was not budging from Nowell's and Dylan's sides.

She made a shooing motion at Alistair, telling him to stick with her family. She would catch up with them soon enough.

"You okay?" She leaned toward Nowell and grabbed hold of his chin, careful as she inspected the redness where Dig's fist had collided with the jawbone.

He gave a curt nod. "Not how I was expecting to spend the Fourth."

"Me either."

He looked down at her, his eyes meeting hers for the first time that evening. "Thank you, for asking him to step in. I'm sure it killed him to have to do it. It was obvious no one else was about to."

She opened her mouth to respond, but had nothing she thought she could say to tell him otherwise. She pushed some of her hair back behind her ear and chewed on her lower lip. "Had I known you were coming, I would've warned you against it. Some people . . . don't really *care* for you 'round these parts."

Nowell exhaled a short breath from his nose, a half laugh. "Yeah, no shit." He wrapped an arm around Dylan's shoulders and brought him closer. "Look, I don't want to keep you from your family. But seriously, thank you for stepping in. You didn't have to."

She gave a happy little shrug. "You get ultra-drunk with a guy and pass out on his couch, you sorta share some kind of special bond with him. Besides, y'know, the *other* stuff." She meant it as a joke, but it sent a chill down her spine, thinking about Nowell's and her shared experiences—and not just Jesse's death. "I'll see you around."

"Yeah, see ya." Dylan wiggled his hand into Nowell's as they walked away from Annemarie. The boy checked over his shoulder several times, hoping to not spot anyone else who might be coming for his dad.

Like every other year, a group of council members and miscellaneous island residents including Alistair, Marissa, and Annemarie hung back to help clean up after the festivities. They worked to empty the many garbage cans sprinkled around the park, clean out now-cooled charcoal grills, break down tables and chairs, and move any extraneous furniture or equipment to the nearby community center storage facility.

Alistair and Marissa emptied trash into larger bags at the north end of Hawthorn Park. She prattled on about a problem at her office, but Alistair's eyes and ears were glued to the scene at midfield.

Nowell, with Dylan bundled up in his arms, chatted with Annemarie. They stood awfully close together, exchanging smiles and laughs, obviously talking about something with deep interest. At one point during their conversation, Nowell said something that made her laugh so hard, she doubled over. Upon righting herself, she playfully slapped his shoulder. As they finished, she gave him a small side hug, trying not to wake up a sleeping Dylan, and Nowell reciprocated the gesture. He headed off east toward the library. With her hands tucked into the back pockets of her jeans, she watched the two disappear with the dregs of the exiting crowd.

Loftily, she swiveled in place and marched toward Marissa and Alistair, who were still wrestling with the unwieldy, rusty trash bins—Alistair's distraction causing them the biggest slow down. As she approached, Marissa was the only one to respond to her arrival.

"How's his jaw doing?" she asked, looking up from her nearly full black bag of greasy paper plates and gooey remnants of food.

"Oh, he'll live," Annemarie replied. She reached out both hands for the bag Alistair was dragging around. He did not bother acknowledging her and kept transferring over garbage.

"That's a shame," he muttered under his breath.

Annemarie slow-blinked while staring directly at him, annoyed with the response. She could not help but think of what Nowell told her, how Alistair acted toward him and Travis the night of the accident. She knew Alistair was an ass, but he often remained collected and impartial while on the job—so she did not believe that part of Nowell's story. Seeing how he acted tonight, however, made her realize it was probably true. She ignored him. "He said it's sore, and I'm sure it'll turn a nice shade of purple by the morning. But he's not too worried about it."

"He should be," Alistair once again muttered to himself.

Marissa quickly interjected, "That's good. Hopefully it won't cause him too much pain in the days to come. He'll have a fun little story to share for anyone who asks." She gave a half-hearted shrug.

"Yeah," Annemarie agreed with a solemn nod.

"I didn't know he had a son. That was kind of a shocker." Marissa genuinely seemed to want to know more about Nowell, if for no other reason than to mask the sass and shade Alistair was dishing out, but her kind prodding shocked Annemarie altogether. She never once thought her sister would care two licks about her husband's murderer, or not be seeing red over his appearance at the festivities the way everyone else was.

"I didn't know about him either until recently. He tried his hardest to keep Dylan out of the public eye during the trial. He's a single dad with primary custody, but because of work and everything, Dylan mostly stays with Nowell's parents, and sometimes his ex. Immediately following the accident and throughout the trial stuff, he barely saw him, so he's been trying to own up to his responsibilities and be there as much as he can be." Annemarie moseyed over to help Marissa tie up the bag and drag it to the flatbed cart. The trio continued along the sidewalk to another set of garbage cans to the southwest.

"At least he's owning up to one of the things he's responsible for," Alistair grumbled.

Annemarie gave him a sidelong glance, staring at him disapprovingly. She shut her eyes, shook her head in disbelief, and continued her conversation with her sister.

"They seem to have a pretty good relationship, despite the lapse in parenting for those few months. Dylan adores him." Annemarie lifted off the top of her next bin, grabbed the overflowing torn bag inside, and hefted it into Marissa's new, empty bag.

"What happened to Dylan's mom? Why doesn't she have custody of him?" Marissa asked. "This state always favors the mom." She knew from experience.

"She's around. She didn't fight the custody stuff, 'cause I guess she didn't want that much on her plate anymore, but she still gets him on certain weekends and whatnot. He hasn't told me much beyond that. It seems to pain him to talk about her, so he kinda avoids it. He says not spending too much time worrying about her allows him to focus all his energy on the kid."

"That's a nice, positive spin to have on all of it. Single parenting is *rough*. There's so little time to do everything. I know if I still worried about Jack, I'd never get anything done." Marissa rolled her eyes. "I'm glad Dylan has the support of his dad, and it sounds like Nowell has the support of his family." Her smile was genuine— Annemarie appreciated it.

"Too bad Jesse's not around to support *his* family."

Alistair did it; he finally crossed the line.

Marissa's eyes went wide as she grimaced, baring all her teeth and sucking in air. She knew what was coming. Hoping to not be pulled into the knock-down drag-out fight about to come to fruition, she stood absolutely still. *"Don't engage, don't engage,"* she chanted quietly. *"If I don't move, they can't see me."*

Annemarie slammed down the half-full bag in her hands, zipped over to Alistair, and grabbed him by the collar with one hand. "*Excuse you.* What the hell's your problem?"

Alistair's mouth dropped open and an alarmed gasp jostled out of him when Annemarie gave him a hard shake. "Annie, I—"

"Jesse was taken away from *me*, Al. He died because of a stupid *accident*. Yeah, Nowell was involved. He was also found innocent. I've forgiven him. He did nothing to *you*. You didn't even like Jesse. So why are you acting like he was your best friend?" At this accusation, Marissa nonchalantly set down her bag and slinked off to find anywhere else to be without being noticed. As much as she was curious to see how it played out, she did not want to be involved, especially after the text exchange she and Alistair had had three days prior. Besides, Annemarie would not want witnesses when she maimed him.

Ripping his collar free from her death grip, he took a step back. "Look, I didn't mean anything by it. I . . ." He flopped his arms down at his sides with a giant huff of breath. "I don't want to see you hurt, and cozying up with the enemy isn't setting you up for success."

"'Cozying up with the enemy?' *Al*, Nowell isn't the enemy. No one is. It was an accident. He wasn't even the one driving." She used both hands to push back her bangs and rested them on her head as she breathed deep, staring at Alistair as she decided what to say next. "You're always doing this. You're always coming to my rescue and I need you to not. No—" She stopped short. "No, I don't mean that. I mean, I need you to trust me. You need to trust that I know what I'm doing."

"I do," he insisted.

"*You don't.* If you did, you wouldn't be standing here looking at me with *that face*—" She tossed an unrestrained hand gesture in his direction. "That face that tells me everything on your brain right now."

Alistair folded his arms over his chest and widened his stance. "And what's on my brain right now?"

"You're regretting pulling Dig off him. You wanted to let him bash Nowell's head into a bloody pulp. You've been pissed from day one, but especially since the verdict found Nowell and Travis not guilty. You're annoyed that I won't let you in all the time or that I won't treat everything you say as gospel." She squinted and copied his folded arms. "You think you know what's best for me and you hate that you're wrong, but will never admit it. You think I've lost my mind and all you want to do is take care of me. You—"

Alistair raised a hand to silence her. "Annie, I *do* want to take care of you. It's all I've ever wanted."

"That implies that I *need* taking care of."

"Fair." He broke eye contact and lowered his head to stare at his feet for a moment.

"I don't know what it is, but you have this . . . this *way* about you where it seems like you don't believe anything I say." She shook her head.

"It's my job to question everything."

"I wouldn't lie to you, Alistair. Ever."

It ended the argument.

Until it did not.

"Where were you the other night?" he pressed.

Her eyebrows shot high up on her forehead for a brief moment but she hoped he had not noticed. "What? When?"

"The night before you found Peter's shirt in your trash can."

Annemarie's mouth opened just wide enough to let out a stunted breath, allowing her a chance to shape an answer. "Brownstone."

"Who with?" His mouth set in a hard line and his eyebrows popped up too.

"Nina."

It was not a lie, but it was not the whole truth. She knew it, and she was pretty sure he knew it too.

"Where'd you stay?"

"I told you," she insisted.

He wagged a finger at her. "Right. At Marissa's." He paused. "Marissa told me she hadn't seen you. At all. For weeks, in fact."

Annemarie's jaw clenched for a tense moment before letting it slacken with her eyes closed. "I was with Nowell."

"Figured as much."

"Then why the line of questioning?"

"To prove that you don't always tell me the truth. And you know what? That's okay. You don't have to. You owe me nothing. Well, as law enforcement, you do, when it matters. But Alistair and Annemarie, you and me?" He shook his head. "I want to know you're okay, because if you're not, I want to help. I can't know you're not okay if you don't tell me." The argument's tone had dramatically shifted from enraged hollering to somber words of support, and Alistair thought it okay to follow up with, "Jesse and I weren't friends. But he meant a lot to you, and your family, and by proxy, that means he meant something to me."

"You had a funny way of showing it," she muttered. She blew a breath of air up her face to flutter her bangs out of her eyes. A string of silence filled the space between them, neither of them thinking anything they could say would be a suitable response to her comment. After it grew too painful to remain quiet any longer, a single, dubious laugh that rocked her whole body escaped her. "We still have a lot of shit to deal with."

He ran a hand over his cheek. "I know. We need to keep being open with each other."

She smirked. "I mean with the party cleanup, dingus."

"That too."

THIRTEEN

Alistair tried not to ride her tailpipe as they drove along Wildwood Highway, keeping a good fifty feet behind her, especially through the tight, blind corners filled with fog and wildlife that often grazed along the road's shoulders. Most summer nights on the island developed gauzy wisps of condensation that infiltrated the road, always obscuring vision; Alistair remembered how the night of Jesse's accident there had been no fog whatsoever, which was strange. Tonight's was extra thick. The stoplight at the intersection of Spruce and the highway was green as they came around the bend, but quickly changed yellow then red. A silver sports car pulled up behind Alistair as the three vehicles slowed their approach.

Annemarie settled right on the white line, impatiently lifting her foot off the brake a hair at a time, scooting forward in inches. The light had turned green for cross traffic, but there was not a single car in sight. She considered blowing through the red, knowing Alistair would not bother to give her a citation, but instead, she waited, much to her chagrin.

Suddenly, the entire intersection went dark. The traffic light dimmed to black, the four lamps on each corner curb blanked out, and the only visibility was from the head- and taillights of the three vehicles. Alistair cocked his head, finding it peculiar. He lifted the lower half of his body up a few inches to reach into a front pocket to retrieve his cell phone. He watched Annemarie ease forward, treating the intersection as a four-way stop. But before she fully pulled away, before Alistair dialed Cami at the station, her driver's side taillight blinked out. It returned as quickly as it had gone, and the passenger's side followed suit. A chill hit Alistair, running the length of his spine and making all the hair on his arms and neck stand at attention. He involuntarily shuddered.

Annemarie sped off, leaving him and the sports car alone. He eased off the brake, slid up to the white line, and stopped again. He peered to his left, straining to see anything through the rolls of fog and the darkness, then turned his head slowly to the right, double-checking no wildlife had charged out onto the asphalt. A glint of something, a flash of silver, caught his eye. He blinked several times, trying to process what he saw. The flare of light happened again, a little more brightly, and Alistair caught sight of the silhouette of a man, facing him from the edge of the woods.

The intersection lit up with the bright lights of the streetlamps and signal. The person in the silver car honked, snapping Alistair out of his deep concentration on what he was looking at twenty feet away. He turned his attention to the intersection, checking one more time for safety, and pulled clear through en route to catch up with Annemarie.

The porch light was on, the front door ajar, and Alistair watched the beam of a flashlight bouncing toward him from the side yard. Moose came tromping out of the bushes along the fence line, head held high, tongue lolling out of the side of his mouth. He approached Alistair and shoved his face against the leg of his joggers, rubbing his nose along the length of the material.

"Hey," Annemarie called as she appeared from the darkness, clicking off the flashlight.

"Hey," he replied despondently. He shoved his hands into his pockets as he made his way up the short flight of stairs and pushed his way into the house with his shoulder. Moose followed closely behind him, then Annemarie. She moved past him to set the flashlight back in her room. He shut the door with the flat of his back, waiting a moment to exhale a heavy breath. A clatter of noise came from her bedroom before she swooped out, dressed down into a pair of black pajama bottoms and a white tank top with her hair out of its ponytail. She stopped in place to stare at him.

"You okay? You look like you've seen a ghost," she said. She walked the few steps over to him and set the back of her hand against his forehead, then at the top of either cheek. "You feel a little clammy. That hot dog coming back to bite you in the ass?"

"I—" He stopped himself before blurting out unintelligible words. He did not know, or understand, what he had seen. He did not know how to even explain it. It did not frighten him, whatever it was. But it left him with a sickly feeling in the pit of his stomach. His insides roiled and the adrenaline coursing through him at the time left him faint, even now. "I don't know. I don't feel . . . right."

She brought her hand back to her side and shook her head. "You're not going home tonight, then. You'll stay here."

He threw a thumb over his shoulder and said, "I should go. I wanted to make sure you got here okay."

"No. I won't hear of it. You're in no shape to drive if something is off."

Alistair began to object, but realized she was right. His head was not in the right place to get back on the road. He was tired, mentally and physically, and he was rattled by . . . whatever it was he saw. So, he agreed with a nod. He pointed to the couch. "I'll shack up here."

"No, you won't. You know there's more than enough room for you in the bed." He knew he could not fight her on the matter. He shrugged and cut across the room toward the kitchen to grab a glass of water. She followed close behind him, doing the same for herself. Though, after he took the first sip, she snatched the cup from his hand and downed half of it. "No use in dirtying two."

He gave her a weak smile. "Guess not." He finished the water, set the cup off to the side of the sink—intending to use it in the morning—and leaned against the lower cabinet. He folded his arms over his chest and sighed. "I . . . I'm sorry about earlier."

She cocked her head and raised an eyebrow. "Sorry about what?"

He shrugged again. "I was being an ass. To you and to Nowell."

"Well, you don't need to apologize to me. Nowell, on the other hand . . ."

"I'm having a hard time letting go of what happened. I *know* it's your thing. I know you were affected the most by it, so it's not my place to be angry with him over what happened. But, his actions, and Travis's, hurt you, and I'm struggling to move past it. And it's not like we're talking about they rear-ended you or something. This . . . this was big. *Is* big."

She ruffled the wavy tresses of her hair, scratching her fingernails over her scalp. "I understand." She set the palm of her hand in the middle of his chest and kept it there. "I appreciate your concern, Alistair. I do. Though, I'd like it a lot more if you laid off him if you see him around."

"I can do that." He gave a slight nod.

"Thank you." She turned in place and glanced at the clock on the stove; it was almost one. "I need to get to bed."

"Yeah, I have to be up at six."

She rolled her eyes. "Fuck work, man."

The corner of his mouth curved into the slightest of grins. "You said it."

She pulled her hand away from him and glided out of the kitchen. He watched her go and waited for her to disappear before letting out another huff of a breath. Without her presence, he was suddenly reminded that he still had no answers as to what he witnessed. The flash of light, the obvious silhouette of a man, the way it stood at the tree line, staring in his direction—what could it have possibly been?

Realizing he had remained in the kitchen for almost ten minutes mulling over the possibilities, he acquiesced in order to give in for the night. He padded into the living room where he kicked off his shoes by the couch, flicked off the lights, and wandered into Annemarie's dark bedroom. The only illumination came from the streetlight barely filtering in through the horizontal blinds over the large window on the far wall. He quietly made his way to the right side of the bed, knowing she slept on the left. Even as far back as high school, the left was hers.

The room was a mite warm, the day having been hot and Annemarie had not been home to air out the house. He opted to strip out of his button-down and tossed it onto the floor into a heap beside the bed. He was careful to pull back the lightweight comforter, not sure if she was asleep yet, and not wanting to wake her if she was. He climbed onto the mattress and let out a soft, uncomfortable sigh. Annemarie rolled onto her side to face him.

"Hey," she said softly, instigating a conversation.

"Oh. You're still awake."

"Yeah. I've been thinking . . ." Her voice came out groggy, sleepy, mere moments from falling asleep.

"Hmm?" He remembered that his cell phone was still in his pants. He fished a hand into the left pocket to pull it out and set it on the night table.

She smoothed the pillow under her head with the flat of her hand. "I think we should—" Her sentence cut off as she drifted to sleep. She snorted awake momentarily to say, "I think we—" and once again, was beaten by exhaustion.

Alistair turned his head to face up toward the ceiling. He intertwined his fingers and set them on his stomach.

He closed his eyes, trying to distract his chattering brain with counting breaths.

He heard a noise in the living room. His eyes shot open. The sound came again and he realized it was Moose snoring. Then the soft snores of Annemarie caught his attention. *Out like a light,* he thought with a mild smile. *Wish that were me.*

As the sun broke the horizon, draping the bedroom with the slightest hint of warm yellows and oranges, Alistair was still wide awake, eyes staring at the ceiling, counting cobwebs. He had not bothered burrowing under the blanket when he climbed into bed hours before and did not get cold enough throughout the night to need to crawl under with Annemarie. He gave up trying to sleep long ago; his brain would not stop thinking about that encounter, the intersection's lights turning off and on on their own, the flash of silver.

He turned over and reached for his cell phone. It was fifteen minutes before his alarm was supposed to sound, but he decided to not bother waiting for it. He turned off the alarm, climbed out of bed, and quietly made his way into the bathroom. Upon returning to the bedroom, he scooped his shirt off the floor and pulled it on. He found Moose deflated in a sploot in the doorway leading into the living room, his eyes tracking Alistair as he moved around. He bent over at the waist and petted the dog behind the ears, giving a good scratch as Moose huffed out his contentment.

In the kitchen, he worked to put together a pot of coffee—he intended to take a cup for the road and leave the rest for Annemarie when she woke up. As he waited for it to brew, he riffled through her cupboards for something to eat. He found an unopened box of peanut butter protein bars and grabbed two. He shoved one in his front pocket next to his phone and peeled open the wrapper of the second to eat while he waited. He munched on it quietly, the crinkle of the foil inadvertently calling for Moose who came prancing into the room with ears perked up and a tilt to his head, letting Alistair know that he, too, would like food.

After opening several other cupboards, Alistair found the bin of kibble, saw the handwritten note taped to the side stating Moose was allowed one cup of food twice a day with half a can of wet mixed in with each meal, and took it upon himself to fill the dog's dish. Always underfoot, Moose licked his slavering lips as he watched Alistair's every move. From the cupboard opening, the handling of the dog-proof container and pulling open of the wet food can, to the shuffle across the kitchen. The clanging of the food hitting the stainless-steel bowl was music to his ears. Alistair held up a hand, freezing Moose in place.

"Sit," Alistair instructed. The big, fuzzy rump plopped onto the floor and a sound halfway between a grumble and a whine squealed out of him. Once Alistair sidestepped, he announced, "Okay," and Moose hoovered his breakfast. Alistair returned to his protein bar, cheeked the rest of it like a chipmunk, and headed for the front door, thinking about what he had to tackle at work.

FOURTEEN

"Yes, mom. I've been working on it since I got home." Annemarie used her bent wrist to adjust the cell phone closer to her ear, trying to avoid touching it with her floury and fruit-sticky hands.

"You didn't start it this morning?" Cecily asked, sounding shocked by her own question.

"No, I didn't have time to peel and soak the peaches. Alistair's alarm didn't go off so I over—"

"Alistair was there this morning?"

"Yes, he spent the night."

"Again?"

"Yes, *again*, mother." She let out an exasperated sigh.

"Hm," Cecily grunted. "Do you think there's anything to that gesture?"

"No. Mom, stop. It doesn't matt—"

"I'm just saying . . ." Annemarie could *see* her mom throwing her hands up into the air, claiming *mea culpa* at a simple question.

"*Anyway*, I didn't have the time this morning, so I'm doing it now. I'm not gonna be able to get it to you tonight, but I'll get up early and take it down to the community center."

"Is Alistair coming over tonight?"

"*No, mom.* He's not coming over tonight." She pushed her bangs off her forehead with the same bent wrist, feeling a tickle of sweat beading at her hairline from the barrage of intrusive questions from her mother. "He offered to follow me home and when we got here—" Red flushed her cheeks as Cecily made puckered-lip kissy noises through the phone. "Knock it off." Cecily stopped, but Annemarie heard her giggling. She rolled her eyes. "I'm gonna let you go. I'll talk to you tomorrow. Good night." She did not wait for a response.

Using the heel of her hand, she carefully balanced the phone flat to pull away from her face, and set it on a clean space of the counter beside her. She used the tip of her pinky to end the call. She shook her head and chuckled incredulously before turning her attention to the empty pie plate waiting for the dough she rolled out prior to the interruption. With deft movement, she folded the crust in thirds in order to transport it to its new home. She gently peeled it open with both hands, using the pads of her fingers to softly squish the dough into the curve of the plate. She cut off all but an inch of overhang, using the excess to fold underneath to build a bulky lip. Creating a V-shape with her left thumb and index finger, she followed the outer edge while poking her right index finger into the crease the other digits made, fluting the raw dough.

As she finished the last crimp, a shuffling of feet and a pathetic soft whimper sounded behind her by the back door. She glanced over her shoulder to see Moose staring at her, eyes wide and puppy-like, the tip of his full, fluffy tail wagging ever-so-slightly at her acknowledgment.

"What's up, pup? Need to go outside?"

His tail wagged eagerly.

"Can you wait?" she asked.

He whimpered.

"Fine, fine." She wiped a hand on her jeans, leaving flour trails down one leg. The space from the counter to the door was only a few feet, but Moose's insistence to be let out, to relieve himself this instant, made it seem like she was traveling a quarter of a mile at a snail's pace. He wargled and *aroo*d emphatically, urging her to hurry. She twisted the knob and cracked the door just enough to be met with a suction of strong breeze. "You sure you want to go out there, bud? You might blow away."

Moose anxiously tap-danced from his left paws to his right. He shoved his nose between the door and jamb, trying to push his way past her. She did not expect such force to come from her usually docile and obedient dog, so he managed to squeeze through and escape into the backyard. With the door now wide open, she realized it wasn't only windy, but raining in solid sheets.

"Make it quick, Moose!" she called after him, knowing full well he would not—could not—hear her over the din of the storm. She did not relish the fact that even a fifteen-second jaunt in this weather would leave him dripping wet, and it had already been a minute.

She left the door open so he could let himself in when he finished; he knew how to find his way home. She needed to get back to making the pie. It was already past ten and it required about an hour to bake. She poured the bowl of diced peaches soaked in rum and vanilla beans into the uncooked crust. She set the dirty bowl aside and reached for the container of cinnamon crumble she made first. The oven beeped at her, stating it was properly preheated. When she finished evenly distributing the rounded chunks of flour, butter, and cinnamon, she dusted off her hands once more and slid the pie into the oven. She set the timer for thirty minutes.

With the dirty bowls in the sink to soak, the next task requiring her immediate attention was drying a dripping wet sixty-pound ball of fluff before he tracked dog smell and mud throughout the house. She glanced around to see where Moose had settled in once returning from his bathroom break. He was nowhere to be found.

"Moose!" she called. No response. She poked her head outside to see if he was waiting nearby, but he was missing. "Moo-oose!" Her voice rang louder, trying to overpower the rain and the wind. "Dammit, dog." She pulled herself back inside in order to grab her jacket tucked behind the open door. It, too, was gone. "Where the hell . . . oh, *whatever.*" She swiped up the LED flashlight that was thankfully still hanging beside where her jacket should have been. Next to the door sat her green rain boots. She stomped outside into the storm and instantly soaked to the bone. She could feel the water already pooling at her toes. She wrapped her arms around herself as she ran across the expanse of the yard, the motion sensor light of the back porch barely illuminating her path, yelling for a dog who could not hear her.

A roll of thunder overhead echoed through the canopy of trees surrounding the house, and within a minute, an exciting explosion of lightning across the pitch-black sky made her skin crawl, followed shortly thereafter by another peal of thunder. When the rumble settled, she heard a distant echo, a familiar noise. A bark. *Moose.* She clicked on the flashlight and tried to find any discernible shapes among the towering lodgepoles, red cedars, and hemlocks.

"Come on, boy!" She let out a high-pitched whistle, his recall signal, and waited impatiently as the rain pelted every inch of her. Another bark came, no closer than before. She trudged to the tree line bordering the backyard, not really wanting to enter the woods, but knowing she had no choice if he did not appear soon. "Moose!" She was screeching at this point, her voice cracking as it strained to gain ardor.

The barking picked up steam, becoming more frequent, more panicked, or maybe more agitated. She entered the woods, alternating the beam of light from the ground to directly ahead of her, making sure she was not about to trip over unearthed roots, thorny bushes, or get a face full of spiderweb. Out of the corner of her eye, she spotted a shape speeding across her field of vision, an already dark blur bobbing over and under other dark blurs. She fumbled with the flashlight to shine it on the moving target and barely caught the tip of Moose's tail skirting around the backside of a girthy cedar. He disappeared completely, quickly, but his barking helped her home in on his tracks.

She called his name once more, hopeful that he could hear her and would obey her now that they were within range of each other. She was not able to pinpoint the source of the barking, echoing and bouncing from tree to tree, disorienting her further. But his noises remained a constant as he raced through the woods, oscillating between barks and growls. Her feet dragged her deeper into the foliage thicket, scanning the horizon for any sign of life. Despite earlier in the day being warm, the wind and the rain forced a whole-body shiver. A twinge of bitter cold came with every gust. Being tucked under the canopy of trees was a double-edged sword: The interwoven branches up above kept much of the falling rain off her, however, occasional intense downpours toppled onto her and the forest floor when the excess water became too heavy to hold and broke branches.

With every step firmly planting her in the muddy ground, the contents of her rain boots sloshed. Picking up her feet as she moved was more difficult than before, as the weight of the water-filled shoes bogged her down. She bent over with the intention of emptying them, but before she could grab onto the heel of either boot, she heard heavy, rapid footsteps echoing around her. These were not like Moose's light, plentiful, purposeful trods.

Not sure from which direction they came, Annemarie focused the flashlight beam in front of her and slowly panned to her left, attempting to make a full circle. The footsteps grew louder. A deep, bellowing roar surrounded her. She assumed the thunder was making another appearance; it did sound different in an echo chamber than in a wide, open space. The roll of noise did not dissipate. Before she could complete her three-hundred-sixty-degree circle, something crashed into her so hard and so perfectly. The flashlight skittered from her hand to come to rest under a nearby bush and she involuntarily lunged forward, sliding across the muddy forest floor on her shoulder. She traveled a good ten feet before coming to a halt in a crumpled pile. Her bones aching from both the cold and the impact, she managed to roll onto her back in time to see a centralized flash of light shimmer not far from where she lay. This was not lightning, or maybe it was lightning incarnate.

The footsteps continued, picking up speed. Ringing in her ears kept her from hearing the huffs of breath and the guttural roar headed for her, but she could feel the vibration of the feet slapping on the ground. The flashlight was pointed away from her, aimed at a forty-five-degree angle, illuminating an overgrown trail leading to the north. A pair of legs crossed paths with the light, causing the beam to flicker momentarily. Annemarie opened her mouth to yell, to scream, but it caught in her throat as a loud bark to her left shocked her. Still unable to make out much more than rough shapes, she caught sight of what was coming at her in a fervor, a flash of silver jutting across its face, and watched it tumble to the ground.

Moose flew through the air to tackle the aggressor, trying to take it down in order to save Annemarie. The sound of him growling with a mouthful accompanied the same surging roar she heard before. Unsure what to do, she pushed herself up onto her knees and tried to stand. The wind had been knocked out of her in the collision. Her ribs felt broken, though she knew they were not. She had had broken ribs before, and while she ached, this was not that. Moose's growling subsided, turning now into vicious barking. Other unidentifiable sounds met the dog's warnings. She could not see either of them.

Moose's barks grew fainter, as if he were leading the threat away, giving her a head start, to allow her to escape. She considered this action for a moment: Was this his intention or was she trying to convince herself this was what was happening to justify leaving him behind?

She took a step backward, followed by another, inching farther away from the dark scene unfolding somewhere in front of her. Whatever had been after her was now engaged in battle with Moose, the dog goading it into chasing him through the dark woods. Annemarie abandoned the flashlight without a second thought, but kept her eyes focused on it as a means to judge distance, to orient herself as she backed out of the clearing. Before long, the rumble of the thunderstorm infiltrated her ears louder than Moose's barking. His chatter repeated, albeit softly. She took several steps forward in order to keep track of him.

With one deep breath, she let out a scream like no other, loosing his name into the blast of the wind, rain, and thunder. This seemed to disrupt the brawl, but it also seemed to give the villain the upper hand.

A pained, heart-wrenching yelp echoed in the trees. A sound Annemarie had never heard Moose make before filled her ears. A repeat of the roar came to her next. There was no mistaking this for thunder. For a brief moment, the wind dissipated and the rain slowed, providing a soft pitter-patter ambience. It was during this break in the weather that her ears were finally capable of tuning in to anything happening with her dog. It was during this break in the weather that she heard it loud and clear: another bark, another yelp, and the sick sound of something snapping. There was no movement. No footsteps. Nothing but the wind picking up, whistling through the trees, tussling her wet, disheveled hair, and the frequency of the rain slamming into the ground.

"Moose?" she called. "Bud?"

Everything in her wanted to force her forward, to force her to retrieve the flashlight and search for Moose, for the attacker, for any semblance of closure as to what happened. A high-pitched chirping distracted her from her thoughts. She whipped around to look over her shoulder, unsure where the noise originated from. *The oven,* she thought.

She sprinted for the house, her boots still sloshing with every heavy step. She barreled through the shut back door—remembering she specifically left it open in case Moose returned during her search—but did not question it as she stumbled shoulder-first into the kitchen full of thick smoke. She pulled the bottom hem of her sticky, wet T-shirt up to her nose and mouth, allowing her to shield her lungs as she navigated the short distance to the oven. This move revealed a gigantic, angry red welt on her stomach, but she felt minimal pain under the influence of adrenaline.

With a free hand, she reached for a towel to swat the billowing smoke away from the digital screen of the stovetop. The temperature of the oven read broil. Her shaking fingers pushed the off button. The cry of the smoke detector wailed on, hurting her ears as the sound banged around the small kitchen.

While she busied herself in locating oven mitts she had left in random places along the counter, hoping to open the oven, remove the smoldering pie, and toss it out into the rain, she missed the soundless sight of a pair of grey feet seamlessly gliding from the living room into the kitchen, barely noticeable in the mayhem, save for the bottom few inches devoid of smoke. The owner exited out the back, bumping the door hard enough to make it creak and rock back and forth on its hinge. Annemarie heard this, but was so focused on the precarious task of discarding the molten mess with one hand, she could not be bothered to investigate. It was the wind, obviously.

With the skill of a professional shot-putter, the pie flew out the back door, landing into a mud puddle with a loud *splat*. Requiring both hands to escort the smoke outside, she dropped the edge of her shirt, held her breath, and began the arm-numbing task of clearing the kitchen. It took several minutes of her constantly fanning the smoke with a small hand towel—all she had available to her then—pushing it outside, before she could see much of anything.

Something on the vinyl floor caught her attention. At first glance, she assumed the puddle was any of the copious amounts of water her clothes held onto; it would have been absolutely feasible considering she was dripping with every step she took. But the medium-brown floor revealed, upon closer inspection, that this particular puddle was blood. Aghast, she checked over her body. She scanned her hands, front and back. She wiped her palms across her face with no results. Her fingertips rubbed along her forearms, the scab, both elbows. She lifted the hem of her heavy shirt once more, looking at her irritated stomach, twisting at her waist trying to spy anything amiss on her back. Absentmindedly, she pulled off her boots, sloshing a large volume of water onto the floor. She searched the soles of the shoes. Nothing. Nothing indicated the blood was hers.

I need to call Alist— She interrupted her train of thought when she saw the muddy footprints. Two, four, six, eight leading into the living room. She reached for her phone, still sitting on the counter where she had left it, and a large chef's knife she had used during the pie prep. She fumbled briefly as she switched around the items, being right-handed, and needing all the strength she could muster to defend herself if necessary. She shuffled across the floor, careful not to touch the blood or the muddy footprints. Smoke still lingered in the upper corners of both rooms. The alarms were silenced with her great effort, but the ringing in her ears had not dissipated.

Cautiously, she poked the top of her head around the doorjamb of the kitchen, peeking into the living area. She gasped and dropped both the phone and the knife. The living room was trashed from top to bottom. The curtains were torn, shredded vertically by something sharp. The couch was on its back and the cushions tossed around the room, covered in what looked like bloody handprints. All of her magazines, bills, receipts, and paperwork she kept in tidy piles littered the space like the aftermath of a ticker-tape parade. Her wall-mounted television had been forcefully ripped from the metal bracket. The coffee table given to her by her grandmother was covered in long, deep scratches and more bloody streaks.

She dropped to her knees, partly in shock and partly to retrieve her cell phone. She tapped the glass face to wake it up, swiped away the screensaver of her and Jesse, and opened up the telephone app to find Alistair's number.

Tears streamed down her face as she pressed the call symbol. She meant to dial the sheriff's line, but instead, got his personal cell. Either way, it was a direct line to him.

FIFTEEN

Stretched out in bed, finally dozing off after a restless day in the office, the ringing of a cell phone brought Alistair back to consciousness. He reached for the vibrating, lit-up device on the bedside table. With squinted eyes and blurred vision, he read the screen. He slid his finger across the phone's face a couple of times until an accurate attempt answered the call.

"Hey, Annie. What's up?" he lazily asked through a yawn.

Any remainder of him being asleep shook free when her response was a high-pitched keening followed by a bluster of words. He did not understand anything coming out of her mouth, but the tone was enough to tell him he needed to be wherever she was *now*. He shot up out of bed, tangling himself in the comforter and almost landing on the floor face-first.

"Annie, hun, what's going on? Where are you?" He switched on speakerphone and set it on the dresser as he wobbled around his bedroom trying to find his pants in the dark. Whatever she said was incoherent. He hoped it was a bad connection more than anything else, but deep down, he knew it was not the case. "Sweetheart, calm down for a beat. Breathe. Are you at home?"

While he waited for an answer, he found a pair of jeans crumpled at the top of the dirty laundry basket. He pulled them on over his boxer briefs. He heard her breathing slow momentarily, followed by a deep breath in through her nose and out her mouth. "Yes. I'm home. Pl-please come. I n-need y-you." She hung up. He hoped it was her own choosing to do so.

He grabbed the phone off the dresser and shoved it in his pocket as he raced into the living room, his bare feet slapping loudly on the hardwood. He turned on the lamp by the couch, letting the light illuminate a small section surrounding it, just enough to see what he was doing. A short-sleeved flannel shirt waited for him, draped over the back of the couch. He dove into it and did not bother buttoning it up over his bare chest. His street shoes by the door were drying after the deluge they endured from his evening run in the unexpected storm. He slid his feet into them with a *squelch* and a dissatisfied, involuntary groan escaped his lips. In the small linen closet off to the side of the room, a digital safe held onto his gun. He anxiously punched in the code, waited for the accepting beep, ripped the weapon free. He checked to make sure it was loaded, grabbed his holster from atop the steel box, and joined the two together as he crossed the living room to leave. He grabbed his keys and wallet and was out the door.

Being sheriff, his work vehicle came home with him, making emergency calls like Annemarie's much easier to access since he already had the light bar raring to go as he peeled out of the driveway and sped along Wildwood Highway. At this time of night, few people were on the road. Those who were around pulled off onto the shoulder to allow him the right-of-way. Even at top speed, it still took him fifteen minutes to reach Annemarie's house. The cruiser pulled into the driveway and barely had time to consider being in park before he ripped the keys out of the ignition, kicked open the driver's side, and barreled out into the night. He pounded his fist on the front door.

"Annie, it's me. Open up," he called at her, his mouth practically shoved into the wood panel. He waited a moment before banging again. "Annie, come on." There was no answer. He fished his keys out of his pocket, found her spare, and let himself in. What he walked into shocked him. Fear clenched his stomach and his throat. He removed the Glock from the holster on his belt and aimed the barrel as he slowly tiptoed through the disaster of a living room looming ahead of him. The furniture was ripped to pieces. Her flat-screen TV was lying on the floor, the center of it shattered. The entire room reeked of smoke. It looked like something had exploded. "Annemarie, where are you?"

He heard a clatter come from her bedroom. He made his way across the debris field, stopping only to poke a head into her sleeping quarters to make sure no one was lying in wait. With the coast clear, he heard another noise, this time echoing inside the bathroom. The door was shut and the light was on, leading him to believe Annemarie was in there. *But is she alone?* he asked himself.

"Annie, I'm here. Are you hurt?" His strong, authoritative voice filled the room.

"In here," she croaked out. "I'm not hurt."

He lowered the gun. He set it on the edge of the bed, knowing bursting into the bathroom with it pointed at her was not going to help anything. He turned the knob and opened the door to reveal Annemarie sitting on the edge of the tub in her dripping wet underwear, tears running down her bright-red face, chest heaving, and digging her fingernails into her thighs so violently, the whitened skin was starting to tear.

Alistair rushed in and slid to a stop on his knees in front of her. "What the fuck happened?" he asked, almost in a whisper.

She leaned forward into him, hoping he would catch her as she continued to cry. He wrapped his arms around her to bring her close. Her skin was damp and cold. Her teeth chattered. She buried her face in his neck and let out a long, low guttural wail. The chill coming from her body made him shiver. Waves of flashbacks from the night of Jesse's death overwhelmed him. He stroked her sodden hair. Still on his knees, he tried his best to reach for the towel hanging on the wall across the room from them. With his fingertips furiously grasping for the edge of the material, he succeeded, and brought it to drape over her shoulders and down her back.

He said nothing for a long time. He allowed her to cry, to dig her nails into his arm, to squeeze, to sob, to wet his bare chest with her tears. He rubbed the palm of his hand up and down over her upper back, trying to generate warmth into her through the friction against the fluffy towel. He waited to say anything until all of her pain and anguish drained out. When she was empty, she pulled away from him a few inches. She grabbed the corners of the towel, tightening it around her as the chill of the evening seemed to finally settle into her bones.

"What happened?"

She opened her mouth to speak, but a strained squeak was all that sounded.

"Come on. Let's get you into some warm clothes and grab something to drink. You're parched." She nodded. He stood first, steadying himself on the edge of the tub. Pins and needles rushed to his calves and feet. He ignored the sensation as best he could. He held out a hand for her, waiting for the connection, and helped her up. She let the towel fall to the floor. He led her into the bedroom where he turned on the light. He retrieved his gun from off the comforter, holstered it, and set her down on the bed. He ransacked her dresser for a pair of warm, fuzzy sweatpants and a thermal shirt from out of the closet. He handed the items to her, which she took without arguing. "Get into these and I'll grab you a glass of water." She nodded once more, still not saying a word.

He left her in the bedroom to get dressed. He surveyed the living room and the state it was in. Bloody handprints marked the couch, the coffee table, and muddy footprints entered but did not leave. His brows knitted; his mouth turned downward. As he walked from the living room into the kitchen, he saw a puddle of blood. It was then he noticed Moose was nowhere to be found.

"Probably at Cecily and Ken's," he muttered. He spied a messy counter covered in flour, fruit skin, and a half-empty bottle of rum. He moved toward the cabinet that housed the drinking cups and slid a little as he did so. The floor was completely covered in water, like a pipe had burst. He grabbed a cup, filled it from the faucet, and returned to Annemarie in the bedroom. She was still sitting upright, rigid at the foot of the bed, but she was at least in warm clothes, defrosting. Alistair handed her the glass of water. She took a deep drink from it, demolishing almost the whole thing in one gulp.

"Thank you," she said softly, her voice still raw.

He sat beside her. "You have to tell me what happened."

Begrudgingly, she launched into the story of her evening. How Moose got out the back door and did not return; how even though she set the oven for three hundred seventy-five degrees, she returned to it on broil and the house filled with smoke; how she believed there was something out in the woods trying to kill her. She showed him her bruising midsection in case he had not noticed in the bathroom. Alistair listened intently. He was there for her as a friend, holding her hand, stroking her arm in comfort, giving her gentle kisses on her forehead when the tears started and stopped intermittently. His desire to get dusting for fingerprints and pulling DNA samples for testing was starting to override.

"Tell you what," he segued. "Take a nap. Get some rest and I'll work on cleaning up the house." She opened her mouth to protest, but he silenced her by holding up a finger to his own lips. "I'll have none of that. You're in no shape to deal with any more of this bullshit right now." He stood, pulling her up beside him so he could lead her to her pillow. He threw back the covers to reveal the soft, inviting sheets. He was exhausted; he could only imagine how far past exhaustion *she* was. She hesitantly climbed into bed. She allowed him to tuck her in. He petted her hair, kissed her forehead one last time, and made to leave the room.

With his finger on the light switch, she called after him. "Please leave it on."

Annemarie woke with a start, bolting upright in bed, her heart beating out of her chest, sweat soaking her back. The alarm clock read 2:47. The light in the room was on. She tossed off the blankets while she waited a moment, listening for any signs of life in the other rooms of the house. Gentle shuffling resonated from somewhere. She exited into the living room. The couch had been set right side up; the broken television was in the same place but the damaged pieces were picked up; the bits of paper tossed about the room were in several tidier piles on the coffee table. The muddy footprints remained, as did the bloody handprints. They could not be scrubbed from the fabric, yet, much like the visions could not be scrubbed from her mind.

"Alistair?" she called, her voice a touch shaky.

His head poked into the room from the kitchen, a slight smile on his face, trying to disguise the utter exhaustion he was feeling. "Hey, sleepyhead. How you doing?"

"I . . . I've been better," she admitted.

He set the broom against the doorjamb and moved across the room to be with her. "Yeah, sorry. That was a stupid question." He paused. "Did you at least get some sleep?"

She nodded. "Did Moose come home?"

"No, he didn't. I've had the door open all night in the hopes he'd make his way back." The look on Alistair's face spoke the truth that he did not expect Moose to ever return.

"I don't think he's going to either. I think he sacrificed himself for me." She scanned the entirety of the room, not sure where she could sit. Everything was part of a crime scene. She ended up sitting on the floor.

Alistair scrunched his face. "Why do you think that? That he sacrificed himself."

"He knew I was in trouble. He knew that whatever took me down was out to get me and if he didn't intervene, I wouldn't be here." Annemarie focused her eyes on the pilling fabric of her sweatpants. She picked at each of the little balls of cotton, mindlessly creating a pile in front of her.

"What *did* take you down?"

"I don't know. I never really saw it. It came out of nowhere and knocked the flashlight out of my hand. I never saw its face. But there . . . there was this flash of light. This . . . *shimmer*. I don't know how to explain it. It was eerie. It was like Now—" She stopped herself. With a heavy sigh, she started over. "When I was with Nowell, I—"

He raised a hand to cut her off. "I don't need to know the details."

She shook her head. "It's not what you think. We had dinner together. So he could tell me about what happened the night of the accident. He and Travis didn't swerve to miss hitting a deer. They were being chased and then were attacked by something with flashing eyes." She did not even have to look at his face to know his own eyes were flashing in disgust. "Yeah, I know, I don't need to hear it."

She continued to explain to him all the details of Nowell's recounted tale and how she came to believe him.

When she finished the story, he stood in front of her, mouth agape, an expression of disbelief mixed with shock. "I don't know what to say," he finally replied. "I'm furious they lied, under oath no less. *But* ... I kinda believe him."

"You do?" The lilt in her voice sounded hopeful, like maybe he would not be angry at her forever.

"I do. And only because I've seen something similar myself. On our way home after the event last night. I don't know what's happening, what this thing is, or what it wants, but I see a pattern emerging and I don't like where it's headed."

SIXTEEN

Wrapped in a black fleece blanket, stationed on the front porch, Annemarie breathed deep the crisp, early morning air. The sun broke the horizon mere minutes earlier as she exited the confines of the warm home and greeted her as she sleepily yawned herself awake. Having rolled out of bed not so long ago, her hair mussed in the way only a night of fitful tossing and turning could create, she managed to put on enough clothes to make herself presentable to the onslaught about to pull up.

Several cars dipped down onto the driveway from the main road, headlights still on from the residual darkness created by the surrounding copse of towering trees. One by one, men and women spilled out from the vehicles: Rita and Jackson Galt from one, along with their teenaged son, Jack Jr.; the Treadwell and the Holland men from an SUV; and Annemarie's parents from Cecily's crossover. Trailing not far behind this crew came Alistair and Riggs in their patrol vehicles. Only a few more minutes behind them appeared a train of a dozen neighbors—husbands, wives, and nearly adult children—walking along the road from where they parked their cars. Most everyone dressed in hiking boots and ratty, stained clothing, and came equipped with flashlights and water canteens, ready for what may come.

Annemarie stood from her perch to solemnly greet the group as they congregated around her. Alistair approached to offer a hug, but Cecily swooped in even quicker to cover that base. She pushed a chunk of tangled hair from Annemarie's face, allowing her to place a loving peck on her forehead. "We're here for you, sweetheart." With her arms draped across Annemarie's shoulders, pulling her in for a deep, long hug, she smiled weakly at Alistair. "What's the plan then, Sheriff?"

Alistair cleared his throat, garnering the attention from the crowd. "Moose McCready was last seen here and last heard from about one hundred and fifty yards from Annemarie's back door out in the woods. We have no idea what sort of situation we're dealing with here, beyond a search to find a red merle Australian shepherd. We'll start out back and slowly comb our way north toward the beach. Deputy Riggs will get us going. I appreciate everyone answering their cell phones so early in the morning and coming out on such short notice. I know all of us have jobs to get to, so I thank you for putting your life on hold for a minute to get this underway. Let's get to it."

As everyone shuffled about for a moment longer, Annemarie waved an arm over her head, hoping to pull their attentions to her without having to raise her voice, further irritating an already raw throat. "One more thing. If at any point you don't feel comfortable out there, or need to get on with your day, don't feel obligated to stay with the group. I'm blown away by the sheer number of you who've shown up for something as frivolous as helping me find my dog. But please leave when you need to. If nothing comes of this search, I can manage to go it alone." She could not be sure if she meant to say she could search for Moose on her own or if she could come to terms with him being one more thing prematurely and unexpectedly ripped away.

Cecily gave her another sturdy squeeze before leaving the porch to spend a minute chatting with Rita Galt. The loose plan was for everyone to venture into the woods, with Cecily and Diana Park volunteering to hang back with Annemarie, in case she needed anything or in the event Moose returned on his own. Comfort and solidarity in numbers. As the rest of the crew figured out a tighter game plan, Diana, a lithe, olive-complexioned brunette who lived six houses down, approached Annemarie and pulled her aside, though no one else existed in their immediate vicinity or within earshot.

"How ya doing, hun?" Diana asked, reaching out an arm to comfort her.

With a tight-lipped grimace, Annemarie responded, "Not great."

"Is there anything I can get you?"

She let out a strained sigh. "No, I don't think I need anything right now."

"Would you mind terribly if I went with the others to search? I volunteered to stay back thinking your mom was gonna go out with everyone too. I know Moose means a lot to her. But now that she's staying . . ." Diana shrugged slightly.

Annemarie and Diana were never the closest of friends, but Annemarie knew she was not the sit-and-wait type, much like herself—so it surprised her when she volunteered to stay behind. "No, not at all. I appreciate you being here in any capacity in the first place. If you think you're of better use out there with them, go for it. I'd be out there myself if I thought anyone would actually let me leave the house." She rolled her eyes and let out a half-hearted chuckle. Diana took her expression to mean it was appropriate to laugh too.

"I've got my cell phone on me and Ji also has his. Don't hesitate to call one of us if you need something. And I don't mean right now either. Whenever. I don't have much to offer in a situation like yours, but I've got two ears and two shoulders." Her smile warmed Annemarie.

Annemarie gave a quick nod and Diana used the silence as her cue to scramble after the others who were already en route to the backyard. Annemarie watched as Diana caught up to Alistair at the tail end of the party, informed him of the change, then fast-walked ahead to join the line beside her lumberjackesque husband, Ji. They simultaneously fist-bumped followed by a mimicked explosion, which made Annemarie smile.

"Honey, do you wanna go inside?" Cecily called up the stairs to her.

Annemarie shook her head. "No, I'd rather sit out back and wait for a little while."

The group of twenty-some family, friends, and neighbors who made up the search party created a line with ten feet in between each, giving them a decently large swath of ground to cover. The forest of dew-laden ferns, tall lodgepole pines and larches, and various berry-bearing bushes spanned for dozens of acres behind and around

Annemarie's property, which made for great privacy, but was less than desirable for the volunteers to cover every square inch in a short amount of time. Many voices called out for Moose. The only sound answering included wild rabbits dashing through the underbrush, startled deer providing a wide berth, and birds chirping high up in the canopy of tree crowns. They continued for a solid hour, combing east and west, before several of the members needed to break off and head south to catch the ferry to Brownstone to start their days. One by one, the group broke up as time passed. There was nothing to be found. Not a shred of fur, no blood, no signs of struggle. Even the mud only seemed to reflect the footprints from the humans marching to and fro. The heavy rain washed away every inch of evidence that may have provided adequate clues.

All that remained of the party was Riggs, Walt Needleham, and Alistair, and that dwindled to one when the station radioed Riggs to come down for assistance in the office.

"Hey, Riggs. Would'ya mind giving me a ride to my shop on your way in?" Walt asked.

"Sure thing," he replied. He clicked on his radio to call Alistair, who was a quarter mile away by this point. "Hey Al, I've got to head in. Cami needs help with . . . I don't even know what." He adjusted the earpiece on his left side waiting for Alistair to respond.

His voice came through. "No problem. Does she need me too or do you have it covered?"

"She didn't mention you. She said Liu's out on patrol and Derrick missed his ferry, so I'm assuming she needs an office grunt to help move banker boxes or something." Riggs rolled his eyes. "I'm taking Walt with me, so it's just you now, buddy. I'll see you at the station later on. Over and out."

"Drive safe. Over and out," Alistair called back. He spun in place from his position further north and waved at his deputy, who returned the gesture. Riggs hiked a thumb over his shoulder to signal their departure to Walt.

Instead of taking the extra time to backtrack the quarter mile to the path that freely led to the beach, Alistair forced his way through the last hundred feet of damp ferns that currently blocked him from arriving at his destination. With little regard for his uniform, he forged forward, careful to not trip on any protrusions in the form of roots, smaller plants, or rocks, but with a quickened pace. His eyes focused on the natural cave eroded out of the rock on the eastern edge of the beach ahead of him. "This has gotta be it," he muttered. His foot snagged on some unidentified object as he neared the end of his impromptu trail. Stumbling onto the sand now beneath him, he took a minute to catch his breath and compose himself. Everything from the tips of his leather boots to his belt were wet, and now covered in large patches of sand from the tumble. He stood and casually brushed at his dirty pants but kept the cave in his sight.

There was no movement. With his hand on top of the unlatched holster at his hip, he briskly moved toward the entrance, unsure of what he was about to find. The closer he got to the cave, the higher his anxiety rose. *Will Moose have suffered a similar fate as Peter Arthur?* He stopped short, shuffled to the right of the opening, and grabbed a loose golf-ball-sized rock. He stepped back, chucked the rock at an inner wall of the cave, waited; he hoped that if someone was in there, it would catch their attention. When his action did not elicit a response, he cleared his throat.

"This is Sheriff Lucas of the Azure County Sheriff's Department. C-come out with your hands up," he called loudly, his voice unexpectedly shaky. After pausing for a solid minute, there came no reaction. "Okay, then," he retorted to himself with a nod. He knew what needed to be done. Being a part of law enforcement was a dream he had from as young as five or six years of age, thanks to his sheriff father; but despite his love of the job, what he was about to do was what he hated the most. Fortunately, it was rare to blindly enter an establishment, gun raised, ready to fight in a place like Port Harrow, but after discovering Peter Arthur's shredded corpse in this exact spot less than a week ago, his nerves were no longer steady and his movements were less than confident.

He closed the gap between him and the cave, holding his breath as he moved. The narrow entrance opened into a larger tunneled-out cavern with a slight twist to the left to a secondary, smaller room. Poking his head in for a peek was not going to cut it. As he lifted his foot to step inside, he noticed a quarter-sized splotch of blood on the sandy rock floor. He first peered in to make sure nothing lay in wait, then knelt to examine the stain. Unlike the night before when he had easy access to his patrol vehicle and the evidence supplies in the trunk, all Alistair possessed on his person included his wallet, cell phone, keys, the Glock, and two rounds of ammunition clipped on his belt; none of which proved to be useful in this exact situation. Steadying himself back onto his feet, he continued the journey inside the hovel, noticing more patches of red along the walls. Some of it seemed fresh while other brushstrokes faded with age.

Steeling himself for come what may, he tensed his muscles, clenched his jaw, held his breath, and took one final step into the antechamber. Everything in him loosened and his shoulders sagged as his eyes fell upon the white, red, and silver body stretched out in front of him. It was obvious Moose's neck had been broken, but otherwise, he looked intact.

"Oh, *Moose*." Alistair squeaked out a small sob as he crouched beside the lifeless body. He reached out a shaking hand to the dog's fur and stroked the tip of his snout, over his head, and down the length of his spine. He knew it was all for naught; the light that was Moose was permanently extinguished. "I'm sorry no one was here with you, buddy." He continued to pet him with long, loving caresses. A couple tears formed in the corners of his eyes and trickled their way down his cheeks, to his chin, where they eventually fell into Moose's fur.

Still hovering low, Alistair brought his fingers to his uniform shirt to remove it. He fumbled with each of the buttons, shaking from his discovery. He slid out of the cotton shirt and used it to cover as much of Moose as it could. He gently tucked it underneath, wrapped his arms around the stiff body, and stood in one swift movement, making sure to keep Moose close to his chest and cradled comfortably for the long hike home. In the past, he would haul up all sixty pounds of Annemarie's beast into his arms and let Moose's big fluffy paws drape over his shoulders, much like a parent cuddled up with a toddler. Those same sixty pounds were like a cannonball encased in concrete now. And so did the lump in his chest.

The hike to Annemarie's property proved difficult, more emotionally than physically. Alistair loved Moose like his own and knew Annemarie relied on him for true companionship and unconditional love, especially since Jesse's death. The entire length of the journey home, Alistair rehearsed what he would—*could*—say to her.

"Sorry, hun, Moose didn't make it."

"It doesn't look like he suffered."

"No clue how it happened."

"He was a good boy."

"We all loved him."

"Rest in peace."

"Fuck."

Nothing was going to be good enough, especially right out the gate. Thoughts swirled around in his head as he drew closer to the house, spying the opening leading to her yard a few hundred meters away. He saw two people sitting on the deck stairs. Annemarie remained wrapped in her blanket despite the temperature of the day rising significantly from when the search started a couple hours before and Cecily perched beside her, robed in her signature wash of grey. He did not want to call out to either of them. He did not want to divulge the truth to Annemarie at all, if he were being honest. This was the worst possible outcome and he drew the short straw to be the bearer of bad news by informing her of her deceased best friend. Again.

Annemarie listened to Cecily list off the variety of vegetables currently growing in her garden, not actually caring but finding the droning of her voice comforting enough to distract her. She let out a slight yawn, rubbed her eyes with the back of her hand, and blinked several times to readjust to the day's light. Once she finally regained her sight, through the tiredness, she spotted a figure moving off in the distance between the trees.

She reached out her hand to grab Cecily's leg to interrupt. "Mom . . ." She pointed. They immediately stood, Annemarie tightening the blanket around her shoulders. She watched the blurry figure sharpen as it steadily came closer. It was Alistair, in his white A-shirt, with his arms full of a shapeless *something*.

She bolted across the yard before Cecily could even attempt to restrain her or offer words of encouragement or condolences. The fleece blanket fluttered behind her like a cape. She reached Alistair easily, even though her knees wanted to buckle and she had not breathed for what seemed like minutes. As she ran, closing the gap, she watched Alistair exit the woods, kneel in the grassy clearing, and set the shapeless lump on the ground. She recognized that his uniform shirt covered whatever he was carrying, and her heart dropped instantly.

"Annie, I—" Alistair stopped as he realized she did not even see him. Her eyes were clearly focused on his work shirt and what was underneath it. He stood and took a step back to let her have adequate space. Cecily joined him a moment later, making sure to grab his hand tightly, making sure *he* was okay.

Annemarie gently removed the now-dirty shirt to reveal the lifeless body. Cecily immediately turned her head and nestled it into the crook of Alistair's neck, closing her eyes as hard as she could. He raised a hand to cup the back of her head, to bring her closer. Annemarie said nothing. Instead, she spent a solid minute scruffing behind his ears, running her fingers through the length of his chest fur, scratching that very best spot where his tail joined his rump. She muttered soft, incoherent words at him. It took a few minutes, but the tears finally overflowed. She glanced up at Alistair through her lashes, opened her mouth to speak, but only wisps of words came out.

She cleared her throat. "W-where did you find him?" Her voice was raspy, as if she had not spoken a single word in years, as if she did not know she had a voice. It reminded her of the accident that killed Jesse, the accident that left her wounded on the side of the road, leading to months of grueling recovery . . . with Moose at her side. But now, Moose was no more.

Alistair hesitated. He scratched at the back of his head, then shoved his hands deep into the pockets of his dirty, wet slacks. "T-the sea cave. Where I found Peter."

Annemarie slow-blinked at him, processing the words. "Was there any—"

Cecily interrupted her before she could ask anything else, not even sure what was about to come out. "Honey, let's get you inside. It's about time you ate something. Alistair can set Moose in the garden until you decide what you want to do with him." She extended her hand to Annemarie who stared blankly at it. Cecily crooked a finger to get her to stand and join her, trying not to give her many options to react or speak—the ol' "Mother Knows Best" routine she often enacted. Reluctantly, Annemarie agreed, took Cecily's hand, and followed her to the house. Alistair did as was suggested and relocated Moose's body to a shaded section of the garden off to the left. The sun would not engulf the area until much later in the afternoon, so Annemarie had time to decide whether she wanted him buried or cremated. Alistair lingered a moment, watching the lifeless dog, as if waiting for him to jump up, give a bark, and play bow. He knew that would never happen again, but he could hope.

SEVENTEEN

In the week following Moose's death, Alistair was called away to Derry to continue cross-training new recruits for the department as well as filling in for an on-vacation Sheriff Bachhuber. Derry, with its considerably larger population, always demanded more of him and the other officers than Port Harrow ever did. On the rare occasion this type of arrangement was made, about once a year, he did not bother ferrying home until the job was done. Instead, the department put him up in a hotel and he tried to pretend it was a mini vacation. A vacation filled with work, work, and more work. He had little time for anything else. In the past, it did not matter that all he did was work, sleep, and shovel down salt-laden microwave meals in between. Now, with Annemarie in distress with the loss of Moose and a pattern of potentially related homicides unfurling, he could not find enough free time to handle everything.

Texts and phone calls throughout the day to a grieving Annemarie yielded zero results. He had better luck retrieving information about her situation from a text message group chat with Cecily and Marissa. Both women tried multiple times to wedge their way into Annemarie's home, going so far as to let themselves in with their sets of keys, but each time, she squirreled away into the bedroom, locking the door and refusing to interact. Everyone saw the warning signs of a repeat downward spiral, so at the very least, they would leave ready-to-eat meals and miscellaneous groceries in her kitchen in the hopes she mustered the will to feed herself.

Hearing the news from her mother and her sister—two of the closest people to Annemarie—left Alistair aghast and annoyed. Not with her, but with the fact that he was stuck on the mainland for the week with so little free time available to try to swoop in and rescue her. After Jesse's death, when she hit her lowest, refusing food, company, and any form of help from those who cared most about her, Alistair resorted to semi-violent tactics. He broke down her door. She had been so deeply asleep on the couch—mostly passed out from too much alcohol and not enough other calories—she did not stir at the sound of his brazen entrance. He had trouble waking her, and when she finally roused, she literally screamed, scared senseless because he was the last thing she expected to see in her living room while she froze everyone out.

Alistair had a bad habit of overstepping boundaries, sometimes unapologetically, and he knew it. He did what he could to separate personal feelings from professional obligation in the line of duty, and in the case of the aftermath of Jesse's death, he did not care that the lines may have been blurred—he knew an intervention was warranted, and he was not wrong. And now that Annemarie had seemed to fuse to the couch once again following Moose's demise, Alistair thought it necessary to step in again.

The minute he finished his last shift at the Derry office, he hopped into his wagon, caught the next ferry home, and drove straight to Annemarie. He dug his fingernails into the padded steering wheel, anxious to see his best friend. He secretly hoped Cecily and Marissa were overexaggerating the situation, that he would end up on Annemarie's front porch, knock, and be let in like any other day. He rehearsed out loud what he intended to say to her: his condolences once again for her loss, apologies for having to bail on her because of work, the offer to do anything in his power to make things better. He did not have it in him to prepare for the worst.

When he arrived at the house, he bounded up the stairs and firmly planted his fist against the door, knocking casually. No answer. He gave it thirty seconds before trying again. Still no answer. "Annemarie, it's me. Let me in," he called to her. Her car was parked in the driveway, so he knew she was home. Another series of knocks and silences greeted him willingly. "Annie, come on." He raised his voice a little. He clenched his fist tighter, banged louder. This time, he heard shuffling coming from inside, but still no answer. He considered using his key, knowing it was a surefire way to get to her. Based on what both Cecily and Marissa reported, however, the sound of keys jingling gave her enough time to scamper away to hide, if she was not doing so already. Instead, he ramped up the theatrics. "This is Sheriff Lucas. I'm performing a wellness check. You have one minute to open this door or I'm kicking it in!"

He glanced at the long hand of his wristwatch, timing exactly sixty seconds. The shuffling grew louder as it approached the door from the other side. The time ticked away, closing in on the one-minute mark, then came the sound of the dead bolt disengaging and the door creaking open. He did not bother saying hi or waiting for the invite inside. He pushed right past her, guarding himself with his shoulder in case she tried to slam the door in his face, said "sorry," and plopped down on the couch among her nest of lightweight fleece blankets.

Annemarie merely responded by closing the door. She did not acknowledge him.

He looked around the room, taking in the sights of her current situation. It was obvious the depression hit her hard again. Several pounds were missing from her already slight frame. Her usually tidy hair was dirty, disheveled. The sweatpants and T-shirt she wore looked like she had been living in them all week. The smell in the room was reminiscent of rotting fruits and vegetables; whether it was produce left alone to decompose, or bits, pieces, and peels discarded in the trash never taken outside, he could not tell. There was a hint of body odor too. He imagined she had not found it in herself to shower recently. To her credit, unlike the past, she looked like her calories were not coming solely from alcohol, even though there were empty bottles littered around the room. There were also empty bowls with dried-up leftover bits caked around the rims and mugs with damp tea bags sitting on the scratched-up coffee table.

"I finally have a day off," Alistair said lightly, like he interrupted an ongoing conversation to make this fact known. Silence. "I thought maybe, if you were feeling up for it, we could get cleaned up and head over to

Brownstone for the night. Dinner, dancing . . . drinks." He hesitated to add in the last part, seeing that she partook in the drinking portion all week long, and did not want to enable her further. On the other hand, it might have been enough of an incentive. "Let me take you out."

Annemarie walked to the other end of the couch, purposely not looking at him. She pushed the blankets away from her, making sure not to touch him, and sat. The night of the incident, Alistair stayed with her until five, organizing the mess, photographing everything, taking DNA samples, cleaning the blood and mud from all the surfaces. He spearheaded the search, brought home Moose, disappeared for a week. Riggs took over the case in Alistair's stead—the DNA test came back inconclusive: There were no matches, nothing in the database. Which they expected, but they still thought they needed to try. It was a crime at minimum, but there were so many unknown details, it was hard to invest too many resources. The leads were nonexistent. Like Annemarie's current want to be in the company of others.

"Come on, you know you'll have a good time. We can see if Nina's gonna be around." He paused, expecting her to respond even though he knew she would not. "It's Grey Barn. You love Grey Barn." Hoping he could dangle her favorite restaurant in front of her in order to get a positive reaction, he was instead met with disinterest.

She barely looked up from her lap. In fact, throughout his visit so far, Annemarie had not spent a single second looking at him. She fiddled with her dirty fingernails as a means of distraction.

"Annie."

No response, no movement.

"Annie."

Nothing.

After another minute of silence, he said, "Annemarie, you're gonna have to look at me at some point. Or at least talk to me."

"No I won't," she said quickly and quietly, like a child trying to get in the last word during an argument. A smirk crept into the corner of her mouth.

Alistair gave off a little chortle. His laugh infected her, making her respond with a snicker of her own. They traded chuckles and cackles, and finally full-body giggles to the point that neither could breathe.

While wiping away tears, she said, "Thank you."

"For what?" He used his sleeve to soak up the water streaming from his eyes.

"For making me laugh. You always make me laugh. You're good at wriggling your way in where you're not wanted and getting people to open up." She paused. "I mean that in a nice way. I'm not implying you're a pest."

"Oh, I'm a pest." He blew a strong puff of air from his nostrils in a half-amused, half-incredulous response.

"You were the one that broke down my door when I was starving myself to death last year. You were the one that *incessantly* bugged me about going for runs and keeping my mental health up when I had bad days."

"So let me being a pest work again and come to Brownstone with me. We'll go to Grey Barn and The Sloe, I can call Nina or Marissa, and if you get me drunk enough, I might be up for dancing." He clenched both hands in front of him and acted out a ridiculous little skit that alternated both fists pumping in the air and wiggling his shoulders.

The tops of her cheeks turned a shade of tomato. "I'm embarrassed for you if that's how you intend to dance tonight."

Alistair knew he could bribe her. He always felt guilty doing so; it was like an abuse of power or taking advantage of her when she was most vulnerable. But in a situation like hers, he knew she needed out of the house, out from under the storm cloud constantly raining shit on her. The trend was starting over and he knew her body and mind could not handle another round of rock-bottom starvation from the depression. He knew that depression was not something a night out on the town would fix; nothing but self-care, time, and getting back to the routine that eased her out of her shell over the last year was the answer. When she emerged from the other end of her first dark tunnel, she made him swear to do everything he could to interfere if she ever headed down the same path. Though he did agree, he assumed she would never be involved in another situation as dire and tragic again. And now, he was not certain he could stop anything from causing her to spiral in an identical way.

"I don't want to leave the house," she said in a hushed tone so low Alistair missed it.

"What?"

"I don't want to leave the house. Ever," she repeated, her voice now strong, adamant. "I'm so beyond broken and all the tips and tricks I learned from Doctor Striker aren't enough and it's like why should I run when my companion is gone why meditate when I won't find calm and peace knowing my dog was murdered by the same *fucking* thing that caused my husband's death?" She sucked in a deep breath, having spoken her piece in a single lungful. "I can't handle this anymore." A tear rolled down her cheek. She did not bother wiping it away.

"Annie—" he started to reply, but she raised a hand to silence him.

"All that being said, you're the first person to make me even consider cracking a smile since ..." She shuddered. "Granted, besides Riggs at the beginning of the week, I haven't allowed anyone near me, so that's not saying much. And after the way I treated him, I imagine he was happy to stay away."

Alistair twisted his lips into a playful frown and nonchalantly shrugged. "I'll take any brownie points I can get."

"Do you remember your promise?"

He cocked an eyebrow. "Yooooou're gonna have to be a little more specific."

"That you'd always look out for me. That you'd pull me out of any dark tunnel I might venture down."

"I will always watch over you, Annemarie. Let me keep my promise to you now," he pleaded quickly before she could interrupt him again.

She nodded. "I will. But I need more than a night out. I want to ask everything of you, knowing you won't say no, because you never say no to me. I'm gonna abuse the power I have over you for once. But I feel like an absolute piece of shit asking you for anything." Her eyes flicked down to her dirty fingernails again. She fidgeted with them for a moment while she waited for any response he might give. Shame colored the top of her cheeks red—she hated asking for favors. But she knew this was necessary.

"Hit me." He did not miss a beat.

"I need help going back to Doctor Striker. I need help setting up a new routine, sans M-Moose, and the support and encouragement to stick with it. I don't know what that means right now. Maybe you come running with me. Or maybe you stick a boot through my front door to make sure I'm out of bed." She shrugged. "I haven't thought that far. *But I just need help.*" She stressed the last part and let her attention float to the scratched-up coffee table, over the mess of dirty bowls and mugs she had not bothered to take to the kitchen. A blank look settled in her eyes and her mouth went slack. "But . . . I also need my space. I love you, but you're a pest."

"Yes. That much has been determined."

A brief smile flashed at him. "Sometimes, I need to be left alone. If I tell you no, you have to respect that. In turn, I'll try to be open to everything." She leaned back on the couch cushion and let a strained sigh escape her. "Moose made me get up every morning. He had needs that only I could fulfill. Even when Jesse was here, Moose came to me first. Without him, I'm afraid I'll melt into my mattress. I can't have that again. But without a—"

"I will do everything in my power to make sure you get what you need. I promise." He was quick to respond before even thinking through what he was agreeing to. She *was* asking a lot of him. Living at opposite ends of the island proved a headache, given that if she needed him banging down her door every morning, that was a long drive. If she needed chauffeuring to Brownstone to meet with Doctor Striker, it would require a lot of coordinating on his part to find the time off from work to get her there.

"I know it's a lot."

He shrugged again. "I love you, Annie. I can't take away your pain for you, but I can help you to take the steps to separate yourself from it. My only question is: Why not ask Cecily or Marissa?" He knew the answer the moment he asked it.

"Mom doesn't have time for me. Not like I need. Dad's a handful in his retirement, and she's often watching Charlie for Marissa. And Mar . . . She's not dependable. I love her to death, you know that. But I can't count on her for anything, but I also can't fault her for how things are. Work, Charlie, allowing time for herself, it's a lot. Plus, her living in Brownstone might help me get to Doctor Striker's office, but it doesn't get me out of bed. It doesn't get me to the ferry on time." She huffed a breath. "Fuck, I sound like a useless child." Her hands shot up to her face and she covered her perpetually red cheeks. "I'm a fucking mess." She waved a hand in the air. "Alistair, forget I asked anything of you. This is . . ."

"Yeah, it's a lot to ask of me. Maybe too much. But you said it yourself, I'll never tell you no. If this is what needs to be done to help you move forward, it's what I'll do. My only hesitation is work. You're the most important person to me, but unfortunately, work is my number-one priority. Like I'll have to respect you telling me no, you'll have to respect that I can't always keep appointments. Anymore, there's no telling what fucking thing is going to happen from day to day."

"I promise to not be upset if you can't be here."

"And I promise to take care of you to the best of my ability."

He extended his hand toward her. He tucked three fingers under the thumb, leaving only the pinky exposed. Annemarie met the gesture with her own, linking little fingers together, then them both leaning in to kiss their thumbs. A smirk spread into the corner of her mouth, reassured things might turn out okay.

She settled back onto the couch cushion. "Now. If you expect me to be seen in public with you over in town, you're gonna have to do better than that." She pointed at his hastily cobbled together dark blue T-shirt and joggers.

"What's wrong with this?" He raised both hands in the air to show off the ensemble.

"You're like a goddamn cartoon character, wearing the same thing all the time."

"*Hey*, I have a work uniform I wear sometimes too," he protested. She stuck out her tongue in playful disapproval. "If I have to change, you need a shower and a shave," he responded, grabbing his nose with his thumb and index finger on one hand and waving the smell away with the other.

She gasped. "You're one to talk! Look at this face." She reached forward and squeezed his cheeks with one hand. "Just one week away from home and you're some kind of wilderness man now." The stubble on Alistair's face scratched at her fingers. Normally, he was impeccably clean-shaven, and to see anything but baby-smooth skin was odd to her.

"Hey now, I was thinking this wasn't looking too bad so far. Cuts ten minutes off my morning routine." He jutted his chin out to show off the three or four days of beard growth.

She chuckled. "Yeah, you're right. It's not hideous."

"You, on the other hand . . ." he said with a wry grin.

She used the back of her hand to smack his shoulder. "Rude!" She stood and tried to brush the wrinkles out of her sweatpants. "If you're gonna be like that, you can go to Brownstone by yourself tonight." They both knew she was joking, but she continued the charade by stomping a foot, throwing her nose up into the air, and walking off in a huff. She did not get far. Alistair bolted out of his place on the couch and grabbed at her waist as she trudged away. He caught her by the tail of her shirt, causing her to stop in place and jerk backward toward him. The force of their collision sent them sprawling onto the couch.

She shrieked with laughter, not expecting to go down in a two-person dogpile. Taking the opportunity to distract her, he tickled her sides, forcing an even louder noise out of her. She writhed around, flailing, trying to break free from his death grip. "Alistair, you g-gotta let m-me go," she stuttered between gasps of air.

"Why's that?"

"I-I'm g-gonna pee!"

"Oh? So I shouldn't do this—" He squeezed her midsection, prompting her rarely heard guttural, guffawing horse laugh. Its sudden appearance caught Alistair off guard, allowing her to flee from his grasp into the bathroom. He could not stop himself from laughing uncontrollably too, maintaining it until his sides ached. When Annemarie returned to the living room, her cheeks were flushed and she still gasped for breath.

She dropped onto the couch beside him, sitting with her shoulder pressed to his. Their breathing eventually equalized, having moved past the ludicrousness of the last five minutes. But as they both stilled, she shuddered; her whole body shook for a solid second.

Before he could look at her, she said, "I miss Moose."

"Yeah, me too."

"I miss Jesse." Tears streamed down her cheeks.

He did not say anything to this and she did not expect him to. After a moment passed, he reached out his hand for hers, gave it a firm squeeze, and said, "I know."

She leaned her head to rest on his shoulder, allowing the physical and emotional weight to slide from her into him. Her body deflated, a tension so tight, so heavy, easing off bit by bit. She squeezed his hand in reply and softly said, "I miss being happy."

Nina was unavailable to join her friends on their last-minute jaunt into Brownstone. She lamented the fact that she had not been able to escape from under the piles of paperwork of her current case, including to come offer her condolences in person to Annemarie when Moose died. She threatened to quit so she could afford the time to hang out. Alistair insisted that was not necessary, but they appreciated the determination and passion to give up on her job in favor of her friends. She promised she would be free soon and they would all have a decadent evening together.

So instead, Annemarie and Alistair sat in the outdoor courtyard of Grey Barn, nursing beers and rummaging around their respective plates of food while he regaled her with stories of the new recruits in Derry. She was only half listening, having little enthusiasm in what the new recruits got up to, but tried to muster the energy to engage with a small laugh or head shake at appropriate times. Alistair was so deep down the rabbit hole, he did not seem to notice her disinterest.

Chomping around a fry, he said, "This kid, Cochrane, he'd been out running radar the night before and . . ."

Alistair continued talking, but another voice in the vicinity caught her attention. It was low and smooth, warm, familiar. She turned her head slightly to the left and the right so her eyes could get a better view of her surroundings. A group of men walked past the courtyard, all of them a tizzy of conversation, all paying attention to one another. That was when she spotted the source— Nowell was in the crowd. Annemarie straightened her spine and opened her mouth to call to him, but the group blew right past without so much a first glance to the restaurant patrons; she had missed her opportunity.

By now, Alistair realized she was no longer paying attention to him. He did not bother finishing the story, especially once she pushed herself out of her chair, did not excuse herself, and disappeared into the restaurant for a brief moment. She popped out through the front door and hurried down the sidewalk after the men. Alistair heard noise between her and them, but could not tell what was being said.

Nowell spun in place on his heel, obviously surprised to not only be called for by name, but that it was Annemarie doing the calling. He motioned at his friends to keep walking ahead, he would join them shortly.

Alistair watched as Annemarie rocked back and forth on her feet as they talked. She had shoved her hands into the back pockets of her pants. Nowell, the towering, stormless statue that he was, mindlessly picked at his fingernails as he listened to her. He gave a slight nod and asked something. She shrugged in response. He returned the gesture. She lowered her head, her face having flushed. A hand flew from a back pocket and quickly wiped away a tear cascading down her cheek.

There was obvious hesitation in their body language. The way she held up her shoulders, but left several feet between them; his constant lowering his head to stare at the sidewalk then back to her face every time she spoke; nary a hitch in their rigid postures. He extended a hand to her shoulder and rubbed it gently, a simple form of comfort as she finally collapsed into her own hands to silently bawl. Nowell glanced around them—was he checking for onlookers who might misconstrue what was happening? What *was* happening? Was he planning an exit strategy?

His eyes found Alistair's and went wide before returning to Annemarie in front of him. The awkward scene continued to unfold until he took it upon himself to wrap his arms around her and bring her to his chest for a long embrace. She kept her watering eyes and red face buried in her hands as he stroked his fingers down her spine. Alistair tensed watching everything. Jealousy ran throughout, but he could not pinpoint why. He knew Annemarie would always confide in him—well, *usually* would confide in him. It was no secret she had kept things from him, and the further along they got in their years, the more it seemed like the secrecy was increasing. Though he was the sole person she had asked for help moving forward, watching Nowell's and her interactions made Alistair feel like a second fiddle. Like she only asked him because he happened to be present.

Before he let himself spiral any deeper, knowing it was a stupid, ridiculous feeling, he mentally slapped himself back to reality as Annemarie scraped her chair across the pavers to scoot herself under the table. Her cheeks were still red, there was a single tear ready to dribble off the tip of her chin, but a small smile remained fixed on her pink lips.

"Everything okay?" he asked slowly.

She chewed on her lower lip to erase any emotion still left on her face and gave a nonplussed shrug. "It will be."

EIGHTEEN

Alistair leisurely flipped through the pages of a file folder splayed out on the cluttered desk, his chin resting upon a balled-up fist supported by his elbow. A stack of documents fastened with a paper clip on the left side was coming apart in a mess while the stack on the right was in a much more orderly fashion. His eyes dragged across each line of information, inspecting and absorbing every word. He had barely slept that morning—a seemingly new, undesired habit—and finding himself wandering the house before sunrise, decided to come to the station to conduct a bit of research before inevitably being called away for one incident or another.

He was grateful that Port Harrow was not a hotbed of criminal activity.

This particular file detailed the drowning death of island resident Soroush Vaziri from eighteen months prior. Vaziri had moved to the island a few years before that, interested in a quiet, retired lifestyle after spending decades traveling the world for work and never being able to settle in just one place because of it. Alistair was not certain, but he believed Soroush was a tech mogul—it would certainly explain how he afforded the multimillion-dollar waterfront home and his collection of seafaring toys. His actions were not unheard of by any means, especially for the area. Soroush found a passion for spearfishing and kiteboarding, and was often out on his twenty-foot bowrider enjoying life to its fullest. Though he mostly kept to himself, he was friendly, thoughtful, and well-liked by the other island residents.

So it came as a huge shock when the crew of the Brownstone-Port Harrow ferry found him face down and lifeless in the water; even more so was that he had been attacked and left for dead.

But given his penchant for hunting the local marine life, the likelihood that he tried to take on the wrong creature, and lost, was higher than not. The bite over the femoral artery proved as much. Jesse was the first marine biologist on the scene and determined that the shape and depth of the wound more or less matched that of a large sea lion. Given that it was January, the migratory pinnipeds chasing prey doubled the population of the locals, and the feeding grounds in the waters around Azure County were chock full of the already territorially aggressive beasts. The case became textbook at that point; as textbook as a sea lion attack resulting in death could be.

Something about the case always rubbed Alistair the wrong way, but he could never put a finger on it. If he were being honest, he did not have enough time in his day to focus on an incident that had been relatively open-and-shut, especially when no family came forward to demand further answers. Soroush had seemingly been alone at that point in his life. Alistair did not know him well. They ran into each other from time to time, maybe at the library or one of the waterfront cafés, and always at the Fourth Festival. They exchanged pleasantries, made small talk about what was new in their respective worlds—all superficial, but nice. A number of times, Soroush extended an invitation to come over for a beer or a trip out onto the water when Alistair had a day off, and beyond giving a noncommittal "yeah, maybe," nothing ever came from it.

Alistair had gleaned a little about Soroush from their brief conversations, however. Including how comfortable, confident, and competent he was in the ocean. He understood what was worth chasing after and what to leave alone. He often spoke of his adventures below the surface—and even picked Jesse's brain once or twice about areas around the shore to avoid for safety—so Alistair knew the man's capabilities. Soroush would never try to spear a sea lion . . . but it did not mean whatever prey he was after was not also the object of another predator's desire.

But because the authorities had their answer and no one was challenging it, he left it alone. Jesse, his team of scientists, and outside help from the Azure County Sheriff's Department and the coroner's office were all satisfied with the absolutely plausible cause of death. Though, with the recent surfeit of fatal incidents cropping up—including Travis Kelly's drowning five and a half months ago—Alistair thought it needed revisiting. Every single one did.

The last hour was filled with devouring the death report, sizing up all the details, scribbling his own notes for anything he could find in common with Soroush, Travis, Peter, and Moose. He lumped Jesse onto the list at first, but given his was a traffic accident at the hands of two men, he removed him as quickly as he had added him. So far, all he could manage to link together was that each death was within reasonable distance of the sea cave on North Beach. But so were a lot of things; the island was not that big.

His brain felt like overcooked porridge left to congeal in the pot. Reading the same words over and over, hoping to find something new, made him think the overwhelming urge to nod off at his desk was a good one to give into.

A heavy-handed knock came at the door, followed quickly by Riggs popping his head into the office. Alistair visibly jumped and flinched at the sound, and appearance, of his deputy.

"Hey, Al, you—are you okay?" Riggs's eyebrows were a jumble high on his forehead.

Alistair let out a long, wide yawn and used his knuckles to wipe at his eyes. He barely nodded. "Yeah, uh, I've been at this for a while now."

Riggs straightened up as he sidled into the office. "What is that?" He lifted his chin to point at the paperwork on the desk.

"A death report." Alistair shook his head a little, hoping to wave off Riggs.

"Is it one of Brownstone's?"

"No, uh ..." He huffed out a stilted breath. "It's Soroush Vaziri's."

"The drowning incident from last year?"

Alistair lowered his eyebrows and squeezed his eyes into almost a squint. "Yeah, um, it's-it's nothing. Uh, did you need something?" He flopped the front cover closed, pushed it away as if to ignore it.

Riggs plopped into one of the chairs opposite Alistair and got comfortable. He set his elbows on his knees and leaned forward, partly eyeing the file and partly trying to get Alistair to say more. "I was gonna see if you could watch the desk while I ran home for a minute, but that can wait. What . . . Why are you in that file?"

Alistair scratched at the back of his head, trying to drag out a response, but he knew Riggs would not relent. "I was thinking about—I-I don't know. Something about it doesn't, hasn't ever really, felt right about it. Even after all this time."

"Well, no, I imagine not," Riggs replied flippantly.

Alistair cocked his head. "What's that mean?"

"A sea lion attack? Here? Does Port Harrow, or even Azure County for that matter, have a history of that?" Alistair shook his head. "Right. So now, we've got this guy who knows his way around the water suddenly the first victim of such a thing? I mean, sea lion attacks happen, just *not here*. There's a first time for everything, I suppose. But yeah, I totally get it sittin' funny with you." The look on Riggs's scrunched-up face was one of incredulity. He gave a shake of his head, the drying, slicked-back mop of hair wobbling with the movement. "I don't buy it either."

"It's not like I think it's some conspiracy theory or cover-up," Alistair interjected. "But, yeah, it's like . . . it's like . . ." He could not form a coherent sentence. Despite spending the last hour poring over the file, coming up with his own conclusions, the words were not there to elaborate any further. But also, he did not want to drag Riggs down into the depths of his private, personal hell if he did not have to. Riggs knew nothing—or at least, very little—about the strangeness truly surrounding the recent deaths, the working theory in Alistair's brain. Of course, he knew the intimate details of Moose's and Peter's demises, but not that they may in any way be tied to Soroush's and Travis's. But the enigmatic nature of the whole thing needed to be said out loud, needed to be fleshed out so Alistair could either continue a potential wild-goose chase, or drop it entirely. He leaned forward, almost conspiratorially, and lowered his voice, lest anyone else in the office hear. "Have you noticed anything, y'know, weird going on lately? Or seen someone who doesn't belong here?"

"You still harping on Nowell Reid showing up at the festival?" A single eyebrow rose on Riggs's forehead.

Alistair clenched his jaw but shook his head. "No, I don't mean Nowell Reid. What I mean is, has anything seemed *odd* to you recently? We all exist in a pretty happy little bubble here, but it seems like maybe something's upsetting that."

"Like what kind of something?" Riggs was leaning in even further now, elbows planted on the edge of the desk.

"Like something, otherwor—"

The cell phone sitting beside the keyboard chirped alive with a loud double beep, startling both men into the backs of their chairs. With a visibly shaking hand, Alistair reached for it to see who the text was from.

[Annemarie]
We're going hunting tonight.
Bring your guns.

NINETEEN

A soft knock came at the front door; Annemarie almost missed it, but happened to be anxiously pacing her way from the kitchen into the living room when Nowell announced his arrival. She fumbled with the knob at first, her hands in sweaty shambles. When the door swung open, he was waiting patiently on the front stoop, head lowered, and the porch light casting a long, sinister shadow across the gravel driveway behind him. It more than set the mood for the moment.

An olive-drab duffel bag slung over his shoulder helped with his forward momentum into the house as Annemarie silently invited him in by sidestepping from the entryway. She pushed the loose strands that had fallen from her ponytail back over her ears, out of her way as she turned to properly greet him.

"Hey," she said meekly.

"Hey," he replied. His lips formed a thin smile. "You ready for this?"

She shook her head without hesitation. "No. Not one bit. But it has to happen. I can't do this any longer." She reached out her hand for his shoulder and squeezed it firmly. "Thank you for coming all the way out here to help me. You didn't have—"

"If this *is* what we think it is, if it's tied to the death of Je—your husband and Travis and whoever else, we have no choice. We have to deal with it, and now." He closed his eyes. When he opened them, he noticed she had her head slightly cocked, her teeth buried into her bottom lip as she gnawed on it, a glisten of a wet eye staring back at him. "Let me, uh, show you what I brought."

He lowered the duffel onto the scarred coffee table and made quick work of the zipper. He pulled out one item after another until the surface was covered. Spread out in the middle was a topographical map of the island; a small, black rectangle that could fit in the palm of Annemarie's hand; a set of walkie-talkies; a heavy-duty flashlight and a larger spotlight; and finally, a semi-automatic handgun with an additional magazine.

Annemarie picked up each of the items as she inspected them. She stopped at the black rectangle. "What . . . is this?"

"It's the dongle for a thermal imaging app I have on my phone." He reached for the device, his fingers dragging across her palm as he retrieved it. With his other hand, he pulled his cell phone from his back pocket and plugged the rectangle into the lower port. "See, I—"

She could not stop herself from laughing. "Wait, *dongle*? That's not a real word."

"It absolutely is, Miss Librarian. Look it up."

She snorted. "Okay, so this . . . dongle . . . makes your phone a thermal imaging camera?" He nodded. "That's cool." She thought for a moment before finally adding, "I hope all of this didn't cost you too much money. I can give you some, if necessary."

He brushed her off. "No, it's fine. I owned everything except the map, and that was an easy acquisition from my local library." He grinned at her. She shared the smile. She was familiar with the exact one—it was framed and hanging in her own branch.

"Why do you just happen to have that dongle?" She tried hard not to laugh again despite finding the word beyond amusing and utterly ridiculous.

Matter-of-factly, he replied, "Hunting. It's good for tracking game in the dark." He neatly organized everything but the map to one side of the table. He knelt on the floor in front of it, allowing better access to it. "Show me what you know."

Annemarie joined him on the hardwood, her shoulder pressed to his as they loomed over the sprawling landscape of Port Harrow. She searched for a moment before pointing at the north end of the island, a spot between Wildwood Highway and the edge of the forest.

"This is me." She dragged her finger, wandering through the scenery. "This is about where I found Peter." Another pause. "Here's where it knocked me down when I was going for help for him." Another. She drew a large, imaginary circle behind her house. "Where Moose—" Her voice hitched. "Where Moose disappeared."

"Hang on a sec." He leaned over to the bag and fished out a red wax pencil and handed it to her. "It'll be easier to track this way."

Her fingers trembled as she retrieved the pencil from his hand. She tried to focus on the task to calm her nerves. One crosshatch, a second, a third. Annemarie marked out each of the incidents on the map, including where Nowell and Travis had killed Jesse. She made it a point to not make eye contact with him when she did it, or when she handed back the wax pencil. He followed suit and tracked his first sighting of the creature and trailed all the way to Annemarie's mark on the highway.

They stared at the blips of red, neither saying anything for a long while.

"So . . ." she started.

"What does it all mean?" he asked.

"Where do we even start?"

Nowell squinted as he scratched at his temple with the flat end of the pencil. "Maybe the most recent area. It seems like a lot happens in the woods."

Annemarie motioned both hands over the map, making a grand, sweeping gesture. "A lot has happened everywhere." She paused. "But I think you're right. We should start directly behind the house and work our way to the cave. Alistair has found two bodies there so far—I imagine that means *something*." They knew what it meant, so it did not bear repeating, but it still weighed heavily on their minds and in their chests.

"All right, then. Let's . . . do this, I guess." He pushed up onto his feet, his knees grateful for the reprieve. Annemarie joined him shortly and excused herself to the bedroom to grab a suitable jacket. As she fished around in the depths of her closet, she looked down to assess her whole outfit: bright colors and lightweight—appropriate enough to avoid getting shot but not quite appropriate for stealthily hunting down some wild *entity*. She had assumed being highly visible would be beneficial for Nowell, but wondered if it also made her a tantalizing moving target with a giant bull's-eye on her back for the creature. They knew so little about it, better to not tempt it. She shimmied out of the neon-green leggings and white T-shirt, dropping them on the floor at her feet.

She had climbed into a pair of dark jeans when she heard, "Annemarie . . ."

Her head popped out from within the closet to meet Nowell's gaze. He stood in the doorway of her room, cautiously keeping his distance in a respectful manner. He immediately noticed her lack of a top, though she was still clad in a sports bra, and immediately averted his eyes to the floor. He was an expert at focusing on an imaginary spot between his feet.

"What's . . . the plan, exactly? J-just so I know we're on the same page, and all."

Pulling her torso and arms into a dark, long-sleeve shirt, she emerged from the little room and stopped in front of him while she continued to fidget with the hem against the top of her jeans. "I don't really know. I kinda assumed we'd go out there, skulk around a bit, and hope it finds us. Put a bullet in its brain maybe?"

"And what happens if we don't find it?"

"I'm willing to stay out there as long as necessary. But I also understand that you have work in the morning. So, we go until it's time to call it, I guess." She shrugged, half nonchalant, half hopeful he would tell her the words she wanted to hear: *I'm all in.* At least that way it would feel less like he was along for the ride or filling his time until he got bored—it would cement that he was a willing participant.

It did not come out the way she had hoped, though. "Yeah, I mean . . ." He rubbed at the back of his head, his fingers scratching against the scalp, making a hollow sound that filled the temporary silence between them. "I can stay at least for a little while. I obviously don't have Dylan tonight, but I *do* have Dylan to worry about."

Annemarie gave a quick shake of her head. "I completely understand. This seems a fool's errand anyway and I would rather us be safe than dead, even if that means we barely make it out of my backyard." Her words were a lie, at least where she was concerned. She did not care if she ended up dead if it meant that *thing* was gone too. She could easily say it now, standing at attention, spine straightened and chin up. But face-to-face with it, should it come to that? Annemarie could only hope for the best.

"Then . . . I guess . . . we head out?" Nowell took his time saying the words, less of a statement than a question. Deep down, he wanted to see the end of this catastrophe that had set in motion the series of events that found him in jail, his best friend dead, and a black stain on his reputation—but closer to the surface, the part of him that yelled louder than the rest, he wanted to disappear into his cozy little life back in Brownstone, never giving his time on Port Harrow a second thought. Now that he was here, though, he did not feel right backing out. He had to try.

They made their way down the front porch stairs, him loaded with the gun, spotlight, walkie, and camera, and her only weighed down with a flashlight and walkie of her own. The sound of squealing tires on the pavement echoed in the trees surrounding the house, and before she could consider the source, Alistair's SUV plowed into the driveway and came to a sudden halt as the gravel dispersed under him. There was no missed beat in between the engine powering down and the door swinging open, allowing a bewildered Alistair to emerge, practically stumbling over his own feet.

"Al, what the hell're you doing? You could've hit one—"

"Annie, what're you doing?" He ran over her words as he righted himself, not even acknowledging the penetrating gaze she shot at him.

She waited for him to come closer before calmly responding, "Nowell and I are gonna hunt down this grey bastard."

His breath escaped him momentarily. "Y-you c-can't," he finally managed to get out. "We don't know anything about it! How do you think this is gonna play out?"

She shrugged. "Not doing anything about it is even worse. I can't sit by knowing this thing is on a rampage. We think we have a pretty good idea of how to track it, or at the very least, bring it to us."

As she continued to divulge the details of their plan, Alistair eyed Nowell suspiciously, wondering which of the two was behind the sudden urge to chase down a ghost. He could not imagine Annemarie having a violent bone in her body—she never proved that to be true in the past—but hearing her confidently speak of their retribution made him second-guess himself. A lot of things going on with her recently made him do that, it seemed.

"So are you with us?" she asked. She widened her stance and locked eyes with him.

He ran flattened fingers over the hollow of his eye and pushed at his temple. A heavy, reluctant sigh left him. "I can't let you go out there alone."

"Then don't."

TWENTY

Despite the nasty knot in Alistair's stomach telling him how much of a bad idea this whole thing was, the louder, more obnoxious feeling overwhelming him was the notion of letting Annemarie go it alone—especially with Nowell at her side. Of what he knew about him—plenty, from a sheriff's stat sheet point of view—he did not trust the man to have Annemarie's back. To be fair to the Brownstone native, Alistair could not be sure *he* had Annemarie's back, either, given the situation. What even were they dealing with? How could any of them be certain that the plan to *put a bullet in its brain* would even work?

She was being a bit too flippant for Alistair's taste, but he thought that maybe the nonchalance, or the ability to turn off the fear, was exactly what all of them needed. She was not wrong in that this thing had to be dealt with. If not them, then who? Not that any of them were experts, but it seemed between Alistair's arsenal of weapons in the back of his vehicle and Nowell's camera, they might at least survive the night.

"So, what'll it be, Sheriff? You in or out?"

Begrudgingly, the reply came, "In."

With a shotgun slung over one shoulder, a gamut of buckshot shells affixed to the buttstock of the weapon, and a holstered handgun at his hip, Alistair was as ready as he could be. Having no experience with weapons, Annemarie opted to be the spotlight carrier who followed behind the men as they surveyed ahead. Nowell had his gun tucked under the waistband at the back of his pants while he booted up the app that turned his phone into a thermal imaging camera. When it finally loaded, he panned a full three-hundred-sixty degrees to see how receptive to light and heat sources it still was. It had been a hot minute since he last used it, seeing as how there had been no real free time for him in the last year.

When Annemarie's and Alistair's bodies radiated a bright white against the black and grey background, he gave them a thumbs-up. "Ready," he said confidently. Even though he was anything but.

The trio made quick work of the length of Annemarie's property, getting to the tree line in under a minute. They stopped where her yard did, all of them holding onto arrhythmic breaths. Alistair heard her mutter, "This is for you, Moose," but she kept the words between her and the self-dug grave to their left. "Flashlights on?" she asked.

"I wouldn't," Alistair warned. "Even though the goal is to find it, we don't necessarily want it to find us first. We have no idea how it hunts and the last thing we need to do is advertise our whereabouts. But keep 'em handy."

Nowell and Annemarie nodded, though it was indiscernible in the pitch-black night. Simultaneously, they drew in deep breaths as they took their first steps into the woods, doing their best to keep close to one another as they moved. Through the cell phone's screen, Nowell could pick up the smallest of critters darting around the forest floor, mice skittering from one hidey-hole to another, something else equally as small running up the trunks of nearby trees, birds nestled on the branches over their heads. Without the aid of the flashlights, they could not see the eyes all around them, staring down in curiosity—though it was probably for the best.

They continued forward as silently as they could; a *snap* from the twig-littered ground or the *woosh* of leaves returning to their starting point as they were momentarily pushed aside were the only sounds heard over the steady breaths.

Alistair let his feet guide him through the dark, shuffling them close to the ground so as to feel what was ahead instead of stumbling and tripping. The moonlight of the clear night barely penetrated the treetops, and what little filtered through was barely enough to see there was a body beside him, but not whose it was. He assumed it to be Nowell, as that was how they started this endeavor, but he could not be sure.

A noise to his left caught his attention. It was a soft but high-pitched squeal that bounced around the thicket of trees. The footsteps beside him stopped too.

"Sorry, that was me," came Annemarie's voice, a couple dozen feet away from them.

"You okay?" Alistair called in a hushed tone.

"Walked into a spiderweb."

"Don't do that," he replied.

He heard a stifled snort come from the same direction. He knew she was trying not to laugh. It made the tension in his shoulders ease a touch, that even with this being so serious and dangerous of a harebrained mission, they could still find some amusement. But they immediately went stiff when another noise rang out hollowly around them.

"F-find another one?" Nowell stuttered.

"That wasn't me," she said on an exhale.

"Are you sure? Be-because it'd be okay if it was."

"Definitely not me."

"Sheriff Lucas?" Nowell asked.

The tension was back in Alistair's shoulders. He tried to straighten his spine and stand as tall as he could, as if the higher he moved his ears, the clearer he would hear. The echo continued, though now faint, and they waited for another noise, or a return call.

Nothing came.

Alistair sidled up to Nowell, trying to catch a glimpse of the camera's dark screen. "You seeing anything?" he whispered.

"Nothing new." Nowell panned to their right, showing off the woodland beasties to Alistair. As he moved to show off the left, they were met with a nearly full screen of bright white. Both men whimpered with their mouths shut, but the sound still carried. *"Don't do that, Annie,"* Nowell hissed.

"I'm sorry. I didn't want to be standing over there by myself anymore."

The noise came again, this time more distinctive in its delivery. "T-there." Nowell pointed, but all it did was light up one edge of the camera, drawing attention from what he had spotted in the frame. Annemarie and Alistair leaned in closer, ear to ear with each other as they watched. Not too far off, a four-legged, bright-white body moseyed into view, alternating between lowering its head to forage for food and lifting it up to let out a mix of a grunt and a sniff—the deer was looking for any predators while grazing.

The problem was the deer had no predators on Port Harrow; its constant checking sent a chill through Alistair's extremities. What did it know that they did not?

The three sighed, but the identification of the source of the noise did not truly alleviate any of the real worry. Annemarie took several steps forward, hoping to coerce the men to move with her.

"Don't scare it," Nowell called softly. He continued to watch the screen as Annemarie came into view, and the deer, still somewhat off in the distance, seemed to be scooting its way toward them. "Let it pass if you can." A fallen branch cracked under Annemarie's step, causing both her and the deer to perk up and remain motionless. She knew better than to keep moving, as did the deer as it assessed the situation. But before it had any time to process what lay ahead of it, a guttural roar and a blazing flash of white light lit up the phone screen and made Alistair stumble back half a dozen steps. Having not seen it herself, being away from the men, Annemarie did not understand what had happened in front of them.

The deer called out a panicked bleat as its body collapsed under the hominal figure, the two shapes becoming one. The camera could not discern between one or the other, and the assemblage the merged thermal imaging created was monstrous. The noises coming from the scene were that of grunts and wails and snarls, though neither Alistair nor Nowell could tell what was coming from who.

Annemarie was frozen in place, too afraid by the familiar sounds to advance or retreat, and not certain what to do. She turned only her head to try to track any sign of her companions behind her, hopeful the ambient light of Nowell's phone might at least show their outline. But as she locked her eyes on the silhouette of one of them, a blast of a voice that was as loud as it was chilling came from the scene directly in front of her; her instinct was to crouch into the smallest ball she could manage. Arms wrapped around her knees, head buried as deep as it could go, she violently shook, unable to do anything else. Memories of being knocked down, twice, while in these woods by an unknown being flooded through her, causing her to regret every moment of the evening up to now. Her body ached like it was muscle memory, like the previous incidents were permanent scars—in some ways, they were.

"Annie," a whisper of a voice called to her. She tried hard to shut it out, worried what answering it could do. It came again, a gentle hush against the din up ahead. "Annie, use the flashlight."

At that, she removed her head from the death grip of her arms, knowing it could only be Nowell or Alistair speaking to her. "And do what?" she asked, still shaken as the words fell out of her.

"Shine it. Directly. Ahead of you," the voice instructed deliberately. She struggled to listen for more of an explanation, but all she heard was the sound of the slide action along the barrel of Alistair's shotgun. Her breathing stilled as her hands soundlessly reached behind her, fumbling for the light she had shoved in her back pocket when they had decided on no lights at the start of the search. It was not there. Thinking it fell when she dropped into the upright fetal position, she traced her hands along the ground around her. Her fingertips stumbled over rocks and sticks and something hard and fuzzy she did not want to think about, until she recognized the smooth, hard aluminum of the flashlight. *"Annie,"* the voice urged.

"I got it, I got it," she replied a little too loudly.

The white shape of the combined creature on Nowell's screen abruptly stopped and he watched as what was once one became two. It was bipedal, though it seemed hunched over at the shoulders. Ever so slowly, it inched closer, growing a mite bigger before Nowell's eyes.

Alistair screamed, "Annie! Now!"

Yellow flooded immediately in front of the trio, lighting up a large swath that only widened as it continued toward the distant, unseen shore. The creature stood still, stunned by the headlong glow, but then it came to its senses, leaned forward, and burst into a sprint in Annemarie's direction. An explosion of sound echoed through the tree trunks as the buckshot left the barrel and spread toward the target some thirty yards away. Several of the lead pellets struck home, causing the grey creature to wince with its humanlike nose scrunching up in dissatisfaction. It curled its upper lip, revealing sharpened, bloody teeth, accompanied by an ululation that caused the spotlight to shake.

It gained ground against her, her still unable to even flinch. "Move, Annie!" Alistair shouted, working to pump the gun once more and level the barrel to his eye. He fired a second shot, but the creature was too fast and escaped the spray of pellets. He refused to line up a third, afraid he might hit Annemarie instead, but he did not hesitate to unholster his handgun and fire several rounds from it. He landed one in its shoulder as it was within reaching distance of her. It skidded to a stop, but not before knocking her backward on her ass. She slid several feet away from the men, separating them even further. But it was okay—she was out of harm's way for the time being.

The creature pivoted and aimed its sights on Alistair and the red-hot muzzle pointed at its head. When he cleared out the cartridge, he pulled the shotgun up from his side once again and fired the last two buckshot, hoping the close space between him and the creature would help each of the pellets land. They did, but it barely flinched as it leaped and flew through the air at him. Nowell backed away suddenly, keeping the camera focused on the scene, but also reaching for the gun tucked under his belt to try to help.

The collision of the creature and Alistair was heavy, an audible *oof* escaping his lips as they both hit the ground hard. The serrated teeth snapped at his face as it tried to muscle its way closer to him, but was held far enough back by the barrel of the gun horizontally slotted across its throat. Alistair pushed as hard as he could, using the strength of his upper body to keep the gnashing mouth at bay. While that worked for a moment, the creature's arms were still able to reach for its victim and managed a swipe at Alistair.

Sharp nails sliced through the uniform material and dug into his shoulder. His knee-jerk reaction of crying out in agony at the feel of his skin ripping apart did not diminish the tight grip on either end of the gun. The creature wielded another wide swipe, this time, its fist connecting with jaw. A sickening crack echoed between the two bodies. Alistair saw stars upon impact and his brief wince allowed for the weapon to be ripped from his hands and thrown aside. Now, there were hot, grey hands wrapped around his throat, squeezing the life out of him.

His eyes grew heavy and a wave of dizziness coursed through his body. The sensation was like a double dose of cold medicine finally kicking in. Alistair knew he could not give in, no matter how tired he grew under the hold of his assailant. But the drowsiness was winning. In a futile attempt to overtake it before blacking out, he reached a hand to push against its face, trying to be mindful of its mouth. It let out a roar, not unlike the one Alistair had loosed when his skin broke, and immediately released the grip it had on his throat.

A series of gunshots echoed around him before his eyes finally closed.

TWENTY-ONE

Splattered in a collection of chunks of mud, dead leaves, and his own blood, Alistair struggled to push himself up off the forest floor. The creature's powerful leap caused them both to hit the ground hard—Alistair onto his elbows first—and slide away from a shocked and stilled Annemarie and Nowell. His entire body ached, especially his arms from the pressure he had to apply to keep the creature's gnashing teeth from penetrating his skin. He took a moment to survey his surroundings, to orient himself before making the trek back toward the light of his companions some ten yards off.

As he leaned down to retrieve his shotgun from the dirt, a twinge of pain overwhelmed his system and several thick drops of red spotted his hand. He lowered his eyebrows into a squint, trying to find the source of the blood. Then he remembered the shoulder wound. He slid his thumb and middle finger over the tear in his shirt, pushing the shredded fibers aside to inspect the scratch. The skin was angry but enough of the blood had coagulated to form a light scab, telling him it was merely superficial; it had felt like it went down to the marrow. A quick cleaning at home was all he would need. He wiped away the spots on his hand, but stopped when a squeal echoed through the trees.

He clenched every muscle in his body to steady himself as he listened for it again, but seeing movement to his left made him recognize the source of the high-pitched trill. Annemarie's spotlight bounced along with her as she cut a path through the underbrush that separated her and Nowell, her elated shriek following her like a celebratory streamer. Nowell held a small, powerful flashlight in one hand and his phone in the other. His light dropped to the ground and rolled in Alistair's direction as Annemarie launched herself into the air, expecting him to grab and hold onto her. In his arms, her fingers raking over the stubble of hair, she pressed her face against his to share a long, passionate kiss.

The aching and pain Alistair felt throughout his body shot directly into the pit of his stomach, collecting into a mass of seething hatred and jealousy. It was obvious Annemarie, whom he always thought was the love of his life, had chosen another. It was her right to choose. He wanted to be happy for her. Truly. But all he could think about was how that *man* was part of the reason the love of *her* life was no longer with her.

He watched for a prolonged minute as they mashed their faces together, one of Nowell's hands cradling Annemarie's cheek while the other supported her body, their lips smacking, tongues visible as they shared a string of saliva. Any longer and Alistair would feel like a voyeur. He overexaggerated the clearing of his throat. They did not budge.

"Hey, guys," he called, hoping his voice would remind them they were not alone, including both himself and the unknown superhuman being that just tried to kill them all. His interruption was ignored once again. "Guys!" he snapped, fed up with the dismissal of his existence. Nowell finally pulled his face away from Annemarie's and shot Alistair an annoyed glance. When the men locked eyes, he continued. "Where's it at?"

Annemarie stuttered out, "O-oh, uh . . ." as she looked over her shoulder to pinpoint the last-known location of the body riddled with bullets from Nowell's handgun.

Nowell gestured with a lift of his chin to an area behind Alistair. "It went down right over there."

"Did you see it get back up?" Alistair asked with a hint of sass in his voice.

A careless giggle escaped Annemarie. "We've, uh, been a little busy, Al." She reached a curled-up hand to Nowell's cheek and pawed at his face to direct his lips back to hers.

Alistair swiped the flashlight from off the ground and juggled it with his shotgun until he was holding them both in a comfortable, ready-to-act position. He turned on his toes to face the opposite direction and solo marched to find the creature. He took a dozen wide strides to a depression in the weeds and roots and practically leaped out of his skin at the sight of the body sprawled out in front of him.

Taking every precaution possible, Alistair set his gun butt-end down in the mud and shoved the handle of the flashlight into his open mouth. He fished out a pair of nitrile gloves from his back pocket and slid them over his clammy hands with a little effort. He knelt beside the creature, holding his breath again to steady himself. His fingers inched over the cold-to-the-touch skin, trying to find a heartbeat, or lack thereof, in the typical human spots. It looked a lot like him or Riggs or Nowell—surely, its anatomy could be similar. With the tips of his index and middle fingers pressed against the carotid artery, Alistair felt nothing. No pulsating, no thrum, no vitality. He exhaled the deep breath he had been holding.

He fell back into a resting position with less strain on his knees. But he ended up flat on his back the moment the creature's right arm swiped out from its side, aimed square at Alistair who was shouting every obscenity he could muster at the top of his lungs. He heard a skittering of feet and assumed the lovebirds were coming to his aid—but he did not care at this point. The creature was still alive.

Despite its attempt at one final, yet meager attack, nothing more came from it. The grey, clouded-over eyes blankly stared at Alistair; its head crooked ever so slightly in his direction to indicate it saw him, it knew he was there, knew he was witnessing its last breath. For the briefest of moments, a pang of sadness and pity for the creature washed over him. But seeing its mouth full of clenched, razor-sharp teeth as it grimaced and its blood-stained fingertips helplessly pawing at its sides as the life force drained into a thick pool under the body . . . Alistair was instantly reminded that this murderous creature deserved no sympathy.

Not for the death of Jesse McCready or Peter Arthur, not for the death of Moose, and certainly not for the attack it launched at him minutes earlier. Its death meant sleepy, quiet, uneventful life on Port Harrow could carry on.

Annemarie slid to a stop a few feet behind Alistair who was still on his back. They both witnessed a brilliant flash of silver illuminating in the creature's eyes before its muscles went slack and the color of its skin darkened. It was gone, officially expired.

Alistair slowly returned to his knees and got back onto his feet on his own. He straightened his spine, feeling pops and cracks along the vertebrae, and twisted his head to the left and the right, stretching out the kinks. One giant pop caused his head to swim, leaving him woozy. He shot out a hand to catch onto anything. He found nothing, and instead, hula-hooped in place for several seconds.

"You okay?" Annemarie's voice startled him; he had not realized she had sidled up to him.

He thought for a moment, delicately nodded, and replied, "I'll be fine."

"Oh, ew, Al, you're bleeding." Her hand shot across his body to point at the large stain on his shirt.

"It's nothing." He slipped the gloves off his hands and stuffed them into a front pocket. "I-I don't know what to do about this."

"What do you mean? You're the sheriff," Nowell said as he joined them, as if announcing brand-new news to the party.

Raising a hand to the back of his head to gingerly rub a sore spot that throbbed, Alistair grimaced. "I'm a sheriff of *people*. This thing—" He gestured to the supine form. "—isn't human. I can't risk us trying to load it into my car in case it's playing possum. And to call the coroner to collect him, it, I-I don't know. Who do you call when you've killed a cryptid?"

256

Nowell lazily shrugged one shoulder. "Dig it a grave. Set it on fire. I don't give a shit. I'm just glad it's dead."

Alistair mulled over the protocol. A wave of exhaustion had been creeping up on him since they started the hunt for the creature; the adrenaline kept his heart rapidly beating and the need to remain quiet while barging through the brush was enough to wipe him out. Add onto that grappling with a being that felt like it was chiseled from concrete, and now every muscle in his body weighed fifty pounds; it exhausted him to take a step.

A loud, muffled noise sounded above him, a voice crashing through the treetops. It came so suddenly that it startled him, causing him to jump six inches off the ground and let out an unannounced shout.

"What's wrong?" Annemarie asked, agog at his reaction.

"Didn't you hear that?"

She raised a single eyebrow. "Hear what?"

"That voice."

"Voice? What voice?" She scrunched up the features on one side of her face and shot him a look of extreme disbelief.

"You seriously didn't hear someone shouting something just now?"

"I heard *you*," she insisted. "Do you know what he's talking about, Nowell?" She looked up at her companion, staring deep into his eyes.

He gave a quick shake of his head. "I didn't hear anything either. What did the voice say?"

"I-I don't know. It wasn't audible. No, I mean—it wasn't intelligible. It sounded like a woman's voice, though."

Annemarie and Nowell exchanged wide-eye stares. "I think maybe you should get your head checked out, hun," she said. Her tone was patronizing, though not entirely unsympathetic.

"Eh, whatever, you're probably right." He flicked his wrist at her. He did not want to fight. He was too tired to argue, to carry on a conversation where it was already two against one, even if they did not mean for it to be. "Let's head back. I'll bring Riggs out here tomorrow to deal with this." He motioned in the direction of Annemarie's house. She huddled into Nowell's side as they plodded their way back home, seeking comfort after a long stretch of unrest. After collecting his belongings, Alistair followed, begrudgingly the third wheel, staying several yards behind them. Their return was uneventful. Until Alistair heard another muffled scream far off in the distance. He spun in place, trying to pinpoint where it came from.

"You okay, Al?" Annemarie called from the stoop at the rear of the house. She pushed her wild hair away from her face and squinted at him through the darkness.

With his back still to her, he asked, "You swear you didn't hear that?"

"Hear *what*?" She descended one step.

The sound came again. This time, it was shriller and lasted a few seconds longer than before. "That! There!" He turned to look at her, to gauge her reaction at the obvious disturbance.

Annemarie's eyes were wide, her eyebrows creating deep creases in her forehead. "I didn't hear anything." She continued down the stairs and cut across the yard to stand beside him. He remained still. He craned his neck to listen harder, to concentrate on how it bounced through the trees. She reached a hand to his shoulder and caught him off guard. "It's probably an animal."

After another quiet thirty seconds, he nodded. "I'm sure that's what it is." His dismissal of the noise prompted them to walk to the house together. Alistair opened his mouth to say he was going home, but he stopped dead in his tracks and fell to his knees. His hands shot to either side of his head and he let out a loud groan as he tried to fold over and bury his head between his legs. The world blurred and spun.

"Al!" Annemarie cried out. It sounded like she was miles away.

He closed his eyes tight as he waited for everything to stop moving. When the excruciating pain behind his eyes subsided and he no longer felt like he was about to expel the contents of his stomach, he popped open one eyelid to make sure all was well.

"Are you okay?" she asked. She rested a cool hand on the base of his neck.

"I-I think so." He climbed onto his feet, slowly but surely, and hung back a moment to ensure he was fine.

"You should get checked out. Make sure you didn't get a concussion when you fell."

He shrugged one shoulder. "I didn't hit my head."

Not wanting to argue, she added, "Well, do whatever you think's best for yourself. Be careful when you're driving home."

He nodded. "Yeah, of course." They idly stood shoulder to shoulder, not saying anything further for another minute. He finally broke the silence. "I'll bring Riggs in the morning. You don't need to be here for it, if you're, y'know, busy." He motioned to the house with a raised chin, meaning Nowell.

"Okay."

"Have a good night, I guess."

"You too."

They gave each other an awkward parting wave. Alistair shuffled to his cruiser at the front of the house in the total darkness; not even a porch light leading the way. He climbed inside, buckled his belt, and started the engine. Rock music turned low filled the interior as he pulled out of the driveway and made his way to the south end of the island. He encountered no traffic on the road, but still found he was hitting all the red lights along the way.

Half a mile from the station, he heard a noise. A whisper. An extraordinarily loud whisper rattling around the inside of his head. He turned up the volume of the radio to see if it was part of the track. Nothing in the song came close to what he heard. He pushed the knob to turn off the music entirely.

In the parking lot of the station, the moment he turned off the engine—making all noises stop—the whisper came again. It was clearer, closer than it had previously been, but it was still impossible to pinpoint what was being said or where it was coming from.

Riggs sat at the front desk, the landline telephone to his left, the communications setup for the police radio to his right, and a thick paperback directly in front of him. The spine of it was so cracked and worn, it had no issue staying open on its own, allowing him to rest his face in his hands in order to read.

"Evening," Alistair said as he entered the small front office.

Riggs finished reading the sentence he was on, set a finger to the page to mark the spot where he left off, and glanced up to greet Alistair. A slight sneer crept over his nose and upper lip as he witnessed Alistair's disheveled appearance. "Uh, hey. You good?"

He shrugged and reached his left hand over his right shoulder to scratch his back. "Eh."

Riggs pointed at him. "You're . . . You've got a bit of . . . uh . . ."

Alistair glanced down, finally able to give himself the once-over he desperately needed, now in full light. Besides the shoulder wound, the elbows of his sleeves were stained brown with dried blood that had soaked through the material. The buttons over his stomach had come undone and the shirt flaps were untucked. The seat of his pants and all the way down the legs were caked in drying mud. He looked a mess. He now understood the look of confusion—of consternation—Riggs gave him.

"What happened to you?"

Alistair ran both hands over his eyes toward his ears and let out a hefty sigh bordering on a groan. "It's been a night."

"I can see that. All you said was you were headed to Annie's. Oh god—*Annie*. Is she okay?"

Alistair raised a hand to quell Riggs's panic. "She's fine. Better than fine."

Riggs cocked an eyebrow. "What was going on up there, then?" He had remained mostly out of the loop with the current events unfolding in Annemarie's backyard. He knew about all of the incidents, of course, but the wild theory that a creature of supernatural origin was the culprit was above his pay grade.

Alistair wanted to go straight home, but he knew he needed to fill in Riggs before dragging him into the woods in the morning. With another sigh, he leaned his hip against the counter and told the tale of the creature's trail of bodies, ending with the final takedown. He left out any mention of him bearing witness to Annemarie and Nowell cozying up—it was not his story to tell.

Riggs was equal parts enthralled and horrified with a touch of dismay that he had not been kept in the loop. He was also a little less than eager to accompany Alistair in the morning, especially after his current late-night shift on desk duty. But he would go regardless. Morbid curiosity had gotten the best of him.

A tickle behind the ear caused Alistair to tilt his head to one side in order to scratch at it. The harsh whisper came on suddenly like a powerful wave of nausea and disorientation. He perked up, straightened his spine, and his eyes went animal-on-alert wide. "Did you hear that?"

he asked. He glanced around the room. He hoped it was static noise or interference from the police radio. With Riggs shaking his head, Alistair knew he was alone—but he still had no idea where the noise was coming from or why. "I'm exhausted. It's been a really, *really* long day."

"Get some sleep and come back in the morning. We'll get to it all then." Riggs bobbed his head toward the door.

Alistair gently pounded a fist on the counter as a means of agreement that, *yes*, he needed sleep. Copious amounts of it. He turned on his heel with a squeak of the sole on the linoleum. As he pushed through the double doors into the dark, dusky night, he unknowingly left a trail of crumbling dirt on the lobby floor.

The drive from the station to his house was unremarkable. In the driveway, up the stairs, into the one-story home, stripped down to his boxer briefs—he did not bother to shower or brush his teeth. He would deal with it when he woke up.

But sleep did not come easily.

He tossed and turned.

He counted sheep to redirect his thoughts.

He tried to power through as many sit-ups as he could to tire himself further.

It was no use.

Lying on his back meant needing to fold his arms over his chest to keep his sore, scabbed elbows from resting on the mattress. On either side left him feeling uncomfortable in an unfamiliar position. In the prone was out of the question too. But it was not all about that; his brain would not shut up. It focused on every aspect of the evening, from tracking the creature as a trio, being taken down by it—albeit temporarily—and suddenly finding himself alone, bleeding in the mud as he watched his best friend making out with the man who was responsible for her husband's death.

It was surreal. It did not make sense. But there it was, unfolding in front of him. No matter how many times he hard-blinked the sight—the memory—away, it remained burned into his brain.

A violent jolt rocked the entire bedroom.

He sprang out of bed and headed straight for the doorjamb. Earthquakes were not rare in their part of the world, but ones large enough to feel were. But for as much as his entire body trembled, nothing inside the house moved. At the very least, the hanging light fixtures in the kitchen should have had some kind of momentum left in them, but they were perfectly still. He could not recall any sounds of things clattering together either.

Maybe I fell asleep and it was one of those hypnic jerk things that woke me up. He nodded to himself. He was embarrassed for making a mountain out of a molehill. Even with this sound justification, he was still rattled.

He walked into the kitchen to grab a drink. On the way back to the bedroom, he detoured to the couch. If he found no comfort under his blankets, maybe the soft, worn cushions of his faux leather couch could lull him to sleep. Maybe being upright was key.

He plopped onto the middle seat and sipped at his water. The mug clinked onto something hard as he tried to set it on the coffee table. Through the darkness, he reached out to feel for the item: his holstered gun. He did not remember leaving it out—he always put it in the safe in the coat closet. Had he been *that* tired when he got home? No excuse could justify that kind of irresponsibility.

While his fingers caressed the grip of the sidearm, contemplating getting up to put it away now, an intense wave of vertigo washed over him accompanied by a distant scream filling his ears. It was so loud, painful, jarring. It was all he could do to not curl up into the fetal position and cry out in harmony with the wail, to let it know he heard it, he commiserated. He closed his eyes and counted to a slow ten while taking deep breaths in between. The panic and upset in him eventually subsided.

But almost immediately, the silent chatter started again. Intrusive, invasive images of him watching Nowell's head, tilted down ever so slightly, mashing his big nose and hungry lips against Annemarie's perfect, delicate, beautiful features. Alistair could not stop focusing on every inch of her. A rush of excessive emotions overtook him. He spent so long suppressing all the feelings he ever had for her, spanning back to their early high school days to that night in the spare bedroom at Nic's house. They were never in sync after that night, and after Jesse's death, there was nothing appropriate about the love that had followed him for two decades. He had long ago given up the chase, knowing it was a one-sided yearning, but his brush with, well, whatever tonight was, would not let him drop the emotions—any of them.

A rage built. Not because of the resentment or a grudge he had no right feeling, but that his mind would not stop replaying the scene. Their kisses, their flippant attitudes, their exclusion of him—*it hurt*. It hurt as much as the endlessly spinning room, the ear-piercing screams and cries that plagued him.

He returned his focus to the gun for a brief moment. He snapped open the strap over the hammer and slid out the firearm. He brought it to rest on the bare flesh of his thigh with his finger nonchalantly, naturally, rested on the trigger. His thumb stroked along the barrel.

A wave of nausea washed over him and subsided as he heard the scream loud and clear: *"You fucking coward . . . do it."*

Without missing a beat, he opened his mouth wide enough to accommodate the cold muzzle of the gun and pulled the trigger.

TWENTY-TWO

There was nothing but darkness.

All around were deep sobs full of panic, dread, and disbelief. "Alistair. Alistair. Wake up. Come on." Annemarie tugged on his lifeless arms. "Alistair. This isn't funny. Wake up." The tears were already streaming down her face the moment she watched the creature's lightning-fast form easily vault twenty feet through the air and land on Alistair's chest, the both of them hitting the ground with an audible thud and a shuffle of crunchy leaves. Her instinct was to run toward the two, but Nowell reached out to grab her by the upper arm to stop her from moving.

"What're you going to do?" he had asked. She did not have an answer. Instead, she stood there and cried. She screamed for him. She kept her distance. Even with all the commotion she made, the creature was focused on Alistair like he was the only quarry in existence.

"Alistair, Alistair, please wake up. Alistair, come on." With her hands firmly planted on his shoulders, she shook him, gently at first, then more vigorously when he did not respond. Overcome with an uninhibited rage coming out of nowhere, she muttered, "You fucking coward. You're not allowed to do this. You can't leave me too. You're not allowed to do it." Fingers to his neck told her there was a heartbeat—slow, faint, but there. She changed tactics.

"Alistair . . ." she whimpered. She let her hand run along the length of his face, stroking his cheek. "Please." Her voice came out as a hoarse squeak. Another tear rolled along and landed on the tip of his nose.

Alistair's eyelashes fluttered for a moment before his eyelids shot open. He was flat on his back, looking straight up, the only light to be found emanating from the flashlight at Annemarie's side on the forest floor. It gave him enough illumination to see her outline but little else. Even in the relative darkness, he could feel her presence, her hand on his cheek, hear her pleading and crying, smell her mix of shampoo and sweat.

Confused, he asked, "Annie, what's wrong?"

In a scream of surprise and delight, she startled him. "Oh my god, Alistair!" She sucked back the snot that had started to trickle out of her nose and wiped her eyes dry with the back of her free hand as she tried to rein in the emotions freely flowing. "You're alive!"

A flurry of noises came barreling toward Alistair's supine form and Annemarie slumped over his torso. Her head shot up to investigate, hoping, praying it was not the creature returning. Nowell headed a cavalry of uniformed men in a straight line over the gnarled tree roots and through the spiderweb-draped bushes. Riggs was hot on the trail, mere feet behind Nowell, and paramedics DJ and Steven were not long after.

"Oh, fuck, man, you're okay," Nowell announced as he reached Alistair and Annemarie first.

Alistair attempted to sit up, using his stomach muscles to propel himself forward. But the moment he reached about one-hundred-fifty degrees, his head physically wobbled on his neck and he went right back down. "That remains to be determined," he muttered.

Heaving out a labored breath, DJ knelt beside Alistair and immediately checked his vitals including shining the pesky penlight directly into each of his pried-open eyes. His head already ached with a massive migraine and the wash of low-beam light constricting his pupils did not help alleviate the pain. When DJ determined his basics were good, his eyes and fingers moved to the wound on Alistair's shoulder.

He gave instructions to Steven. "This has gotta come off." He tugged at Alistair's shirt to indicate what he meant by *this*, but Steven was already pulling out a pair of shears to accommodate the request.

Alistair protested. "Whoa, hang on a sec. I can unbutton the damn thing. No need to ruin a perfectly good shirt."

"Uh, Sheriff, this thing's a goner." Steven pointed to the dinner-plate-sized bloodstain as well as the remnants of material that stood zero chance of being repaired. "This is faster." The shears zipped up the front of the button-down, leaving Alistair in his bloodied A-shirt. Pain sizzled over his skin as DJ worked on cleaning out the wound and determining whether or not it needed stitches. Alistair directed his attention to find Annemarie in their small crowd of six. She had been pushed aside by Steven and was now standing a short distance away, talking to Nowell in a hushed voice.

She reached an arm up to him, patted his shoulder, and the gesture turned into a hug. But before Alistair could even try to shake away the image of what came next—her leaping into his arms and them sharing a passionate kiss—Nowell turned in place and made his way away from the scene, alone. Annemarie shuffled up alongside Riggs, who leaned his head to one side to exchange a few quiet words with her. She responded in kind. They both faced away from Alistair and took several steps deeper into the woods, her pointing and gesturing in the distance.

"All right, let's get you up," DJ said. Strong hands gripped in his armpits as both paramedics hoisted him into a sitting position. His head still swam, but he had their support to keep him upright. "No signs of a concussion, so you're good there. No stitches needed on that wound either. We'll walk you to the rig and see how you're feeling by that point. If you want a ride back to your place, we can do that."

Alistair shook his head, but immediately regretted the motion. "Let's play it by ear."

"One, two, three." DJ and Steven got Alistair up onto his feet, and after a brief bout of vertigo that passed as quickly as it came on, he thought he was steady enough to walk unassisted. The migraine lessened to more of a throbbing at the base of his skull. The pain in his muscles caused him to take stiff steps while he monitored his balance, like the second day after running a marathon he had poorly prepared for. The tug of the medical tape holding the gauze over the shoulder wound was a constant reminder that he had not escaped unscathed, but at least everyone was alive. *Alive.*

"Wait," he said, and stopped suddenly. "Annie!" He spun in place to find her out in the woods behind them, her flashlight giving away her position. The move made him want to puke when it finally caught up to his brain.

She interrupted her conversation by setting a hand against Riggs's chest to quiet him. "What's up?"

"Where . . ." His eyes scanned the horizon, trying to piece together any details of what happened once the creature bailed. "How did . . ." A coherent sentence could not form in his mind. He saw her and Riggs, he saw Steven and DJ beside him, he knew where he was and he mostly knew what happened, but he could not stop focusing on what he had seen transpire between her and Nowell. The last thing he remembered prior to Annemarie's tear dripping onto his face was being in his living room, the drastic measure he took with his sidearm, the complete darkness and nothingness.

Annemarie's goodbye with Nowell was nothing more than two friends parting ways; there was nothing lascivious or uncouth about that. Did that mean they had not shot and killed the creature either? "Annie, where's the—" He stopped himself short as he watched her approach, taking big steps over fallen forest detritus.

She sidled up to him and threaded her arm underneath his, both as a means for comfort and to guide him as they made their way to the ambulance. "What's going on?" she asked quietly.

"What *happened*?" he finally managed. "Where's the *thing*?" He stressed the word as quietly as he could, not wanting Steven or DJ to overhear.

"Gone," she whispered back. She cuddled into his side a little deeper and took a big breath, relieved he was okay.

"So, it's still out there." Not a question.

"Unless it bleeds out from all the bullets Nowell put in it, yes."

The wind picked up, fluttering dead leaves across Annemarie's backyard as the group silently made their way to the collection of vehicles at the front of the house. She loosened her grip on his arm when she thought he was capable enough of staying upright on his own, allowing her to make her way back to Riggs. She exchanged a few more quiet words with him before he turned his eyes to Alistair, then back to her, accompanied by a shallow nod.

"Well, Sheriff, how you feeling?" Steven asked.

Alistair made a quick movement with his head, jerking it from side to side to see if the wooziness had abated. He flashed a thumbs-up and shrugged. "Seems good enough to get me home."

"All right, then we'll head out. You know the drill: Any redness or swelling from that cut, or feelings of fever or the dizziness returning, give us a call. We're off in about an hour, but we'll make sure Des and Ilya know what happened." DJ gave Alistair a comforting pat on his unharmed shoulder before climbing into the rig.

Alistair stood beside Riggs and Annemarie, watching the paramedics drive away, lights off and at a leisurely pace. Riggs turned on his heel to face Alistair. "I'm gonna follow you home. Just to make sure you get there in one piece."

With a nod, he replied, "Probably for the best. You're back on desk duty anyway, right?"

"Yep. Till five, when you're supposed to come in."

Alistair rubbed at a tender spot at the back of his head. "Would you mind hanging out till six? I think I'm gonna need a little extra time to wind down from tonight's bullshit."

"Not a problem. Let me know if you need longer. Worst case, I can call in Cami to cover the desk or get one of the other deputies to do it when they get in." Riggs gave Alistair that same comforting pat on the same shoulder. "Get some rest." He faced Annemarie. "Both of you." His tone was stern.

She could not help but smirk. "Yes, mom."

"*Someone's* gotta look after you two when Cecily isn't around."

They shared a laugh, but they dwindled into a quick silence that saw them all head in different directions when it was obvious no one had anything else to say: Annemarie to her front door, Alistair to his SUV, Riggs to his cruiser. The engines of the two vehicles started up, and before Annemarie could turn to give a parting wave, Riggs was already backed up onto the asphalt and Alistair was seconds behind. She watched their taillights disappear along the curve of the road before considering sleep might come much easier if she had a drink.

Her nerves were shot. No one would, or could, believe what she, Nowell, and Alistair had experienced. *Alistair.* What the fuck had happened to him? Why did he keep looking at her with that expression that spoke volumes without ever uttering a word? She was certain she had lost him tonight, certain that his demise alongside Jesse's and Moose's would be the thing that ended her too.

She sat with the thought as she warmed a dram of whisky between her hands. She brought the glass to her lips, but it rested there a long moment before she took a sip. The glass returned to the coffee table without so much as a drop gone, and she was up off the couch before the liquid could quit sloshing in the snifter.

TWENTY-THREE

Alistair's SUV gradually rolled to a stop at the bottom of his shallow driveway. With little effort, he placed the car in park and turned off the engine. Riggs followed a solid thirty seconds behind him, making sure to flash his light bar in recognition of Alistair's arrival home and that he was headed back to the station. With a sore hand, he gripped the handle of the door, pulled it toward him, and pushed his body out of the car. Having sat for the duration of the trip home after his little tumble with the creature left his legs feeling tight, causing him to shuffle toward the front stoop. Up the stairs to the unlit front door, he fumbled for the right key to get inside. With it being so late at night, there were few sounds in his vicinity. When the door swung open a little too fast, it banged against the wall behind it and echoed loudly. He flinched at the sound, mostly sensitive to the fact that it left a dent in the drywall.

He closed the door behind him. He flipped on the light with the nearby switch, casually kicked off his black boots, and peeled off each sock by tucking the big toe of the opposing foot under the elastic band holding them against his calves. They were to be left in an untidy pile until the morning, he decided. Lately, it seemed like *everything* was left in an untidy pile until the morning.

"Should probably do something about that," he muttered as a quick scan of the room revealed many procrastination piles. He set his keys on the small table beside the door where he normally left them, wallet, and cell phone: essentials for any time he left the house. He emptied his pockets and found a couple small rocks had wriggled their way in. His hands reached for the buckle of his duty belt, fingers deftly maneuvering to remove it and the gun holster, to leave on the coffee table in the middle of the room. As he glided through the house, from the living room to his bedroom, he unbuttoned and unzipped his muddy, brown work pants and let them fall to the carpeted floor as he peeled off the bloodied A-shirt. He swapped into a clean one and entered the adjacent bathroom to retrieve a washcloth to clean his wounds.

With intent to head back to the living room, he wet the cloth with hot water, wrung it out, and beelined to the big, soft, well-worn couch. He flopped onto the middle cushion with a heavy sigh. He propped up his feet on the edge of the table to take a quick peek at his knees and legs in the hopes he would find no additional scratches. He was happy to report—to himself—that they were in good condition. He twisted his right arm toward his body, trying to spy on his elbow, which had a thin layer of caked-on blood. Nothing a little moistening and gentle rubbing could not fix. With a few dabs and one hefty wipe, the scrape came clean and did not weep any further. He repeated the motion for his left elbow. Letting the length of his arms air-dry, he tossed the damp cloth onto the coffee table beside the pile of outdoorsman magazines and his holstered gun. He shuddered, thinking about the vision he experienced in the woods. Everything about it was incredibly realistic, vivid like a waking dream. He eyed the gun again, practically sneering at it.

A knock on the front door startled him. He glanced at his watch and saw it was a few minutes after eleven. Internally fighting with himself—not wanting to touch his gun at this moment, but not sure who would be standing on his front stoop this late at night—he relented and popped the Glock from its leather holster, removed the magazine to double-check it was at capacity, and inched toward the front door. Without a peephole, he could not see who awaited him. Gun in his right hand, he turned the knob with his left and peered out into the darkness. The lights from the street barely illuminated his property, but it was enough to recognize the telltale ponytail belonging to Annemarie. Another sigh of relief.

She stood on the stoop with her hands firmly tucked into her folded arms. "Hey," she said unemotionally. Alistair peered past her and saw her vehicle sitting behind his personal car in the driveway.

"Hey." He did not budge from the door for a moment. Realizing she did not drive all this way to keep the front porch warm, he stepped away to allow her entry without saying a word. He took a moment to holster his gun and placed the entire unit under the table, out of sight. He would put it in its safe later.

As Annemarie entered the house, she, too, noticed the large number of untidy piles throughout the living room. Socks and work boots by the door; a pile of crumpled receipts on the side table where he kept his keys and wallet; magazines strewn across the coffee table and spilling onto the floor; a pile of laundry draped over the armrest of the couch—dirty or clean, she was not sure; and a stack of empty cereal bowls on the pass-through countertop leading into the kitchen. Alistair normally kept his place clean, so seeing things in this level of disarray worried her. *Maybe he's been busy,* she thought.

She did not wait for an invitation to jump into the overstuffed easy chair she loved so much. She made herself comfortable. He moseyed over to the couch and before sitting, said with a laugh, "I don't apologize for being half naked in my own living room." Annemarie smirked and gave him a little wink.

"You're not forgiven, then."

He sat on the couch cross-legged, but quickly reached for a throw pillow to place in his lap for modesty's sake. "So, what's up?"

"I wanted to make sure you're okay. Tonight was . . ." The word caught in her throat for a brief moment. ". . . intense." She used the tips of her fingers on both hands to push stray hairs behind her ears.

He gingerly rubbed at the back of his head and concurrently showed off one of his torn-up elbows, which was now without blood. "I'll be okay. I was fortunate to not wang my head when I fell, but I've been feeling dizzy ever since that sonofabitch touched me."

"Maybe it's vertigo. Maybe it dislodged one of those little nuggets in your ear."

"'One of those little nuggets'?" he asked with a half laugh.

"You know what I mean."

His smile dissipated. "This isn't like vertigo. No ear nuggets are free moving. This is more like the occasional swimmy-head. Cotton candy for brains." He lowered his elbow when he realized there was little to see. "Elbows seem intact. Butt's a little sore. This thing—" He pointed to the gauzed wound on his shoulder. "—that's gonna be a pain to deal with, but I can pop a pill and all'll be well. Well, as well as can be." He laughed again, more of a huff of breath, at this last sentence.

"You seem kinda shaken," she replied to his self-diagnosis.

With a slow blink, Alistair retorted, "Are ya serious?" He pointed over his shoulder with a thumb sticking out of a balled-up fist. "I just got attacked by a flesh-eating, blood-thirsty superhuman monster in the woods behind your house. I shot it multiple times and it didn't even flinch. And now it's at-large. *Yeah*, I think I'm a little shaken." His intention was not for it to sound so callous, but he did not regret it; he was not wrong. The high-eyebrowed look of concern on Annemarie's face turned to sadness at his outburst. He noticed the change immediately; then the regret came. "I'm sorry. I didn't mean to snap. I'm . . . I don't even know what's going on. This is all too—" He interrupted himself. "Annie, what're we gonna do?"

She shook her head, a look of incredulity on her face. Her lips tracked to one side, pursing them as she thought. "I honestly don't know. I thought tonight would be enough." A heavy breath escaped through her nose. "I'm out of ideas. Nowell's out of ideas. We both thought . . ."

Her eyes darted to her lap where she fiddled with her fingertips.

With the words hanging open between them, the silence stretching on, Alistair finally interjected. "What's going on with you two?"

She suddenly looked up. "Huh? What do you mean?"

"This guy ruined your life and now you're out cavorting in the woods together, trying to—"

"I am *not* cavorting with him," she snapped. "I already told you: I've forgiven Nowell. Honestly, there was nothing to forgive. He and Travis were in the wrong place at the wrong time, and now that we've both witnessed this motherfucking thing, and Nowell could give me all the details to describe it to a T, I know he's telling the truth. I forgave him and we've been bonding about this . . . *this thing*." She huffed. "So can you please stop asking about it?"

Alistair chewed on his bottom lip then begrudgingly nodded. "If you tell me to leave it, I will."

"I've told you a million times, dude," she pushed back.

His head tilted and a perked-up cheek revealed the slight smile on his lips as he replied, "More like once. But 'a million,' 'one,' potato, potahto." He gave a friendly shrug. But then his expression turned serious. "How long was I out for?"

"Huh?"

"In the woods. After it . . . How long was I out for?"

"Fifteen minutes, maybe a little more. I mean, I wasn't timing it, and it felt like a lifetime. But Nowell was on the phone pretty quick and ran off not too long after."

Her lips tightened as she thought about his question further. Alistair shook his head. "What?"

"It couldn't have—" He paused mid-sentence. "It had to have been more than that."

She tapped a finger against her philtrum. "I honestly can't think that it was more than that. Going full speed in the rig and with no traffic at this time of night, the guys absolutely could've gotten here in that time. They may not have even been at the garage when they got the call." She shook her head. "Yeah. I don't know. It wasn't, like, an hour or anything."

"You're sure?"

"Why?"

"I—" How did he explain what happened when *he* was not even sure himself? "My . . . hm. I guess . . . My recollection of things is fuzzy."

"The guys cleared you of a concussion," she reminded.

"Not like that. It's more like—you ever have a dream that's so vivid that when you wake up, you're convinced what you experienced in your sleep actually happened?"

"Yeah, sure. That's happened a lot since Jesse died."

"This is like that. I remember fighting with the thing. We were wrestling on the ground, it tore into my shoulder, took my gun from me, and had its hands around my throat. But then Nowell started shooting at it and it left me alone. He killed it, and you and him—" He stopped himself short but Annemarie took over the conversation.

"But Nowell didn't."

"No, I know that. But this is also in my memory." The wound on his shoulder throbbed and he set the flat of his hand against it, hoping to steady the thrumming of the pain. "I decided that I'd bring Riggs back in the morning to deal with the body. Which seemed strange to even suggest. I mean, why would we just leave it there? I started hearing these noises and they followed me all the way home."

"Noises? Like what?"

"Screaming."

"Screaming?" she echoed.

"I can't describe it any better than that. I got home and into bed and I started feeling these, like, jolts. I honestly thought we were having an earthquake. But between these electric sort of movements and the noise getting louder and louder, I . . ." He was not sure he wanted to finish the story. "I ended up . . . killing myself." The final two words came out barely above a whisper.

"You *what*?"

Alistair could not tell if she was incredulous or unable to hear him, so he repeated himself. "I killed myself. Stuck the gun in my mouth and—" He mimed the barrel of the handgun in his mouth and an explosion from the back of his skull.

Annemarie shuddered and let out an audible noise to accompany it. "That's dark, Alistair." She sucked in a deep breath and held it for a moment before letting it slowly ease out of her, giving her time to collect her thoughts. "So, obviously, that didn't happen. You're still here."

"But I remember everything. I even remember the taste and feel of the gun on my tongue. That's . . . I've *never* done anything even close to that in my entire life, yet, I *know* what that sensation is now."

She readjusted herself on the armchair, tucking her feet underneath her to sink in even deeper. "Do you think it's some kind of 'this is your future' scenario?"

He thought for a second, then shook his head. "No. Well, I mean, I can't know for sure, I guess, but it was too similar to what actually happened to feel like I'd ever repeat it." He sighed. "I don't know. Everything about this is messed up. Nothing makes sense."

"By 'this,' you mean . . ."

"That there's a monster hunting and eating us on the island. Or anywhere, for that matter." Neither of them had anything to add. Alistair took the silence as an adequate time to break away to the kitchen. "Want something to drink?"

"I'm good."

He leaned into the fridge to grab a beer and popped off the cap. On his way back, he studied Annemarie's face. She was stoic, not even looking like a thought was infiltrating her mind. The blank expression across her eyes dissipated when he returned to the couch and flopped down on the cushion, accompanied by a tight hiss as the ache in his entire body reminded him of what he had endured.

He dug his thumbnail under the label of the bottle and sighed. "I wish . . ." He took a drink and waited until it hit his stomach before he continued. "I wish I knew what this was. At least then we'd be able to make an actual plan. We know what it looks like and how it acts." He leaned forward and set his elbows against his kneecaps, but immediately regretted it when he was met with another shock of pain. "If we knew what it was, maybe we could figure out what it wanted. Or why it's here. Or ev-even how to kill it. Because bullets definitely don't seem like they do a damn thing. It moves too fast to ensure a headshot. And okay, what if we *do* find out what it is: How do we find it again? Is it smart enough to know we're hunting it? Is it possible . . ."

He continued his rambling at such a rapid pace that Annemarie found herself zoning out. She did not mean to, but he was asking too many questions with zero answers to be had. She wanted to figure this out as much as he did—she had been the most affected by it—but so late at night, after a traumatic evening in the woods, after almost losing him . . . she could not feign enough interest.

She was not even sure he had finished talking when she blurted out, "I don't know what to tell you, hun."

"No, I know you don't. I'm just talking to talk at this point. I'm at a loss for *anything*." He got quiet suddenly, out of words or out of gas, then finally opened his mouth. Annemarie only heard a sharp intake of breath. "I . . . have something to admit."

She dug her top teeth into her bottom lip. "What's that?"

"I've encountered this thing before, I think." Her eyes grew wide at the admission but then her brow furrowed and a deep crease set itself between her eyebrows. "Yeah. On the night of the Fourth—"

She cut him off. "You mentioned something about that before. The other day. We—"

He returned the interruption and nodded. "Yeah, we didn't get into it. But, uh, on the way back to your place, I think we ran across it on the highway."

"*We?*"

A stilted sigh left him. He proceeded to detail what he watched happen in front of him, the ethereal body crossing his path, the feeling of overwhelming dread seeping into his bones. He studied her expression as he spoke and that same unemotional facade he had seen earlier remained.

"Why didn't you say something before?"

"I didn't think it mattered. Figured I was, I don't know, exhausted from the heat and sunshine and the fight and the cleanup and *life* and was seeing things. But after tonight, I know it's important." He paused. "The one thing I can't figure out—"

"You haven't figured out *anything* about this," she reminded.

He scrunched up his features and shot her an annoyed glare. "*What I can't figure out* is why something as simple as me fighting back with a push of my hand in its face was the thing that made it let go. I shot it. Repeatedly. And it didn't even flinch." He snapped his fingers a few times, thinking, and then pointed a finger at her. "You got your phone on you?"

She nodded and fished it from her pocket to hand over. He spent several minutes typing away on the screen, frowning, typing some more, and then finally letting out a defeated sigh, his whole body deflating.

"What's up?" she asked.

"It was a crapshoot anyway."

"What was?"

"I was trying to see if I could find any information about it online. A lot of different cryptid-centric sites came up, but nothing worthwhile." He handed her the phone and leaned back into the couch. He closed his eyes and breathed deeply.

"I need you to know something." Her voice made Alistair's eyes gradually open.

"Hmm?"

"The reason Nowell and I have been . . ." She trailed off, still forming a coherent sentence.

He raised his free hand to stop her, the other still holding onto the beer. "You don't hafta explain anything about your relationship with him. See who you want to see."

One of her eyebrows shot up. "What? I'm not dating him, you idiot."

He shrugged. "I don't know that. I don't *need* to know that either. What you do with your free time—"

"Will you just shut up for a sec?" She set her fingers to her forehead and closed her eyes while she gathered the nerves and energy to continue. Without looking at him, she said, "What I'm trying to say is that the reason he and I have gotten so buddy-buddy recently is because we've had something awful to bond over. In the time that this particular crap has been going on, you've . . . Well, you've kind of brushed me off. And . . . that didn't—*doesn't*—feel good." Alistair's mouth opened a little, more of a sign of being aghast than wanting to say anything in protest or in his favor. She glanced up through her eyelashes at him. "It hurt, knowing that you were chalking up my experiences to hallucinations, not being in the right frame of mind."

"But I honestly thought that. I wasn't using it as an excuse to not believe you. I promise."

"I know. But it doesn't change how it made me feel."

His throat was tight and dry at this and he desperately wanted a drink of the beer, but assumed it would come across as a type of nonchalance he did not want to give off. "I'm sorry, Annie. I really am. I never meant to hurt you. You know I never would on purpose."

Annemarie blinked a few times in quick succession while she processed his apology. "I do know that." She paused again. "My point isn't to make you feel bad or anything, even if you do. It's to make note that Nowell and I had something really fucking strange in common and that's why I'm kinda sorta friends with him . . ." The last part trailed off into a quiet mumble like she, herself, was still coming to terms with this new development.

"That absolutely makes sense." He gave several short nods as he thought about his behavior over the last year. But in his ruminations, he lowered his eyebrows and shot his gaze over to her. "Hey, do you know if he was recording?"

"What?"

"Nowell. Was he recording with his phone, or just using the infrared, night vision, whatever it was?"

She shrugged. "I honestly don't know. I could find out easily enough, though."

"Would you mind doing that? If he recorded it, I'd like to take a look at the footage. If, y'know, he has the capability of transferring it to a thumb drive or something and getting it to you. Of course, assuming he even *has* any footage.”

She chewed on her lower lip. “Yeah, I’ll text him.” Even with how late it was, Nowell still had to catch the hour-long ferry to Brownstone, get to his place, and wind down for the night—the likelihood he was asleep was slim, so she shot him a message.

With her phone finally face down on the armrest, she let go of a sigh mixed with exhaustion and exasperation. Even after everything they had been through that night, she had nothing left to say, nothing that would make any difference, at least. Alistair finally smacked both hands on his thighs with a silence-shattering *slap*.

“Well, despite probably almost dying tonight, I still have to go into work in the morning.”

Annemarie shifted to get up as well. “Yeah, totally. I should . . .” But before she could finish her sentence, Alistair pointed at the bedroom.

“You know you’re welcome to crash here tonight. Save you the drive. Especially with the beastie still on the loose.”

She gave a visible shudder. “Yeah, that’s not a bad idea.”

“I’ll take the couch.”

“I’m not kicking you out of your own bed,” she protested.

“You’re not kicking me out. I’m offering. Besides . . .” He wiggled in place on the couch cushion. “This is feeling pretty comfortable right about now. I could fall right over and conk out.”

"You need to be able to stretch out. You've had a bad night and the last thing you need is to go all fetal on the couch. Take the bed. End of argument." She followed through on standing and hurried off to his bedroom to grab a blanket from his closet and a pillow from off the bed. She returned to stand in front of him, her meager height now towering over his seated form. She leered at him, trying to urge him to acquiesce.

Alistair raised a hand. "Fiiine. I'll take the bed." As he stood, she threw her bedding onto the couch, freeing her hands, and caught him in an unexpected embrace. She wrapped her arms up under his armpits and rested her fists on his shoulders.

"I'm glad you didn't die tonight," she said softly.

He hesitated a moment before setting the flat of a hand between her shoulder blades. "Me too." He paused. "Good night, Annie."

She disengaged herself and stepped back, allowing him an easy exit toward the bedroom. The bedroom light flicked on as the living room light turned off; it gave Annemarie enough glow to spread out the blanket, to climb underneath, get comfortable. She reached for her cell phone, set the alarm, and put it on the coffee table.

The bedroom light turned off too, the sound of the mattress groaning under Alistair's weight. Annemarie closed her eyes, somehow drifting off into a dreamless sleep.

But then her eyes shot open in the pitch-black room; her chest heaved and beads of sweat traced the edge of her hairline. She sat up, feeling around herself for her phone. Remembering it was on the table, she reached for it to wake it up. A bit after three o'clock. She had managed to sleep for a few hours.

She climbed off the couch to shuffle her way into Alistair's bedroom. Trying not to make any noise, she tucked into the bathroom, closing the door behind her and not bothering to turn on the light. When she flushed the toilet, he stirred in his sleep, and a gentle creak of a hinge fully brought him to.

Instead of heading back into the living room, Annemarie tiptoed her way to the foot of the bed, trying to judge which side Alistair was sleeping on. He often liked to take up the whole middle—it was his bed, why would he not?—and she did not want to trod on him when she climbed in. The faint illumination from the streetlight outside the window gave her enough of a silhouette to figure it out, and onto the mattress she went.

The only acknowledgment he provided was rolling onto his side, allowing her more room in the bed and the ability to climb under the blanket. She adjusted herself as best as she could, still unaware that he was completely awake. Her head nestled against the pillow, smelling a touch of his tea tree shampoo, where sleep found her quickly; but Alistair remained awake.

Try as he might, pressing his eyes closed, slowly counting from ten to zero, thinking up random words to distract his brain from any other thoughts . . . Nothing but hyperfocusing on the night's events came to him. Truthfully, he had not gotten much sleep prior to Annemarie shuffling through the house, him jerking awake as quickly as he had dozed.

He still could not wrap his brain around what he had experienced, from the grappling with the creature, to the vivid and lucid vision of his suicide, to the fact that it was still at-large—and after an hour of staring at the ceiling, he was done trying to sleep.

Annemarie's steady, soft snores let him know that he could ease himself out of the room without disturbing her; she was usually a deep sleeper and if she was snoring, she was dead to the world. He nonchalantly rolled out from under the blanket and set both feet on the hardwood. He reached for his cell phone on the side table, checked the time—just after four—and headed for the living room.

He was not sure what to do with himself. It was too early to get ready for work. He wanted to let Annemarie sleep for as long as possible. For as tired as he was, he knew she was tenfold. He sat on the couch, taking care with his bruised backside and the rest of his banged-up body, and settled deep into the cushion. He let his legs stretch out a little, trying not to put too much taut pressure on his kneecaps. His foot hit something.

He immediately leaned forward to fish for the gun holster under the coffee table. After all of their talking, he had completely forgotten to put it away in its safe. As he started to push himself off the couch to go to the closet, he hesitated long enough for gravity to pull him back down. The holster now rested on the table in front of him.

His lips moved back and forth as he chewed on the bottom one, giving the sidearm a good, long look. Without thinking, he pulled the gun from the leather cradle. But he kept it on the table while staring hard at it, never breaking eye contact or focus. His shoulders slumped, the tension in his neck feeling like it slid entirely down his spine. The gentlest huffs of breath left through his nose.

Daylight streamed through the horizontal blinds over the window, dancing long beams over Annemarie's face, gingerly bringing her back to consciousness after the deepest sleep she had had in a while—at least, one that was not alcohol fueled. Her eyelashes fluttered open, allowing bits of the morning to seep in. She turned her head to look at Alistair beside her, but he was not there.

"Alistair?" she called quietly. No answer came. She pushed herself out of bed, finding one foot still asleep, and she shook it awake while she hobbled toward the door leading to the living room. She spied Alistair's body slumped over, the side of his face caught on the pillow of the couch's back. Her eyes darted to his gun on the table and her breath caught in her throat. "No . . ." She gasped. "Alistair, Alistair, come on. Don't . . . don't have been so stup—" She raced to his side to grab him by the shoulder. His skin was chilly to the touch, but the longer she held onto him, dug her fingers into him, he felt warm. "Alistair!"

His eyes popped open as he jolted awake. "What the—Annie? What . . . what are you doing? What's wrong?"

"You!" she cried, tears streaming down her cheeks, wetting her shirt in an instant. "I thought you were . . ."

Alistair sat up a little straighter, craning his neck from one side to the other as he worked out the kinks. "I don't . . . You thought I was what?"

Both of her hands shot out to gesture at the gun on the table. Then they moved to point at him. "You know . . . Your dream. Vision. Whatever." She shuddered. Wiping the tears from her face with the back of one hand, she exhaled a shaky breath.

He closed his eyes for a moment, his jaw going slack. "I found it, under the table. I-I couldn't sleep so I came out here and forgot that I hadn't put it away. I was going to. But then you came by and I forgot." He hesitated. "I've never forgotten to put away my g—oh *god*, Annie. I'm *so* sorry." Realization finally dawned over his features, his eyes and mouth open wide. "I can't even imagine—"

"No, you *can't*," she snapped. She pushed a hand through her bed-mussed hair.

He checked the time on his phone: six thirty. Despite not thinking he could sleep, he had apparently collapsed under the exhaustion and gotten at least two hours. "Let me make us some coffee."

He did not wait for her response as he launched off the couch to head into the kitchen. He desperately needed the caffeine to wake up his brain, to get him to a better state of mind to process what happened. But he was using it as an excuse to put a little space between them. He knew she was angry—more sad-upset than anything else—and he did not have it in him, yet, to plod through everything.

While he waited for the coffee to brew, he picked up half a dozen empty, label-less soup cans and put them in the recycle bin across the room. He pulled the stack of dirty bowls from off the pass-through and set them in the sink. He let hot water fill each of them, hoping it would lift some of the rings of dried *whatever* had been in them so he would not have to scrub so hard when he cleaned them later on.

After pouring two cups of coffee, he spent a minute leaning against the countertop, still blinking himself awake. His hesitation to join Annemarie in the living room had been apparent, so instead, she came to him. He handed her the steaming cup; she thanked him with a single, solemn nod.

Her mouth opened to speak, but she was interrupted by ringing. It was Alistair's work phone. He set down his mug and cut across the living room to grab it off the table.

"Oh, Riggs, you're still at the station. Shit, I'm sorry, man."

"Don't worry about that right now," he replied.

"Then what's up?"

"Uh, it's not an emergency or anything, but I need you to come over as soon as you can. There's . . . something you're gonna want to hear."

TWENTY-FOUR

The ride along Wildwood Highway to North Beach rarely took more than forty minutes, even when puttering along, barely going the speed limit. Island resident Merle Doss was never in a hurry, no matter where he was headed, and hitchhiker Liam Peck did not mind the slower rate of speed; so long as he arrived before sundown, he was fine to take in the scenery at thirty-five miles per hour. The weather was sublime the day of the ride north—blue skies for miles, warm but not hot, a breeze slight enough to tussle hair—and continued to be halfway into Liam's annual camping trip.

On day four, he woke with the sun. The earliest rays of light broke over the long stretches of sand, creeping across the landscape before reaching the green nylon of the lone tent on the beach. As the warmth of the morning engulfed Liam's quarters, he stirred gently with a yawn and a single sweep of a hand over his tired eyes. The best part of his camping vacation was not needing to be anywhere at any particular time or doing anything he did not want to do. So far, he had spent his trip rockhounding, swimming, fishing, and even doing a bit of trail maintenance in the woods behind his site.

The entrance of the tent zipped open wide, allowing Liam to shuffle into the day. He stood outside his temporary home, taking a moment to smooth the creases from his flannel overshirt and stiff cargo shorts. He cleared his throat, sucked in a deep breath of fresh air, and exhaled, all accompanied by a big grin. The sea was smooth this morning, the water gently lapping at every inch of sand, giving the scuttling crabs a clean slate as they rushed from tide pool to broken log to rock in search of breakfast. The occasional shrill call of seabirds pierced the fizzling of the foam dissipating on the shore. Everything was perfect.

The firepit he set up upon arrival had been well used thus far. With a cobble of kindling made of wood he scavenged from the forest and paper he packed in, he started a morning fire to cook breakfast over. He always brought coffee grounds and basic food staples like eggs, oats, beans, and a variety of vegetables that could withstand a week without refrigeration. He caught fish daily in order to bulk up his meals, which is what he intended to do next. After a visit to the woods, he retrieved his fishing pole from beside the tent and made his way down to the water. With the tide in, he did not have far to trek.

Fish were plentiful in the waters surrounding Port Harrow. A seemingly never-ending supply of turbot, lingcod, sand dab, salmon, halibut, and rockfish made fishing a favorite pastime among residents and visitors. Rod, reel, line, and bait, and Liam easily procured himself a hearty meal of a small chinook to go alongside the last of his eggs and a couple hunks of rye bread.

As he settled into his sandy seat in front of the crackling fire, the skillet sizzled as the hot oil met the fresh ingredients. Armed with a fork from a family heirloom set passed down from one camping enthusiast to the next, he poked and prodded the fish he had expertly filleted. The combination of sounds between the ocean, the fire, the cooking food, and his contented sighs pleased him, but there was an additional noise he could not pinpoint: a rustle of branches, limbs, shrubbery. It sounded close, right behind him. But the closest vegetation was at least fifty yards away.

He turned around to look at the trees. Stillness. No breeze. No movement. The sound did not continue for the moment. He returned to his meal. Within a minute or two, the rustling started again. As quick as he heard it, he whipped his head to look over his shoulder. A blur of grey streaked across his field of vision from right to left. It disappeared behind a thick evergreen. Liam shrugged it off. Wildlife was everywhere on Port Harrow; he knew that. In years past, he had encountered deer wandering through the lodgepoles, grazing on grasses growing up from the dirt and berries budding on the bushes. The grey he had seen did not seem deerlike, but what did he know? It was not bothering him, whatever it was.

His attention returned to the meal once more, the fish almost ready to be eaten. He flipped the salmon over, its skin crisp from the cast-iron skillet. The eggs were perfectly runny, the yolks thick and gelatinous and the whites solid with golden-brown edges. He balanced a small metal plate in the palm of one hand as he gently scooped out the finished food. The remaining fat in the pan absorbed into the soft rye slices, allowing them to gradually toast over the heat.

Coupled with another mug of hot coffee, he was ready to eat. He was starving, but wanted to savor every bite. In his day-to-day, his job as an office manager kept him ridiculously busy to the point that he ate most meals leaning over the sink in the break room, rarely having the time to cook anything more than a frozen tray of beige in the microwave, and practically spinning in counterclockwise circles to offset the metaphorical downward spiral into the toilet that was his life.

He took every advantage he could to get out of the city; Hyland Grove was pretty in its own way with a skyline full of modern, window-lined office buildings overlooking the ocean; streets littered with cars chugging to and from work, appointments, and shopping; and little dollops of pine, juniper, and moss greens bringing color to the otherwise bland surroundings. Doing the same thing day in and day out made Liam ache for his annual vacation to Port Harrow—it broke up the monotony of everything and rejuvenated him enough to carry on for another fifty-one weeks. If given the opportunity, he would never return home. The wilderness man life suited him; the blinding fluorescent bulbs and cubicles did not.

He fished a pin bone from between his teeth and dropped it into the fire. He took a mouthful of coffee and let it lazily drain down his throat. As he reached for a piece of bread in the skillet, he heard a series of huffs of breath not of his making. The toasted surface scratched along the plate as it sopped up the remainder of the egg yolk and dripped golden-yellow dribbles into his patchy, short beard as he stuffed the too-big piece into his mouth. The short hairs on his neck pushed back and forth with the breeze. A chill ran down his spine. There was no wind. Everything was absolutely still save for the roaring beating of his heart in his chest.

In one slow, fluid movement, he glanced over his shoulder again to peer back at the woods. Inches from his face was that of a mouth full of razor-sharp teeth sneering at him. Opaque, muddled eyes the color of ash bounced Liam's reflection back at him. A thin, hooked nose protruded from the face and drifted closer with every breath.

Startled, but unable to process what he was seeing for thirty seconds, Liam finally took in the full length of the thing in front of him. It was crouched in position, ready to pounce at a moment's notice. Liam dared not move a muscle, unsure what its intentions were. Its bare, smooth chest inflated with an inhalation of air and it seethed out of that hawklike protrusion, which was now touching its tip to Liam's own small button of a nose.

Trying not to draw attention to what he was doing with his hands, Liam opened his mouth to say, "Hello," the way a child might greet a strange but friendly dog, to distract it as he slowly, soundlessly set down the mug and plate. Nearly inert, he used his hands to brace himself on the log seat. He did not know if he meant to make a break for it or wait for its own first move. The more Liam looked at it, the more he realized he might be in trouble.

In an instant, it had him laid out in the sand, his shoulders pinned. It set a hand to Liam's throat, the eerie, long fingers clutching onto his neck, jagged nails digging into the skin. All of the oxygen escaped his lungs, being forced out solely by the incredible weight on his chest.

The creature's eyes flashed silver and raised its head upward to the sky to let loose a roar unlike anything Liam had ever heard. It was bearlike in resonance and shook him to his core. The fingers squeezed tighter and tighter around his throat, blood trickling from the wounds created with the fierce grip.

Liam kept his eyes focused on the creature's face, though his vision blurring did not bode well for his long-term plan. His hand slinked up alongside his body, moving it as slowly as he could so as to not incur the attention of the thing that was sizing him up as a threat or its next meal. With his hand above his head, he groped for anything he could find. The hot skillet was beyond his reach, and even if he could grab it, he was not sure he could swing it with any real meaning as he slowly lost consciousness. His fingers fumbled over a long, sturdy handle, giving it a firm grip before heaving his arm at the creature. The tines of the fork penetrated the smooth shoulder, causing another blast of screams to escape the being's lungs. The creature's grip tightened. Its force was stronger. The stabbing only emboldened it, leaving Liam uncertain what to do or what was to come next.

It was not until loose sand trickled into his mouth that he realized what was happening: The brute strength of the creature pinning him down, shoving its weight against his body, was pushing him *into* the earth, into the shore underneath them. Liam was being buried alive; or at least, he was alive for the moment. The longer the creature held its grip, gnashing its teeth in front of his face, stringy, hot saliva dribbling onto Liam's nose, the harder it was to keep conscious. His eyelids were weighed down, the breath in his lungs left him too many minutes ago, the sounds that once filled his ears—filled him with joy—were gone. All he could hear was the unmistakable sounds of bones crunching, followed by an explosion of pain in his chest cavity. Darkness settled over him. He could not even open his mouth to do anything more than gape like a suffocating fish, like the salmon he had caught an hour ago.

For all of the years he spent his one week of vacation out on this beach, in this little slice of heaven, for all of the hard times he experienced where the spot of sunshine was this shoreline, he never once considered it would also be the place where he would die. He had told coworkers he could die happy on the Mondays he returned to the office after the long-awaited vacations; this was not what he had in mind. This was not happy; there was no peace to be found buried under the sand, taking his final breaths of life.

TWENTY-FIVE

With a gasping start, Liam shot up from his bed of sand and immediately checked his surroundings. His vision was blurred for a moment, that same sort of impairment when he first woke up in the morning. He rubbed at his eyes as his chest heaved. His sternum hurt, his lungs burned, the taste of blood was ever present in his mouth, but the scratch of coarse sand against his lips, his gums, was missing. Anywhere he looked, it was obvious he was alone. He squinted in the morning sunshine, partly in surveillance, but mostly in thought. A jittery hand made its way to his aching throat. He winced and the fingers came away bloody.

"What . . . the hell . . ." he choked out. "H-how . . ." He winced as the breath of words skated up his aching throat; the windpipe itself felt heavy and bruised.

Liam was the only soul on the beach.

He climbed to his feet, taking his time to make sure he was steady enough to be upright. He tested each of his limbs, twisted his head back and forth—only hesitating a moment when the blood drying on his neck pinched— wiggled his fingers, his toes, even twitched his nose. He was in one piece.

"I'm fucking dead," he muttered. "I have to be."

It took ten minutes for him to come to terms with this realization. The creature, whatever it was, had killed him, had crushed his chest, stolen his breath, shoved him so far into the ground; there was no way he could have survived.

Out of the corner of his eye, he noticed something out of place that interrupted the hopeless line of thought regarding his demise. He took several steps in its direction. Lines. In the sand. Movement lines. Not footsteps, no. But scuttle lines, belonging to something as big as a human. And they stretched for a good hundred feet before disappearing into the lapping water's edge.

A flash of silver off in the distance, near a jetty of rocks jutting out of the ocean, grabbed his attention. It left as quick as it appeared. Liam blinked hard several times, willing the distraction to reappear or this bucolic dream to wash away. The waves coming up on the shore filled his ears. His hair rumpled in the gentle wind. He could smell the remnants of food burning in the skillet—*the skillet*.

He whipped around and beelined for the campfire. One piece of bread remained in the cast iron, charred to a crisp on one side as it continued to cook while he was off being murdered. Thinking himself invincible in death, he reached for the bread to wing it out into the sand and burned his fingertips.

A sharp breath sucked in through clenched teeth. "Fuck," he muttered. He shoved the scalded fingers into his mouth and sucked. The sensation was familiar. He raised an eyebrow as he peered around him again. The knife from the heirloom set lay strewn across the sand with the drained tin cup of coffee and the mostly empty metal plate. With the knife in hand, he carefully and shallowly dragged the serrated edge against his opposite palm. He winced again, but did not cry out as the dribble of blood welled up.

"Why did that hurt?"

Another idea popped into his head.

He dove into the tent and dug into his rucksack for his cell phone. He always kept it off on his trips, but handy in the event of an emergency with a solar charger just in case. He impatiently waited for the device to start up—realizing how inconvenient the slow boot would be were he in a matter of life or death. He navigated to his contact list and pulled up the first name: Amara Tzavellas. He tapped on it and let it dial. He urged it to ring, knowing it was fruitless. There could not be any reception in the afterlife, could there?

"Liam? Aren't you on vacation?"

He dropped to his knees with a *thud*. "Ama, hi!" He did not care how eager he sounded. "How are you?"

Amara, his immediate supervisor at work, was slow to respond. "I'm fine. A little confused, if I'm being honest. Why exactly are you calling me?"

"I—" What *was* the point in calling? Was it to verify that he had not, in fact, perished under the weight of the creature? Or was it to verify that he *had* died? He was not certain himself. The first step was making the call, assuming there would conveniently be no signal or that Amara would not answer. Now that there was, and she had, he had no idea what to say. "I wanted to . . . make sure that . . . my phone was still working. I dropped it in the ocean, and uh, I needed to make sure it made calls. In case of, y'know, an emergency. Y-you happened to be the first name in my c-contacts."

"Oh. Yeah, I guess that makes sense. Well . . ." She cleared her throat. "I'm glad it seems to be working, then. Are you having a good time out there?"

He opened his mouth to respond, but the breath that escaped quivered as if suppressing a cry. "Yeah. The best." He nodded, hopeful the answer would convince her he was fine, and maybe even himself. "All right, Ama. Well, thanks for picking up. Appreciate it. I'll see you next week."

"Have a good one, Liam. Have fun catching fish or whatever it is you're doing out there. Remember to shower before you come back into the office!" The line went dead at the sound of her laughing.

The phone dropped into the sand as his chin fell to his chest.

He was not dead. He could not be. Not if he was making phone calls. Not if Amara had answered. He had gotten the answer he needed, not necessarily the one he wanted—he wanted to be told he *was* dead, because living after such a horrific experience did not seem like a good idea. How did you come to terms with the event? How did *anyone* deal with a brush with death, let alone one at the hands of another person—no, not even a person, something unhuman?

However, here he was, Amara having provided the truth of it all, having given him a glimmer of hope—and he felt worse than ever. He could deal with the physical and mental trauma later, though, he decided. He needed to get back to town and tell someone what had happened.

But what *had* happened?

He looked to the rocks in the distance once again, waiting for a sign. Any sign. He tried not to blink, but his eyelids were still so heavy. Letting his eyes close for a long moment, he exhaled a deep breath and his entire body shuddered.

TWENTY-SIX

Riggs scribbled on the messy stack of forms on the counter. His head hung low as he transcribed missing information from the traffic collision he oversaw earlier, his notes from those involved scrawled in his little notebook. He paid no further attention to the man sitting in the lacquered chair across from him in the small office—he had already heard his story and there was nothing more to do until Alistair arrived.

Upon Liam entering the station, Riggs did a double take, closely assessing the man he did not recognize. His blond hair was short but unkempt, sticking up in several cowlicks around the crown of his head like he had recently woken up from a long night of fitful sleep. A scrub of blond and brown grew across his chin and cheeks; nothing out of the ordinary. He had a scrap of grey flannel material wrapped around the palm of his hand and a chunk of the bottom of his shirt was missing. The buttons of the flannel were done up all the way to his neck, though haphazard in their fastening. Matched with a pair of stained cargo shorts reinforced Riggs's thought he may have been a vagrant. Though, they were rare on Port Harrow.

Regardless of who Liam was and where he came from, Riggs listened to his story. One of how he was camping on North Beach, how he had been alone this entire time—until this morning—and everything changed when the grey thing attacked him. Concerned not only with the validity of his story, but how similar it sounded to Alistair's experience when he tracked the unknown creature with Annemarie and Nowell, he called him in the hopes he was available to swing by the station to field the situation.

Until then, Riggs focused on the pile of pressing work in front of him and the man who introduced himself as Liam Peck stared blankly at a water stain on one of the ceiling tiles.

The chime of the bell over the front door called attention to Alistair casually striding in, a protein bar still halfway in its wrapper hanging out of his mouth, a tall thermos tucked under one arm, and a black leather briefcase in the other hand.

"Mmff," he said with a tilt of his chin, greeting Riggs behind the counter. Alistair's eyes darted around the room, looking for the reason he had been called in. When they landed on Liam, who looked petrified, a deer stunned in the headlights, he picked up the pace. He disappeared into the small side room, only to reappear a moment later, hand stuck out to make Liam's acquaintance. "Apologies for the wait, Mister . . ."

"Peck. Liam." The man rose to meet him and shake hands.

"My deputy said you've got something I'd want to hear." Liam nodded several times, but stopped with a wince of pain in his eyes. "Why don't you come into my office and we'll get this all on file," Alistair offered. He extended a gesture of *right this way* and followed a hesitant Liam into the shoebox office. He did not close the door completely, but it was enough to give them privacy. He sidled up to his desk and took a seat, keeping his eyes on Liam who was attempting to do so too. His movements were stiff, his entire body seemingly tense as he eased into the chair. Alistair jiggled the mouse to wake up the computer and set his fingers on the keyboard, ready to work. "So, tell me your story, Mr. Peck."

It took a moment for Liam to gather his wits. The hitchhiked ride in the back of someone's pickup truck followed by a quiet wait in the station lobby where he had time to decompress from the morning—if that were even possible—and to think through every logical, and illogical, explanation for what happened and by whom, gave him the opportunity to forget the little details. He was not sure what would be of interest to the sheriff's department, but with his knack for oversharing on every subject, he wanted to make sure he was doing this right.

He explained who he was, where he was from, why he was visiting Port Harrow to begin with. He tried not to get lost in the weeds of the mundane-to-everyone-else things he had experienced over the last few days, wanting to focus on what mattered. When he got to the point in his story where he was face-to-face with the creature, Alistair held up a hand to stop him.

"Before you continue, will you give me an in-depth description of what it looked like?"

Liam nodded.

Grey skin.

Milky eyes.

Sharp teeth.

A terrible roar.

Lightning fast and whisper quiet when it wanted to be.

The hairs on Alistair's neck stood at the first mention of its physicality. It took a moment for his writing to catch up, not because Liam rattled off the attributes quickly, but because Alistair was shaken to his core. There was no way this could be anything other than what he came up against last night.

The two men spent another hour together, Alistair reading back what Liam had told him, trying to help him suss out every detail—his duty meant listening, recording, understanding; his own run-in with the creature meant gleaning whatever he could to hunt down the bastard and finally end this.

With a heavy breath released, Alistair asked, "Is there anything else you can think of?"

Liam's eyes shot from the wringing hands in his lap up to Alistair's face. He stopped his nervous fidgeting and brought the fingers to his throat where the top button of the flannel rested. He unfastened the first three mother-of-pearl snaps to reveal the dried-blood wounds the creature had inflicted. Alistair believed every word he had said, but if anything about the story seemed too much of a bald-faced lie, this would make him rethink his stance. The five punctures—four on one side and one on the other—dotted around his neck were proof positive. But what could he say to Liam?

Alistair leaned back in the leather chair, grabbing the lower portion of his face with his hand as he thought. "I have one question for you . . ."

But before he could continue, Liam beat him to the expected punch. "I swear I haven't consumed any hallucinogenic drugs or alcohol on this trip."

Hands up in front of him, Alistair shook his head. "No, no, that's not it. The thing is . . ." He rubbed at the back of his head. "Did you experience anything, I don't know, nightmarish? Or like, not an out-of-body experience, but akin to an alternate reality maybe?" It was the only thing Liam had not mentioned that was different about Alistair's attack.

Liam's eyebrows dropped. His lips twisted to one side. "I don't know what happened. I felt him—it— crushing my sternum and ribs as it shoved me into the sand. I blacked out, I think. But when I woke up, I was fine. I actually kinda thought I was dead. I don't know how much of what I experienced was real. Obviously, there's this—" He gestured to the marks on his throat. "— and I'm definitely sore. But it made me feel like every bone in my chest had shattered into a thousand pieces. I don't know if I was choking on all the sand in my mouth or from my lungs being popped. It was surreal. L-like, have you ever had a dream feel so real you don't realize it was a dream even after you wake up?"

Alistair perked up especially tall at this; it was the same way he described his encounter to Annemarie. He nodded. "Yeah, I do."

"That's like this was. I woke up and there was no one around for miles, far as I could see. Truth be told, my idea of paradise is a beautiful beach with no one else on it." It came out almost wistful. But then, Liam cocked his head.

"That's a pretty specific question, Sheriff. Do you know what that thing is?"

Alistair leaned forward and planted both elbows on the desk. "If I'm being completely honest, Mr. Peck, I have no fucking clue."

Liam declined a medical assessment from paramedics, even for the cut on his hand, especially when he heard that Alistair was en route to North Beach. He asked for a ride back to his campsite, which Alistair did not balk at; Liam could show him where he was attacked, where he saw the final silver flash. He shot Annemarie a text that something had transpired and wanted to know if she was interested in tagging along with him—her response came quickly and Alistair let Liam know they were making a quick pit stop.

For a brief moment, Alistair wondered if it was a good idea to bring her along. Given that she was not a part of that particular incident, it was best for her to stay out of it. But . . . the very thing that may have been the reason Jesse was dead, that Peter was dead, that Moose was dead, that tried to claim another victim this morning, and had come for them both, might be at their fingertips.

Or they might have been walking into another dead-end, or even something far more dangerous.

The patrol vehicle pulled into her driveway where she waited anxiously, dressed in highlighter pink running shorts and a black long-sleeve shirt. She did not bother bringing anything but her phone and the house keys, which she held in her hands as a means of hiding the nervousness. She watched as Alistair motioned to the driver's side back seat, signaling it was empty. When she climbed in, she stopped midstride as she saw Liam, who was scrambling to button up his flannel.

"Hi," she said kindly. Alistair only told her he was on his way to the beach to follow up on a potential lead, not that there would be anyone else with him.

Liam drifted from Annemarie's brown eyes down to what she was wearing, then back up to her face. "Afternoon." Alistair briefly explained to him they were picking up someone with interest, but she was not at all what Liam was expecting.

Darting his eyes from the road to the rearview mirror in order to look at Liam, Alistair asked, "Where did you say Merle dropped you off at?"

Liam scooted forward, hindered by the seat belt, but attempting nonetheless. "There's a bend in the road as you're coming up the highway. It has a road headed to the west and there's a surfboard that's been cemented into the ground. I think it's a memorial. I've never really paid attention 'cause it's on the opposite side of the road. But there's a trail just beyond it."

Alistair's eyes shot to Annemarie in the mirror, studying her face as Liam described Jesse's roadside memorial the island community decided would be a good idea to erect. At first, she agreed to the gesture, thinking it was a sweet way to remember a well-loved member of Port Harrow. Because Annemarie did not leave the house for an extended period of time after it was put in place, she was never subjected to seeing it. But once she made the daily drive to the library, to the ferry, to anywhere outside the few-mile radius of her home, it became a constant reminder of what she had lost. Any time she brought up possibly taking it down, as the widow of said well-loved transplant, the town's government overrode her, insisting Jesse would have loved it. She had even gone so far as to try to dig it out on her own, but the concrete persevered.

She did not flinch. She kept her eyes focused on the trees passing by out the window of the SUV, wondering what mess they were about to get themselves into.

They parked alongside the road, Annemarie having launched herself out of the car before Alistair even put it in park. He took a moment to gather a few items in the front seat as Liam slinked out of his seat belt and landed in the weeds and wildflowers on the shoulder. The three congregated at the front of the vehicle and Alistair gestured toward the woods with a flattened hand.

"After you, Mr. Peck."

Liam's nerves—the uneasiness of the morning—rattled around inside of his stomach, unsettling him and each of his purposely placed footsteps en route to the beach. He clenched his fists and released each finger slowly as a means of working through the nervousness, being careful to not split the knife wound on his palm. The more he thought about it, the worse it got. But knowing he needed to do this, needed to be the lead for his party, he pushed himself to remember every step he took.

They made their way through the woods, taking care to dodge low-lying branches and high-topped roots, and Annemarie especially on guard for spiderwebs after having made their acquaintance face-first last night and disliking it entirely. The roar of the beach was echoing through the trees, growing louder as they approached. Upon emerging, they were within throwing distance of Liam's campsite, the fire now a pit of the burnt logs and everything he owned in disarray. If someone else had come upon the scene, unaware of the circumstances, no doubt they would call the police to report a crime of some sort.

"So, uh, here's where it happened," Liam started. He pointed to the fallen log he had been using as a seat in front of the fire, then traced a line to the deep depression in the sand. Except, there was no death pit where the creature tried to bury him alive. The surface immediately surrounding his campsite was smooth, nary a speck out of place. "Wait, but I—" Liam's hands shot to his head, intertwining fingers in his hair and grabbing hold of it tight. Alistair walked around the space, making mental notes of what Liam was saying as he retold bits of his story.

When he finished speaking, Alistair said, "You never said how you escaped."

Liam's eyebrows lowered, his gaze narrowed in on the sheriff's face. "I don't rightly know." He scratched at his scalp, unturning more chunks of his already unruly hair. "The last thing I remember was everything going dark. Maybe it wasn't interested in me anymore. Maybe it likes to toy with its food. Oh, Jesus. Do you think it's coming back for me to finish the job?"

Alistair ignored the bit of overflowing panic. "But if its intention was to kill you, why didn't it? Do you remember if something, or someone, interrupted you?" He was grasping for straws.

"No, I—*food*." Liam's eyes brightened.

"Huh?" Alistair asked.

"Breakfast. I was eating breakfast when it jumped me."

"Right, you said as much."

"But my fork. Where's my fork?" Liam stuttered in his step a moment as he scoured the campsite. He was down on his knees, scooping through shallow layers of sand.

Annemarie stepped close to Alistair, her face nearing his ear to ask, "Is this guy okay?"

He only shrugged. "Your guess is as good as mine," he mumbled as he crossed his arms over his chest.

Liam's head popped up as he took a break from his search and he locked eyes with Alistair. "My fork. When it was attacking me, I-I grabbed my fork and stabbed the damn thing."

Alistair's arms dropped to his sides and his mouth went slack. "At what point did that happen?"

"Well, it had to be before I blacked out. 'Cause when I woke up, there was no one around, no sign of—*wait*." Liam pointed toward the shuffled marks in the sand that disappeared into the water. "I didn't see it leave, but these were new when I woke up. A-and when I was looking around, trying to figure out if I was dead—" Annemarie's nostrils flared and her eyebrows lowered, causing enough of a bewildered expression to catch his attention. "Yeah, I wasn't convinced I was alive when I got back up. Anyway, I looked over there." He pointed to the barrier of rocks. "There was a flash of light. I kinda figured it was like, the sun hitting some of those flying fish things that are out here in the ocean."

Annemarie and Alistair exchanged knowing glances. "Then we should head over there."

Unknown to Liam, the jetty was a stone's throw from the sea cave; the two connected at low tide. But because of the curve of the shoreline, the cave was not visible around the copse of trees. They plodded their way across the sand, keeping quiet, not knowing what to say. It did not seem like a good time to crack jokes, muse about what they might find, or anything that could alert the creature to their approach—assuming it was even in the vicinity anymore. It was a long, silent walk, save for the occasional sound of Annemarie muttering "fuck" every time she accidentally flipped sand at the back of Alistair's or Liam's legs.

Alistair knew from having found Peter and Moose in the cave that the creature spent *some* amount of time in there, but was it home base? Was it a dining room of sorts, out of sight from anyone who might happen across this part of the beach? Was it a storage unit, and Alistair kept coming in and clearing it out before the thing could do more than kill?

The same dread he felt the other times gripped his throat and his spine at the same time, sending waves of chills up one and a searing-hot deluge down the other. As he reached for the gun at his waist, Liam and Annemarie noticed the visible tremor.

"This is Sheriff Lucas of the Azure County Sheriff's Department. Come out with your hands up," he called, slightly proud of himself that he was able to get it out without a hiccup in his voice this time, especially with witnesses. But he also felt like a buffoon, announcing who he was and expecting compliance, as if the thing were just another criminal hiding out from the law. He looked over his shoulder at Annemarie and Liam and motioned for them to stay put. He pointed a finger at himself and gestured to the opening of the cave, then reiterated they needed to remain exactly where they were.

"You can't go in there by yourself," Annemarie hissed, protesting his instructions.

"I can and I will. It's my job. Now stay put. The both of you." His word was final—they all knew it.

The little step up into the cave seemed feet-high now, but he knew he needed to advance. At first, he popped his head around the corner of the entrance, peeping to see if anything was lying in wait. When nothing seemed amiss, he stood a little straighter, readjusted his grip on the gun, and took in one giant, deep breath before slowly exhaling it, centering himself to make the next move.

He stepped up into the mouth of the cave, inspecting the surroundings. It all looked the same from when he was last here. Except . . .

He spotted a foot.

He extended his leg as far as it would go without getting too close to the lone appendage and gave the sole a push with his boot. It did not flinch. He crept closer, being sure to hold his breath should he deign to alert the foot's owner of his presence. As he inched toward the antechamber, reliving in aggressive flashes having found Peter missing much of his lower body and Moose with his broken neck and blood-splattered fur, he closed his eyes in an attempt to push away the memories. It took every ounce of his willpower to keep moving forward, even with the insides of his nostrils suddenly assaulted by the metallic and iron tang of blood and the constant flares of hot and cold rushing through his body.

"You can't go in there," Annemarie insisted in a hushed, hissing tone, holding onto Liam's wrist as he tried to trudge through the sand to the entrance of the cave.

"It'll be fine. The sheriff's got a gun. What's the worst that can happen?" Liam insisted, wrenching away his hand from her surprisingly tight grip. He rubbed at the skin where she had been digging in her nails, inspecting it for any damage.

"If Alistair says to stay put, we have to stay put. Once it's safe, he'll let us know." She laughed at herself, wondering when the last time she obeyed anything Alistair had told her. Why she was fighting so hard against this complete stranger, she did not know. Was it concern that he might endanger Alistair? Was she jealous that he had the courage to run in blind and she was left terrified, unable to move, outside? "Give him a few more minutes," she urged.

Liam stopped and turned to look at her, one eyebrow lifted halfway between intrigue and suspicion. "Just a peek," he said softly while holding his fingers an inch apart. "That won't hurt anything."

She could not argue with that.

As Liam moved closer to the entrance, he gripped the stone edge of the cave mouth and poked his head into the opening, as Alistair had. Not too far from him stood the sheriff, his back to Liam, hunching over as he inched toward a secondary room of sorts within the cave. Liam surveyed the first chamber—red marks covered the walls, sand spread over the floor, but much of it was not the same shade of the beach, rather an umber hue.

His eyes finally landed on the wayward foot, which elicited a giddy tingle below his sternum. It *had* to belong to whatever attacked him, and if it was the creature, that might mean his fork was within striking distance too. He heaved his weight up into the cave, taking care to not make any noise. Liam held more confidence in his steps as he made his way to Alistair, who still had no clue the gap between them was closing—as far as Alistair knew, Liam had listened to him and was waiting outside with Annemarie. But as Liam neared, setting eyes on the body stretched out on the floor, he could not contain himself.

"Holy fuck! That's it!" His shout echoed so loudly and thoroughly in the small space it startled Alistair more than it should have, and the noise shot out the mouth of the cave to where a waiting Annemarie could hear it crystal clear.

"What're you doing in here?" Alistair snapped, keeping his voice low. He had only managed to make it to the feet of the seemingly dead creature but had not done much else. Practically face-to-face with the terror of Port Harrow had him losing all of his confidence.

Liam's arm shot out in front of them, pointing at the fork stuck in the creature's shoulder. "I need that."

"Are you kidding me right now?"

"Why would I be kidding?" Liam emphatically frowned, trying to convince Alistair how serious he was.

"I told you to wait outside with Annemarie."

"The thing's dead. What's gonna happen?"

Alistair pointed toward the entrance of the cave. "Mr. Peck, not even an hour ago you were scared shitless that this thing was going to come back and 'finish the job.' Now you're obsessing over a *fork*." Liam shrugged, casually pushed Alistair out of the way up against the wall, and leaned over to retrieve the utensil. "This isn't two buddies stumbling across a cool find. This is a crime scene. I need you to back—"

The moment the tines left the punctured skin, tendrils of blue-grey smoke danced up from the wound. Liam noticed it first, being in such close proximity, but Alistair was quick behind him. "What the . . ." Liam drawled.

Before either of them could react, the creature's eyelids zoomed open, revealing its grey sclera and iris, and it slashed out with one clawed hand, missing the buttoned pleat of Liam's flannel by mere inches. He stumbled onto his ass with such speed that inertia forced him onto his back and his head cracked on the stone floor. An unearthly reverberation came from the creature's open mouth as it tried to get onto its feet, the clatter sounding like bone scraping against itself and the rasp of air escaping through a fissure.

After a moment of shocked hesitation incapacitated Alistair, he was quick to aim and fire his gun, planting two bullets in the creature's forehead. Liam's hands went up to his ears, shielding them from the resonance bouncing around the small space. A brilliant flash of silver lit up the antechamber, forcing both men to shut their eyes and cringe away from the brightness. The creature's body slumped to the floor, but the rasp remained as it struggled with its final breaths.

"Alistair!" Annemarie shouted from the mouth of the cave.

"We're fine!" he called back.

"Speak for yourself," Liam grumbled as he sat up, gingerly rubbing the back of his head. "I think I've had enough adventure for one lifetime." He climbed onto his feet, using the wall behind him as a steadying surface, and tucked the fork into the pocket of his pants. He shoved the edge of his boot into the creature's ribs, prodding for any further movement.

"Mr. Peck," Alistair forced out. He pointed toward the cave's entrance. "You need to leave immediately."

Liam raised his hands in front of him with an expression of *mea culpa* on his face. "I got what I came for." He backed out of the space, leaving Alistair to do whatever he intended to do. When he met up with Annemarie, she grabbed him by the shoulders and shoved him out of Alistair's view. Whatever had happened to them, she knew it was serious because of the tone he had used with Liam.

Alistair did the same as Liam had, using his boot to push at the now-lifeless corpse. It had stopped making any noise at this point, so he was certain it was dead now. He crouched beside it and set his index and middle fingers on either side of the fork wound Liam had inflicted. It no longer spewed smoke, but the longer his fingers stayed in place, the hotter the creature's skin got—to the point he thought his own skin might blister if he stayed there any longer. He ripped his hand away to inspect himself. Above the ring on his index finger, a small, red patch was popping up. He grunted in displeasure and then stood, ready to be done with this whole thing.

The only problem was: Did he call this in?

He exited the cave and found Annemarie and Liam where he had originally left them. Liam was in the middle of explaining to her why the fork was so important. He was not some crazed, possessive freak, he just greatly valued his family's heirlooms—the source material for the set came from a hoard of intricately inlaid blades found and dated to the late 1700s and were melted down to create the silverware that was passed down from generation to generation. As he mused about how he would have to eventually end up with a child of his own in order to keep the chain going, Alistair breezed right past them and headed straight for the tree line where the forest met the sand.

He rested a hand on the stone wall beside him, doubled over at the waist, and took in several deep, almost painful, breaths.

TWENTY-SEVEN

Riggs cleaned out the squad car of several manila folders, a couple empty water bottles, and a pile of crumpled-up food wrappers as Annemarie pulled alongside him in the parking lot. She was nonchalant in her climbing out of her vehicle, but made herself known once she got onto the sidewalk.

"Heya!" she called.

He was still partially tucked inside his car, rooting around for any other trash. When he extracted himself, pleased with the cleanup, he meant to wave at her, but ended up letting loose the wrappers; though luckily for him, they fell back into the car's interior. "Hey, Annie."

"Alistair in?" she asked. She had one hand tucked into the back pocket of her jeans and the other was a clenched fist.

"His car's here, so, yeah, I think so?" It was not the most confident answer, but Riggs had recently arrived at the station himself after a morning patrolling the island; her guess was as good as his.

Annemarie made to head to the double doors but stopped. She stayed frozen in place for a long moment. "Hey, uh, what all do you know about what's been going on?" She knew he had been there after the takedown of Alistair, but did he know the intimate details? Had Alistair explained anything to anyone else?

He tilted his head ever so slightly and lowered his eyebrows. "Uh, what do you mean?" There was an unusual high lilt in his voice, as if this were a game. She opened her mouth to attempt an answer, but the hesitation overrode everything. Riggs met her on the sidewalk, bumped her with his shoulder, and said, "Just tell me what's going on."

She opened her fist, showing off a red thumb drive, wiggling it in the air. "It might be best if you come with me."

He held open the door into the lobby and beelined it for the trash can to dispose of his garbage. The manila folders came with him as he followed Annemarie toward Alistair's office. The door was shut, but a knock on the frosted glass pane prompted him to call, "Come in."

Annemarie creaked open the door and poked her head inside. "You busy?"

"Give me ... just a sec ..." He typed for several seconds, darted his eyes back and forth as he read the short email he had finished, and clicked send. He turned slightly in his chair and asked, "What's up?"

She lifted the thumb drive and announced, "I'm back from seeing Nowell." Riggs's eyes locked onto Annemarie's face. He had not expected her to say that. "He said it's pretty good, but told me not to involve him in whatever we're doing."

"Huh?" Riggs managed.

"Does he know what we intend to do? Is he okay with it?"

"What?" Riggs asked.

Annemarie crossed the room to slide in beside Alistair. "He said he can't imagine either of us wanting it for, y'know, a keepsake collection so he could only surmise. When I asked him if he wanted to be involved, or wanted any updates, he emphatically noped out of the whole thing."

Riggs raised both hands in the air, unintentionally dropping his files. "What are you talking about?"

Annemarie motioned to the computer monitor with one hand while handing the thumb drive to Alistair. "It's easier if you join us." She gestured for Riggs to come to the other side of the desk. The space was tight, but they all packed in shoulder to shoulder with little issue.

Alistair plugged in the device and waited for his computer to recognize it. He double-clicked on the pop-up in the corner. It opened a single file labeled "North Beach." Before he proceeded, he looked up at Annemarie who loomed over him. His eyes momentarily darted to Riggs's face, but they returned to hers.

"Ready?" he asked.

She only nodded.

"What . . . the fuck . . . did I just see . . ." It was not a question. Riggs's mouth hung open and his eyes remained fixed at the dark, paused screen. At some point during the viewing, he had planted a hand atop his head and dug his fingers into the mop of hair, holding on for dear life, and had not let go.

Annemarie and Alistair exchanged uncertain glances, his more worrisome than hers. He turned his attention to a still-flabbergasted Riggs. "We don't know, to be honest."

Riggs's arms shot out in front of him, fingers splayed as if literally grasping for a feasible answer. "And you . . . you fought this thing. You were face-to-face with . . . whatever the fuck it is." Again, no questions, only pure statements bubbling out of him while he came to grips with what all of them had watched—what Alistair and Annemarie had been silently dealing with. "How . . ." A stilted breath was the only thing he could muster. Riggs made his way over to one of the chairs on the opposite side of the desk; he had to sit, he had to take a minute to collect his fraying thoughts.

"We *really* don't know anything," Annemarie insisted. "I know what I saw—"

"*I* know what *I* saw!" Riggs exploded. "Except, I don't . . ." He dropped his head into his hands. "Al, make it make sense."

"I wish I could, man. But that's why I wanted this video. I-I thought maybe we could post it online somewhere. See if anyone might know what it is. Annemarie's dealt with this, what? Three times now?" She nodded.

Riggs's head shot up, bewildered at the information. "How are you not fucking dead, Annie?"

She gave an emphatic shrug. "Maybe because there was always someone else. Peter. Moose. I mean, Nowell told me about the night . . ." Her voice cracked and she huffed out a heavy breath. "About *that* night. He and Travis—Riggs, they didn't kill Jesse. Obviously, the impact did, but it was be-because of that thing. It was chasing them. And they blew through the stop sign because it—" She had both men's eyes on her. "And, I think . . ." Her continuation was still shaky in its delivery. "I think I might have had a run-in with it before all this." She whirled a hand at the computer screen. "On *that* night."

"What?" It barely left Alistair's mouth before he was scrunching up his face, trying to pick apart what she meant.

"I *know* Jesse would've buckled me into the seat. That's what he did. Plus, I would have launched out of the car from the impact had I not been buckled in."

"You can't know that," Alistair protested.

She shook her head at this. "How far away from the car did you find me?"

"A hundred, hundred-twenty feet," he replied.

She counted on her fingers. "No sign of me hitting my head anywhere inside the car despite having a scalp full of blood. No fingerprints on the passenger handle inside the car—at least not mine. No drag marks or blood in the grass leading to my body."

"Are you suggesting it took you out of the car?" he asked. Riggs flicked his attention to Alistair, then looked back to Annemarie, awaiting an answer.

She clenched and bared her teeth in a grimace, accompanying it with another shrug. "How else do you explain how I got there? I was covered in blood when you found me, but forensics only found some hair in the car, right?" Alistair nodded. "I can't know for sure, but I have a gut feeling it was still there at the scene."

"You also had a broken collarbone and cracked ribs," Riggs reminded her.

"Seat belt injuries," she replied without missing a beat. "Or . . . It did to me what it did to Liam Peck."

"Crushed him," Alistair mused.

"But he only had the cuts on his neck," Annemarie said.

"And his hand," Riggs added.

"That was his own doing. And we don't know for sure there isn't something else wrong with him. Broken ribs or something, y'know?"

Riggs shook his head. "If he had broken ribs, we'd have all known about it. Those hurt."

Annemarie lowered her eyelids and gave him a flat, "Yeah, I know."

Alistair had stopped listening to their banter as he focused on the details of Jesse's death. The airbag had deployed on impact, but even that and his seat belt could not keep him from destroying his skull against the windshield. It was not an unheard-of scenario, but it was the first of its kind for everyone working on Port Harrow that night. The crews were split between extracting him from the wreckage and taking statements from Travis and Nowell, followed by their arrests. It was not until they were almost ready to pack up the scene that they found Annemarie, broken, left for dead alongside the road had Alistair not heard a noise; more than a noise, it was the echo of a wail.

For the last year, he never questioned that it had been Annemarie crying out for help. But now . . . *Was she right? Had the creature still been there at the scene? Did their arrival with the lights and sirens catch it off guard, causing it to leave her alone and flee to safety, and it was waiting for them to leave without her so it could have a meal? And what if. . . what if the creature was responsible for killing Jesse? What if Jesse had been alive at the time of impact? What if his death was at the hands of this creature and not bad luck with a car accident?*

Annemarie's scream startled Alistair out of his swirling thoughts. The air conditioning unit in the window had kicked on with a loud whine and scared her enough to warrant her yelp. Her hand went to her chest and a shaky, annoyed breath escaped her flared nostrils.

"I'm fucking *tired* of being scared all the time," she grumbled.

None of the three knew what else to say. Her eyes shot to her hands where she fidgeted with a chipped nail. Alistair opened his mouth to say something but stopped short. Riggs leaned back in his seat and looked at both of their faces.

Finally brave enough to say something, Riggs started, "I think we—"

A knock came at the closed door, Annemarie having shut it when she brought in the footage. "Come in," Alistair called.

Brown-pigtailed Cami entered the office with a hesitant smile on her face. It disappeared entirely when she felt how tense the air was. "Sorry to bother you, Al. You've got a phone call. And Riggs, there's been a small fender-bender at the park. You're the closest." Riggs gave a knowing nod as he hoisted himself out of the chair. He did not look at anyone before exiting.

"Line one, boss," Cami added.

"Thanks, I'll grab it in a sec." He watched her leave and waited another moment before turning to Annemarie. "Will you come by the house after work and help me upload the video?"

She nodded. "Yeah. Of course. I'll text you when I'm done for the day." She made to move, but stopped. "Do you think it's the right thing to do?"

"I'm running out of ideas, Annie. I'm all ears if you have any of your own."

Alistair traced a fingertip over the touchpad of the laptop to hover above the green button on the screen. "So then I click upload and . . . that should do it." He reclined on the couch the moment the website started churning through the video's data, rendering the images and compressing the resolution. He let out a breath, a mix of relief and annoyance. He had hoped to make quick work of the task so as to not take up much of Annemarie's time, but the laptop demanded a series of updates first. It took half an hour before they could even get to the website to build a profile for themselves and the video.

But now, with the video loading, the progress bar inching closer to the finish line, he could relax for a moment. "How was work?" he asked.

"Same as always. Though, I'm starting on a new project cataloging a bunch of old material someone from Brownstone donated. It has a lot of archived stuff about the island. It's—oh! It's at a hundred percent." She pointed to the screen. The green bar was full and the site confirmed it was ready to view. Alistair returned to his original position, his elbows digging into his knees as he leaned forward to tap away at the computer; a slight hiss escaped his lips from the lingering pain of his twin wounds. With another click of a button, the website redirected them to their profile page where the video waited for all to see.

"Just wanna make sure it's all there," he muttered as he clicked play.

They shuddered alongside every bestial roar. It had already been a lot reliving every moment of the panic, the fear, and the horror in the office with Riggs earlier that day. But with the two of them sitting side by side on the couch, alone with only the noise on the screen, a deep sense of dread truly set in. They experienced different emotions from the second watch-through; him, a tightness in his throat and gut at the thought that he could have died at the hands of the beast, and her, a moroseness at her screaming his name and being drowned out by the bullets Nowell fired into the flailing creature that would always be imprinted on her.

Prior to the upload, they stringed together a narrative for the about section, explaining the date, the events that unfolded, a reassurance that they were all okay after the incident, and that they were looking for answers as to what the unidentified *thing* in the video might be.

Alistair was not necessarily tech inept, but the understanding of how they would not have immediate answers, or even any interaction, escaped him. After refreshing the page several times over a ten-minute span and seeing zero views and zero likes, he hastily snapped, "This was a stupid idea."

"Patience," Annemarie said with a roll of her eyes.

He tapped his fingers on the edge of the coffee table. She reached forward to pull his hand back, knowing he was seconds away from hitting F5 to reload the page. He turned to look at her, eyebrows high up on his forehead, and she quickly let go. "I don't know what I was expecting . . ."

"You were expecting instant answers. And honey, that's not how this sort of thing works."

"I thought something as sensational as this would go viral," he admitted. "That's still a thing that happens, right?"

She nodded. "Yeah, of course. But that kind of content doesn't hit a million views in ten minutes. I mean, the video itself is over thirty minutes long. People are impatient—" She cleared her throat loudly and obviously while she gestured to him with a tilt of her head. "—but they need enough time to actually get through the video first."

"So, what? I should go to sleep and check it in the morning?"

She chewed on her lower lip for a moment before answering. "Probably. Though, knowing you, you're not going to get any sleep."

"And you're saying you will?"

"Alistair, I've had an incredibly long day. I could fall asleep standing up in your kitchen if you let me." She settled back into the corner of the couch, facing him at an angle. A yawn overtook her and she covered it with her hand. "That being said, I should go. Unless you need me for anything else."

He hesitated at the vague offer. There was nothing else he needed, not in terms of what she was offering, but he could use the company. He wanted to ask her to stay the night, simply to be another body in the bed; it was not something he was used to, having another person there with him, but after the last few weeks, it would not be unwelcome. But as he opened his mouth to suggest such a thing, a yawn overtook him and he found himself suddenly hit with a wave of exhaustion he knew would see him pass out the moment his head hit the pillow.

"No, I should be good. Thank you, though. For coming over. Are you good to drive home?"

She nodded. "As good as I'll ever be."

"All right, great." He stood as if to usher her toward the door, but she helped herself out. "I guess we'll talk tomorrow. Maybe there'll be something of use for us in the next twenty-four hours." She shoved her hands into her back pockets as she crossed the threshold to the front stoop. She turned on her heel to face him.

"And if not in twenty-four hours, then maybe forty-eight," he added, trying to sound hopeful instead of put-out by the idea he needed to be patient. He wanted answers now. It had not occurred to him they might never come.

"Have a good night. Try not to obsess over it." She lifted her chin to gesture at the computer behind them on the table.

"I promise I won't." A meek smile crept into the corner of his mouth as he raised a hand to wave her off. She was down the steps and inside her car before she waved back, and then the engine started and she was gone down the road.

A cursory glance the next morning while he prepped for work showed that it had been viewed about a hundred times, but there were no comments, no interactions beyond a thumbs-up or thumbs-down; there were far more positive ones, at least.

His day got away from him—the moment he set foot in the office, he was running. If it was not an official call of some sort directing him out of the building, it was Riggs or Liu or Cami needing some semblance of help around the property, including troubleshooting one of the cruisers because Port Harrow's mechanic, Peter Arthur, well . . .

It was nearing five o'clock when Alistair had an opportunity to sit and breathe—and even then, his inbox was full and required his attention before he could leave. As he hit send on the final email to Sheriff Bachhuber, his cell phone chirped. He pulled it from his pocket and woke up the screen.

[Annemarie]
You check the video today?

[Alistair]
First thing this morning. Not a
lot of movement with it at that
point. Why? Is it doing anything
now?

[Annemarie]

335

Nothing helpful, but it's getting
seen at least.

At that, Alistair popped up from his seat, pocketed his phone, and shut off the computer monitor. Anything else that came his way could wait until the morning. Rainey was behind the counter on the phone, talking loudly and slowly at the person on the other end. Alistair could see the annoyed expression on her face as she tried her best to keep it from her voice. He raised one questioning eyebrow and flashed a thumbs-up followed by a thumbs-down. She responded with a roll of her eyes and a flick of her wrist—she would be fine without him. He gave a little wave on his way out the front door, then could not contain another ounce of his intrigue. Into his car, on the road, and home in minutes, he could only imagine what their little video had gotten up to in the last twelve hours.

Six thousand views and a dozen comments.

"So fake. You can see the actor's green suit."

"The way that thing pounced on that deer = me IRL when it's food time during intermittent fasting."

"Movie trailers are getting really weird these days."

And in response to the last comment, someone bothered to chime in with: *"This is def one of those where the best parts was in the promo. Not gonna bother seeing this when it comes out."*

The frustrated groan that left him was one that rivaled the rumble of tires halting in his gravel driveway. It caught his attention and he left the couch, still in his half-undressed state—he had not bothered to do more than take off his button-down and shoes—to investigate. He poked his head out the door in time to see Annemarie hauling herself and a small crockpot out of the car.

"Hiya," she said with a big smile on her face.

"Hi?"

"I brought dinner."

A little confused, he looked over his shoulder into the house then back at her, then cocked his head. "Did . . . did I know you were coming over?"

She stopped at the bottom of the stairs and locked eyes with him, the crockpot hoisted up in both hands at her chest and a reusable grocery tote hanging from the crook of one arm. "Don't think so. I figured since you had a stupid-busy day, you could use a little good home-cooking." What she was not going to bother mentioning was that she knew he had been living off of protein bars, canned soup, and cereal in recent weeks—the pile of empty, dirty bowls had been a dead giveaway, and after he rushed off to work the other morning, she hung around and snooped through his belongings. What she found verified her hunch.

"How'd you know I had a busy day?" He sidestepped as she made her way up the stairs, careful to not let the sides of the crockpot touch him.

"You said so yourself."

"Yeah, like fifteen minutes ago. There's no way you cooked something and made it down from your house in fifteen minutes."

"Okay, *maybe* I made a phone call earlier today to the station to ask you a question and Cami said you'd been out most of the day on back-to-back calls. And *maybe* I noticed you've been losing a little weight and your eating habits haven't been all that great . . ." She trailed off.

When Alistair shut the door behind them and leaned against the wood panel, he tried to force out his stomach a little to hide the fact that he *had* lost some weight and he *had* been neglecting himself. But he had not thought anyone noticed. He raised an arm behind his head to rub at his neck while a half grimace rested on his lips. "Yeah, well, I—"

"I had an unexpected afternoon off and so I figured this was the least I could do." She was already in the kitchen setting down what she brought with her. She continued talking to him via the pass-through while she worked, the sounds of the glass lid clanking on the quartz countertop and the susurration of plastic and canvas bags against each other accompanying her words. "You take care of me, I take care of you."

"That's . . . really not necessary, Annie. I'm fine."

She pressed her lips together to form a thin line and raised both eyebrows. "So, then, you're saying you want me to pack up this here beef stew with all the big chunks of skin-on potatoes and carrots and the loaf of garlic bread and the pint of dark chocolate ice cream and go home?" She made an overexaggerated gesture, showcasing all of the food she had brought with her.

"I mean, you came all this way . . ."

The spoon clinked against the licked-clean bowl as Alistair set it on the coffee table. They had spent the impromptu dinner eating in an amiable silence, and now he waited for Annemarie to finish her food so he could whisk away both their dishes. He busied himself with tooling around their video's page, refreshing it once to see if the view count had increased any since the last time he checked twenty minutes earlier. Another five. *Big whoop.* And two new comments that were less than helpful, and instead, focused on how much better *their* night vision equipment was.

Annemarie leaned forward to set her bowl aside too, but he was quick to swoop in, gather their things, and head into the kitchen—making it a point to let the dishes soak and to grab another slice of bread. He stuffed a corner of it in his mouth as he returned to the living room and hesitated a moment when he saw Annemarie had moved positions. She was in his seat now, scrolling up and down on the webpage with her head tilted.

"You look perplexed."

She turned her attention to him and gave a slight nod. "Yeah, maybe. Your computer made a little noise, and I saw some kind of notification pop up in the corner." She pointed to the lower right-hand side. "But before I could see what it said, it disappeared. So now I'm trying to figure out what it was."

He crowded beside her and joined her in hunching over the keyboard, squinting a little as he perused every inch of the screen in search of something different. "Mm, wait, go back up." She scrolled to the top. There was a little green icon on the left, something he had never noticed before. "Can you click on that?"

It took them to a direct message page where there were several notes from a myriad of accounts. Three of them advertised cam-girls, one of them was offering an uptick in views for a fee, and the last one had the subject line of: "I have information regarding the being in your video."

Annemarie let loose a tiny gasp, a sharp intake of breath, as she popped her head up to look at Alistair. His heartbeat increased at what they both had read. "Is there more?" he asked, gesturing to the screen.

"I don't know." She clicked on the sender's name—it said VL—and that took them to another page with a short message attached. Annemarie read the words out loud. "Hello. No doubt you'll receive any number of messages and comments in response to the video you posted, but I would like to share with you what I think the creature is. I have information regarding its identity." She looked at Alistair again with her mouth slung open. "Do you think this is legit?"

He could only shrug. "Your guess is as good as mine."

"There's a reply button. I could try sending a message back, see if we can get anything more out of them."

"Yeah, try that."

Annemarie spent a few minutes typing away at the laptop, deleting and retyping several times over, before deeming the note good enough.

"Hi, VL. Thanks for contacting
us. We're at a loss for what this
thing could be, so any
information you have would be
great."

"Hello, again. I'm afraid that the knowledge I have of this thing is best provided in person. It's not a simple matter of giving you a name so you can do a search of your own."

"How do you intend to share the information?"

"I see based on the details you left for the video that you live on Port Harrow. I live just down the road in Cedarbrook. I'd be more than happy to host you for an afternoon."

"I don't like the sound of that." She buried her teeth into her lip to gnaw at some of the anxiety the message exchange caused. "Randomly showing up at someone's house?"

Alistair straightened his spine, giving his back a rest from the unnatural hunched position he had been in while reading the back-and-forth between Annemarie and the person on the other end of the conversation. "I don't like it either. But, supposedly, they're local. Cedarbrook isn't Azure County, but I can still do a background check on them if we can get all their details."

She stuffed the nail of her ring finger against her clenched teeth and gnawed on that for a moment too. "I don't trust this."

He stood from the couch and stuffed his hands in the pockets of his work pants. He paced in front of the coffee table, head hung low. "I mean, worst-case scenario we get their info, I look them up, and they're some kind of dangerous felon and we don't go."

"How about worst-case scenario we get their info, you look them up, they show up as all clean and harmless, and we end up missing our kidneys in a bathtub full of ice."

Alistair stopped moving to gawk at her. "Are you okay?" he asked.

She pushed her hair back off her forehead. "Are you?"

"Don't you want to get to the bottom of this?

"Of course I do. More than you, probably," she snapped, though she did not mean for it to sound so harsh.

His incredulity turned into a frown. "So then why don't we pursue this?"

"Why are you so willing to jump right into it?"

"I told you we wouldn't do anything until we know for sure that this person is legit."

"But *how* will we know they're who they say they are? Is the background check going to tell us every little thing about them?"

He huffed a breath through his nose, a touch indignant, but more at being made to see reason than anything else. "Well, no."

"It's going to tell us about anything they got caught doing, right?" He nodded. "So we *can't* ever know if they're *legit*." She was trying hard to hold her tongue; she desperately wanted to verbally shake him so hard to knock sense into him—*him*, the goddamn sheriff.

He sat in the easy chair. "Look, I understand what you're saying. But just because we can't get their whole life history from a name and an address doesn't mean this is already dead in the water. If you're not wanting to do this, that's fine. I'll go by myself."

"And if you get hurt while you're there?" She raised an eyebrow.

"Then I'll only have myself to worry about and to blame. I won't have dragged you into anything."

"You can't go alone," she protested.

"Then come with me."

Annemarie opened her mouth, then closed it. She reached for the laptop and typed again.

> "We don't get down to
> Cedarbrook all that often, but
> we could make something work.
> Give me your name, number,
> and address, and we'll see what
> all of our schedules look like for
> us to come down to talk to you."

TWENTY-EIGHT

Alistair and Annemarie agreed to meet at his house at eight in order to catch the ferry to Brownstone thirty minutes later. She was running ten minutes late. Alistair reclined on the couch with his sneaker-clad feet propped up on the edge of the coffee table.

"Come on, Annie," he muttered, seeing the clock showed eight fifteen. Thankfully, the dock was less than ten minutes away, and the eight thirty on Saturday rarely filled by even half. Still . . .

His restless leg bounced. It was not so much that he worried about missing the boat—he was concerned about their impending day. The visit with Victoria Lucia—a woman he could only find so much on in the databases he had access to—may or may not give them the answers they required to put the lid on this bubbling-over problem he had on his hands. What would the next step be should they get useful information? What would the next step be if they *did not* get useful information? Being cooped up in the car with Annemarie for six or more hours, hopeful their only squabble would be over what music to listen to, could easily go sideways. Would she even talk to him, based on how their last conversation went?

The thoughts of the unknown swirled around in his head so fast it made him dizzy. A rapid knock sounded at the door, startling him. He lifted off the couch and rushed to the entryway to pocket his wallet and car keys from off the side table. Another series of loud knocks rang out as he heard a muffled, "C'mon, Al, we're gonna be late!" He closed his eyes and let out an amused exhale of breath as he opened the door. Annemarie was caught mid-stroke of her fingers through her ruffled, windswept hair. "C'mon, slowpoke," she urged.

His eyebrows raised on his forehead, creating creases that aged him, and his tiny smirk turned into a mouth-gaping look of disbelief. "I'm the slowpoke?" he asked. He made an emphatic gesture of looking at his watch. He stepped out of the house and pulled the door shut behind him, giving the knob a jiggle to ensure it was locked.

She gave a tense chuckle. "Sorry I'm late."

He led the way to the car, climbing inside first, quick to clean up the paperwork piled on the passenger seat before letting her in. He unlocked the door, enabling her to get situated too. "Sorry. I forgot I brought some work home." He tucked the manila folders in the pocket behind her seat.

"No worries," she replied with a slight smile. She pulled her cell phone from her purse and glued her eyes to the screen, scrolling through a series of text messages.

Alistair turned the engine over and backed out of the gravel driveway. While the ride to the ferry terminal lasted mere minutes, the awkward silence between the two seemingly lengthened the short journey. Annemarie could not stop herself from thinking about their last fight, but kept any further opinions to herself. Occasionally, Alistair glanced over at his solemn travel companion in the hopes of catching her attention, even to give a smile, but her phone proved to be more entertaining.

Aboard the hour-long crossing, she opted to stay in the car to nap while Alistair wanted to stretch his legs in front of the four-hour drive to meet Victoria in Cedarbrook. Alistair often paced the length of the vessel during the journey, sometimes to have peace and quiet, sometimes to work through a problem in his head, or more often than not, to quell boredom. Today was a combination of all three.

Meeting Victoria was a task he was simultaneously gung-ho and apprehensive over. He needed answers. He needed to know what was happening to his island and to his loved ones. But . . . all of this could be a wild-goose chase. Since the first time Victoria contacted them, a red flag flew freely in the back of his mind. As a sheriff, he was trained to read into situations, to look below the surface. As a civilian, and perhaps a little less logical than his professional side, he was paranoid. She was a complete stranger to them. Annemarie had it right when she asked why he was so eager to throw himself at the situation, especially when *stranger danger* had been firmly drilled into their heads from a young age, and he actively taught children about it when he spoke at schools.

After Annemarie left his house that night, having agreed to meet up with Victoria if nothing about her seemed too out of the ordinary, he read through the online conversation several times, trying to suss out anything more from a handful of emotionless words. It carried over into the next day when he started the background check on her. He needed to be quiet about it, given that it was a grey area—there was no probable cause for investigating her, or at least one good enough to keep him out of trouble if anyone were to find out.

When he finally had a chance to review the results, he called Annemarie to tell her the good news—Victoria Lucia had nothing on her record. They had agreed to meet with her that Saturday, thinking they would not show up if something was flagged about her, but now they could move forward. The conversation took a bizarre turn and ended with them shouting at each other because Jesse had been brought up and she did not want to talk about it.

It left things awkward, as was obvious from their interaction in the last hour. Alistair pinned the source of it as them both being scared, skeptical of the truth, frightened of finding all the answers. Or finding *no* answers whatsoever.

At the thirty-minute mark of the ride from Port Harrow to the mainland, the island's northwest shore came into view. No matter the time of day or the weather, this section, with its drastic mocha cliffs topped with perpetually fog-laden evergreen trees was always a sight to behold. If he could manage it, Alistair stopped to sit and admire his home. Because the ferry remained relatively quiet at the moment, he had half a dozen seats to choose from for watching the cliffs roll by as the boat pulled away from the channel to veer toward the mainland. He watched the white and grey seagulls soar low over the water as they searched for a suitable spot to land. If he squinted and concentrated enough, he could see the small colony of tufted puffins nesting within the steep, nearly inaccessible nooks. This time of year, they were still incubating their eggs. A tidbit of information he inadvertently learned from Jesse. *Jesse . . .*

Images involuntarily flashed through his mind: of Jesse's beaten, broken, bloody skull planted firmly in the middle of a spiderweb of windshield glass; his body hunched over the deployed airbag, arms askew with compound fractures; the vacant, dead-eyed stare of irrefutable death; of absolute destruction of property and pers—

A hand touched his left shoulder. He visibly jumped, lifting from his seat an inch or two, his breath catching in his throat. He turned to look up at whomever the hand belonged to, and seeing it was Annemarie, the worry melted from his face, softening his features and relaxing his tense body that came from thinking of Jesse's horrific death.

"Sorry," she said.

"No worries."

"Figured I'd pee before we hit the road again." She crossed in front of him to take the seat on his right.

Alistair stood immediately. "That's a good idea."

He silently excused himself, leaving Annemarie to stare at the backside of him as he walked to the restroom halfway across the boat. Her attention turned to the chiming of her cell phone. A text from Nowell asking if they were on their way yet. She shot a concise "no" as she spotted Alistair exiting the bathroom, heading toward the car, not her. She silenced the phone and slipped it into the small pocket of her dress.

The cars piled off the boat one by one. The duo was quickly on the road in Brownstone, en route south to

Cedarbrook. Both of them having spent so much of their lives in Port Harrow and the neighboring towns of the mainland, there were many memories they shared.

Along the main drag cutting Brownstone in half, Alistair spotted the coffee shop all of their friends used to go to before and after school. He pointed it out, then immediately asked, "Do you remember when Nate finally got the balls to ask out that one barista?"

Annemarie covered her face with both hands. "That was a nightmare to watch. I still feel bad for him all these years later."

"Did you hear the most recent news about him?"

"Last I heard, he went to college in Mayfair, but we lost touch right after that and I've never crossed paths with him or his family again. What's going on with him?" she asked.

Alistair straightened up in the seat but relaxed his shoulders and his grip on the steering wheel. It was nice to not think about the utter chaos plaguing their lives, just for a moment. "Do you remember the one super shy barista? The redhead?" He glanced over his shoulder to see her nod. "She apparently was madly in love with him, but never had the courage to say anything, especially after Nate spent so much time drooling over, uh, what was her name . . ." He snapped his fingers as a means of thinking. "B-B-Brenda?"

"Oh man, uh . . ." Annemarie thought for a moment. "Becca!" she blurted out.

"Becca, right! So Dierdre, the redhead, never said a thing to Nate because he was so hung up on Becca. But what neither of them knew was that they were both going to the same university and were living in the same dorm. He eventually saw her in the dining hall and flagged her down. They got to talking, an extremely long story a little shorter, they got married a couple years ago."

"Aw, that's really sweet. I'm glad to hear something good happened for him." Annemarie pushed strands of her hair back as she stared out the passenger window. She noticed an empty lot. "Wait—what happened to Vince's?"

"The skate shop?"

She nodded.

"They demo'd it about six months ago. I heard they plan to build apartments."

"That's a shame. So much of my youth was spent there trying to pick up burnout skater boys and seeing how many wheels I could steal without Vince catching me."

Alistair glanced over at her and blinked several times. "What?"

She giggled as she lifted both hands in the air, touching at the wrists as if ready to accept a pair of handcuffs. "You caught me, Officer. I used to shoplift."

"But *why wheels*?" he asked.

She shrugged. "Why not? They were small, easy to pocket, easy to not notice they were missing."

"I—okay. That's fair enough." He stared at her a moment longer as they waited at the red light and he finally burst into laughter with a shake of his head. "I don't think I ever knew that about you."

"What? That I had a bad-girl streak in me?"

"Well, I mean, we used to steal beer from people at the Fourth parties and go get high in the woods and behind the high school, so I *knew* that about you. But where was the harm in that?"

"Where was the harm in taking wheels from Vince? Not like he had any shortage of them." She snorted. He emphatically cocked his head to the right and aimed his rolling eyes directly at her. "I know, I know. Stealing is stealing. If he was still in business, I'd take the whole box of them back."

"You still have them?" he asked.

"Yep. Well, they're at mom and dad's in my old room."

"How many do you have?"

She shrugged. "I dunno. Like fifty or sixty?"

He choked on his own spit. "Anne*marie*!"

Her laugh was one of mania. "Didn't take too long to get them either."

"Yeah, you really were there all the time."

The conversation dissolved into silence until Alistair finally said, "I guess the good news is that Vince moved his shop to Dearborn, so you can go return them."

She gasped and stuttered out, "O-oh, well, uh, I . . ."

He shot her an impish grin. "I'm only messing with you." Her cheeks flushed red, but a smile spread across her lips at the realization that he was not expecting her to be true to her word. On top of everything else she— they—had going on, the last thing she wanted to concern herself with was wandering back into Vince's skate shop and having to explain the fifteen hundred dollars' worth of products she had stolen over twenty years ago. Maybe Vince would have a good laugh; maybe he would call the cops. She never could tell with him and she was not about to test her luck—so far, it had not been all that good.

TWENTY-NINE

"That's how Sierra used to make me feel. Until I found out what a smoldering piece of garbage she was." Alistair did not feel the need to glance at Annemarie for a reaction to a statement he considered fact.

"Seems harsh to say that about an ex-girlfriend, or a woman in general," Annemarie replied casually.

"Fiancée."

"What?" Her voice came out as a confused half croak and her head shot to the side to look at him.

"We were gonna get married." Again, he kept his eyes staring forward, not looking for sympathy, or questioning, if he could help it.

"How long ago was this?" Her eyebrows lowered and she squinted one eye.

"Uhh . . . well . . ." He thought for a long moment. "We met, like, fifteen years ago, I think. Something like that. I don't keep track of time too well." He paused in thought, realizing how odd that statement sounded to anyone other than him. "I try not to think about it, is what I mean."

Annemarie was not sure how to respond in that moment; he was not offering up any additional intel willingly. That piercing, awkward silence returned. She finally cleared her throat. "Can I ask what happened?"

Without missing a beat, he replied, "Of course you can," but once again did not elaborate further.

She hesitated. "I can ask, but will you tell me?"

In one breath, he uttered: "We met in undergrad, fell in love, I proposed, she said yes, our career paths took us in different directions, she eventually found someone else to carry on an affair with for several years, and when I accidentally caught her trying to leave the apartment with all her things, she raged at me, threw my mom's ring in my face, told me how unhappy I made her, and that she wished me many years of loneliness." His chest heaved. "We broke up and went separate ways. Selfish silver lining: Freedom enabled me to pursue this position one hundred percent unhindered after that." He shrugged one shoulder.

Annemarie nodded, now understanding why he was not thrilled to talk about the relationship and why he felt the way he did about her. But she needed to know more. "So . . . you met in undergrad and you ended it how long ago?"

He corrected her, trying not to sound like he was still bitter, "*She* ended it. Despite years of doting on each other and her seemingly intense desire to marry me, she found something more worthwhile in someone else. And fairly soon into the relationship, from what she admitted."

Annemarie stuttered for a second on her words before she could clearly say, "I-I've known you all my life, Alistair, but I have to ask: W-were you awful to her? Were her feelings of anger and unhappiness j-justified because of your behavior?"

Alistair shot an agitated glance at her, thinking she was being difficult on purpose, but he saw the look on her face—the honest, wide eyes and the biting of her lower lip—and calmed down to a simmer instead of boiling over. He wanted to blurt out *"How could you ask me that?"* but despite their decades-long friendship, the chunk of time saw them apart, pursuing lives independent of the other. People changed, and not always for the better. It was a legitimate question.

With a sigh, preparing for a story time he did not anticipate, he replied sheepishly with, "I don't think so." He paused. "I probably wasn't the best partner. I've never been abusive, I've never intentionally put someone in a position that made them uncomfortable, I've never had any want to make someone feel like they're not worth something. The way I treated you in our relationship?" He paused to watch for her acknowledgment, which she gave with an ajar-mouth nod. "Exact same way I treated her. But I definitely put a lot of passion and energy behind my career. I won't skirt around the fact that my want to get excellent grades and do the best I could in each of my jobs was just as important as making a loved one at home happy. I mean—" He interrupted himself to take a breath, but to make a point. "I think anyone who knows me knows that to be true." He cleared his throat. "Could I have made more time for her? Sure. Could I have gone out of my way to make sure *all* her needs were met? Maybe, but maybe not. She expected a lot out of me. I only had so much time in my day and divided between her and school or work, it was a tough juggle."

Annemarie nodded. "I often went weeks without seeing much of Jesse when he was fast-tracking through his degree. It was hard not to feel . . . neglected."

"And that was the last thing I wanted her to feel, but I didn't know how to do both well. We met when things were easy, y'know? Dating her was effortless. She was studying to be a nurse and her school life wasn't so taxing back then either. But the deeper we got into our respective fields, the harder things got. I always thought we were okay, though. Honestly. I'm not placing blame on her, but had she at least told me she was unhappy, I would've worked harder to do better. I can't fix something if I don't know it's broken. Men can be pretty dumb sometimes. And I wasn't always the most observant of people."

"Which is hilarious given how incredibly anal you are with your job."

He blew a little raspberry with his lips. "I like to believe I've matured and gotten at least a *little* smarter since then."

"So, then, when did you guys split?" She was trying to picture the timeline.

"When did you get back?" he asked.

She counted on her fingers. "Five years ago."

"She left me maybe a year before you moved home."

"Wait. You were together for ten years and in all that time, you never told me about her? You never talked about being with someone." She looked to him, intrigued to see a reaction.

He glanced along his shoulder to meet her gaze. "It never came up."

"But we talked about *everything*," she insisted.

"Obviously not that." He nonchalantly shrugged. A little defensively, he added, "And besides, you never mentioned Jesse."

She blurted, "Well, that was because—" but stopped. She had asked herself many times before why she kept the secret from Alistair and her answer always came back to not knowing if she had truly moved past her feelings from their high school days; she never wanted to confront the possibility that she might still have been hung up on him when she was also so in love with Jesse. Their weekly phone calls were a constant reminder that they had been more than a puppy-love adventure, and though they broke off the relationship amicably, she knew they were both deeply affected by it. Because he never talked about his love life, she did not want to rub her happiness in his supposedly single face.

But how did she tell him that now?

Before she could answer with a nonanswer, Alistair pointed off into the distance at a building in the middle of being demolished. "When did they shut down Blacktop Brewery?" he asked, drawing her attention to the construction site.

"Probably when the wrecking ball hit it."

Alistair could not help but snort at the response. "Thanks, Captain Obvious. Man, I used to go there all the time. I guess it's been a while since I've come out here, though. A lot's changed."

"A lot's changing," she added, the corner of her bottom lip perpetually stuck under her top teeth as she gnawed on it. She waited for a response, or any kind of expression to fill his face, but he kept his eyes forward.

When he did not give her what she wanted, her eyes drifted to his mounted phone to see how far out they were from Victoria's house. "Looks like we're getting close."

He glanced down for a moment; it was another dozen miles. His breath caught in his throat before he could get out the words he had been thinking the last several days. "What are we doing?"

"Hmm?" Her eyes were back on him.

"This. This whole thing. What the fuck are we doing?"

"I—"

"I mean, I did a background check on this lady, I dug deep to find any dirt I could that might be a red flag, and she came up clean . . . But I still don't feel like what we're doing is safe."

"She's a harmless old lady, right?" Annemarie cocked an eyebrow.

"She's not old, but seemingly harmless, yes."

"Then we give her some of our time, we ask our questions, we listen to what she has to say, and we go." She shrugged. "I know I was against this at first, but I don't think anything about that is to our detriment."

"But we're entertaining the idea that anything she says will be the truth. How do we know she's not lost her mind and is preying on the vulnerable, leading us into a trap that's going to see us hurt or robbed or . . ."

The roles were now reversed from the other night. Annemarie reached a hand out to his lap and pressed it against his thigh. "Are you okay?"

He looked at her, a little shocked at her touch, but mostly curious about her question. "Yeah, of course I am. Why?"

"You did your research on her. And still you think she could be dangerous?"

"I'm in law enforcement, Annie. My brain goes to worst-case scenario whenever I do anything."

"That . . . sounds awful."

"The job takes a toll. I mean, my life's not rainbows and sunshine."

"Mine hasn't been for the last year either."

The silence between them hung languidly the last fifteen minutes of their drive, neither of them exchanging words or stealing glances. Annemarie's revelation of his long-term relationship she knew nothing about prior to this car ride made her question what else he had not been open with her about; but she could not balk at the omission for all those years—she had done the same to him. Given it was a personal matter, she could understand it, but she worried he was holding back information regarding what they were currently embarking on, what they had been experiencing. Her learning of his deepest, darkest desires from the night the creature attacked him and seemingly sent him to an alternate reality had been alarming, but she also remembered how he seemed hesitant to share the details. Was he withholding pertinent information? Or was it a series of events that propelled the narrative forward that he figured was not relevant?

His wagon dragged along the street, headed toward a cul-de-sac with several homes positioned around the curve. They were simple houses, suitable for families of three or four. Nothing glamorous or over-the-top, but seemingly quaint and quiet. Each of the yards were a little overgrown, some dry patches here and there, with shrubs and trees in desperate need of pruning. One of the houses stuck out more than the others. Its teal paint was pristine, as if recently touched up, especially compared to the others that showed signs of obvious weathering and wear. The three steps leading to the front door were decorated with brightly colored flowers in big ceramic pots and the rest of the veranda was teeming with a clutter of hanging plants, patio furniture, and several cats lazing about.

"This is the place," Alistair announced as he pulled up alongside the curb in front of the teal house.

"Doesn't look like a felon lives here."

"That's what she wants you to think." But he said it accompanied by an overemphatic wink. "Victoria Lucia, sixty-two years old, widowed, no children, a bank teller for half of her life followed by a career of volunteer work for local food banks, soup kitchens, and animal shelters. She currently lives alone, doesn't have any registered firearms, and as far as I can tell, she likes shades of blue."

Annemarie raised her eyebrows at the last remark. "What? 'Cause the house is teal?"

Alistair pointed at the house where there stood an older woman with dark tresses streaked with silver, a tan complexion against her age-worn face, wearing an aquamarine housedress dazzled with bright blue embroidered flowers and matching slippers. She had a hand raised above her head as a means of greeting.

He did not waste any time pushing open the driver's side door, relishing in the ability to stand and stretch his lower back and legs. He strode over to Annemarie's side of the car to help her out, but she was on her own two feet before he could make it. She lifted a hand to her brow to shield her eyes from the bright sunshine before directing her attention to the woman on the porch.

"Good afternoon!" Victoria called in a cheerful tone so sweet, it seemed fake.

"Hey there," Alistair responded as he took a moment to ensure the car was locked before joining Annemarie up the path to the house. "Victoria, I'm assuming?"

"And Alistair and Annemarie, so nice to meet you." She was already reaching out to embrace Annemarie who seemed taken aback at the woman's simple gesture. Victoria noticed her reticence and immediately segued to extending a hand instead. Annemarie was far more obliging to this. Alistair was right behind her, waiting his turn to greet the woman in a standard, familiar fashion. "Please, come in. I hope you're hungry. I've made *campechanas* and *mantecadas*, and there's always plenty of coffee to go around." She turned on her delicate heel with a flourish of her housedress and pushed her way in through the screen door.

Alistair and Annemarie exchanged glances, the corners of her mouth dragged into a frown and his eyebrows high on his forehead. He gave a simple shrug and followed Victoria into the house; Annemarie was close behind him, unsure whether her apprehension to hug the stranger plus her lack of eagerness to enter the unusually cheery abode would give off a bad first impression.

Victoria's home was as bright inside as it was outside, and both matched her sunny disposition. Even when Alistair had called her to discuss their meeting, Victoria had been nothing but high-spirited, including when speaking about the dark information she claimed to possess. Juxtaposed were the vibrant white walls splashed with orchid, sapphire, blush, and daisy and the looming menace overtaking Port Harrow—and none of the overwhelming embellishments calmed the saturation of what was happening back home.

The sound of soft footfalls echoed through the house and Alistair was not sure where she had disappeared to. To his right was a modest living room with a large, well-worn couch draped in blankets to protect the leather from the small pack of cats bouncing around the furniture. An all-white shorthair bounded up a carpet-covered tree in the corner while an overweight Persian tried to chase its companion and failed when gravity kept its heavy bottom from jettisoning off the ground. Meanwhile, three tortoiseshells rocketed between Alistair's legs, causing him to lift a foot in the air to stop from being knocked over.

"Don't mind the babies," Victoria said from behind the two, the sweet hum of her voice enveloping them like the hug she did not receive on the front porch. Annemarie jerked her head to one side, unexpecting, and watched as the woman carried a tray of baked goods in one hand and a collection of mugs, a glass carafe filled with steaming coffee, and smaller containers with lids in the other. "Sit, sit. You've driven a long way." She nudged Annemarie with her elbow, encouraging her toward the couch. "I promise, I don't bite. And neither do the babies,"

At her insistence, Alistair shuffled to the opposite side of the couch and lowered himself onto a cushion, remaining rigid in his posture. Annemarie followed suit, desperately hoping he would take the lead in the whole scenario. "You've got a lovely home, Victoria," he finally managed. The Persian sat at the base of the cat tree, its attention now turned to him, its puffball of a tail flicking back and forth. Feeling a bit unnerved at its ice-blue eyes trained on him, Alistair cleared his throat and tried to focus on anything else in the room.

"Don't mind Archie. He's a gentle fellow. But those eyes—they'll make you feel you were a bad person even when you haven't done anything wrong." A smirk pressed itself against Victoria's puckered lips. "Please help yourself to food and drink."

Annemarie was not certain what either of the baked goods were, but if they tasted anything like the house smelled—perfume-strength citrus enrobed in a thick cinnamon blanket—she was certain she would like them. She reached a hand forward to grab one of the small ceramic plates on the second of the two trays. Serving herself one of each, she set them in her lap while she poured herself a cup of coffee. She waggled the carafe in the air at Alistair, offering him a helping.

"No, I'm good," he said softly. Truth be told, while they looked great, his stomach was in a knot—and had been since before Annemarie's delayed arrival—and the thought of stuffing food in him in any quantity made the knot tighten further. With her face pointed away from

Victoria, Annemarie raised her eyebrows and bulged her eyes, silently insisting he take some of the concessions being so generously offered to him. "In a bit," he added through tight lips and a huffy breath.

Noticing the quiet exchange between them, Victoria piped up. "So, Port Harrow. That's a beautiful island. Have you both been there long?"

Their attention snapped back to her, almost forgetting she was in the room with them, and their serious expressions melted away. "We were both born and raised there," Annemarie said. To quell herself from oversharing, she shoved a corner of the flaky, delicate *campechana* in her mouth.

Alistair picked up the slack. "Yeah, born and raised. Annemarie left after high school for a decade or so and I came over to the mainland for school and work, but we're both back now."

Victoria nodded along. "It seems like true love brought you back together."

With a sudden, sharp inhalation, part of the pastry shot down Annemarie's throat without her having chewed it, causing a series of choking coughs as she worked to dislodge it. Alistair set a hand on her back to give a couple good pats between her shoulder blades. Red in the face, she reached for the coffee to take a long drink. "You okay?" he asked.

She held up a hand to signal she needed a moment, but nodded. "Yeah, sorry," she wheezed.

As she gathered her breath, Alistair interjected. "We're not together. We've been best friends pretty much all our lives, but that's it."

Victoria tilted her head and gnawed on her bottom lip. "But you have a history of romance." It was not a question.

Another round of coughs prompted Annemarie to set down the pastry and put the whole thing on the coffee table—she did not think she could trust herself to not choke if the conversation continued in this manner. "Ah, yep. We did date briefly. But that was a long time ago."

Victoria arched an eyebrow. "But that love is still there."

"Well, sure, I mean, Alistair's my best friend. We—"

"I think we're getting off topic here," he interrupted. "We'd like to know what you know, Victoria. This whole thing has been . . ." He could not fathom finishing the sentence. "We could really use some answers."

She nodded again, her eyes closed this time as she took a moment before responding. "What would you like to know?"

"What . . ." Alistair started but immediately stopped himself. He had been thinking about this meeting all week, stressing, being anxious, summoning up all the ways it could go sideways. But he never once thought about questions to ask Victoria; he had not been sure they would even get out of Brownstone before fear of the unknown turned them around.

"You haven't thought this far, have you?" she asked, an amused smile tiptoeing across her lips. "You were so worried about whether I was going to serve you poison in your coffee or maybe that I was a lunatic serving up falsities to get attention that you didn't bother to compile a list."

Annemarie scoffed into the coffee cup set up to her lips, but finished the sip she had already taken. She turned only her eyes to glance at Victoria, then turned her whole head to look at Alistair who was still frozen with an unformed response in his mouth. She indelicately elbowed him in his side to set him back on course.

"I'm sorry, you have to understand that we needed to ensure our safety," was all he could muster.

The grin never left Victoria's face. "Oh, Sheriff, I'd never want it any other way." She leaned forward to pour herself a cup of coffee and immediately took a long glug from the still-steaming cup. "Let's start with something a bit easier: What about the video are you wanting to know?"

Without thinking, Annemarie blurted, "What is it?"

It was an apt question.

"Well, it's not an animal. A mammal, yes. But its existence is not unsubstantiated the way your Bigfoot or Loch Ness Monster is. That much is obvious." A sip. "Maybe to your eyes, it seems as feral and uninhibited in the way a cheetah pursues its prey. Or maybe what you've witnessed is more like an ambush predator—lying in wait for the perfect moment to attack. It's not an animal, but neither is it a human." Annemarie swore Victoria paused for dramatic effect. "It's as tall as a man, it looks like one too, but it's not one. It never was one." Another drink from her cup. "It's a hunter. It tracks. It watches. It waits. It's patient."

Alistair held back an eye roll. Whatever they had been dealing with might be patient, but he was not. "Does it have a name?"

"It has many names: devil, djinn, firebrand, *cazador*, ogre, fomenter, beast—"

"Those are adjectives," he interrupted.

"If you would let me finish," she cut back. "It has many names. But they're all descriptors of its persona, yet not what it truly is. It has no taxonomy. It's not just one thing. It's something from ages past and never once is it called anything but an *adjective*." It seemed to Alistair that she spit out the last word to coincide with his accusation.

"You used a word . . . what was it? Gin?" Annemarie asked.

"*Djinn.* It's a spirit deeply rooted in Middle Eastern cultures. It can be good, bad, or neutral. It's a valid description, but it's not what this is. Not really." Victoria set the cup of coffee on the table in front of her and leaned back in her overstuffed chair, letting her intertwined fingers rest on her belly.

Alistair rubbed a couple knuckles along the hollow of one eye. "How do you know about it?" he asked.

"How does someone know anything about anything?" she returned. But before he could snap at her about more nonanswers, she added simply, "Stories."

"Stories?" He squinted at her, focusing on the fine lines around her mouth, waiting to see them flex and bend with the smile he knew was coming—she was taking them for a joyride at the expense of their time.

"*Erudition*, Sheriff."

"I . . . What?" He stared at her blankly.

Annemarie leaned over and mumbled, "It means book learning."

Victoria nodded. "Gold star for Miss McCready." Annemarie's eyes widened; she was not aware Victoria knew her last name. "You see, Sheriff, I've spent a good chunk of my life outside of this country, absorbing information through reading and oral tradition and exposure to different cultures. And what this enigma boils down to, this *story*, is a thousand years in the making."

Despite his anger rising, he kept his mouth shut, letting Victoria know the stage was hers. But she was done talking, it seemed.

With a bit of a drawl, Alistair started, "Okay, so, you've told us what it's not. You've danced around the idea of what it is. What can you tell us that's actually helpful?" He was losing his cool, but trying as hard as he could to stop himself from calling her out on what he perceived to be bullshit.

Annemarie set a hand on his arm to calm him. She knew what was coming if she allowed him to keep talking. She could not blame him—Victoria's ability to wax poetic was not lost on her, but they did not come all this way to be sent in pretty, wordy circles. "What Alistair means is, we understand it doesn't have a name. That's fine. But we still don't know where it came from, how we can stop it, or even if it *can* be stopped. Do you have any information in that regard?"

Victoria puckered her lips and brought them to one side of her mouth, creating an in-thought expression while remaining silent a moment longer. "I don't have all the answers you seek—" Alistair exhaled an annoyed breath at her admission. "—but what I *can* tell you is this: Soroush Vaziri."

THIRTY

At that, Alistair straightened his spine, his eyes went wide, setting all of his focus on her. "How do you know that name?"

"Who's Soroush Vaziri?" Annemarie asked as she let her gaze flit between his face and Victoria's.

"I met my husband here in the States, but shortly after our marriage, he took me abroad to return to his homeland where he was tasked with caring for his widowed mother. I didn't continue my career there, but instead took to volunteering where I could. I needed something to do with my time. One of my colleagues was a man named Soroush Vaziri. He was a philanthropist of sorts, having made his money early on in life, and was trying to do good where he could. More often than not, he donated money, but sometimes he rolled up his sleeves and did the dirty work alongside the rest of us." A smile rested on her lips. "Soroush and I became friends and kept in touch regardless of where he was in the world. It was the kind of friendship where he would drop what he was doing to take my call and he would go out of his way to keep me abreast of his adventures."

"Sounds like someone had a crush," Alistair added unnecessarily.

"I would be kidding myself if I thought anything else was true. But he knew I was happily in love with my Mahdi. Not to mention, I was his mother's age." She chuckled. "When my mother-in-law passed away, Mahdi and I decided to return to the States. We ended up in this area, and imagine my surprise when Soroush ended up on Port Harrow."

As she paused to collect her thoughts, two of the tortoiseshells rocketed into the room, both scaling the cat tree in order to continue their play-scrap on top of the white shorthair who had been content to snooze while the humans talked. This created a terrible noise, causing both Annemarie and Alistair to tense up their shoulders and cringe their features. Victoria stood and wriggled her hands into the hissing, crying pile of fur to extract the white cat. She pulled it close to her, stroked its head, and returned to the chair. Alistair could not get the thought out of his head of a movie villain announcing its plan for world domination all the while petting their cat. He tried not to let out the smirk that accompanied the thought.

"Mahdi died shortly thereafter. Bad heart. Rest his soul. Soroush remained in contact with me, always the gentleman, always the good friend. During one conversation after a lapse of a month or so, he told me he had returned from burying his mother back east. And while that's an anticlimactic element of our story, the one thing that gave me pause was his admission that he thought something had followed him home. He said something felt wrong at his mother's, but he couldn't pinpoint it. It didn't feel like the same place from even a couple years before when he was last there. He assumed it had something to do with illness in the air. Upon her dying, he experienced the expected grief that comes with losing a loved one, but it was more than that. He specifically used the word *haunted*, though I'm not certain if he used it for lack of a better one."

Annemarie glanced over her shoulder at Alistair who, while was still a touch annoyed that this meeting had taken on a story-time quality, was at the edge of his seat waiting for an answer to his dozens of questions. His jaw slacked as he watched Victoria, looking seconds away from interrupting her, but he kept quiet, if only out of politeness.

"I encouraged him to tell me more. I wanted him to be reassured that whatever he was thinking or feeling was safe in my ears. Though . . ." She leaned forward, still petting the snow-white ball of fur. "I admit, I am not much for gossip, but this had thoroughly piqued my interest. Partly because I wanted to help Soroush, partly because I was intrigued." The cat, obviously tired of sitting still, leaped from Victoria's lap and bounced onto the back of the couch behind Annemarie. "He told me bits and pieces over the months, never really committing to a certainty. But as the days and weeks progressed, the Soroush I knew seemed to be slipping away from reality. His phone calls came at random hours of the night, or we would drop a call mid-conversation and I wouldn't hear from him for another day or two. *Erratic*, I believe is the word to best describe the behavior. Which was very much unlike him."

A growl grew in Alistair's throat, one he wanted to unleash in a display of annoyance, but for once, Victoria seemed to be heading in a progressive direction, so he kept his cool. Annemarie noticed how he tensed, his fingers dug deep in the cushions on either side of his lap. She slipped an elbow into his side again, silently telling him to knock it off.

"He came here one Friday. Earlier in the week, I had told him I was busy that day and couldn't host him, to which he said he understood and promised to find another day that worked for him. But come Friday, as I was making my way out for an appointment, he was on the veranda, banging a fist on the screen door, begging me to let him in." Alistair cocked an eyebrow at this. Victoria noticed. "I'm getting there, Sheriff." She took in a huge rush of air as if preparing herself for the longest run-on sentence in history. "He pushed his way into the house despite my insistence that I would be late and he wouldn't let me leave. Not like he was holding me hostage, Sheriff, since I know that's what you're thinking." Annemarie glanced at Alistair's face to see what expression he would give based on Victoria's announcement. He gawked at her, seemingly wondering how she knew.

"He told me he thought he was losing his mind, that he needed help. He was desperate. There was no doubt about that. I made a phone call to postpone my previous engagement so I could give him the attention and care he obviously needed. In all my years of knowing him, I'd *never* seen him like that. Disheveled in appearance, ghost white in tone, skinnier than he'd ever been, and obviously coming apart at the seams. I don't know if either of you have ever witnessed someone in a manic spiral, but it's not pretty." She paused as she put a finger to her lower lip. And answering herself, she added, "Of course you have.

Annemarie has suffered much this last year, and Alistair, you've bore witness to her self-destruction."

"How . . ." Annemarie started, but stopped herself. "It wasn't . . . I mean, I . . ."

Alistair's hand shot out to stop her from continuing, knowing the triggering *self-destruction* would be enough to turn the conversation from Soroush Vaziri to the chaotic months leading up to this moment. A selfish streak spread through him, not wanting to zig when Victoria was finally zagging, but a deep part of him did not want Annemarie to have to dredge up any terrible emotions relating to Jesse's and Moose's deaths. "Please continue," he urged.

"There was a lot of mindless chattering, none of which I'll bore you with. But what I do want to share is that as our night came to a close, he admitted that whatever was causing this ever-increasing distress needed to disappear, otherwise, *he* would. I honestly didn't know what to do with that information. You see, I believed that he thought he was under duress, but I wasn't sure what to believe it was, or could be. There are stories from his and my husband's homeland that tell of these kinds of hauntings, where an entity attaches itself onto some poor, unsuspecting soul and torments them until it's time to move on."

"'Move on'?" Alistair echoed.

"Death, Sheriff."

"Its', or the person's?" he asked.

Victoria only gave a little shrug.

"But why? What's the purpose?" Annemarie piped in.

"What else? Malevolence." Victoria delivered the answer so smoothly and matter-of-factly, it unnerved her guests.

A pallid expression washed over Alistair. "You said that was Friday." She nodded. "When—"

"This was the evening before the Brownstone ferry crew found his lifeless body in the water. January 14." Annemarie gasped, a hand simultaneously shooting up to her mouth to cover the noise. Suddenly, she remembered why Soroush's name was familiar even if she had not known it.

"His death was ruled a suicide." That was public information so Alistair did not feel it necessary to keep quiet about the case file, but the other details of his drowning were for his department's and the marine biology crew's sole knowledge.

Victoria nodded. "And perhaps it was. Maybe he felt he had no solutions to his problem. Maybe he had tried everything and this was the only thing he thought would end the torment. Maybe the large bite on his neck was truly from a sea lion. Or . . ." She trailed off, egging on Alistair with information she should not have possession of.

"Wait, that's classified. How do you—"

She interrupted him with a waving of her hand, dusting away the question. "That doesn't matter, Sheriff. What's most important is that he *did* die, and if he were truly haunted, and hunted, where did it go? It doesn't survive unattached. It needs a host, so to speak, though parasite is not a word often used to describe it."

"But that's something else it is?" Annemarie asked in a small voice.

"Soroush's death—" She paused to make the sign of the cross. "—was ruled suicide, or at the very least, accidental. That was just about eighteen months ago. Think about the timeline since then: What sort of deaths have occurred on or near Port Harrow?"

Alistair mulled over the question. "Pretty common deaths. Old age, mostly. Port Harrow's a bit of a retirement community in places. Nothing truly out of the ordinary up until . . ." He looked to Annemarie, hoping she knew where he was going and that she understood his bringing it up. He slipped a hand across the gap between them and curled his fingers into hers, offering comfort for what came out of his mouth next. "Jesse McCready's death was the start of a series of deaths that were less than usual."

"A car accident, correct?" Victoria asked. Annemarie's grip on Alistair's hand suddenly tightened.

"Correct. Six months after Soroush's death came the car accident caused by Travis Kelly and Nowell Reid. Five or sixth months after that, Travis Kelly died in a similar fashion to Soroush. Drowning. Then, a month ago, we had an islander who Annemarie claims to have seen immediately preceding his death—" At that, she tossed aside his hand, willing to go it alone if he still was not of the mind that she absolutely found Peter in the throes of death. "—die in an extremely brutal fashion. Then three weeks ago, Annemarie's dog was murdered." He paused to take a breath, but Victoria continued for him.

"And what you cannot seem to figure out is whether or not they're related, and what to do in either scenario." He could only nod. "Here's the thing, Sheriff: You have a big problem on your hands. Soroush absolutely brought with him this demon, and it is *hungry*. It doesn't know satiation. It never will. It will continue to hunt its desired prey, and for every person that cannot resist its traps, it will move to the next. So far, it's winning. And it sounds like Annemarie, or even yourself, is the next target. It's kill or be killed, Sheriff, and I sure hope you're packing more than your handgun."

THIRTY-ONE

Victoria stood in the doorway of her home, waving them off as they drove away. Annemarie returned the gesture, but as soon as the teal house disappeared from sight, silence returned to the car's interior. Both their faces turned to stone. Staring straight ahead, Alistair gripped the steering wheel with such intensity all color drained from his strained knuckles. Annemarie sat with her mouth slightly agape and her eyes steadily set, without movement, save for the occasional blink. Even that was slowed.

For the first hour of the drive, absolutely no words were exchanged. Alistair glanced down at the fuel gauge, knowing they would need to fill the tank sooner than later. When his eyes returned to the road, a lifted black pickup cut across two lanes of traffic, directly at their vehicle. Alistair slammed on the brakes, causing their car to swerve for a moment, lurching him and Annemarie forward. He shoved his hand against the horn, letting the other driver hear about his displeasure.

"Fucking asshole! Watch where you're going!" he shouted and let a middle finger fly, too, for extra emphasis. "Fucking shit, man." He shook his head, willing the adrenaline to subside as fast as it came on—he was not sure he could take more of the elevated heart rate right now. He shot a glance at Annemarie who still had a hand pressed against the dashboard. "You okay?"

Four nods came shallow and fast, her eyes not leaving the road ahead of them. But then she turned to look at him. "Or are you talking about what we learned today?"

He sucked on his teeth for a moment, buying some time, but also trying to swallow the road rage in him that had not yet subsided.

"Because I'm not okay," she said quietly.

He huffed a breath through his nose. "Neither am I."

At the gas station, Alistair was transfixed on the screen of numbers ticking upward, but he saw nothing. Annemarie cut across the small but busy parking lot with a fountain drink in one hand and a small bag of cheese crackers in the other. She noticed that the pump had stopped dispensing gas, but Alistair did nothing to finish up the transaction. Over the roof of the car, she called, "Alistair," but he did not respond; he did not hear her. "Earth to Alistair." It came a little louder, a little more singsongy, but there was zero movement from his side. More concerned than upset with him, she snapped, "Al!"

He hard-blinked several times and shot a look over his shoulder at her. "Yeah?"

"You're done." He squinted. She gestured with a quick, upward lift of her chin to the pump. He turned back to see what she meant and the tension in his shoulders and across his forehead slid away.

"Right." He removed the nozzle from the tank, set it back in the cradle, and declined a receipt. They climbed into the car at the same time, slammed the doors shut, and both shuddered at how loud the sound was. Alistair set his hand on the key already in the ignition, but did not turn on the engine. "I'm worried, Annie."

It took her a moment to process the simple words. "About what?"

He fixed a look of incredulity at her. "About what? About *what*? Were you not with me at Victoria's house?"

"I meant, we've got a lot of things going on right now. *Which* of them is immediately on your mind?"

He filled his cheeks with an excess of air and breathed it out slowly. "I'm sorry. I didn't mean to overreact."

"It's warranted."

He set out a hand in front of him. "This whole thing is . . . is ridiculous. I mean, hi, I'm Sheriff Lucas. I look after a sleepy island community whose worst offenders are litterbugs, fender benders, and loose household pets getting stuck in obnoxiously awkward places. Except now, I'm dealing with mutilated corpses and suicides-turned-murder and something that's actively hunting me and my friends. And I've been told that it's a supernatural being that torments its prey until they kill themselves or it gets to feeds off the humans it stalks. Oh, oh, and to boot, my best friend is *numero uno* on its hunt-and-kill list and my work best friend is probably in danger now that he's been introduced to this whole mess." It came out fast and unhindered, a kind of bewilderment in his voice that rose an octave every few seconds as he delved deeper into his increasing panic. Annemarie recognized this was something he needed to get out, get off his chest. He blinked several times after his conclusion, as if he had blacked out and was just now coming back into himself.

He glanced over at her and said, "*That's* what's on my mind. What about you?"

"All that, and more," she said quietly. "Something Victoria said has been gnawing at me. She said silver was something that could be used against it. Isn't . . ." She trailed off, her eyes scanning him for a moment. When they landed on her target, she continued. "Isn't your ring silver?"

"My—" He looked down at the thick band on his right index finger, the ring that had been his dad's. "Yeah, I think so." He wiggled his fingers a little, the later afternoon sunshine glinting off the ring's surface, giving a sudden flash of silver.

"Did it maybe touch the creature when you were fighting it?" She popped up one eyebrow, curiously anticipating an answer.

"It's always a possibility." He thought back to that night, to the attack. The creature snapping its teeth, trying to take a bite, trying to overpower and subdue. He had pushed with all of his might to get the thing off, and at some point, it was likely his silver ring touched its skin, prompting the horrid scream and its retreat. But the longer he thought on it, the clearer another thought became. "The fork."

"Huh?"

"Liam Peck's fork. The one he was so obsessed with getting back."

She blinked at him a couple times, a frown prominent on her face. "Yeah, it was part of his family's heirloom silverware—oh, *silver*ware." She slapped her forehead. "Doy."

"He stabbed the creature right before he blacked out and that was enough to get it to leave him alone. When I found it in the cave, it was comatose up until Liam took the fork back." Something else struck him. "And this—" He extended his hand to show the bandage wrapped around the still-healing finger.

"Is it a cut?"

"A blister."

"From what?"

"This happened when I was inspecting the fork holes in its chest. Its skin got so hot, to the point that I wasn't surprised at all that I got this." He brought his hand back to his lap.

The silence reared its head again, them contemplating what the silver revelation meant. Victoria *had* said silver was a weakness, so this was further proof that she might actually know what she was talking about. The entire afternoon, listening to her tell these outlandish tales of malevolence and hunger and horror skulking around every corner when one of these creatures was involved . . . Alistair could not get it out of his head that what was most unbelievable—besides this sort of creature existing—was how he and Annemarie had been so lucky to *just* run across someone who knew many of the seemingly occult details. In all the world, something that happened to be from thousands of miles away landed in their backyard *and* even for as confusing as they were, the details were handed to them by someone in the know, like it was everyday trivia.

Alistair thought that some random woman knowing all these facts was more far-fetched than the existence of the creature; but he realized how unfair that was to Victoria. She was a sweet woman trying to help them—if not put the fear of some deity into them too—and despite everything they had experienced recently, he was still willing to doubt her. But how much of it was doubt and how much of it was denial?

"What if . .. Victoria's wrong?" Her question interrupted his swirling thoughts.

"About the silver?"

"About everything."

Alistair opened his mouth as he pondered it. "Then I guess we're no worse off than we were this morning before we left Port Harrow."

"But we're no better off either."

He gave a shallow shrug. "I mean, we've known that could always be the case. But, our last encounter was Liam's attack. It's absolutely dead. There's no way it survived two bullets to the brain. That's been, what? A week and a half? We haven't had any other encounters, right?" She shook her head. "Maybe it's good and gone."

"Maybe. Did you ever go back and check on it?"

"I—" He had not. Even though he told himself he would go back to the cave, find the corpse, and torch the bastard, he never did. He thought about it every day but could not will himself to return. And he regretted every evaded opportunity. "No. But there's no way it could have survived."

She wanted to believe that was the truth. Alistair was not wrong—it had been a few days with zero signs of life or the feeling of being watched. That sensation had been nonstop in the past month since finding Peter on the beach. But something about it felt anticlimactic, like they were robbed of some kind of epic showdown. She decided she was a lunatic for being disappointed that this was not like some blockbuster horror movie. The only reason she was waiting for the other shoe to drop was simply because she had found herself wearing so many pairs of shoes the last thirteen months that it felt *wrong* to be optimistic, to feel like things were done.

She shrugged back at him and said, "Yeah, sure."

They returned to the uncomfortable silence, both of them mulling over what was fantasy, what was reality, and what would be waiting for them when they—

HONK

A driver behind them made a fast shooing motion; they were holding up the gas pump spot. Alistair started the engine, put the wagon in drive, and eased out of the parking lot to get back on the road to Port Harrow.

THIRTY-TWO

The only nonwork email in her inbox that morning was from the company she had commissioned to make Moose's grave marker, stating the item was done and it was being sent that day; a tracking number would later follow. A twofold emotion swept over her: the eternal sadness of losing *another* loved one and a mite of contentment that she was one step closer to finishing the memorial for him. Though she had opted to have him cremated, and was still awaiting his homecoming, she knew she needed to do this too. Moose loved rolling around in grass, often leaving him green-streaked against the reds and silvers of his fur. But for as much as he adored hoisting his paws up into the air and wiggling his whole self in a kind of happy dance, his most favorite place to kick up his feet was in Annemarie's garden. Much to her chagrin, he was the murderer of many a squash plants and nasturtiums in his lifetime.

It seemed only fitting that his little corner of worship would be in and among the crops he so loved to destroy.

But to properly honor the beast, Annemarie first had a load of weeds to purge and a new batch of starts she picked up at the library's plant sale earlier in the week. Donning paint-stained leggings and a ratty T-shirt and her hair pushed back and out of her face with a bandana, she descended the back steps of the house and beelined for the shed in one corner of the yard. The grass was overdue for a trim; she had been lax in her outdoor housekeeping lately—she had other priorities and the lawn was not one of them. Her shoes crunched over the clumps of crabgrass that proliferated. She stopped a moment to pluck a dandelion out of the ground, grasping tightly at its base in an attempt to get the whole root. It came out in shreds and she simply muttered, "Fuck."

A bit of rust on the wheels of the sliding shed doors caused a squeak as she pushed them open, allowing herself entry as a wave of a warm, green scent greeted her. A small table was shoved into the right-hand side, decorated with a variety of tools all cobbled together from the last time she worked. Like the lawn, the garden had not been much of a priority as of late. But now, she was making it one.

On the left-hand side was an unkempt pile of larger tools that had no place on the little workbench: shovels, long shears, rakes, an electric edger, a rusted but still sharp machete, and a scythe that was last used as part of a Halloween costume that got Jesse in a bit of trouble at a party in Brownstone. The scythe had not been used since, and she kept meaning to get rid of it, but it always made her smirk when she thought about how when the cops showed up and tried to arrest him—something that never should have happened in the first place, but the concerned citizen said he had been "wielding a dangerous weapon in a large crowd"—he simply thought it was a person in a cop costume playing the role. He was a little less amused when they cuffed him and led him toward the cruiser.

She needed the bow rake and a shovel, both of which had fallen on their sides at some point. Being mindful of any spiderwebs she did not want her face to meet, she swiped at the air for a solid ten seconds as she shuffled her way into the ten-by-eight shed. The *thunk* and *plonk* of metal on wood on fiberglass echoed loudly in the small space, and was met with that of a grunt.

But not Annemarie's.

She stilled in her movements, straining to listen around the noise of the birds high up in the trees. A caw here, a flap of wings there, and *there*—the grunt came again. It sounded of a hog rooting for fungus, snuffling hot on the trail to somewhere it could not get to. And it grew louder the longer she waited. But it finally subsided. She wondered if a deer had wandered into the yard. Given that the whole greenbelt between her house and the beach was full of wildlife, and she did not go a week without finding at least one deer plundering through the yard, it was the likeliest scenario.

However, as she turned in place to head out the shed door to take a peek, her breath caught in her throat and she had to cover her mouth with a hand to stop the sound of her choking from ringing out. A hand that swung in the air, mid-gait, disappeared past the opening. Had she looked two seconds later, she never would have seen it; had she looked two seconds sooner, would it have seen her? Did it know she was in there? Was it trying to ferret her out of the space?

Her knee-jerk reaction was to call out. But her fingers gripped her lips and pinched them tight, physically forcing her to keep everything inside, including her breath. She waited a prolonged moment to see if anything reappeared in the shed's doorway, and when she thought she was truly alone, she took a step back and pressed herself flat against the wall, tucked into the dark corner. As slowly and steadily as she could, she lowered herself to the dirt floor, frantically feeling with one hand for the set of loppers she had seen earlier. When the cold aluminum of its handles met her skin, she tightened her fingers around one side and held them close to her chest.

A mix of wanting to disappear behind them and wanting a means to defend herself should anything poke its head inside overwhelmed her. She needed to empty her lungs, she needed to refill them with something other than the mingled odors of gasoline and dried grass and rust. Her breath left her nose in a steady, slow release, but her entire body threatened to shake against the metal wall and give away her position; assuming her exact location was not already known.

When she was able to collect herself and her thoughts a bit better, she relaxed a little. The tension in her shoulders slackened and her jaw unclenched itself. She had spent the last five minutes with her muscles in one giant knot; letting go was such a relief. As she lifted a foot to step over the jumble of tools separating her from the shed door, ready to sprint to the house, a thunderous explosion of noise erupted to her left. The sound of fists battering against the wall, of claws scraping down the side.

This time, she could not help but scream—a strangled, blanched sound. She ducked into a low crouch, not even minding where the blades of the loppers were, and covered her head with her balled-up fists. She shoved knuckles into her ears, trying to drown out the horrendous sound. It was like the entire shed would fall on her head. And as quickly as it came, it instantly ceased.

It took her several long seconds to realize the shed was still standing, and despite tucking in on herself, so was she. Her fists slid down her cheeks to her jaw, still clenched and pressing against her skin as they gradually fell to her sides. She hesitated before making the conscious effort to get back onto her feet. But deep in the pit of her stomach, she worried the moment she let her guard down, it would return. The noise, the panic, the uncertainty—it all made the breath coming from her lungs hitch in her throat.

Several minutes passed without a sound, from her or otherwise. She took several large—silent—gulps of air to center herself. If all remained in this same manner, she could make it across the yard to the porch, to the safety of indoors. She leaned the loppers against the wall of the shed, close enough to grab again if necessary, but out of the way so as to not trip on when she decided to bolt. Her foot lifted an inch off the ground, but froze instantly when she heard it: the unmistakable crinkle of a foot crunching against grass.

It was just the other side of the shed wall. Whatever it was, she could have reached out to touch it had it not been for the sheet of metal separating them. Another plication of skin on grass echoed. Her hand shot behind her, desperately grasping for anything she could find without moving her eyes from the opening. Despite being right there, the loppers were nowhere to be found, but she did find the looped handle of a shovel, and that would do fine. As she lifted it from its spot, it caught on something else and would not come free, forcing her to decide between abandoning the tool or temporarily changing her focus.

She chose the latter, knowing her time was limited; if it was hunting her, it would not be much longer before she needed to defend herself. It undoubtedly knew where she was. And now, she needed protection. For a brief moment, she set her sights on the shovel, noticing a bit of plastic string from the weed whacker was woven around the notched edge of the step on the blade. It required a hearty tug with both hands, drawing her attention fully. But the moment it was free, she whirled around to the shed's entrance.

Just in time to see a grey shadow pass by the door and the sound of the shuffle of footsteps followed.

She sucked in both of her lips and bit down hard to try to muffle the cry that struggled to break free of her, but it was in vain—a pathetic mewl escaped. The footsteps stopped. The sound had been traveling away from her, but now they were retracing and returning to her position. As the noise grew louder and louder, Annemarie made a tight hold on the handle and shaft of the shovel and speared it forward as the grey form reappeared in front of her.

"What on—Annemarie! What are you doing?" Cecily cried, almost stumbling off her feet as she backed up quickly, narrowly dodging the cutting edge.

"Mom? Mom!" The confusion and ease came simultaneously. "I-I thought—"

Cecily cocked her head, her hair cascading with the gesture. "What are you doing in there anyway? Were you gardening?"

Annemarie's grip on the shovel loosened, allowing it to slump to her side. "Yeah, trying to at least. M-Moose's—"

A shrill cry pierced the conversation, sticking a pin in the words she was about to say. Cecily spun a hundred and eighty to look down the driveway. "Oh, Charlie, honey, did you fall, sweetheart?" She was off in a grey flash before Annemarie could comprehend everything that had happened.

The heat of the day dwindled the chunks of ice in the plastic cup that swirled in Annemarie's anxious hand. The sloshing of the pieces as they rattled together was a reminder to stay in the present, to not let her mind wander back to two hours prior. But it was difficult. How could she *not* replay every single moment? With the sudden appearance of Cecily, how could she *not* question what was real and what was made-up?

Was the creature stalking her? Was it even what she thought it was? It had to know she was there—why else would it have attacked the shed? Did Cecily's arrival scare it off? Was it even able to feel fear? It was not human, it could not be, so did it experience emotions the way she had? Was it possible that—

"Rude."

Annemarie opened her eyes a little wider and asked, "Who is?"

"You." Marissa huffed a breath that fluttered her bangs off her forehead for a moment.

"What? Why am I rude?" Annemarie shot back, a mix of annoyance and genuine confusion in her tone.

"I came all this way to hang out with my little sister and I get nothing but a brick-wall expression in return. I'm trying to talk to you, you know," she whined. She set down her drink a little too hard on the metal lattice table, causing it to wobble on the uneven patio outside the Ferry Café.

A slow blink came from Annemarie before she responded. "You came here to drop off Charlie with mom and dad so they can babysit her while you're away for work."

"*And* to see you," she added quickly.

Annemarie raised one eyebrow as her lips formed an unimpressed thin line. "I happened to be at home when mom came by with you and Charlie in tow. It was coincidence and opportunity more than the actual intention."

"Well *regardless*," she spat with a bit of a huff, "you agreed to grab lunch with me before I headed back and now you're completely ignoring me."

"I'm sorry. I don't mean to. I've got ..." She considered the next set of words out of her mouth, wondering if she should—*could*—share the details of what had been happening with her recently. Or if she attempted to, would Marissa even believe her? Or would she once again accuse her of making everything about her so she could be the center of attention—a pattern often visited by Marissa since they were young girls. "I'm not sleeping well and it's been hard to stay present for anything." It was not a complete lie, but also not the whole truth. "I promise, it's not you."

Marissa rolled her eyes and gave a little shake of her head, knowing it was just a line, but also letting go of the annoyance. "It's fine. I wanted to spend some time with you. That's all."

Annemarie extended her hand toward her, palm side up. "We hung out the whole time at the Festival. And it's not like we never see each other."

"But we never *talk*. Charlie's always there wanting attention, or mom's commandeering conversations, or I get a phone call."

"Then let's talk." She sat up straighter in her chair and scooted closer to the table. She folded her hands in front of her, showing that she was at one hundred percent attention. "What's been going on in your life?"

A smirk crept into the corner of Marissa's mouth, accepting the overexaggerated gesture Annemarie was performing. "I've been seeing someone."

Annemarie lifted both eyebrows, genuine intrigue taking over; Marissa had not dated in years. "Oh, really? Where did you meet them?"

"Through work. He doesn't work for my company, but he's a consultant and has a contract to come in one day a week. We kinda started flirting and things have gone up from there. I don't think anything—"

"Afternoon, ladies." The familiar, smooth voice interrupted them, catching them both off guard, prompting them to look up and spot Alistair walking across the patio from the parking lot. In his uniform, in between calls, he approached with a big smile on his face. "Good day for an outdoor lunch, huh?"

He reached for an empty chair at an adjacent table and settled in between them. "Hey," Annemarie said softly.

"Hey, Sheriff," Marissa said with an expression that matched his. "What brings you to these parts?"

"I could ask the same of you." He leaned over to give her a hug.

"Depends on who you ask. I came here to have lunch with this one—" She threw a thumb at Annemarie. "—but she says I came over here to drop Charlie off with mom and dad."

Having thought the nonissue debacle was over, a layer of heat rose in Annemarie. She both did and did not want to argue with Marissa; she was tired of the game. Alistair cast an unsure glance at Annemarie, spending an extra moment studying her face. Her blank stare and stoic lips gave him no inkling as to the water he had treaded into, so he continued with caution.

"Well, whatever the case, glad to have you back on the island, even if it's only for an hour. What's been new with you?"

Marissa grinned as she pushed back a swath of bangs off her forehead. "I've been seeing someone."

"Oh, yeah? What's that all about?"

"Well, his name is Marc, and while we don't work for the same company, he's a consultant who comes in once a week to . . ."

Even though her shift did not start until one that afternoon, Annemarie was awake at an ungodly hour to roll the trash, recycling, and yard waste bins to the curb. She had forgotten to take them up the previous night, and by the time she remembered, she was already tucked tight under the covers and seconds away from dipping into a comfortable sleep. She promised herself to get up early, with an alarm, if she was allowed to doze off right then and there—and it worked.

But the second the annoying jingly jangle alarm on her phone started, she regretted not getting out of bed when she first realized she had forgotten the chore. So now, at four thirty, she was climbing into a lightweight fleece jacket and her house slippers to make the shuffle along the gravel driveway with the bins in tow.

The chilly early morning air enveloped her the moment she set foot on the back porch. The floodlight clicked on, illuminating the stoop in a harsh yellow glow. She shut the door behind her and padded down the four steps to the little nook that held the three bins. She could handle two at a time, meaning she would have to retrieve the yard waste can by itself once the others were at the street. She started the long walk, the plastic wheels of the cans chuttering along as they bounced over rocks, little potholes, and the occasional tuft of grass or weeds growing through the dirt. She heard the floodlight click off.

She set both cans in place and turned on the balls of her feet to head back to the third; the sooner she could finish the chore, the sooner she could climb back into bed—even though she was certain sleep would not find her. The idea of being horizontal again sounded lovely.

The toe of her fuzzy slipper kicked a rock and it skittered across the driveway. The sound of it was *loud*. Its subsequent skipping echoed in Annemarie's ears in a way that she found peculiar; it was a normal chunk of gravel: Why was it making such a racket?

Then it hit her. The early-morning birdsong and stridulatory cricketsong was no more. Not even a breeze stirred the copse of the trees surrounding the house. It was dead silent, and had been prior to launching the rock down the driveway. She took several shuffling steps forward, just enough to trigger the floodlight again.

Straight ahead of her, at the threshold where the forest turned into the furthest reaches of her backyard, silver eyes watched her. At the realization that all the usual sounds of the morning were now nonexistent, her eyes darted around. When she finally landed on the pale, statuesque frame some fifty meters in front of her, her breath hitched and the sudden urge to flee overwhelmed her.

But she could not move.

And neither did it. With their eyes fixed on each other, its blazed silver—that iridescent flash of headlights rolling over a shiny object along the road. The wash of the floodlight did not reach as far as the forest's edge, making her strain her eyes to figure out how she was capable of seeing its muscular frame in such detail. The moment she understood that it was emitting a faint, ethereal glow was the same time the floodlight clicked off.

A tremor shook through her, the thundering of feet on the ground and the uptick in her heartbeat filling her ears as she took off in a sprint. Only ten feet to the bottom step. She could get there in a blink.

She tore up the stairs two at a time, lunging for the doorknob, praying it had not locked behind her, admonishing herself for not double-checking when she started the task. But her body slammed into the wood panel and blew open the door, allowing her entrance as the sound of feet clawed across the gravel at the base of the stoop. She spun so fast on her feet in order to shut the door behind her that she nearly fainted. It was like whiplash, inertia working against her.

Her shoulder slammed into the door and a hand fumbled for the dead bolt as a mighty weight pushed from the other side. It nearly sent her to her knees, but she summoned all of her waning strength and shoved hard, the door clicked shut, the bolt locked in place, and she wedged her body between the frame and the wall of the nook, using her legs to fortify the barrier her back created.

The door bent and bowed from outside. With every thrust came a rabid grunt, a frothing zeal to get at the coveted prize inside. Annemarie shoved the second knuckles of her thumbs as deep into her ears as she could, drowning out the noise. She kept herself from crying, though much more of this assault and she was not certain it could be stymied. She focused on her breathing, a heavy lungful coming in and a peaceful exhalation out.

A whir of grating metal and hydraulics penetrated the imperfect seal of fingers-in-ears, signaling the arrival of the refuse workers; the recycling truck would follow shortly thereafter, she knew. The clawing at the door and the audible lamentation subsided. After a clatter of gravel spraying against the side of the house filled the gap in between trucks, she knew it had given up. *Hoped* it had given up.

She remained in the rigid position for another fifteen minutes, watching as the kitchen gradually lit up with the warm glow of morning. She fought off sleep, accepting she could not let her guard down for even a moment. But a hot cup of coffee, tucked in under a blanket in her nest of a bed, sounded pretty enticing . . .

When she thought it was safe enough to get up, and her bladder begged for release, she climbed off the floor and crept her way toward the bathroom. She hoisted herself onto the vanity and peeked over the sill of the one-foot-wide window above the toilet. Morning was in full bloom and nothing stirred in the driveway. The garbage can's lid was flopped open, but nothing else was amiss.

She made her way to the kitchen, tiptoeing as if a single creak of a floorboard would indicate to anyone outside that she was theirs for the taking. Her fingers weaved through the base of the curtains covering the large window over the sink as she pulled them back ever so slightly to see if the coast was clear to the west. Then she moved to the back door, undid the locks, and poked her head outside, peering toward the trees to the north as best as she could without ever leaving the confines of the house.

All was clear.

As she rounded in on herself, ready to breathe that final sigh of release and relief, she noticed the deep punctures in the wood of the door. Had it not relented, it would have gotten a hand, claw—whatever it had—

through the panel in another few strikes. She visibly shuddered at the thought.

She closed the door behind her, locked the dead bolt, and quickly padded into the bedroom. She changed out of her pajamas into a pair of lightweight capris and a grey T-shirt. Her hair got shoved into a one-handed messy ponytail while she tried to brush her teeth. A splash of cold water and a pat-dry was the extent of her skincare. In the kitchen, she nuked a frozen breakfast sandwich in the microwave while she filled a travel mug with freshly brewed coffee. She shoved a variety of necessities into her bag, cobbled together her breakfast and keys while trying to slip into her shoes hands-free, and was peeking out the front door to make sure she was alone.

THIRTY-THREE

She habitually checked the time on her phone while she waited in the lobby of the sheriff's station. Cami and Deputy Lozano were present, one manning the phone line and the other filling out paperwork at the end of their shift, respectively, with Riggs and Alistair nowhere to be found. The door to Alistair's office was locked, barring Annemarie from being able to tuck inside, away from Cami's suspicious gaze.

When she arrived thirty minutes earlier, Cami had asked if there was something she or Lozano could help with. Annemarie shook her head, shaking them off, and offered to sit quietly in the corner. She flickered between playing with her phone, cleaning one set of fingernails with the other, and thumbing through her paper planner, occasionally glancing at the set of double doors at the entrance.

An hour had passed when Alistair finally rolled into the building. He first caught sight of Cami standing at the counter on a phone call and lifted his chin at her in a silent greeting. He turned to the left to head to his office and kept rolling when his eyes briefly met Annemarie's; he did not even hesitate. He knew she was there, thanks to a discrete phone call from his office manager.

"Everything okay?" he asked as he shoved the key into the old knob on the door, not bothering to make eye contact with her. She did the same, her face pointed straight down at her lap.

"Yep."

The door swung open and before he entered, he extended a hand, palm up, in a means of *ladies first*. She saw that. She gathered her things and hurried in, making a break for the plushest of the chairs in the room. It was an old wingback Alistair had no use for at the house and figured it might find love in the office—Annemarie usually gravitated toward it.

He settled into his own chair at the opposite side of the desk, jiggled the mouse to wake up the computer, and leaned back as he suspended his folded hands over his lap. "So . . ."

"So?" she asked back.

"It's seven o'clock."

"Are you adding clock tower to your resume now?"

He narrowed his eyes, willing her to look at him. She would not budge. "What's going on, then?"

"Nothing."

"It's not nothing for you to be here waiting for me, at some ungodly hour of the morning no less." She shook her head. He tried a different tactic. "All right, Mrs. McCready. Doooo you have a crime to report?"

Her eyes darted up to his face, but they immediately shot down again. "No."

An exasperated sigh slipped past his clenched teeth. He leaned forward to rest both elbows on the desk, adding a level of severity to his concern. "Then *what* is going on? Why are you here?"

It took a long, drawn-out minute for her to say anything. When she did, it was a whisper. "I had an extremely vivid dream about Jesse's death and I . . . didn't want to be alone." She paused and looked at him, her voice coming a bit harsher. "You happy?"

"No, I'm not happy, Annie. You know I'm not."

"Yeah, well, welcome to the club."

The admission killed any semblance of the conversation moving forward. "Is that all that's going on?"

She gave the slightest of nods, being sure to not delay the response in case he was doubting her. *She* knew it was not the truth, but maybe she could keep him convinced. "Look, I shouldn't've come here. I'll go to my mom's or something."

She made to get up, but he held out his hand. "It's fine that you're here. I'm trying to figure out if you're okay because this—" He motioned at her and out toward the hallway. "—this isn't normal behavior for you."

"Not a lot is normal right now anyway," she replied.

"No, but it's my duty to make sure that Annemarie McCready *and* Annie are both okay."

With a huff, she sat back down and let her bag drop to her feet. "I . . . needed to get out of the house. I work this afternoon and figured if I could kill some time till then, I'd be fine."

"Then by all means, hang out here as long as you need. I'm in and out all morning. I have a meeting in Brownstone at ten. But Cami is here until two, Riggs'll be here most of the day. You've got people here, Annie. You've got company."

It was the first moment all morning where she felt light, or at least a little less heavy. Knowing that Alistair was not going to kick her out of the building—not that she thought he would—she closed her eyes for a long moment in order to breathe. She was safe here, even if left alone when he needed to catch the ferry, and Riggs was inevitably on a call, and Cami took her lunch. *Safe* was all she craved.

Behind her eyelids, flashes of silver infiltrated her vision, lighting up the darkness. Her eyes shot open. Alistair was reading something on the computer screen, entranced by whatever email had come through his inbox, and therefore, did not witness her moment of silent panic. As exhausted as she was, she knew sleep was not the answer, not right now. Taking a page from Alistair's book, she dug out her phone and planner from within her bag and got to work on library emails. She knew of several that required responses and now was the perfect time to deal with them.

Annemarie had drifted off into a deep doze after Alistair left for his meeting on the mainland. He bade her goodbye, closed the door, and miraculously, she was *out*. It was fitful, not restful, and the fact that the side of her face was planted against the upholstery of worn leather and diamond-pattern buttons, creating creases and divots in her skin while she slept, added to the overall pain of the day.

A series of footsteps echoed past the office, causing her to stir enough to realize someone was close. She opened her eyes in time to see a grey form standing in the corner, tall and lean, getting ready to lunge at her. She shoved herself as far back into the chair as she could and screamed, her voice high but hoarse.

The office door swung open a heartbeat later. Riggs stood in the entry, eyebrows high on his forehead, a look of panic spread across his cheeks paired with a heaving chest. "Annie, what's wrong?" She pointed at the corner silently, arm shaking violently. He quickly turned his attention to it. "I don't . . ."

"Can't you—" She stopped short when she looked again and saw the tall, narrow, grey storage cabinet that had always been in the office.

Riggs took several steps in her direction and knelt in front of her. He set a hand to her forehead, then down to one cheek. "Are you okay?"

"I g-guess I fell asleep after Alistair left. A-and when I woke up, I-I saw . . . I-I don't know what I s-saw." Her bottom lip quivered noticeably; she reached a hand up to physically stop it.

"I was about to head out to grab lunch. Do you wanna come with?" His eyebrows returned to nearly touching the tousled blond locks falling down his forehead. Annemarie could see the genuine concern on his face.

Besides the breakfast sandwich she fisted into her mouth on the drive down to the station, she had not eaten anything else; the protein bars she brought with her were the least appetizing things she could think of. She gently nodded. "Yeah, I'd be up for that."

He stood from his crouched position and offered her a hand up from the chair. She willingly grabbed hold, for a moment feeling the gentleness Riggs naturally exuded calming her too. But as soon as she let go, the anxiety and exhaustion and fear of the morning overwhelmed her.

"Got anything you're craving?" he asked.

She shook her head. "I'm up for whatever." She wrinkled her lips. "Maybe not anything super greasy." Her hand shot to her stomach.

"So I'm guessing deep-fried butter is off the table?"

Annemarie and Riggs sat across from each other at a two-person table outside the small bistro next to the library. He had ordered and wolfed down a meatball sub while she casually poked at the half of the club sandwich she had not finished. She figured she could have it for dinner while on shift.

Riggs usually took half an hour for lunch, rarely needing more than that to shove food in his face, take a walk, and clean up before heading back to patrol or desk duty. Today, however, he allowed an hour—or as much time as Annemarie wanted—to make sure she was okay. He did not know what was going on with her, besides the obvious happenings that had befallen her and Alistair, but her outburst in Alistair's office had him beyond worried. If offering up a little companionship was what she needed, it was the least he could do.

So, as they sat at the bistro, her plucking the tiniest pieces of bread off her sandwich and leaving them in a pile on the plate and him leaning back in the chair while he gabbed at her, he kept an eye on her body language, listened to what she was saying when she did manage to say something. He wanted to report back to Alistair to compare notes, see if they could use their detective skills to figure out the puzzle that was a quiet and reserved Annemarie.

She suddenly lifted her head. "Hey, how's your mom?"

He screwed up his face for a moment. "My mom?"

"Yeah. She had surgery recently, right?"

Understanding washed over his face and he let his expression untwist. "Oh, yeah. Things went great. She stayed in the hospital for one night and they released her and she's been doing well. My stepdad's been taking good care of her, or at least that's what he said."

"What was she going in for?"

"Hip replacement."

"Oh, ouch."

"She says she's feeling a lot better, so that's something."

"Well, that's good to hear. I'm glad. Tell her I said hi the next time you talk to her."

A warm smile spread over his face. "I will."

Annemarie glanced at her phone; it was almost one. She reached for the to-go box she had asked for earlier, knowing she would have leftovers, and packaged up the remainder of the sandwich. They had already paid—Riggs insisted he buy her meal—so now she needed to walk to the library in order to relieve Katherine.

"I gotta head out."

He checked his watch. "I should too. Alistair'll be back soon and I know he's gonna want to fill me in on whatever the meeting with Sheriff Bachhuber was about."

"Ooh, a meeting with the big guy himself, huh?"

He gave a little nod. "Yep. Just my luck, he's gonna tell me Bachhuber wants him transferred to the mainland." They both stood and tucked their chairs under the table.

"Oh, bite your tongue. Why would you say that?!" A big grin accompanied the outburst, the first genuine smile she had had all day.

"If I say it's going to happen, it won't."

"I'm gonna hold you to that," she replied. They stood in the parking lot for a moment longer, neither of them far from their destinations. "Thanks for lunch. I appreciate it."

"Thanks for letting me take you to lunch." He paused. "We should do this more often."

"I think I'd like that." They both hesitated, but she broke the silence and leaned forward to give him a hug. "I'll see you later."

"I hope your day gets better."

She gave him a half wave as he climbed into the patrol car and pulled out of the lot.

THIRTY-FOUR

The evening in the library had been slow, not a patron in sight for close to an hour, and Annemarie took her time closing up the building. She had gotten sidetracked by a project setting up a new display for the children's section and neglected to check in and shelve all the day's returns. So with her unwieldy stack of books finally put away, she locked the front door, double-checked the back exit was secure, and dawdled a few minutes longer behind the circulation desk, dusting and straightening the area for Tish in the morning.

Armed with a feather duster, Annemarie cleaned off the countertops, the computer monitors, and was about to get down onto her hands and knees to clean the towers under the desk when she heard a muffled smash coming from the basement. She paused in place, thinking about what it could be. She had not been down there for several hours and she knew she was alone in the building—she had been for some time. She dropped the duster onto the counter and cautiously made her way toward the door with a big EMPLOYEES ONLY decal plastered across it. She reached a shaky hand to the doorknob, but stopped the moment she heard what sounded like a shuffle of footsteps followed by a susurration of papers scattering.

She took three steps back, each one a little wider than the last. She bumped into the edge of the circulation desk and startled herself. Another sound of things crashing to the floor echoed up the stairwell. Blindly, her fingers scrabbled behind her for the phone, never once taking her eyes off the door. The entire console came with her hands as she brought it closer to her. She peeked down once to orient her fingers and punched in the number for the sheriff's office.

"Azure County Sheriff's Department, Port Harrow office, how can I help you?" came an unfamiliar voice.

"Hey, uh, who is this?"

"Deputy Liu. Who's—"

"Oh, hi, Shaun. Is Alistair there?"

"He's out on a call right now. Is there something I can—"

"What about Riggs? Is he around?"

It took a moment, but the deputy finally recognized her voice. "No, Annemarie, he's out too. What's going on?"

"I-I need to talk to one of them." Annemarie tried her best to keep the wavering emotion tamped down.

"Derrick is in the area, if that helps."

After a long, pregnant pause, Annemarie blurted, "I think there's someone in the basement," and did not wait for Liu to process what was said before adding, "and I need Alistair to come here now."

"Where are you?"

"At the library." A resounding *whoomp* filled Annemarie's ears. "I'm gonna try to call his cell, but can you radio him too?"

"Yes, of course. Let me send Derrick to you too. Whatever you do, don't pursue the assailant. Get to a safe place, even if that means going outside to your car and waiting for one of us to show up. Lock your doors, start your engine, whatever you need to do to make sure you're safe."

"Thank you, Shaun, I will." Annemarie hastily set the receiver on the base and leaned as far over the counter as she could to fish around for her bag. The tips of her fingers gained purchase on the cloth strap and it came whipping around into view. She held her breath as she tiptoed to the basement door and made sure it was locked. If someone *was* down there—though, how anyone could have gotten in, she could not say—they were not about to get out up the stairs. She pocketed the old skeleton key and made her way to the exit. Before finally stepping outside, she held her breath, listening once more for any additional noise coming from the basement. Liu's suggestion to wait in her car was a good one—she could remain safe but also keep an eye on the building. The sheriff's station was not far from the library, but without Alistair or Riggs in the vicinity, and Deputy Derrick Vernon en route—but who knew coming from where—she was tempting fate by lingering upstairs too long.

No further sounds echoed around the room, giving her a moment of doubt that made her question whether someone was down there at all. She had not been sleeping well since Moose's death—since Jesse's, really—and her exhausted mind was known for playing tricks on her. After another hesitation, she decided she needed to leave it up to the cops; they would know what to do. But how embarrassing would it be if it turned out to be a raccoon stuck down there?

A sudden clatter of crashing items startled her out the front door, into the parking lot, to her car. She climbed inside, leaving the driver's side open, searching for anything out of place.

The library's entrance seemed in order. No signs of anything out of the ordinary. Each of the windows were intact. They were the single-hung variety and Annemarie knew she had closed every one of them when she locked the doors for the evening. Except . . . one looked open, as if the spring-loaded sash had popped up six or seven inches. Had someone forced their way in and snuck downstairs while she was in the bathroom or shelving books with her back to the circulation desk? Did she mean to leave it like that for fresh air while she finished her evening and forgot to close it in all the commotion of the potential intruder? Did the sometimes-faulty frame rear its head again?

Against her better judgment, she walked back to the building to investigate. If she had forgotten to close it, despite being sure she closed them all, there was a good chance everything she thought was happening was another defect in her tired mind. With her cell phone tucked into the back pocket of her capris, she inched closer to the facade in order to check for fingerprints or any obvious signs of someone getting in.

Finding nothing—as she hoped—she stepped back and released a loaded sigh. She could not be certain, but she was mostly confident the intruder had not used this window as a means of entry.

Along the bottom of the building, inches above the gravel landscape, stood five rectangular, frosted windows that led into the basement. Wondering if she could see through them, she cupped her hands around her face to shield the light from the parking lot's lampposts behind her from obscuring her view. She squinted at first, struggling to see much of anything in the darkness of the room that was filled with tall shelving units that made up long corridors, but her eyes grew wide when a shadow passed by the window.

In a lurch, she fell back onto her ass, terrified out of her mind, but also shocked that she was right. Something was down there—*someone*.

Before she pulled herself up, she glanced over her shoulder to see whether anyone was en route. No flashing lights in the distance, no echoes of sirens. Back onto her feet and giving her phone a quick once-over to check for damage, she found herself idling closer and closer to the library's landing, debating her next move. She meandered into the lobby, letting the door silently close behind her. She crept across the carpet, remaining as quiet as she could. She did not have a plan, though she considered she might catch whoever it was off guard. She was not law enforcement with the means for subduing an intruder with a weapon, but both Alistair and Jesse had taught her how to defend herself. Surely, something had to overlap when it came down to taking on a perp, or so she hoped.

With a shaky hand pulling the skeleton key out of her pocket and placing it in the lock, she swung open the door just wide enough to slink in sideways. She wanted to make her presence as little known as possible.

The staircase leading down was built of cold concrete and padded with strips of thin carpet to provide grip.

Every step Annemarie took, she made sure to land perfectly on the soft material, cushioning and muffling any sounds. From her view above the shelves as she descended, the room was still and silent; there were no signs of movement. Once both feet were on level ground, she peeked around either corner to see if anything was amiss. All clear, she dashed across the open space to the first set of bookshelves, using their height as a wall to block anything from attacking from the sides. She nervously glanced behind her after every few steps as she made her way forward.

She shuffled along and her breath caught in her throat the moment the tinny clack of metal fell upon the floor in the next aisle over, though it was hard to pinpoint the exact direction or source. An unknown item rolled across the painted concrete for several yards, slowing down as it approached the intersecting row, barely within Annemarie's line of sight.

Animal, human, whatever it was, it, too, remained still.

There came a breath—heavy, loud, drawn out. It did not belong to Annemarie. She strained to listen to each of the labored inhales and exhales. If it was an animal, its movement and mouth breathing would be accompanied by other animal-like noises. Growls, cries, gurgles, chitters. Nothing. Even still, how on earth could an animal make their way into the basement? To access the space, anything would have had to waltz directly past her at the circulation desk, opening the heavy, creaking door without being noticed, and that was not possible. Especially when the animals on Port Harrow lacked obvious thumbs. Hooves and paws only. The only other option was to open or break the windows that barely peeked above ground; coincidentally, they were providing the sole source of light. Upon her descent into the basement, she did not notice any broken panes of glass, but she had not been looking.

Another footstep led Annemarie closer to the intersection of aisles. She identified the noise as coming from one of the old archive canisters that housed even older physical photographs, documents, and microfilm that she and Tish regularly worked on upgrading to digital for long-term preservation. She was far more concerned about the intruder, but secretly hoped that whatever archives were now on the floor were not collateral damage of an angry or hungry entity.

The unidentified breathing grew louder. So much so, Annemarie turned to look behind her in case it snuck up without notice. Much of its movement had not been overtly boisterous, so it was not out of the realm of possibilities. Hell, the last month, apparently, had no limits when it came to the realm of possibilities. Annemarie caught herself thinking about the creature, about the stories Victoria told her and Alistair. She never considered herself a skeptic, but calling herself a believer was not quite right either. A year ago, she would have said she was open to the possibilities of strange creatures lurking in the woods or little green men visiting from beyond the Milky Way or malevolent forces. Now, she did *not* want to believe no matter what the truth was.

She placed her left hand at the edge of the bookcase, gripping hard as she slowly eased forward to peek, to help her tiptoe quietly. As she mustered enough courage to propel herself around the blind corner, the fine, loose hairs fallen from her ponytail at the nape of her neck moved, like they were caught in a rhythmic breeze. Annemarie froze in place. Her brain told her to turn around, to check again for reassurance that she was alone in that dark, isolated room; but her body could not—would not—move. The hair wafted back and forth again and a sense of warmth enveloped her, causing a wave of hot panic to eclipse the bravery she had found only a moment before. She wriggled her right hand free of the invisible hold on her body and slowly, uncertainly, reached behind her to see what she could find without looking. She felt heat. She felt roughness. She felt pulsation. She felt *flesh*.

Closing her eyes, she waited. She still could not move more than her arm. Her left hand remained glued to the corner of the bookcase while the right was stuck in place against skin belonging to the unknown. She looked like a freeze-frame of an interpretive dance in that moment. Her breathing was rapid-fire, near hyperventilation. The breath behind her matched in speed and frequency. Both her and the uninvited guest remained motionless, save for the heaving of their chests. On the inside, every ounce of her strength and willpower struggled to move a limb, her torso, *anything*. Her toes moved. Her shoe slid ever so slightly across the concrete. Instead of a flat palm against flesh, she made a fist. Her faculties pushed away the paralysis.

As she regained the ability to move her neck, she attempted to turn her head to the right to peer over her shoulder. Despite the parking lot lights flooding in through the windows, the dark recesses created by the tall, shadowing shelves made it impossible to detect anything more than shapes and silhouettes. Without turning her entire body, she saw the figure: much taller than her; lithe, but almost awkward and gangly; intimidating. A noise like low, guttural moaning came, and it took a moment for Annemarie to realize it was not coming from her.

The warmth inched closer without movement from the wall of flesh she touched. A wave of dread washed over her. Her chest tightened as something brushed against the skin of her extended forearm. She opened her mouth with the intention of speaking, but all that fell out was a squeak, followed by an explosion of music.

Startled, she involuntarily released her grip of the bookcase, causing her still-rigid body to collapse backward. At the same time, she heard a grunt, a panicked shuffle of feet, and the sound of oil-hungry hinges echoing off to her left.

In her daze, it took Annemarie a solid fifteen seconds to realize her phone was ringing and that she was currently alone. She fumbled for a moment before answering.

"Annie, where are you?" Alistair sounded worried.

"In the basement. Where are you?"

"Riggs and I both just pulled up in the parking lot and *oh holy shi*—" Before he could say any more, she heard a voice yelling in the background of their call and a round of bullets firing. It echoed in the basement from both the phone and from outside.

"Alistair?" she asked. More gunfire.

She disconnected the call and rushed to the flight of stairs leading into the main room of the library, no semblance of the paralysis present, but a persistent tingling in her toes and calves. The noise was muffled in the lobby, more so than it was downstairs. Regardless, it was still happening; she could hear that clear as day. She locked the door to the basement, in case the creature returned. If it was smart enough to understand how hinged windows work, it probably also knew how to turn a doorknob. That thought was frightening.

The gunshots and yelling ceased. She took this moment to speed walk to the entrance. With a hand on one of the double doors, she pushed herself out into the cool air of the night. The sound of the heavy wood groaning against the metal frame and creaking shut echoed into the newfound stillness of the parking lot in front of her.

There came one more loud explosion. The sound of a bullet launching from the barrel of a rifle, whizzing through the air, and finding its target with a soft but forceful *squelch*. In the lot, positioned behind the open driver's door of his vehicle, Riggs stared down the length of his gun. His sure, steady expression morphed into one of abject horror as he saw Annemarie's body crumple to the ground.

THIRTY-FIVE

Unable to move, Riggs watched Alistair holster his handgun and sprint to the stairs of the library to slide to an abrupt stop at her side.

"Annie!" Alistair cried out as he cradled her neck and head in his arms. A stain of deep red spread across her T-shirt. His want to comfort her and his need to attend to her sparred internally. Her brown eyes remained open as she stared up at him. Her whole body trembled. The bleeding continued. Alistair gazed down at her with a certain fondness in the gesture of stroking the hair on either side of her face, brushing away loose strands on her forehead. The sound of Riggs dropping the rifle and the scraping of his boots on the cement snapped Alistair out of his own shock.

"Oh, fuck. Oh, fuck, Annemarie!" Riggs repeated as he ran to her side. "I'm so sorry, I'm so sorry." Tears rolled down his cheeks, blurring his vision as he came to a stop beside her and Alistair. "I didn't see her. I didn't know it was her. I—"

Alistair interrupted him. In a loud, stern voice, he said, "Officer Riggs, step away from the victim." The anger in Alistair bubbled over. He reached for his phone to call for a medevac lift to Brownstone. He hoped they were not busy on the mainland. He hoped there was still time.

"Al, please. Let me help. I'm sorry. It was an accident. I swear, I—"

Alistair raised a blood-covered hand to silence his deputy. "Medical kit. Trunk. Now." He was furious and the most he could muster was brevity. Riggs wiped the cascade of tears from off his hot, red cheeks with the back of his hand. He scrambled across the parking lot to the squad cars, approaching the ajar trunk with lightning speed. He tore apart the contents of his vehicle, pushing aside the rifle duffel, the extra bulletproof vest, bolt cutters, and finally, the army-green canvas first aid bag tumbled into his hands. Riggs ran faster than he knew he was capable of to close the gap between him and his dying friend.

Alistair waited with an outstretched arm, opening and closing his hand in order to signal a quick delivery without saying a word. Riggs tossed the midweight bag to him, hoping his aim was true.

"What do you want me to do?" Riggs asked.

"Nothing," Alistair replied curtly.

"Al, come on. Let me help."

"You've done enough. Now step off." Alistair turned his attention to Annemarie who had remained quiet and still during their interaction. He, as well as the other members of law enforcement, were never formerly trained to confront medical emergencies meant for paramedics and doctors, but he knew enough tips and tricks to keep Annemarie afloat until help arrived. He knew the contents of the first aid kit could prevent the traumatic death of a victim, of Annemarie. He never needed to utilize this knowledge and know-how in a real-life situation.

He hastily unzipped the bag, unveiling a small roll of gauze, a tourniquet, trauma shears, gloves, tape, antiseptic solution, and more. He realized he was going to need Riggs's help despite not wanting it.

"Get over here," he ordered.

A few yards away, keeping his distance as commanded but hoping he would be allowed to jump into action, Riggs took a deep breath and stepped forward. "What do you need from me?" His voice was calm despite his whole body shaking.

"Take over for me here. Keep her flat. I need to stop the bleeding and she may need her shoulders pinned down when I start putting pressure on the wound." Alistair carefully slid out from underneath her, allowing space for Riggs to cozy in.

Alistair plucked the scissors from the bag and ran them up the center of her blood-sticky tee, revealing that her normally fair skin was now coated in viscous, red blood. He was careful in how he peeled away the remnants of her shirt, but once exposed, he double-timed it. With a roll of gauze partially unwound, he placed several layers over the gunshot wound and set a hand against it.

"I'm sorry, Annie. This is gonna hurt." He pressed against her abdomen with a lot of force, and knowing she was bleeding heavily, leaned into it with all his weight. He used his knee to push against the gushing, which was enough for her to cry out in agony. "I'm sorry, I'm sorry, I'm sorry," he chanted quietly.

The more Alistair pushed, the more her shoulders rose, calling Riggs into action to use both of his knees to pin her to the concrete stoop. He used his hands to brush back her hair, to try to soothe her, even though he knew none of it would help. Her entire body convulsed with shock waves of her crying and the pain coursing through her, but Riggs did what he could to keep her in place while Alistair continued to apply pressure. Her whimpers were drowned out by the sound of the ambulance siren, screaming from off in the distance and getting closer every second. It took a sharp turn into the library's parking lot, its tires squealing on the pavement. It pulled up to the walkway that led directly to Alistair, Riggs, and Annemarie, and out piled DJ and Steven.

Steven moved to the back of the rig while DJ approached the trio on the stoop with his jump bag ready to go. "What've we got?" he asked.

"GSW to the abdomen. She's awake, not really talking, but letting us know the pain is there. I've been trying to stop the bleeding." Alistair pulled back on the pressure he had been applying and did not attempt to pick at the gauze stuck to her skin for fear it would gush again. He moved out of the way for DJ, who was pulling on a pair of nitrile gloves, to sidle into place.

"Riggs, go help Steven, will you?" DJ asked, gesturing toward his partner tucked behind the ambulance. Riggs got up and scrambled down the stairs. "Hey, Annemarie, it's DJ. You with us?" Her glassy eyes were slow to track the penlight he was flashing back and forth across her vision, assessing her pupils. "Did she hit her head?" he asked, though he did not move his focus off of Annemarie.

"I-I don't know. She got hit and then crumpled right here. W-why?"

"Her pupils are sluggish."

"What does that mean? I mean, why would they be sluggish?"

"Any number of reasons. Trauma to the head, lack of oxygenation because of blood loss—hey! Steven! Hurry it up, man!" DJ investigated the gauze attached to her stomach and deemed it in good order; he checked her airways to ensure she was still breathing on her own, not in need of a bag valve mask or field intubation; he tried to get her to verbally respond to several simple questions, but had minimal luck beyond a grunt or groan.

Steven and Riggs rushed alongside the ambulance with the wheeled stretcher in tow. Alistair stood to get out of their way, but remained close in case they needed help. Riggs sidestepped with him, waiting anxiously.

Steven and DJ worked to gently straighten out Annemarie's body on the stoop. They used a scoop stretcher to cradle her and get her up onto the gurney. Steven strapped her onto the bed as DJ made other adjustments for her comfort and their speed.

"Either of you coming with?" Steven called as Alistair and Riggs followed close behind.

"No, we've got shit to deal with here," Alistair replied. "Is she headed to Brownstone General?"

"Yeah. Medevac is about three minutes out and they'll take her straight over."

"Take care of her, guys," Alistair called. DJ gave him a thumbs-up as they secured her in the back of the rig, Steven staying with her while DJ peeled out of the parking lot, en route to Hawthorn Park where there was enough clearance for the helicopter that would take Annemarie to the mainland to land.

Alistair and Riggs watched from afar as the helicopter approached the island, coming in for a swift, expert landing in the middle of the parking lot. It was a couple minutes before it took off, both of them tracking the flashing light until it disappeared to the west.

"How can I fix this?" Riggs asked, finally breaking the silence between them. "Tell me what I can do." When Alistair did not answer, he continued. "I didn't mean to. It was an accident." He fought back the tears rising in him again, a burn of anxiety and anguish gripping tight on his throat, threatening to strangle him.

Alistair's closed lips moved back and forth as he mulled over the situation. His breathing had calmed, and with the emergency now out of his hands, he could focus a little better. He turned in place to face his deputy and set a hand on Riggs's shoulder.

"Yes, it was an accident. I know that, you know that, Annie knows that. It fucking sucks that it happened and the paperwork isn't going to be any fun. I can't guarantee there won't be disciplinary consequences from Bachhuber's office, but with me? It'll be fine. I will stand by you as much as I can." Riggs shuddered at these words, the almost-violent convulsion of his body emanating into Alistair's own. "Right now, though, I need you to go back to the office and start the report. I've got a couple phone calls to make about this—" He gestured at the pool of blood seeping into the concrete stoop. His eyes dropped to his feet. "—and then I have to go tell Ken and Cecily."

Alistair shut the door to the SUV and stood at the base of the stairs leading to the Mitchells' front door. He took in a deep breath through his mouth and slowly let it eke out of him via his nose. He had been trying to calm himself the entire drive north, knowing nothing he could say would lessen the blow he was about to deliver. But if he could do it with a confident and cool demeanor, there was hope that he could keep Annemarie's parents calm too.

But now that he was here, every ounce of him wanted to melt into the ground. In all of his career, he did not have a lot of experience with delivering this kind of bad news. Port Harrow was never the place where "bad news" was ever anything more than a "you're the one at fault for this collision" or "I'm sorry to report Fluffy was found runover a mile up the road." And now, in the last year, he was doing this *again*, and it never got easier.

One step at a time, he made his way up to the door. He raised a fist to knock, but hesitated a moment longer before following through. There was no answer at first; there was only one car in the driveway—Cecily's—but that did not necessarily mean she was home. He knocked again, this time a little harder to have the sound carry further.

"Just a minute!" He heard a cheery, singsong tone come from behind the door. He stepped back a foot, affording them both a little space once Cecily arrived. When the door swung open, she appeared framed in the doorway, tea towel fumbling over her hands as she dried them. "Hey, Alistair. What are you—*oh my god.*" She dropped the towel.

"Cec, I—"

"No, no, Sheriff. Do *not* say what I think you're going to say," she begged. A hand shot out to the doorframe to steady herself. He chewed on the inside of his bottom lip, torn on what to do. She needed to know, but she did not want to hear it. "What . . . Who? Who is it? Oh god, please, please tell me it's not Ken." He could only shake his head. "Marissa?" She could read the stoic expression on his face. "Oh, no, Annemarie? What happened to Annemarie?"

"Cec, there was an accident. Annie, she . . . she got shot."

All of the color drained from Cecily's face as she collapsed to her knees under the weight of the news. Alistair was quick to react, wrapping his arms around her to stop her from completely hitting the floor. "My baby . . ." she croaked out. She buried her face in Alistair's shoulder and the wetness instantly soaked through his shirt.

"She's alive," he whispered. "They took her to Brownstone General."

Cecily pulled away from him for a moment, stared deep into his eyes, and then cuffed him on the shoulder. "Goddammit, you *lead* with that, Alistair!"

He rubbed at the sore spot for a moment while he asked, "Is Ken home?"

She shook her head. "He's out of town on a golfing trip. What's her prognosis? Can I go see her?" The words came out rapid-fire.

He raised a hand to calm her. "I don't know all the details yet. Riggs and I saw her get flown out of the park, she was conscious but in a lot of pain. She's in good hands. We know that much."

"Will you go with me over there? Even if I call Ken home now, he won't get back until tomorrow at the earliest."

"Absolutely. Get your things and we can go." She did not wait for another prompting and spun on her bare heel to collect her purse, cell phone, and house keys. Alistair stepped over the threshold to retrieve the tea towel she had dropped and set it on the console table in the hallway. Cecily hurried toward him, one arm tucked inside a jacket and hobbling along as she tried to walk and pull on socks. "Cec, we've got time before the next ferry. You can stop and dress properly."

They booked it out of the house and climbed into the vehicle. He turned on his light bar as he pulled onto the main road, beelining it south to the dock while Cecily called Ken and Marissa to tell them what was going on.

THIRTY-SIX

Cecily slumped over in the hard, plastic chair, her red face shoved into her shaking, cupped hands, bawling, inconsolable. The brays and lows filled the waiting room and drew looks from other patrons. Alistair could not tell if they were concerned, annoyed, or empathetic—Cecily would not care one way or another, so he tried to not let the glances bother him either. Seated beside her, an arm wrapped around her shoulders to provide comfort, the two of them looked a mess; his uniform stained with blood did not help matters.

Annemarie remained in surgery with no details from the emergency room staff regarding her condition. The gap in time between Alistair's patchwork job at the library and the helicopter landing at Brownstone General placed her life in critical danger. All they could do was hope.

The sniffles subsided long enough for him to ask, "Can I get you a cup of coffee?" She only nodded, fearful her voice would not work if she tried. Alistair silently excused himself to wander toward the cafeteria where two women in powder-blue scrubs shared their break together. He recognized them immediately. "Cherise, Malia, hey." His voice was tired, lacking emotion.

The brunette, Malia, darted her eyes from her chewed-on sandwich to his face. "Oh, hey, Alistair. What are you—oh my god. What's . . ." She zigzagged a finger at his torso where the bulk of Annemarie's blood had dried.

Petite, spunky Cherise pushed away from the table as she asked, "Do you need—" But he cut her off with a wave of a hand.

"I'm fine. This isn't mine." He felt obligated to wipe at the blood as a means of hiding it, getting rid of it. "Accident back home." He threw a thumb over his shoulder. "By chance either of you have anything to do with a GSW surgery?"

The women exchanged unsure glances and simultaneously shrugged. Malia pursed her lips. "I've been in the ICU all afternoon and no GSWs. Sorry."

"Same. We don't get too many of those, so I'm pretty sure I'd remember if we did. But ..." She unceremoniously shoved a corner of her sandwich into her mouth then continued to talk. "We've been on lunch almost an hour so there's no telling who's rolled in since."

Alistair gave a gentle, knowing nod. "Thanks anyway." He lifted a hand to indicate his appreciativeness and signal goodbye before turning toward the coffee pot. He topped off a paper cup for Cecily and decided against one for himself. It was a slow wander back to the waiting room, taking advantage of being able to stretch his legs after two hours of sitting.

A familiar voice came: "How long before I can see her?"

Alistair rounded the corner in time to see a doctor with a surgical mask hanging from his neck speaking to Cecily, who was wringing her tear-wet hands at his words. "The anesthesia's wearing off right now so it shouldn't be much longer. I know it's been a long night for you." He glanced up and locked eyes with Alistair. With a quick nod, he said, "Officer," then turned back to Cecily as if Alistair had been passing through, the incident none of his business. "I'll have a nurse come get you when she's awake."

"Thank you, Doctor Hassan." She reached her hand for his to shake but he gave her a reassuring squeeze of the shoulder instead. The tension in her body subsided under his touch. As the young surgeon walked away, Cecily looked to Alistair who only tilted his head as an inquiry. "She's out of surgery. H-he said there was some complication. I-I didn't understand what he was saying, but she's done, she's good."

"She'll be okay." It was a statement, not a question.

"She'll be okay," Cecily repeated.

He handed her the coffee, the liquid quavering in the cup as he tried to steady himself. From start to finish, he had no time to process the evening. Even the silent hours he and Cecily spent on the ferry ride over and in the waiting room had him with a head full of protocol and paperwork and professionalism. There was no time to feel anything. Except now.

He blinked away several tears—a combination of relief that Annemarie was in recovery and assuagement that Riggs would make it out of this in one piece too. There was still a lot to do regarding the incident, but there was time now.

His hand slipped into his pocket to pull out his phone, eager to share the good news with his deputy. Cecily had the same idea—Ken was on his way to Brownstone, but wanted updates as they came in. In separate corners of the waiting room, they made their respective calls, providing the necessary relief in order to move forward.

A nurse eventually came—Annemarie was awake. Groggy, but awake. Cecily managed to hold herself together from when the surgeon spoke to her up to the second she rounded the corner into the recovery room. The moment their eyes met, she lost all composure. It was the car accident all over again. It was Jesse's death. It was finding Annemarie along the side of the road covered in Peter's blood. It was Moose. It was every scraped knee, every fall, every broken bone, every sickness she ever experienced. The emotions from each overwhelmed Cecily to the point that she almost did not make it through the door.

Alistair remained a few steps behind to allow mother and daughter their time together. He was in no rush.

"Oh, baby!" Cecily cried out as she cradled Annemarie's face in her hands. She placed kiss after kiss on her forehead, being careful but struggling to restrain herself. "I was so worried. I've been . . . I can't even think . . . I don't know . . ." Her brain short-circuited.

Annemarie raised both hands to meet Cecily's and extracted them to hold onto in her lap. She slurred slightly, seeming to have trouble getting the words out. "I'm o-okay, mom. I'm f-fine."

"When Alistair showed up at my door . . ." She trailed off.

"It's thanks to h-him that I survived," Annemarie mused, announcing it to the room, but mostly reminding herself she owed her life to Alistair—which seemed to be the case more often than not. Between him finding her alongside the road after the accident, to practically busting down her door when she was in the depths of her depression, keeping out of a relapse with Moose's death, and now intervening after the shooting—he was not wrong when he said he would always have her back. She habitually rolled her eyes when he insisted it was the truth; now, she was beyond grateful he was a man of his word.

The thought overwhelmed her, but she was too tired to cry, too tired to do anything besides let her heavy eyelids droop shut. Cecily struggled to turn off the waterworks despite seeing Annemarie would be fine. She was finally pulling herself together when an older woman in scrubs and a heavy-knit sweater entered the room.

"I know you've just arrived, but it's time Annemarie got her rest. You'll be allowed back tomorrow morning," she announced. That made Cecily howl, and as a result, everyone else in the room flinched.

"Mom, it's fine. S-seriously." Annemarie released a pained groan. Her hand shot to her stomach.

"How's the pain, hun? Maybe the meds from the surgery are starting to wear off already," the nurse said. Annemarie could only nod. The nurse took the few minutes Cecily rambled at Annemarie about everything and nothing—as a means of saying goodbye without saying those words—and readied the next dose of morphine. With the narcotic fully administered, the nurse waited by the entryway for Annemarie's guests to leave. She picked at imaginary hangnails so as to not seem nosy.

"Let Alistair take you home, mom. I'll be . . ." She trailed off as the drug hit her hard.

Alistair extended an arm to escort Cecily out of the room, and she begrudgingly followed. But before he could set both feet in the hallway, he heard, "Alistair." He stopped midstride to backpedal into the room. The nurse continued tinkering with her hands, but wandered a few feet into the hall when she caught sight of Alistair's softer features focusing on Annemarie's face.

Alone and in silence, she forced open her eyes to gaze at him. The smallest of smirks crept into the corner of her mouth, noting she knew he was with her. "What's up?" he asked, shoving his hands into his pockets, playing it casual.

"I-I w-wanted to say . . . t-thanks. Thank you." She struggled to get out the words. "Y-you r-really—"

He interrupted. "Don't overexert yourself. You need to rest. Sleep now."

She gave a little shake of her head, barely noticeable. "I d-don't think you understa-stand what you m-mean to me, A-Alistair. I was-wasn't lying when—"

It was his turn to deflect her words. He was familiar with drug-induced emotions; he knew she was talking for the sake of talking. "Annie, I did what any other person would have done. It's a part of my job."

"Your job, your job. It's a-always you just doing y-your job. Own u-up to the f-fact that you're an in-incredibly good human being w-who does more for-for the people he l-loves than the average p-person." She sighed, a mix of exasperation and contentment. Her eyes fluttered shut and remained closed.

"I-I would do anything for you, Annie," he managed to stutter out. "I'm sorry I can't save you from everything." He lowered his head.

"This wasn't your fault. It was-wasn't Riggs's either. Oh—" Her breath caught in her throat. "Oh, poor Cassidy. How is he? Is he o-okay? I-I won't press ch-charges. I know it was an ac-accident. P-please tell me he's okay."

"Riggs will be fine. He's a mess, but knowing you'll recover will help. He sends his apology and his love."

There was a prolonged moment of silence. Alistair awkwardly stood at the foot of her bed, wondering if it was an appropriate time to say goodbye. The morphine coursed through her body, her fists unclenching and her body slackening. Another deep breath escaped her, deflated her. He turned to excuse himself, but not before she could squeak out an unintelligible noise that caught his attention. Then:

"You've always been here for me. You've always taken care of me. You've always been my best friend." It was slurred and slowed, but the words were all there.

Alistair added, "And as long as I breathe, I always will be."

A morose Cecily begrudgingly climbed the stairs to her front door, often glancing over her shoulder at Alistair who was right behind her.

"I wouldn't leave you if I didn't have to," he said in a solemn tone. "Ken said he'd be at the hospital in the morning. I've got to get back to work and make sure Riggs is doing okay." What he failed to mention was that Riggs was waiting for him at Annemarie's house, ready as ever for what he hoped was the final showdown with the creature. Alistair did not care if it took them all night hunting the bastard—it was all going to come to an end.

Cecily opened the front door and turned on her heel to face Alistair. "*Will* Annemarie be all right?"

He gave a curt nod. "Absolutely. You heard her surgeon."

"I mean long-term. She . . . she's endured so much, especially in such a short period of time. Most people don't experience that in a lifetime. I worry that—"

Alistair reached out to grab her hand, giving it a hearty squeeze. "She'll be okay. I promise."

"I hope you're right."

"Let me know if Ken ends up not making it in the morning. I can try to go with you again if need be."

Cecily nodded. "I will. Thank you, Alistair. I appreciate you more than you know. And please send my love to Riggs. It sounds like we've all had a terrible night."

"Anything for you guys." He pulled back his hand and tried to smile, though it came across as a grimace. He trekked back to the SUV, waving once before he casually pulled from her driveway. The moment the house was out of sight, he floored it—Riggs was waiting and Alistair was beyond antsy. The drive from Cecily and Ken's to Annemarie's normally took ten minutes, but in his haste, Alistair timed it in barely six.

Sure enough, Riggs's patrol car was parked in Annemarie's driveway, though there was no sign of him. Alistair pulled up alongside, giving a quick whirl of the light bar and a *whoop* of the siren—an announcement he had arrived. Within a minute, Riggs appeared from around the far side of the house. He raised a hand to wave.

There were no set plans beyond hunting down the creature. Past experience provided a few of its regular haunts: the sea cave, the long stretch of the north shore, and the woods behind the house. The locations were a wide, vague swath of the island, but at least they could narrow it down to one end. For that, Alistair was grateful. Riggs did not know what he agreed to, even after witnessing the video footage, but he was certain he would do anything to make up for the Annemarie incident.

As Alistair sorted through his cache of guns and ammunition in the back hatch of the vehicle, Riggs sidled up; he was dressed down in cargo pants and a long-sleeve shirt—hopeful protection from what may come.

"I brought you a change of clothes too. Figured you wouldn't have had time to get out of the bloody uniform."

Alistair shook his head. "I'm hoping the bastard can smell her on me. I want every opportunity available to catch it." But he did take a moment to untuck the shirt.

Riggs nodded. "Sure." He paused, then cleared his throat. "So, what's the plan?"

Alistair fished around in the bottom of the duffel. He retrieved two small cardboard boxes and handed one to his deputy. "Use these," he instructed.

Sliding open the box, inspecting the contents, Riggs saw six shotgun shells. "Okay, slugs. Going for a killing not a maiming. Got it. I think I've got more in my kit." He made to shuffle over to his car but Alistair grabbed his forearm.

"No. Only use these. They're silver."

"When did this become a werewolf hunt?" Riggs meant it as a joke, but the stern, solemn expression on Alistair's face gave him pause. "Where did these even come from?"

"Victoria. She gave them to me when I went to see her today. She said if I was stupid enough to try to kill the thing, I should at least make one good decision."

Riggs did a double take. "Wait. Where did you get the time to go see her? That's a really long drive, isn't it?"

"I . . . didn't have a meeting with Bachhuber."

"What?"

"I set up another meeting with Victoria and she agreed to meet me halfway so we could talk more."

"But why?"

"I had more questions."

"Did you get your answers?"

"I guess we'll have to wait and see."

After a brief pause, Riggs trying to figure out what that meant, he said, "Well, I've got a question for you."

"Shoot."

"The lady *who knows all about this thing* thinks taking it out is a bad idea?" Alistair nodded. "Then what the fuck are we even doing?"

"Ending this."

THIRTY-SEVEN

An hour passed without incident. Knowing so little about its habits, there was no telling as to whether light would attract or deter, or if the scent of blood was strong enough to goad it or turn it off, or if there were other options they had not considered. It was obviously intelligent, but more than them? Did it follow instinct or desire? Did it understand traps?

They decided to go in blind. This time, Alistair did not have the benefit of Nowell's camera. They possessed their eyes, their guns, and two spotlights to be used only as a necessity. It would have to do. But even so limited in their equipment, they were as ready as they could be. They had to be.

Each of their steps were purposeful, taking care to miss roots and trenches, to dodge low branches and bushes. They could not see in the darkness. Any illumination that may have come from the moon in the patchy, overcast sky was shrouded by the tree canopy, making it impossible to see the hand in front of their faces. Still, they persevered, they moved forward, making a slow, steady trek toward North Beach.

Pushing into the second hour, Riggs was running out of steam. His steps turned to a shuffle, he no longer held the shotgun at attention, letting the shoulder strap do the heavy lifting. If he were to stop moving, he could fall asleep upright. It had been a long day—the adrenaline from responding to Annemarie's distress call at the library to his part in the accident had pumped him up, made him ready to go, fight or flight. But now he was faltering and he was not sure how Alistair was still soldiering on.

A noise to their left caught both of their attentions. They halted in place, strained to listen better. The sound of hammering, thundering footsteps filled Alistair's ears—a stampede headed in his direction. But the deer population on the island was not so large for this type of roar. It sounded more like—

An explosion of pain hit Alistair like a duffel bag of bricks into the torso, forcing a labored groan out of him as he fell to the ground with a sickening *thud*, a sound of crunching bones, squelching mud. He slid across the forest floor from inertia, from the impact, the weight on his chest unbearable. He did not understand what was happening, what *had* happened, until his head started swimming and a familiar sensation of feeling out-of-body overcame him.

He opened his mouth to scream, but something large and dry obstructed his throat. Everything in him constricted. After several struggling breaths, he let loose: "Riggs! On me!"

The sudden outburst echoed in the trees, startling Riggs, rendering him useless as he tried to comprehend what Alistair said and where it came from. He flipped on the spotlight to scan at eye level. Greeted by nothing but stillness at first, he finally spied a flash of silver—a burst more than a reflection—to his far left. He tracked it as best as he could; its movements were erratic, chaotic, but also pointed and measured, like his and Alistair's had been upon entering the woods.

It free-fell from a high branch of a withered lodgepole, the tree barely supporting its weight. It landed with no noise, but quickly released a roar as it scrambled across the ruddy ground, aimed straight at Alistair who was still in a supine position, transfixed on the monster.

Riggs's breath rattled around in his rib cage, the creature's noise so penetrative, reverberative, it shocked him. But it only diverted him for a short moment—Alistair's screams as he was grabbed by his uniform collar and hastily dragged away caught his attention.

"Take the shot!" he hollered, hoping Riggs could hear him despite the distance widening between them. The creature seemed to be taking Alistair toward the sea cave.

Unsteady hands worked to balance the spotlight and shotgun, but with a lot of effort, Riggs lined up his sight and pulled the trigger. The slug whizzed past the creature's right ear, though it gave no pause. He took a moment to steady his breath, to slow his heart, and squeezed again.

The creature's shoulders buckled backward and its head faced skyward in a guttural howl as the silver shell pierced the grey flesh over the spine and launched out through a pectoral muscle. It stumbled in its gait, releasing its grip on Alistair who could do nothing as his back and shoulders collected their own assortment of wounds and bruises while dragged over every rock and root in their path.

Another slug skimmed its way from the barrel of the shotgun and landed square in the creature's shoulder, never to see the light of day. Its eyes flashed grey, flashed anger, as it spun around on its muddy heel, lowered its bald head, and barreled straight at Riggs. He was not sure if he should try to land another shot, run, or play dead. Indecision paralyzed him to his detriment.

Before he could choose, the creature launched itself into the air, eyes a silvery blaze, sharpened teeth bared. At the last second, Riggs dropped to the ground, but even with the creature overshooting, it was no problem—it landed five feet away, rounded, and extended a lithe arm to catch an army-crawling Riggs. Dragged back by his ankle, his nails failed to dig deep into the patch of compact dirt he had fallen on.

"Al!" he yelled, hoping the one syllable was not falling on deaf ears. "Al!"

As soon as Riggs was tucked beneath the creature's body, it struck. Without hesitation, it swiped at his midsection, slashing the bulletproof vest and the T-shirt underneath it to shreds, revealing a hint of the pale flesh of his stomach and drawing a swath of blood. Riggs whimpered at the sharp nails serrating his skin. He screamed for Alistair a third time. He was met with a heavy fist in his face—the creature wanted to silence Riggs; knocking him unconscious seemed the logical answer for its next meal. It did the trick: The contact of its skin on Riggs's started to lull him into the nightmare-like alternate reality, allowing the comatose opportunity to be feasted upon.

Straddling his limp body, the creature snarled. The adrenaline pumping through Riggs made his carotid artery thrum—music to the creature's ears. It pulled back its chalky, cracked lips, proffering the yellowed teeth in its mouth, ready to sink into the smooth skin of its prey's throat, ready to puncture, ready to sup.

A terrible roar escaped the creature and it collapsed onto Riggs. Blue-grey tendrils snaked up from its back as it writhed and groaned. It snapped its jaws open and shut, desperate for even the tiniest of taste of its catch. But Riggs's head was too far below it.

Standing ten feet behind the two was Alistair, the shotgun now devoid of its ammunition. He landed both shots in the back of the creature's skull. He was wobbly on his feet, the aftermath of a nightmare realm not coming fully to fruition. The last time it happened to him, he did not think he could stand, let alone now, accurately aiming and hitting his target.

"Riggs!" he cried out, unsure where his partner was. Alistair fumbled for the flashlight in his front pocket to shine over the bodies. The creature had collapsed atop Riggs, and at first, it was a sobering silence. But he caught something moving at the bottom of the pile of flesh; several fingers flapped away, trying to wriggle free to catch Alistair's attention. "Riggs!" he called again. He set one hand on the arm of the creature and tried to tug him off, but in its death, it seemed to have solidified into concrete. It took all of Alistair's strength to budge it even an inch, but it was enough to unbury Riggs's face.

Riggs gasped in a deep breath, a bluster of air sweeping in and out of his mouth. "Get 'em off me!" he said in between wheezes. He tried pushing from his angle; looking for an advantage between his efforts and Alistair's, they were able to free him. Alistair extended a hand to get Riggs back on his feet, but instead of letting him go once he was up, he pulled his deputy into a tight embrace.

Alistair buried his face in Riggs's shoulder and muttered, "I thought I lost you, man."

They broke apart, but not before Riggs patted Alistair's shoulder and gave a knowing nod. "Me too. That was . . ." There was no need to finish the sentence.

Looming over the creature's body, Alistair followed suit from his last encounter with one—he used his boot to push it, to goad it back into existence. When it was obvious the thing was good and dead, they worked in tandem to drag the thing to Annemarie's property. Riggs grabbed hold of the ankles to pull it along while Alistair kept a gun trained on the head and a flashlight pointing in front so they could see where they were walking. But it did not take long for Riggs to drop its legs onto the ground and yelp out in pain.

"What's wrong?"

"My hands . . ." Riggs lifted them to his face, trying to see through the darkness. "They felt like they were on fire for a second there."

Alistair rubbed his thumb against the area of where his burn blister had been, remembering where it came from. "Shit, I didn't think about that."

"Think about what?" Riggs pushed his palms together, trying to bypass some of the uncomfortable twinges arching across the skin.

"I don't think this thing is safe to touch."

"Huh? What do you mean?"

"I think touching it burns you. The day I brought Liam Peck up here, I was inspecting the creature's wounds and I ended up with a blister, like I'd touched a pan hot out of the oven."

Riggs made a sound halfway between a squeak and an indignant scoff. "Then how are we supposed to deal with this thing? We can't set it on fire in the woods. That's too risky."

"Yeah, no, that's absolutely not an option. Maybe we can wrap its ankles up with something so you aren't touching it skin to skin." Alistair flashed the light over the creature's face, double-checking it was still where Riggs dropped it, that it was still dead. He was taking no chances this time, the creature obviously never knowing a true death despite receiving several bullets in its skull at their last meeting.

The two quickly figured out how to tackle the problem; Riggs removed the bulletproof vest to get at his claw-torn shirt and Alistair climbed out of his work button-down, and then Alistair wrapped the fabric around Riggs's hands. But they only made it so far before the material started to slip off, prompting brief skin-on-skin contact that made Riggs cry out again. They tried to secure the shirts to the ankles, creating looped handholds for Riggs to tug on. That worked for a while, but the creature's deadweight coupled with the encroaching exhaustion slowed Riggs considerably.

Alistair had to make a decision: Did he continue to protect them from the possibility the thing was still alive or did he let down his guard, put away the gun, and double-team it to Annemarie's yard in the hopes it did not suddenly wake up? He wanted this over as soon as possible, so the choice was clear, even though every noise he heard en route to the yard buried him deeper in paranoia.

It did not take long to soak its body in gasoline and flick half a dozen lit matches; it went up in flames immediately. The acrid smell of burning flesh surrounded them as the grey skin crackled and separated from the thick muscles and bones underneath.

Riggs kept his eyes focused on the flames, a hose at the ready in case they should spread much beyond the creature. The fire danced in Alistair's eyes; he could not look away from the shrinking, ashy body, gaining some pleasure from watching it eternally burn.

In Annemarie's driveway, the floodlight allowed them to check each other over. Alistair sustained several tears in his shirt across his back where he had been dragged and blood was faintly trickling through and staining the material. He already knew it was trashed, thanks to Annemarie's earlier incident. There were a few superficial scratches over his cheekbones and forehead, nothing a little time and bacitracin could not fix.

Riggs, on the other hand, was a little more worse for the wear. He internally thanked himself for wearing the vest—had he not, his organs might be spilled over the forest floor at this moment. The claw marks on his torso were minor, but still could use a thorough cleaning. The bridge of his nose, where the creature had punched him, was swollen and would inevitably lead to a deep bruise. His whole body held onto a mild ache, one he could not place its origin at first. Upon further inspection, he pieced together that anywhere his skin had touched the creature's while its dead body pressed against him before Alistair freed him, he had developed ruddy burns. He checked the undersides of his hands where he had gripped the ankles and found the skin pink and tender. The pain of it all was minor while his adrenaline was still high.

None of their wounds were worth a visit to the emergency room on the mainland, even if it meant getting to check in on Annemarie. Alistair made a call to the firehouse, seeing who was on duty—hoping it was still DJ and Steven—so that they could meet them in a nonemergency fashion to get a professional once-over.

THIRTY-EIGHT

Take it easy. No extraneous, wild movements. No lifting. Take short walks to prevent clots if you can. Only take the painkiller when you absolutely need it. Accept help from others, no matter how prideful you may be. No one will think you weak if you can't dress yourself in the beginning or can't walk for more than a minute unsupported.

Orders from Doctor Hassan, verbatim. He knew Annemarie and her need to be constantly moving. So she sat perfectly still while Riggs and Alistair busied themselves in the kitchen. Because of the layout of the house, she couldn't see what either of them were doing and could only surmise by the sounds of banging pots, pans, and dishes. Occasionally, Alistair popped his head into the living room to remind her it was doctor's orders she remained calm and relaxed or to reassure her that all was well after a worrisome cacophony of noise escaped the kitchen.

Her need to be in and amidst the action started to overpower the necessity to stay still in order to help her heal. It had been six days since the shooting and her first night home from the hospital. Annemarie, torn between wanting company and craving solace, bent to Alistair's insistence that he help her for a couple days. "Not doing everything, but some of the basics to make life easier."

When Riggs heard that Annemarie was begrudgingly accepting assistance, he volunteered to cook her meals. Even though she said no repeatedly at first, Doctor Hassan's words resonated sharply: *No one will think you weak* . . . She finally gave in when she struggled to get to the bathroom *with* a nurse's guidance before leaving the hospital. She could do everything on her own, just in double or triple the amount of time than if she welcomed help.

So, the statue game played on: Annemarie was wrapped like a sloppy, partially supine burrito on the couch, eyes glued to the kitchen entryway, both hopeful dinner would emerge soon and that the men were not trashing her kitchen. *At least I won't be responsible for cleaning up their mess.* The silver lining made her smirk.

At the same moment her lips migrated into a happy little grin, Alistair appeared in the entryway, met with the look not intended for him, and smiled back in response. "We're almost done in here. What would you like to drink?"

Annemarie stiffly turned her head to peer into the mug sitting on the table beside her. "I could use a top off of my tea."

"Absolutely." Alistair glided across the floor to her bundle of blankets, swiped the empty ceramic cup from off the table, and stopped. "How's the pain?" He sat on the edge of the table where the cup had been.

"I'm better than I was, if that means anything, but about as good as a gunshot victim can be." Her gaze casually drifted up to his face as she spoke. They locked eyes for a brief moment, but both broke contact when the lingering silence accompanying the dual stare was interrupted by Riggs bursting into the room with arms full of food.

"Soup's on!" he announced. Alistair popped up quickly in order to help liberate Riggs from the bowls and plates he precariously balanced and to dole them out to everyone. Alistair knew there was a foldable breakfast tray stored in the entryway closet, so he scarpered off to find it.

In front of Annemarie sat a bowl of a thick stew, filled mostly with vegetables and a little meat; the small plate beside it hosted half of a toasted cheese sandwich and several apple slices. Her throat was still healing after a complication from surgery intubating caused a laceration in the trachea, so the prospect of eating solids after days of lightweight or liquid meals elicited both elation and dread.

Riggs plopped himself on the easy chair, using the armrest to hold the sandwich. Alistair sat on the couch at Annemarie's feet. Her toes wiggled under him as he settled into the cushion. His whole body jumped and she snorted at the reaction. The three of them ate in a comfortable silence, only crunching and spoons clicking against the ceramic bowls.

After several swallows of the stew followed by one bite of the crispy, crunchy bread of the sandwich, Annemarie grimaced, garnering attention from the men.

"Is everything okay?" Riggs asked. Her tightened features were not an answer.

"Do you need another painkiller?" Alistair made the motion to stand to fetch one from the kitchen. Annemarie raised a hand to stop him, unable to say anything as she worked through a bout of intense pain in her throat, but by the time her fingers were high enough to catch his gaze, he was already gone. He rushed back into the room with a glass of water and her pill bottle. He sat back down beside her, set the cup on the table, and popped off the lid of the orange pharmacy jar. "Here," he said as he fished one out and handed it to her.

With hands shaking, she reached one for the pill and the other for the water. Doctor Hassan told her that while she was lucky enough to not have had anything major punctured when the bullet entered her, on top of her perpetually sore throat, she was still going to feel extremely uncomfortable for many days to follow. Inflammation from the intestinal manipulation while he surgically fished around for all the bullet fragments would be the main culprit.

Knowing this, she requested a mostly liquid diet until she healed, but broths only afforded so many calories and Cecily's suggestion of pureeing everything—and she meant *everything*—repulsed Annemarie to no end. When Riggs stepped in as her personal chef, he agreed to keep all ingredients out of the blender.

Both men sped through their meals, making quick work of the food in front of them and ready to move on to cleaning up their mess in the kitchen. Alistair was a clean-as-he-went type, whereas Riggs left a wake of destruction behind him. The combined personalities made for a half-cleaned space that needed a little elbow grease to tackle the rest. When Annemarie sipped down the last of the stew, she waited patiently for either of the men to check on her, to take the dirty dish away. When it was obvious neither was coming, she took it upon herself to free her body from the blanket burrito and cautiously walk the bowl and plate into the kitchen. *After all, Doctor Hassan said I should take little walks often.*

Alistair jumped when she barged her way to the sink when her noisy arrival did nothing to alert them to her presence. It was the first time all night—at least since Riggs took control of the operation—that she was given the opportunity to see how much they trashed the kitchen. Much to her surprise, it looked fine. Either they were adept at cleaning up messes quickly or it was all bark and no bite—based on the noises coming from the kitchen over the last hour, she expected to see everything she owned broken.

"What are you doing?" Alistair asked, gently grabbing her by the shoulders to lead her back into the living room to plop onto the couch.

"I can get up to pee, thank you very much. Unless you have a solution for that too," she said with her arms folded across her chest, giving half of a grumbled *hmph* in protest.

"Twenty-foot-long catheter."

She lowered her eyebrows in a partial squint and her nostrils flared. "I am *not* hooking up to a catheter. Again." She was immediately reminded of the discomfort of the hospital stay.

"That wouldn't work anyway," Riggs piped in. He rounded the corner, wiping his hands dry on a towel.

Annemarie extended a hand in a gesture of gratitude and scoffed. *"Thank you!"* she exclaimed.

"Fifty feet would be better. That way the line isn't taut. If she's got to roll to one side or the other, we don't want it coming undone accidentally."

"You have a point, but fifty seems a bit excessive. You don't want so much slack that the line could pinch," Alistair added.

"So, what? Thirty? Thirty-five?" Riggs asked. He snickered and Alistair struggled to hide his amusement at Annemarie's reddening face.

"I hate you both." She stormed off in a slow, pathetic flutter to use the bathroom, leaving the men alone in the living room.

"You headed back to the station, then?" Alistair asked. He tucked his hands into the pockets of his dark brown pants. Once his shift ended, he had booked it up to Annemarie's house to join her and Riggs for dinner. He managed to change out of half of his uniform, but the slacks remained.

"Yeah, I think so. I have a little more paperwork to finish, then I'll probably do a ride-along with Shaun. Are you gonna stick around here for a bit?"

Alistair scratched the back of his head. "No, I wanna get out of her hair. Give her some space. I'll make sure she's all set before heading out, though."

Annemarie returned from the bathroom, pain shooting through her midsection causing her face to scrunch up. "Did I hear you guys are leaving?"

"I've got to get back to work," Riggs announced.

"And you don't need me hovering around you," Alistair added. He looked at his watch. It was almost nine. "Besides, I've got an early shift tomorrow."

"Oh, okay." Her tone came across as dejected. While she loved her independence and hated being waited on, she did appreciate the company. Having not truly been alone the last handful of days, knowing a nurse was always within earshot and friends and family were checking in with her regularly, she was secretly nervous for her first night home alone. "Well, thank you both for coming by and helping. I appreciate you two."

"Of course, Annie. It's the least I can do, given the, y'know, circumstances." Riggs would never forgive himself for the accident. Alistair patted him on the shoulder as he made his way past the couch and to the door. "Have a good night. Call me or Shaun if you need anything. We'll be out and about."

"Thank you, Riggs. Love you, bud." She waved at him as he excused himself outside. She turned to look at Alistair. "And you too? Headed home?"

He nodded curtly. "As much as I know you'd love for me to stick around, I do have to leave. But you know I'll come to you in a heartbeat if you need anything. I'm a phone call away."

"You know realistically I'd call my mom, right? She's ten minutes away and you're, like, forty." She knew she did not have to remind him—none of it was news to him.

"I know, I know." He leaned toward her and planted a kiss on her cheekbone. "Last call before I leave. Do you need anything? Anything whatsoever?"

She shook her head. "I'm gonna take my other meds and head right to bed, I think. Hosting the two of you, even though I did absolutely nothing, wore me out." She lifted her hands to run her fingers through her hair but hesitated in the movement, taking care with the way the skin of her torso stretched. "Marissa's coming by in the morning. Though, I'm hoping she drops Charlie off at mom and dad's first."

"Sounds good." He paused. "Okay. I'm out." He kissed her cheek once more and this time she reciprocated with a peck on his stubbled chin. As he pulled away, he hesitated. Their eyes met. She inched closer, her hand raised at her side to reach out to him, but he sidestepped and cleared his throat. "Good night, Annie."

"Good night," she replied softly. She watched him as he let himself out of the house. He looked up at her one last time, locking onto her face, and shut the door before either of them could do or say anything else.

Alistair arrived home at nine thirty. He was exhausted. Between work earlier in the day, entertaining Annemarie, cleaning up after Riggs's kitchen disasters, and then the long slog home, he was ready for bed. He locked his gun in the safe in the front closet, leaving the holster perched atop. He dragged himself across the living room toward the bedroom, messing with the button and zipper of his pants.

He stripped down to his boxer briefs, taking care to hang up his slacks in the closet. He paced between the bathroom and bedroom as he brushed his teeth, anxious for an undetermined reason.

He climbed into bed, piling the lightweight blankets over him. He double-checked that the alarm on his phone was set for four forty-five. Not long after shutting his heavy eyelids, he was out.

He woke with a start, a heavy feeling settled against his sternum. His hand shot to the warm-to-the-touch skin and winced; the remnant of the large bruise from the night he and Riggs killed the creature was still sore. He checked the time—a little after three. He still had time before his alarm. But the nagging in his bladder forced him out of bed; he knew he would not be able to ignore it.

After he finished up in the bathroom, he dragged himself back to bed, falling face-first onto the pillow. The familiar *bzzt bzzt* vibration coupled with the ringtone made him turn his head to the nightstand. He sat up as he grabbed the phone, the bright face of the screen forcing him to squint in the darkness and blurring the name of the caller for a moment. He swiped to answer.

"Annie, hey," he answered groggily. "What's—"

"Someone's in the house!" she cried out in a strained, hushed tone.

Her words did not register in his brain.

"What?"

"Someone is in my house. I tried calling Riggs and Shaun and neither answered their phones. I need you, Alistair. Please." He had trouble making out her words, her voice was so quiet.

He pushed himself upright so he was kneeling on the bed, facing the headboard. "Where are you right now?" He put her on speakerphone but kept his voice low too, in the hopes of not giving away her location to whoever was in her house.

"I'm under the bed. They're in the living room."

"Good. Stay there. I'm on my way."

He whipped his body around to fling himself out of bed. His feet hit the floor and he was racing out the bedroom door toward the living room. But the moment he stepped over the threshold, he instantly went down flat on his back and his phone clattered away across the hardwood. Pain erupted from his trachea, having taken a solid hit across the throat, and he gasped for breath. His hands shot to his neck, feeling like it was broken and struggling to take in, or let out, any air. Mouth gaping like a fish out of water.

He closed his eyes as he listened to Annemarie's labored breathing turn frantic. Her high-pitched scream echoed throughout his bedroom. She begged and pleaded and cried out for help, shrieking for Alistair, calling for mercy, devolving into muffled yelps and pained groans that eventually subsided. Then silence.

Alistair still could not take a full breath. Upon opening his eyes, he saw someone standing above him. He gasped, but it made him choke on his spit. In the darkness of the room, little could be discerned. The sliver of a moon outside the bedroom window barely illuminated the figure, who remained motionless, and as far as Alistair could tell, looking straight ahead.

"Annie?" Alistair croaked, his voice hoarse and painful. "Annemarie!"

No answer.

He tried to move, to collect himself from the heap on the floor. A flash of light filled the room, like headlights bouncing off the wall. His gaze returned to the figure. It cocked its head as it listened. Alistair watched as it lowered itself onto all fours to look at him. Its eyes blazed silver, then absolute darkness filled the room.

ACKNOWLEDGMENTS

Woebegone had been in existence in some form for well over thirteen years at the time of its publication. It started as one silly idea way back in 2004 or 2005 that I genuinely tried to flesh out in 2011, and after some fits and starts, its plot and villain changed to closer to what you have in your hands. It has been a labor of love, figuring out if our female main character was an Annette, Elle, or Annemarie; if Alistair was an Ireland transplant with an appealing Irish brogue; whether the setting was going to be based on a real place or if it needed to be in its own little world; and whether or not to make Annemarie and Alistair end up together. It has been a long thirteen years, but I designated 2024 the year it all came to fruition, in the hopes that readers will come to love what I created.

And to get the damn thing out of my head once and for all.

My thanks goes out to anyone who has been cheering me along, whether they were with me from the beginning or are more recent additions to my life.

To readers who pick this up—whether because you know me personally or you were just intrigued by the cover art or blurb: I hope you enjoy reading this as much as I enjoyed writing it. Thank you for your support.

To my extraordinary partner, Daren: I appreciate every ounce of support you have given me since day one. You have encouraged me every step of the way. And I do not know if you will ever know just how much your belief in me and my ability means.

ABOUT THE AUTHOR

Kasey Kubica lives in the Nevada desert with her partner of nearly two decades. Prior to the transition to a southwest lifestyle, she spent fifteen years in Washington state and about seventeen years on Maui (though there will be a special place in her heart for her birthstate of Michigan).

Writing has always been a part of her life, but it has also always taken a back seat to everything else. Her published works include a nonfiction travelogue, three full-length erotic romance novels, a light and fluffy Christmas romance novel, and a short story entitled "The Fish, the Wish, and Vinny" in an anthology of magic. Kasey's other hobbies include traveling; reading; cooking and baking; games of all sorts, especially jigsaw puzzles; kayaking and paddle boarding; and fiber arts.

CONTENT WARNINGS

Death of the suicide and animal variety—though neither are described in great depth or graphic detail.

Discussion of ongoing depression and the lack of self-care (and self-destruction) that can come with it.

Abuse of alcohol—though it is not described in great detail.

Passing mention of a character being mentally abused by a parent and bullied by kids at school.